Sir Walter Besant

The Holy Rose

Sir Walter Besant

The Holy Rose

ISBN/EAN: 9783337419097

Printed in Europe, USA, Canada, Australia, Japan

Cover: Foto ©Andreas Hilbeck / pixelio.de

More available books at **www.hansebooks.com**

E T C.

By WALTER BESANT

AUTHOR OF 'ALL SORTS AND CONDITIONS OF MEN,' 'CHILDREN OF GIBEON,'
'TO CALL HER MINE,' ETC.

WITH A FRONTISPIECE BY FRED. BARNARD

London
CHATTO & WINDUS, PICCADILLY
1890

CONTENTS.

THE HOLY ROSE.

THE INNER HOUSE.

THE HOLY ROSE.

PROLOGUE.

ALL night long, until within a couple of hours of daybreak, the ships' boats were rowing to and fro between the fleet and the shore, swiftly, yet without haste, as if the work had to be done without delay, yet must be done in order. They were embarking the English and the Spanish troops, for the town was to be abandoned. All night long the soldiers stood in their ranks, waiting for their turn in stolid patience. Some even slept leaning on their muskets, though the season was mid-winter, and though all round them there was such a roaring of cannon, and such a bursting and hissing of shells, as should have driven sleep far away. But the cannon roared and the shells burst harmlessly, so far as the soldiers were concerned, for they were drawn up in the Fort Lamalque, which is on the east of the town, while the cannonading was from Fort Caire, which is on the west. The Republicans fired, not upon the embarking army, but upon the town and upon the boats in the harbour, where the English sailors were destroying those of the ships which they could not take away with them, so that what had been a magnificent fleet in the evening became by the morning only a poor half-dozen frigates. They burned the arsenal ; they destroyed the stores; not until the work of destruction was complete, and all the troops were embarked, did they turn their thoughts to the shrieking and panic-stricken people.

What do we, who all our lives have sat at home in peace and quietness, know of such a night? What do we, who, so far, have lived beyond the reach of war, comprehend of such terror as fell upon all hearts when—'twas the night of the eighteenth of December, in the year of grace one thousand seven hundred and ninety-three—the people of Toulon discovered that the English and Spanish troops were leaving the town, and that they were left to the tender mercies of the Republicans? Toulon was their last camp of refuge ; Lyons had fallen ; Marseilles had fallen. As the English gathered together in the fens and swamps to escape.the Normans, so the Provençal folk fled to Toulon out of the way of the Republicans. As for their tender mercies, it was known already what had been done at Lyons, and what at Marseilles. What would they not do at Toulon, which had not only pronounced against the Republic, but had even invited the English and the Spanish to occupy and hold the town ? And now their allies were embarking, and they were without defence.

It took time for them to understand the situation. They did not learn that Fort Caire and the Pharon had been taken by the Republicans, until the cannon of the forts were turned upon the town, and the bombardment began. Then they ran out of their houses, because it is better to die in the open than to die in a hole, and congregated—some in the churches, some in the Place d'Armes, and some on the quays. It was dreadful, even there, because the shells which flew hurtling in the air sometimes burst over their heads, and the cannon-shot sometimes flew through the crowd, making long lanes where the dead and wounded lay. It was more dreadful when the English sailors fired the arsenal and the stores, and the lurid flames leaped up into the sky, and roared and ran from place to place. It was more dreadful still when the lubberly Spaniards blew up the powder-ships instead of sinking them, and that with so terrible an explosion that the boats in the harbour were blown clean out of the water. But it was most dreadful of all when it became known that the English had abandoned the town, and were even then embarking at Fort Lamalque, where . they were secure from the fire of the other forts ; because then the people understood that they would be left to certain death.

Then with one consent they rushed upon the Quai. The women carried their little ones and dragged the elder children by the hand ; the men snatched up whatever, in the terror of the moment, they could save that seemed worth saving, and there, crowded all together, they shrieked and cried to the English boats, and implored the sailors to carry them on board.

All night long they vainly cried, the men cursing the English for their inhumanity, the women holding up the children—for the flames of the arsenal made the Quai as light as day—if the sight of the tender innocents would move their hearts. All night long the sailors, unmoved, went on with their work of destruction in the harbour, and of embarkation on the fleet. But in the early morning, two hours before daybreak, they had done all that they had time to do, and they thought of the wretched people.

When the boats touched the Quai there arose a desperate cry, for it seemed here indeed, as with those who of old time stood or lay about the Pool of Siloam, that only he who stepped in first would come out whole. Then those behind pushed to the front, and those in front leaped into the boats, and some in their haste leaped into the water instead and were drowned ; and, to make the terror worse, the forçats, who had been released when the arsenal was fired, came down upon the crowd, six hundred strong, yelling, 'The Republicans are upon us! They are coming! They are coming!' Then even those who had been most patient, fearing above all things to lose each other, and resolved to cling to their treasures if possible, either lost their heads and rushed forward, or were forced to the front by those behind and separated ; and in the confusion they dropped their treasures, which the convicts picked up. And some were pushed into the water, and some, especially the women and children, were thrown down and trampled to death ; and at this moment the cannon-shot of Fort Caire fell into the densest part of the crowd. And some went mad, and began to laugh and sing, and one or two fell dead with the terror and distraction of it. But the English sailors went on steadily with their work, helping the people into the boats, and when those were full pushing off and making room for others, as if they were Portsmouth wherries taking holiday folk to see the ships at Spithead ; so that, although at daybreak they were forced to desist, out of twenty thousand souls who were in Toulon, they took on board, all told, fourteen thousand five hundred men, women and children.

Among the groups on the outskirts of the crowd there was one of four, consisting of two ladies, a man, and a boy. One of the ladies sat upon the arm of an anchor, holding the boy by the hand. She had stuffed his ears with wool and covered his head with her shawl, so that he should see and hear as little as possible. The other, who stood by her, was dressed as a nun. In her hands she held a golden crucifix, and her eyes were turned to the heavens. The man stood silent, only from time to time whispering to the lady with the boy :

'We can die but once, Eugénie. Courage, my wife.'

Then came the false alarm of the forçats, and a surging wave of humanity suddenly rushed upon them, bearing them along upon the tide. And as for the lady called Eugénie, she was carried off her feet, but held the boy in her arms, and knew nothing until the strong hands of two English sailors caught her as she was falling headlong into the water, crying :

'Now then, Madam Parleyvoo, this is your way ; not into the harbour this time. Lay down, ma'am ; lay down, and sit quiet.'

When it was daybreak, the refugees upon the deck looked around them. They were seeking for brother and sister, husband, wife, lover, parent, or child ; with them Madame Eugénie. Alas ! the husband was nowhere on the ship. They comforted her with the hope that he might be on one of the other vessels. But she was to see him no more. Presently her eyes fell upon a figure lying motionless beside a cannon on the deck. It was a nun in blue and white.

'Sister !' cried Madame Eugénie ; 'Sister Claire ! You are saved ! oh, you are saved !'

The nun slowly opened her eyes, looking about her.

'I thought,' she said, 'that we had passed through the pangs of death, and were on our way to the gates of heaven.' The terror of the night had made her reason wander for the moment. 'Where are we, sister ?'

'We are safe, dear. But where—oh, where is Raymond ?'

'I know not. What has happened ? What have I here ?'

In her hand she carried a bag.

I have said that in the hurry of the moment each snatched up what seemed most precious. This lady, for her part, held in her hand a large leather bag, containing something about eighteen inches long. If we consider how weak a woman she was, in what a crowd she was pressed, how she was carried into the boat and hoisted on board, and how her wits fled for terror, it seems nothing short of a miracle that she should have brought that bag on board in safety. But she did, and thus a miracle, she always believed, was wrought in behalf of her and those she loved.

She sat up and began to recover herself.

'Oh, my sister !' she said, bursting into tears, 'you are safe ; and I have saved the Rose, the Holy Rose, the Rose blessed by the Pope.'

'And I,' said Eugénie, 'have lost my husband. Thank God, the boy is safe. But where is Raymond ?'

Then followed the sound of a fierce cannonading ; the last, because the Republicans now discovered that the place was abandoned.

The nun kissed the crucifix.

' Those who are not with us,' she said solemnly, ' are with God. If they are not dead already, they will be presently killed by those who are the enemies of God and the King. Let us pray, my sister, for the souls of the martyrs.'

In the afternoon of that day, the English and Spanish ships being now under full sail and out of sight, there was the strangest sight that the Toulonnais had ever seen. The performance took place in the Place d'Armes, under the trees which, in summer, make a grateful shade in the hot sun. Generally there is a market there, which begins at daybreak, and is carried on lazily, and with many intervals for sleep and rest, until the evening. But to-day the market-women were not at their stalls, and the stalls were empty. The smoke of the still-burning arsenal was blowing slowly over the town, obscuring the sky ; some of the ships in the harbour were still on fire, adding their smoke, so that, though the sky was clear and the sun was bright, the town was dark. Under the trees at the western end of the Place sat four Commissioners, forming four courts. They were dressed in Republican simplicity of long flow-ing hair, long coats with high collars, and their throats tied up in immense mufflers. They were provided with chairs, and they were surrounded by a guard of soldiers. The fellows were in rags, and for the most part barefooted ; but every man had his musket, his bayonet, and his pouch. They carried nothing more. Their hair was longer than that of the Commissioners ; their cheeks were hollow, partly from short rations long continued, and partly from the fatigue of the last week's incessant fighting. And their eyes were fierce—as fierce as the eyes of those Gauls who first met a Roman legion. In the open part of the Place, where there were no trees to shelter them, were grouped a company of prisoners, driven together at the point of the bayonet. They were the helpless and unresisting folk who had been left behind by the re-treating English. The men stood silent and resigned, or, if they spoke, it was to console the women, who, for their part, worn out by terror and fatigue, sat as if they could neither hear, nor see, nor feel anything at all, not even the wailing of the children.

At the east end of the Place were more soldiers, and these were engaged in turn, by squads of six, in standing shoulder to shoulder and firing at a target which was continually changed.

A strange occupation, surely, for soldiers of the Republic ! For the target at which they aimed, at ten feet distance, was by turns a man, a woman, or a child, as might happen. They always hit that target, which then fell to the ground, and became instantly white and cold, and was dragged away to be replaced by another.

For the Republic, revengeful as well as indivisible, was executing Justice upon her enemies. With this Republic, which was naturally more ruthless, because less responsible, than any Tyranny, Justice was always spelt with a capital, and meant Death. So exactly was Justice at this time a synonym for La Mort, that one is surprised that the latter word should have survived at all during the early years of Revolution, when the thing was signified equally well by the word Justice. The judges here were those pure and holy spirits, Citizens Fréron, Robespierre the Younger, Barras, and Saliceti, all virtuous men, and all fully permeated with a conviction of the great truth, that when a man is dead he can plot no more. Therefore, as fast as the traitors of Toulon, who had held out for the family of Capet, and had invited the detestable and perfidious English into their city, and had been contented with their rule, were brought before them, they were sentenced to be done to death incontinently, and without any foolish delay in the investigation of the case, or in appeals to any higher court, or any waste of time over prayers and priest.

Presently there was brought before Citizen Fréron a Gentleman. There could be no doubt upon this subject, because, even at this moment, when the result of his trial was certain, he preserved the proud and self-possessed air which exasperated the Republicans, who easily succeeded in looking fearless and resolute, but never preserved calmness. It wants a very well-bred man to possess his soul and govern himself with dignity in the presence of a violent death. When it came to the turn of the Robespierres, for example, one of them jumped out of window, and the other shot himself in the head. Yet in the dignity of the Nobles the fiery Republicans read contempt for themselves, and it maddened them. This gentle-man was a handsome man of five-and-thirty, or thereabouts, with straight and regular features, black eyes, and a strong chin. You may see his face carved upon those sarcophagi of Arles, where are sculptured a whole gallery of Roman heads belonging to the second century. It was, in fact, a Roman face such as may be seen to this day at Tarascon, Aiguesmortes, and Arles ; a clear-cut face, whose ancestor was very likely some gallant legionary born in the Campagna, who, his years of service accomplished, was left behind, grizzled and weather-beaten, but strong still, to settle in the Provincia, to marry one of the black-haired, half-bred Gaulish maidens, to bring up his family, presently to die, and then to be remembered for another generation at least in the yearly commemorative Festival of the Dead.

'Your name?' asked Commissioner Fréron.

There were no clerks, and no notes were taken of the cases. But certain formalities must be observed in the administration of justice.

'My name is Raymond d'Arnault, Comte d'Eyragues,' the prisoner replied in a clear, ringing voice.

'You have been found in the town which for two months has harboured and entertained the enemies of the Republic. You were on the Quai, endeavouring to escape. Why were you endeavouring to escape?'

The prisoner made no reply.

'Friends of the Republic do not fly before the presence of her soldiers. What have you to say?'

'Nothing,' said the prisoner.

'Is there any present who can give evidence as to the accused?' asked the President.

A man stepped forward.

'I can give evidence, Citizen Commissioner.'

He was a man, still young, whose face bore certain unmistakable signs denoting an evil life. Apparently his courses had led him to a condition of poverty, for his clothes were old and shabby. His coat, which had once been scarlet, was now stained with all the colours that age and rough treatment can add to the original colour ; its buttons had formerly been of silver, but were now of horn ; his hair was tied with a greasy black ribbon ; his shoes had no buckles, and were tied with string ; his stockings were of a coarse yarn. As he stepped to the front, he seemed to avoid looking at the prisoner.

Some of those who assisted at the trial might have noticed a strange thing. The man was curiously like the prisoner. They were both of the same stature ; each of them had black eyes and black hair ; each of them had a shapely head and strong, regular features. But the face of one was noble, and that of the other was ignoble, which makes a great difference to begin with. And one was calm in his manner, though death stared him in the face ; and the other, though nobody accused him of anything, was uneasy.

'What is your name?' asked the Court.

'My name, Citizen Commissioner, is Louis Leroy.'

At these words there was a murmur among all who heard them, and the Court itself showed its displeasure.

'It is my name,' said the witness. 'A man does not make his own name.'

'Citizen, your name is an insult to the Republic.'

'I will change it, then, for any other name you please.'

'What is your profession, citizen ?'

'I am '—he hesitated for a moment—'I am a dancing-master at Aix.'

'A dancing-master may be a good citizen. As for your name, it shall be Gavotte—Citizen Gavotte. For your first name, it shall be no longer Louis, but Scipio. Proceed, Citizen Scipio Gavotte, and quickly. Do you know the accused ?'

'I have known him all my life.'

'What can you tell the Court about him ?'

'He is an aristocrat and a Royalist, therefore the enemy of the Republic ; also a devout Catholic, therefore the enemy of man-kind.'

'What is his business in the city of Toulon ? Why is he found here ?'

'He was one of those who invited the English into the town. It was thought that Marseilles, Lyons, and Toulon would all hold out together, and be three centres for rallying the Royalists. The Count was strong in favour of English intervention.'

'Have you anything further to depose, Citizen Gavotte ?' asked the Court.

'Nothing more.'

'Accused, have you anything to ask the witness ?'

'Nothing,' replied the Count.

'Citizen Arnault,' said the President, 'you have heard the evidence. You are charged with inviting the enemies of the Republic to insult with their presence the sacred soil of the Republic ; you have delivered into their hands the fleets of France ; you have destroyed the arsenals and the munitions of war. Have you anything to urge in defence ?'

'Nothing.'

'You admit the charge, then ?'

'I admit the charge. It is quite true. I would not willingly waste the time of this honourable Court. There are many hundreds of honest people waiting their turn to be treated as you treated the people of Lyons. I have nothing more to say.'

'Death !' said Commissioner Fréron.

The Count heard the sentence with a slight bow. Then the soldiers led him away to the other end of the Place, where the prisoners already sentenced were gathered together waiting their turn, men and women. As for the former, they affected indifference; but the women, with clasped hands and white faces, gazed into the light of day, which they were to see no more, and some hung upon the shoulders of husband or lover, and some sat together, their arms about each other's necks, whispering that they should not be separated for many moments, and that the pang of death was momentary.

The Count spoke to no one; but he turned his head slowly, surveying the scene as if it was a very curious and interesting spectacle, full of odd and amusing details, which he would not willingly forget. The ragged soldier, the mock dignity of the Court, seemed to amuse him. But among those who stood among the soldiers, he suddenly observed the fellow who had given evidence against him. He was crouching in the crowd, his eyes aglow with hatred and eagerness to see the carrying out of the sentence. With a gesture of authority the Count beckoned him. The man, perhaps from force of habit, obeyed. So for a moment they stood face to face. Truly, they were so much like each other that you might have taken them for brothers.

'Louis,' said the Count, speaking as one speaks to a dependent or a humble friend, 'it needed not thy testimony, my friend. I was already sentenced. Pity that I could not die without finding out that you were my enemy—you.'

The man said nothing.

'Why, Louis, why?' the Count continued. 'We were boys together; once we were playfellows. I loved thee in the old days, before thy wild ways broke thy mother's heart. It was not I, but my father, who bade thee begone from the village for a vaurien. Why, then, Louis?'

'Your name and your estate should have belonged to me, and gone to my son. I was born before you, though my mother was not married to—your father.'

'Indeed!' said the Count coldly. 'So this rankled, did it? Poor Louis! I never suspected it. Yet my death will not undo the past. Louis, I shall be shot, but thou wilt not inherit the name or the estate.'

'I shall buy the estate,' said the man. 'Estates of émigrés and traitors can be bought for nothing in these times; so that after all the elder brother will inherit.'

'And yet, Louis, 'tis pity; because thy brother's death will now be laid to thy charge. There can be, methinks, little joy for one who murders his brother.'

The man's face flushed.

'What do I care?' he said. 'Go to be shot, and when you fall remember that the vineyards and the olive-groves will be mine— the property of the brother who was sent away in disgrace to be a gambler, a poet, a dancing-master—anything.'

'My brother,' the Count replied, 'thou hast changed thy name. It is no longer Leroy, nor Gavotte, but Cain. Farewell, brother, enjoy the estates and be happy.'

He dismissed him with a gesture cold and disdainful.

'Enjoy thy estates, Cain.'

Citizen Gavotte slunk back; but he waited on the Place watching, until his brother fell.

Meantime the Commissioners of the Republic continued to administer justice, and the file of soldiers continued to execute it, and every man and woman had his fair turn and no favour, which the Republic always granted to its prisoners; and each one, when his turn came, stood before the pointed muskets, and then fell heavily, white of cheek, his heart beating no longer, upon the stones.

When justice was thoroughly satisfied, which took several days, and the remnant of the Toulonnais was reduced to slender proportions, they threw the bodies into the Mediterranean, where they lie to this day.

CHAPTER I.

IN MY GARDEN.

THE village of Porchester is a place of great antiquity, but it is little, and, except for its old Castle, of no account. Its houses are all contained in a single street, beginning at the Castle-gate and ending long before you reach the Portsmouth and Fareham road, which is only a quarter of a mile from the Castle. Most of them are mere cottages, with thatched or red-tiled roofs, but they are not mean or squalid cottages; the folk are well-to-do, though humble, and every house in the village, small or great, is covered all over, back and front, with climbing roses. The roses cluster over the porches, they climb over the red tiles, they peep into the latticed windows, they cover and almost hide the chimney. In the summer

months the air is heavy with their perfume ; every cottage is a
bower of roses ; the flowers linger sometimes far into the autumn,
and come again with the first warm days of June. Nowhere in the
country, I am sure, though I have seen few other places, is there
such a village for roses. Apart from its flowers, I confess that the
place has little worthy of notice ; it cannot even show a church,
because its church is within the Castle walls, and quite hidden from
the village.

On a certain afternoon of April, in the year of grace one thousand
eight hundred and two, the colour of the leaves was just beginning
to show on the elms, the buds were swollen in the chestnuts, the
blossom was out on the almond, and the hedges were already green.
The sunshine was so warm that one could bring one's work out to
the porch, with a shawl round the neck ; the village was not quiet,
and yet it was peaceful ; that is to say, there were the ordinary
sounds which are expected, and therefore do not annoy. The
children were playing and shouting, the soldiers were disputing
outside the tavern door, the village blacksmith and his two appren-
tices were hammering something on a tuneful anvil, which rang
true at every stroke like a great bell ; the barber was flouring a
wig at the open door, and whistling through his teeth over the job,
as a groom whistles while he rubs down a horse ; a flock of geese
walked along the road croaking and calling to each other ; a dog
barked after his sheep, keeping them in order, and the cobbler
sitting in his doorway was singing aloud while he cut the leather,
adjusted it, and hammered it into place. Sometimes he sang out
merrily, sometimes he sang low. This was according as the work
went easily and to his liking, or the contrary. 'Twas a rogue who
always had some merry ditty in his mouth, and to-day it was the
famous ale-house song which begins :

> ' I've cheated the parson, I'll cheat him agen ;
>   For why should the rogue have one pig in ten ?
>   One pig in ten,
>   One pig in ten,
>   Why should the rogue have one pig in ten ?'

Here something interrupted his song and his work, but immediately afterwards he went on again :

> ' One pig in ten,
>   One pig in ten,
> Why should the rogue have one pig in ten ?'

When I had resolved to write down my history, and was considering how best to relate it, there came into my mind, quite un-

expectedly, a single afternoon. At first there seemed no reason why this day more than any other should be remembered. Yet the memory of it is persistent, and has so forced itself upon me that every moment of it now stands out as clear and distinct before my eyes as if it were painted on canvas. Perhaps in the world to come we shall have the power and the will to recall day by day the whole of our lives, and so be enabled to live each moment again, and as often as we please and as long as we please. I confess that I am so poorly endowed with spiritual gifts, that I should desire nothing better than to prolong at will the blessed years of love and happiness with my husband (who, to be sure, has never ceased to be my lover) and my children. But Madam Claire (who was never married) says that the joys of our earthly life will appear to us hereafter as poor, unworthy things, and that subjects of more holy contemplation will be provided for us which will more fitly occupy our thoughts. That may be so, and if anyone now living in this world should know aught of the next it is Madam Claire, a saint, though a Roman Catholic, and formerly a nun. Still, for one who has tasted the joys of earthly love and been a mother of children, the memory of these, or their renewal, would seem enough happiness for ever and ever. Amen.

The day which came into my head is that day in spring of which I have just spoken. The porch in which I was sitting belonged to a house in a great garden, which stretched back from the village street. The garden was full of everything which can grow in this country. Apple and pear trees were trained in frames beside the beds. These were bare as yet, except for the cabbages, but in a month or two they would be green with peas and beans, asparagus, lettuce, and everything else of green herbs that is good for food. There were glass frames for cucumbers and melons ; a great glass-house for grapes and peaches ; there was quite a forest of raspberry-canes, gooseberry and currant bushes ; and there was an orchard full of fruit-trees, apples of the choicest kinds, such as the golden pippin, the ribston and king pippin, and the golden russet ; there were also pears, Windsor and jargonelle, plums and damsons, cherries and mulberries, Siberian crab and medlar. Again, if the beds were full of vegetables, the narrow edges were planted with all kinds of herbs good for the still-room and for medicines—such as lavender for the linen, to take away the nasty smell of the soap ; the tall tansy for puddings ; thyme, parsley, mint, fennel, and sage for the kitchen ; rosemary, marjoram, southernwood, feverfew, sweetbriar, for medicines and strong waters. Among the herbs flourished, though not yet in bloom, such flowers as will grow without trouble, such as double stocks, carnations, gillyflowers, crocus, lily-of-the-valley, bachelors'-buttons, mignonette, nasturtium, sunflower, monkshood, lupins, and tall hollyhocks. In short, it was, and is still, a beautiful, bounteous, and generous garden, the equal and like of which I have never seen.

The house stood in one corner of the garden, its gable-end turned to the road. Like all the houses in the village, it was covered with roses, and, except the Vicarage, it was the most considerable house in the place. It was of red brick, and had a porch in the front, facing a broad lawn, which served for a bowling-green. The porch was of wood, painted white, and was so broad that there was a bench on either side, where one could be sheltered from north and east winds. At the back of the house a brick wall marked one boundary of our land. It was an ancient broad wall, with no stint of red bricks, such as I love, and covered with moss and lichen— green, gray, red, and yellow. In the places where the mortar had fallen out grew pellitory and green rue, while the top of the wall was bright with yellow stonecrop, tall grasses, and wallflowers already in blossom. The wall ran from the road to within a short distance of high-water mark, where it was succeeded by a wooden paling. Thus our garden was bounded on three sides by road, wall, and sea ; on the fourth side it was separated from the Castle by a field of coarse grass, growing in tufts and tall bents. Under the shelter of the brick wall was a row of bee-hives ; a mighty humming the bees made in summer evenings, and a profitable thing was their honey when it came in, for, of all living creatures, the sailor has the sweetest tooth.

There is always work to do, and someone doing it, in this great garden all the year round. This afternoon the boys were busy among the beds. Sally stood over them, rope's-end in hand, but more for ornament and the badge of office, as the bo's'n carries his cane, than for use, though every boy in our employment has tasted of that rope's-end. Her father, sitting on a wheelbarrow, had a broom in his hand and a pipe in his mouth, thus giving his countenance, so to speak, to the boys' work. To look at him you would have thought that his working days were now over and done, so wrinkled was his face and so bent his shoulders. Yet he was only seventy-five, and lived for twenty years longer.

He it was who managed the boat, taking her down the creek every morning, summer and winter, wet or dry, fair weather or foul, high tide or low. Every sailor in the King's ships knew the boat and the old man, commonly called Daddy, who rowed or sailed her ; and every sailor knew Porchester Sal, the bumboat-woman, who came alongside in the morning with a boat-load of everything belonging to the season ; who knew all the young gentlemen, and even had a word for the first lieutenant. As for the tars, she freely talked with them in their own language, and a rough language that is. She would also, it was said, drink about with any of them, and in the cold mornings, when the air was raw, smoked a pipe of tobacco in the boat. At this time she was five-and-forty years of age, and single. She dressed in all seasons alike, in a sailor's jacket, with a short petticoat and great waterman's boots. For head-gear she never wore anything but a thick thread cap, tied tightly to her head ; round her neck was a red woollen wrapper, the ends tucked under the jacket. Her face was as red and weather-beaten as any sailor's, her hands were as rough and hard ; and I verily believe that her arms were as strong with the daily handling of the oars, the carrying of the baskets, the digging, weeding, and planting of the garden, and the correction of the boys.

This garden was my own, mine inheritance, bequeathed to me by my mother's father, and a providential bequest it proved. The boat was my own. Daddy and Sally were my own, I suppose, for they belonged to the garden. And they sold for us, on board the ship or in the town, the fruits and vegetables in due season. They also prepared and sold to the purveyors of ships' stores, and for those who sold smuggled tea secretly—there are many such in Portsmouth—a great quantity of leaves picked by the boys from the sloe, ash, and elm trees, dried ready for mixing with the real tea. And Sally also grew for the herbalists a great quantity of plants for those concoctions which some people think better than any doctors' stuff.

We had not always lived in Porchester. We lived, when I first remember anything, in a great house in Bloomsbury Square, close to Bedford House. Here we had footmen and a coach, and were, as my father daily in after years reminded me, very great people indeed, he being nothing less than an Alderman. 'But, my dear,' he was wont to say, 'I persuaded myself to retire.' Here he sighed heavily. 'In the City we are born to amass wealth, but I retired. I was already but three years off the Mansion House—but I retired. Well,' here he would look about the room, which was, to be sure, small and ill-furnished, 'the world seldom enjoys the spectacle of a substantial merchant retiring into obscurity in a country cottage.' Here he sighed again.

He retired when I was a little girl of eight or nine, so that I knew nothing of the circumstances connected with his retirement, but I understood well enough that he deeply regretted that step, and longed to be back again on 'Change.

In two words, we now lived in this small house ; and my father, instead of directing the affairs of a great London business, took the accounts daily from Sally on her return from the harbour. And a very flourishing and prosperous business it was, while the war lasted ; and, though I neither knew nor inquired, it not only kept us in comfort, but enabled my father to keep up the appearance of a substantial merchant ; gave him guineas to jingle in his pocket, and preserved for him among the officers and others who used the best room at the tavern of an evening, the dignity and authority which he loved.

At this time I was nineteen years of age. Alas ! it is more than twenty years ago. Good King George is dead at last, and I am nearly forty years old. The garden still lies before me, with its fruit-trees, its flowers, and the bees, but what has become of the girl of nineteen ? Oh, what becomes of our youth and beauty ? Whither do they go when they leave us ? Whither go the fresh and rosy cheeks, the dancing eyes, and the smiling lips ? What becomes of them when they disappear and leave no trace behind ? Those were blue eyes which Raymond loved, and the curls which it pleased him to dangle in his hands and twirl about his fingers, were light brown ; and as for the pink and white of the cheeks— nay, it matters not. The girl was comely, and she found favour in the sight of the only man she could ever love. What more, but to thank the Giver of all good things ? Love and beauty are among the fruits of the earth, for which we pray that they may be given us in due season.

I was sitting in the porch, pretending to be engaged in cutting out and making a new frock. I remember that the stuff was a gray camblet, which is a useful material, and that the frock was already so far advanced that the lining was cut and basted on the camblet. But I was not thinking at all about the work ; for, oh ! what should a girl think about the very day after her lover had spoken to her ? Spoken, do I say ? Nay, kneeled before her and prayed to her, and sworn such vows as made her heart leap up, and her cheek first flush with joy and then turn pale with terror ; for it is the property of love to fill us first with gladness unspeakable and then with fear. And, besides, I heard voices in the parlour, the window being open, and I knew very well whose voices they were, namely, those of the Vicar and my father, and that they were talking of Raymond and myself. For the Vicar had always been the patron and protector of the Arnolds, but it could not be denied that they came from France, and my father hated all Frenchmen.

Presently, however, the conference was over and they both came out together, my father carrying himself, it seemed to me, with more than his usual dignity. Heavens! what a Lord Mayor he would have made, had Heaven so willed it! Authority sat upon his brow; wealth and success were stamped upon his face. He spoke slowly, and as one whose words bring a blessing upon those who hear them. A corpulence above the common, joined to a stature also above the common, a commanding nose, thick eyebrows, and a deep voice, all joined in producing the effect of great natural dignity.

While my father walked upright, swelling with consequence, the Vicar beside him might have been the domestic chaplain to some great nobleman in the presence of his master. For, being tall and thin, and with a stooping figure, he seemed to be deferring to the judgment of a superior. Yet, as his eyes met mine, there was in them a look of encouragement which raised my hopes.

'Ha!' he said, standing before the porch, 'your garden is always before mine, Molly. There is goodly promise for the year, they tell me. Well, Naboth's vineyard was not more desirable. Perhaps Ahab looked down upon it from the keep of his castle, which, I dare say, greatly resembled yon great tower. It is a goodly garden. It is a garden which in the spring should fill the heart with hope, and in the autumn with gratitude.'

''Tis well enough,' said my father, taking my seat. ''Tis well enough, and serves to amuse the child. It grows a small trifle of fruit too, sufficient—ay, 'tis sufficient—for the modest wants of this poor house.'

No doubt one who has known such greatness as my father had enjoyed could talk in such a manner concerning the garden. But— a trifle!

'In former days, Vicar,' my father continued, 'we had our early peas and hothouse grapes from Covent Garden. But a merchant who retires into the country has to content himself with whatever trifle of garden he may light upon.'

'True, sir; 'tis very true. But to our business. Molly, I have this evening been an ambassador to thy father from—nay—thou canst surely guess, child; indeed, in thy cheeks I see that thou hast guessed rightly.'

'From Raymond, Molly,' my father added kindly. 'From the young man, Raymond Arnold.'

'I have pointed out to thy father, Molly, that a gentleman of the ancient county of Provence is not a Frenchman, though he may for the time be under French rule. He speaks not the same tongue; he hath not the same ancestry. Wherefore, thy father's first objection against Frenchmen doth not hold in the case of Raymond.'

'This I grant,' said my father.

'Did not his father die in support of those principles for which we are still contending? And, again,' the Vicar continued, ' 'tis a lad of honourable descent and of illustrious foreign rank, if that were of importance.'

'It is not,' said my father. 'There is no more honourable descent than to be the child of a substantial London merchant. Talk not to me, sir, of French nobles. Heard one ever of an English peer teaching a mere accomplishment for a living?'

'Very well, sir; but it is to the point that he is a lad of good morals and sound principle; no drinker or brawler; who enjoys already some success in his calling.'

'These things, Vicar, are much more to the point.'

'In short, Molly,' said the Vicar, turning to me, 'thy father consents to this match, but it must be on a condition.'

'Oh, sir!' I kissed my father's hand. 'You are all goodness. Is it for me to dispute any condition you may think well to impose?'

'The condition, Molly,' said the Vicar, 'is that no change may be made in the existing arrangements.'

'Why, sir, what change should be made?'

'When daughters marry, my child, they generally go away and leave their fathers; or they even turn their fathers out to make room for the husbands.'

Lovers are a selfish folk. I had not considered the difference which my marriage might make to my father.

'Sir,' I threw myself at his feet, 'this house is yours. If there is room in it for Raymond as well, we shall be grateful to you.'

'Good girl,' he said, raising me, 'good girl; I will continue to manage this little property for thee, to be sure.' He looked at the house with condescension. 'The cottage is small, yet it is comfortable; in appearance it is hardly worthy of a substantial merchant, yet my habits are simple; the situation is quiet, and the garden fruits are, as I said before, sufficient for my wants. I have retired from the City; I desire no more riches than I have. I would willingly end my days here. Enough said, child; I wish thee'—

he kissed me on the forehead—'I wish thee all happiness, my dear.'

This said, he rose with dignity, as if no more need be said, and walked out to the garden gate, and so to the tavern where the better sort met daily.

'So,' said the Vicar, 'here is a pretty day's work—two young fools made happy. Well, I pray that it may turn out well; a fools' paradise is a very pretty place when one is young. He loves thee, that is very sure ; why, thou wilt be a Countess—Ho ! ho !—Countess Molly, when thou art married, child ; Sally will leave off taking the boat down the harbour, I suppose, unless Raymond paints a coronet upon the bows and thy new name, Madame la Comtesse d'Eyragues.'

Then the Vicar left me and departed ; but he stopped in the road, and listened to the cobbler singing his eternal refrain :

' One pig in ten,
One pig in ten,
Why should the rogue have one pig in ten ?'

'Jacob,' he said, 'must thy song ever smack of the pot-house ? And when did thy Vicar ask thee for a pig ?'

'With submission, your reverence,' said Jacob, hammer in air. ' What odds for the words so the music fits the work ?'

'Idle words, Jacob, are like the thistle-down, which flies unheeded over the fields, and afterwards produces weeds of its kind. Would not the Old Hundredth suit thy turn ?'

Jacob shook his head.

' Nay, sir,' he said, 'my kind of work is not like yours. The making of a sermon, I doubt not, is mightily helped by the Old Hundredth or Alleluia ; but cobbling is delicate work, and wants a tune that runs up and down, and may be sung quick or slow, according as the work lays in heel or toe. I tried Alleluia, but, Lord ! I took two days with Alleluia over a job that with "Morgan Rattler " or "Black Jack " I could have knocked off in three hours.'

' In that case, Jacob,' said the Vicar, ' the Church will forgive thee thy fib of one pig in ten.'

When they were gone I sat down again, my heart much lighter, though my mind was agitated with thinking of what we should have done had my father withheld his consent. And for some time I heard nothing that went on, though Sally administered the rope's end to one of the boys, and the cobbler went on singing and the children shouting.

'Presently, however, I was disagreeably interrupted by the trampling of a horse's hoofs, the barking of dogs, the cracking of a whip, and a loud, harsh voice railing at a stable-boy. The voice it was which affected me, because I knew it for the voice of my cousin Tom, who had been drinking and laying bets with some of the officers all the morning, and was now about to ride home. Then the horse came clattering down the street, and he saw me in the porch, I suppose, for he drew rein at the gate and bawled out, his voice being thick with drink :

'Molly, Cousin Molly, I say! Come to the gate—come closer. Well, I have to-day heard a pretty thing of thee—a pretty thing, Molly,' he said; 'truly, nothing less than that you want to marry a Frenchman, a beggarly Frenchman.'

'What business is that of yours ?' I asked.

'You may tell him, Mistress Molly, that I shall horsewhip him.'

I laughed in his face. A girl always believes that her lover is the bravest of men.

'You, Tom? Why, to be sure, Raymond does not desire to fight his sweetheart's cousin ; but if you so much as lift your little finger at him, I promise you, big as you are, that you will be sorry for it.'

At this he used dreadful language, swearing what he would do when he should meet the man I preferred to himself.

'And him a Frenchman, Molly,' he concluded. 'To think of it! Wouldst throw me over for a beggarly Frenchman ? But wait, only wait till I have made him roar for mercy and beg my pardon on his knees. Then, perhaps——'

'Oh !' I cried, 'go away quickly, lest he should come and take you at your word.'

He began to swear again, but suddenly stopped and went away, cantering along the road, followed by his dogs ; and, though I knew my Raymond to be brave and strong, I was glad that he did not meet this half-drunken cousin of mine in his angry mood.

Tom Wilgress, my mother's nephew, and therefore my own first cousin, who afterwards broke his neck over a hedge fox-hunting, was then a young man about five-and-twenty. He was of a sturdy and well-built figure, but his cheeks were already red and puffed up with strong drink. He had a small estate, which he bequeathed to me, part of which he farmed, and part let out to tenants. It was situated north of Portsdown Hill, under the Forest of Bere. But the greater part of his time he spent at the Castle or the village tavern drinking, smoking tobacco, making bets, running races, badger-drawing, cock-fighting, and all kinds of sport with

the officers of the garrison. He professed to be in love with me,
and continually entreated me to marry him, a thing which I could
not contemplate without horror. Sometimes he would fall on his
knees and supplicate me with tears, swearing that he loved me
better than his life (he did not say better than a bowl of punch),
and sometimes he would threaten me with dreadful pains and
punishments if I continued in my contumacy.

This evening I clearly foresaw, from the redness of his face, the
thickness of his voice, and a certain glassy look in his eye, that he
was about to adopt the latter method. Heaven pity the wife of
such a man as my cousin Tom! But he is now dead, and hath
left me his estate, wherefore I will speak of him no more evil than
I can help, yet must speak the truth.

When he was gone, I returned to my work.

Presently, I was again interrupted, this time by Madam Claire.
She had with her one of the French prisoners. It was a young
man whom we all knew very well. He was a sous-lieutenant,
which means some kind of ensign in a French infantry regiment,
about Raymond's age—that is, between twenty-three and twenty-
four—and had been a prisoner for three years. We knew a great
many of the French officers ; this was natural, because we were the
only people in the village who could talk their language. I say we,
because the Arnolds taught me, and in their cottage we spoke
both French and Provençal. But this young man was our special
friend ; he was the friend of Raymond, whom he called his
brother, and of Madam Claire, whom he called his mother. Of
course, therefore, he was my friend as well. The reasons for the
affection we bore him were many. First, he came from the South
of France, and was therefore a countryman of Raymond's, and had
spoken, like Raymond, the language of the South when a child.
Next, when he was first landed he fell ill with some kind of
malignant fever, which I believe would have carried him off but
for Madam Claire, who nursed him, sitting with him day and
night, a service for which he was ever grateful. Thirdly, he was
a young man of the happiest disposition, the kindest heart, and
the sweetest manners possible.

As he came from the same part of the country, it was not strange
that he should be like Raymond, those of Southern France being
all dark of complexion, and with black hair and eyes. But it was
remarkable that he should be so very much like him that they
might be taken for twins. They were of the same height, which
was something under the average height of an Englishman ; their

heads were of the same shape, their eyes and hair of the same shade, their chins rounded in the same way ; even their voices were the same.

The resemblance was the greater this evening because, his own uniform having fallen into rags, Pierre wore the dress of a civilian, a brown coat and a round hat. His hair was neatly tied and powdered, his linen was clean ; he might have passed very well for what they call the country Jessamy.

Of course, those who knew them well, knew the differences between the two, just as a shepherd knows each sheep, though they seem to the general world all exactly alike. So many were their points of difference, that it was impossible to mistake one for the other. Pierre was of a larger and stouter frame, in manner he was more vivacious, his step was livelier, his gesture more marked, he talked more. It was strange to note that Pierre, as well as Raymond, had what is called the air of distinction. No one could fail to remark that he looked, as we in England should say, every inch a gentleman, and carried himself accordingly, yet with something of the French gallantry and swagger which was not unbecoming. Yet he was by birth a son of the people ; he came, like General Hoche, the soldier whom most he admired, from the gutter, and he was proud of it. Raymond, for his part, was of a more quiet habit—you would have taken him for a scholar—who talked little ; a dreamer, contented to accept whatever fortune offered. Had he been a soldier, he might have had the same ambitions as his friend, but he would have talked about them less.

'Their faces,' said Madam Claire, 'are those of my countrymen. Some call it the Roman face ; you may see it on the old monuments in the cemetery of Arles. Bonaparte is reported to have this face, though he is but a Corsican.'

I have never seen any nuns, but when I hear or read of them I must needs think of Madam Claire, who had been what is called a religieuse, but I know not of what kind. In religion she was named Sister Angélique, but her Chrissom name was Claire. She wore a frock of blue stuff with a long cloak of the same ; on her head was a cap or hood of the same, with a white starched cap beneath ; she had also a large white collar, round her neck was a gold chain with a crucifix, and in her hand she always carried a book, because her rules obliged her to read prayers at certain hours all through the day. She spent her time chiefly in the Castle infirmary, where she nursed and comforted the sick prisoners. Her face was pale, but sweet to look upon, and to me it seemed always as if she never thought of herself at all, but always of the person with whom she was speaking.

We are taught that to hide in a convent is but to exchange one set of temptations for another, but it would surely be a blessed thing if our Church allowed men and women to renounce the things in which we weaker creatures place our happiness (such as love, marriage, and tender children, or place, power, and wealth), and to give all their labour and thought for the good of others. This is what Madam Claire did.

'Great news!' cried Pierre. 'Great news indeed! Peace is concluded and signed. We are all going to be returned.'

This was news indeed. For four or five months nothing else had been spoken of; but though there was a cessation of hostilities, there was always the fear that the negotiations would be broken off.

'Peace!' I replied. 'And what have they done for the émigrés?'

'I believe they have done nothing. Vive la paix!—until we are ready to go home again. Then, tap-tap goes the drum, and to the field again, and I come home a colonel at least.'

'I understand not,' said Madam, 'how peace can be concluded unless the King returns with the nobles, and the old order is established again.'

'The old order!' Pierre laughed. 'Oh, ma mère, the old order is the old world before the Deluge. But you do not understand. Whatever else returns, the old order will never return. Why will a people once free return to slavery?'

'But for what else has Great Britain fought, except for the old order?'

'I know not, indeed. But this I know, that the old order is dead and buried.'

Certainly there was never any man who more honestly believed in the Revolution than Pierre. Yet not like the wretches who were our first prisoners in that war, who shouted the Carmagnole and tossed their caps in the air, filled with hatred for priests and aristos. They were gone, and they would never come back again.

'How, then,' said Madam, 'are we to go back again, unless they return us our property?'

'Your property is sold, and your rights are lost,' Pierre replied. 'Come back and join the people. You are no longer a separate caste; we are all French together. Well, if you please, we will carve a slice out of Germany and give it to you. And your share, ma mère, I will conquer for you with my own sword.'

In the evening, when they were gone, I had another visitor—Raymond himself—and we talked together, as lovers do, of nothing but ourselves. The peace was signed. It was not possible that Great Britain had abandoned the émigrés ; some compensation would be made. For his part, he loved not the new order in France, and decided not to live there ; he would be an Englishman ; but with this compensation, he would do this and that, always with me. Oh, the dear, delightful talk !

I went with him at nine o'clock to the garden gate. Sally was standing there waiting for us, her arms akimbo—well, with her short petticoats and big boots she looked exactly like a sailor.

'So, young gentleman,' she said, 'I hear that my mistress has promised to marry you.'

'Indeed she has, Sally.'

'A lucky and a happy man her husband will be.'

'He will, Sally.'

'We have known you a long time, Mr. Raymond.'

'More than eight years, Sally.'

'And yet it can't be denied that you are a Frenchman, much the same as those poor fellows now in the Castle.'

'I am an Englishman now, Sally, because I shall have an English wife, which of course naturalizes a man.'

'I hope,' said Sally, 'that it's more than skin deep, and that we shan't have no fallings off.'

CHAPTER II.

PORCHÉSTER CASTLE.

THE Castle, which, now that the long wars are over, one hopes for many years, is silent and deserted, its ruined courts empty, its crumbling walls left to decay, presented a different appearance indeed in the spring of the year 1802. For in those days it was garrisoned by two regiments of militia, and was occupied by the prodigious number of eight thousand prisoners.

I am told that there are other ancient castles in the country even more extensive and more stately than Porchester ; but I have never seen them, and am quite satisfied to believe that for grandeur, extent, and the awe of antiquity, there can be none which can surpass, and few which can pretend to equal, this monument. It is certainly ruinous in parts, yet still so strong as to serve for a great prison, but it is not overthrown, and its crumbling walls, broken roofs, and dismantled chambers surround the place with a solemnity which affects the most careless visitor.

It is so ancient that there are some who pretend that parts of it may belong to British times, while it is certain that the whole of the outer wall was built by the Romans. In imitation of their camps, it stands foursquare, and has hollow round towers in the sides and at the corners. The spot was chosen, not at the mouth of the harbour, the Britons having no means of attacking ships entering or going out ; but at the very head of the harbour, where the creek runs up between the shallows, which are banks of mud at low water. Hither came the Roman galleys, laden with military stores, to land them under the protection of the Castle. When the Romans went away, and the Saxons came, who loved not fighting behind walls, they neglected the fortress, but built a church within the walls, and there laid their dead. When in their turn the Normans came, they built a castle after their own fashion, within the Roman walls. This is the stronghold, containing four square towers and a fortified entrance. And the Normans built the water-gate and the gate tower. The rest of the great space became the outer bailly of the Castle. They also added battlements to the wall, and dug a moat, which they filled with sea-water at high tide.

The battlements of the Normans are now broken down or crumbling away ; great patches of the rubble work have fallen here and there. Yet one can walk round the narrow ledge designed for the bowmen. The wall is crowned with waving grass and wallflowers, and up the sides grow elder-bushes, blackberry, ivy, and bramble, as luxuriantly as in any hedge beyond Portsdown. If you step out through the water-gate, which is now roofless, with little left to show its former splendour, except a single massive column, you will find, at high tide, the water lapping the lowest stones of the towers, just as it did when the Romans built them. Instead of the old galleys, which must have been light in draught, to come up Porchester Creek, there are now lying half a dozen boats, the whole fleet of the little village. On the other side of the water are the wooded islets of Great and Little Horsea, and I suppose they look to-day much as they did a thousand years ago. On this side you look towards the east ; but if you get to the south side of the Castle, and walk across a narrow meadow which lies between the wall and the sea, you have a very different view. For you look straight across the harbour to its very mouth, three miles away ;

you gaze upon a forest of masts and upon ships of every kind, from the stately man-o'-war to the saucy pink, and, twenty years ago, of every nation—because, in those days, we seemed at war with half the world—from the French-built frigate, the most beautiful ship that floats, to the Mediterranean xebecque, all of them prizes. Here they lie, some ready for sea, some just arrived, some battered by shot, some newly repaired and fresh from the yard ; some—it seems a cruel fate for ships which have fought the battles of their country—converted into hulks for convicts and for prisoners ; some store-ships—why, there is no end to the number and the kind of the ships lying in the harbour. They could tell, if they could speak, of many a battle and many a storm ; some of them are as old as the days of Admiral Benbow ; one poor old hulk is so old that she was once a man-o'-war in the old Dutch wars of Charles II. and carried on board, it is said, the Duke of York himself.

In the dockyard, within the harbour, the wooden walls of England are built ; here they are fitted up ; from this place they go forth to fight the French. Heavens ! how many ships we sent forth every year ! How many were built in the yard ! How many brave fellows were sacrificed year after year before the insatiable rage for war which possessed one man, and through him all Europe could be overcome, and the tyrant confined in his cage, like a wild beast, until he should die !

Standing under those walls, I say, we could look straight down the harbour to the forts which guard its entrance ; we could see in the upper part the boats plying backwards and forwards ; we could hear the booming of the salutes ; we could even see the working of the semaphore, by whose mysterious arms news is conveyed to London in half an hour. And the sight of the ships, the movement of the harbour, the distant banging of the guns, made one, even one who lived in so quiet a village as Porchester, feel as if one was taking part in the great events which shook the world. It was a hard time to many, and an anxious time for all ; a time full of lavish expenditure for the country ; a time when bread was dear and work scarce, with trade bad and prospects uncertain. Alas ! with what beating of heart did we wait for news, and gather together to listen when a newspaper was brought to the village ! For still it seemed as if, defeat his navies though we might, and though we chaised his cruisers off the seas, and tore down the French flag from his colonies, the Corsican Usurper was marching from one triumph to another, until the whole of Europe, save Russia and England, was subjugated and laid prostrate at his feet.

As for bad times, we at Porchester—so near to Portsmouth, where all the shopkeepers were making their fortunes, and the ships caused so great a daily expenditure of money—felt them but little, save for the cost of coals, which were, I remember, as much as fifty shillings a ton ; and the lack of French brandy, which we women never wanted to drink, and of Gascony or claret wine, which we replaced, quite to our own satisfaction, with the delicate cowslip or the wholesome ginger, made in our own homes. Think, however, if there were so many men afloat—a hundred and twenty thousand sailors in His Majesty's Navy alone, to say nothing of those aboard the merchant ships, coasters, colliers, and privateers— there were also so many women ashore, and so many hearts torn with anxiety at the news of every engagement. Custom hardens the heart, and no doubt many, even of those who loved their husbands tenderly, rose up in the morning and went to bed at night with no more than a simple prayer for his safety. You shall hear, however, one woman's history, by which you may learn to feel for others. What am I, and what have I done, that, while so many poor creatures were stricken with lifelong grief, my shadow should have given place to sunshine, my sorrow to joy ?

The outer ward of the Castle was open every Sunday, because the church stands in the south-east corner. It is the old Saxon church altered by the Normans. Formerly it was shaped like a cross ; but one of the arms has long since fallen down. The nave is long and narrow, and rather dark, which pleased Madam Claire, because it reminded her of the churches of Provence, which, it seems, are all kept dark on account of the hot sunshine outside. On one side of the nave is hung up a great wooden picture of the Royal Arms, with the lion and the unicorn, to remind us of our loyalty ; at the end is a gallery where the choir sit on Sundays, and below the gallery an old stone font, ornamented, like the chancel, with round arches curiously interlaced, very pretty, though much worn with age. In the churchyard outside, there is an old yew among the graves. As for tombstones, they are few, because, when a villager dies, the mound which marks his grave is known as long as his memory lasts, which is as long as his children, or at most his grandchildren, survive him. What need of a tombstone when the man, obscure in his life, is clean forgotten ? And how many, even of the great, are remembered longer than these villagers ?

To this church we came every Sunday ; my father and I sitting in the pew on the right-hand of the chancel, and, after the prisoners' return, Madam Claire and Raymond with us. The left-hand pew was occupied by Mr. Phipps, retired purser, and his wife, a haughty lady, daughter of a Portsmouth purveyor to the fleet. In the long nave, never half filled, sat the villagers ; the choir were in the gallery at the end, where we had music of violin, violoncello, and flute ; in the transept were the soldiers of the garrison, near the church door, so that in case of trouble they might troop out quickly.

There were no gentlefolk in the village, unless we count ourselves. I am well aware that people who sell fruit and vegetables from a market-boat, even though the head of the family be an alderman, cannot be regarded as belonging to the quality. But if a woman is by marriage raised to her husband's rank, it is beyond question that my own position, had everyone her rights, should be among the noblest in the county, even though the boat still goes down the harbour (the profits being very far short of what they were in the war-time), and though some persons, jealous of my connection with the old French nobility, sniff, as I am informed, at the pretensions of a market-gardener. Sniffing cannot extinguish birth ; and perhaps now that we are in easier circumstances, and have succeeded to my cousin Tom's estate, my son may one day resume the ancient title.

Outside the gates, the village tavern, now so quiet the week through except on Saturday evenings, was crowded all day long, with soldiers drinking, smoking tobacco, and talking about the war. There was a canteen in the Castle, but the men preferred the tavern, because, I suppose, it was more homelike. In the evening there was a nightly gathering, or club, held in the upper room, where the officers, with a few gentlemen from the village, assembled to take their punch.

The regiments in garrison in the year 1801 were the Royal Dorset Militia and the Denbigh Militia, under the command of Colonel the Hon. George Pitt, afterwards second Lord Rivers, at this time a man of fifty years.

There were in the Castle at that date no fewer than eight thousand prisoners. It seems an incredible number to be confined in one place ; but in this country altogether thirty-five thousand French prisoners were confined, of whom four thousand were at Forton near Gosport ; nine thousand in the hulks in the harbour, and I know not how many at Waltham, in Essex ; at Norman Cross ; at Plymouth, and up the Medway. These men were not, it is true, all French sailors; but they comprised the very pick and flower of the French Navy. Why, the pretended peace of 1802, for what purpose was it concluded but to get back those sailors whom we fought again at Trafalgar? As for exchange, 'tis true that France had some ten thousand English prisoners, with a few thousand Hanoverians; but the advantage was all on their side.

A great fortress, with eight thousand prisoners and a garrison of two thousand men within a stone's throw of the village, yet their presence disturbed us little. In the day-time those prisoners who were on parole walked out of the Castle, it is true, but they made no disturbance; the common sort, of course, were not suffered out on parole at all, so that we never saw them unless we went into the Castle. Their provisions were sent up the harbour from Portsmouth; it was by the same way that most of the visitors came to see them. Within the Castle, among the prisoners, were farriers, blacksmiths, tailors, shoemakers, and tradesmen of every kind, so that they had no occasion to go outside for anything except for poultry, eggs, and fresh butter, which the farmers' wives brought to the Castle from the country round. As for the fare of the prisoners, it must be owned that it was of the simplest. Yet, how many a poor man in this country would be thankful could he look forward confidently to receive every day a pound and a half of bread and half a pound of beef, with vegetables! No beer or rum was served out, but those who had money might buy it in the canteen, and that of the best and at a cheap rate.

All that we heard of the prisoners was the beating of the drums and the blowing of the whistles in the morning and evening. At night there were a hundred sentries posted round the Castle, almost close to each other, and every half-hour the sergeant of the main guard went his round and challenged the sentries. Then those in the village who were awake heard the hoarse answer of the men— ' All's well '—and the sergeant marched on, and you heard the same words a little farther off, and so on, quite round the Castle, getting fainter as the sergeant reached the water-gate, and becoming gradually louder as he returned to the main guard station outside the Castle gate. Also, at nine o'clock, the Curfew bell was rung, when all lights had to be put out, and the men turned in. Once there was a great scare, for the man whose duty it was to ring the bell, an old man named Clapham, fell asleep just before nine and woke up at midnight; thinking he had been sleeping only for a minute or two, he seized the rope and rang lustily. Then the garrison was hastily turned out, and the whole country-side, roused by the alarm of the midnight bell, and all the men in the village, and from Cosham Wymering, Widley, Southwick, Fareham, and even Titchbrook, all with one consent came pouring into Porchester armed with whatever they could snatch, thinking it was a rising of the prisoners. At the head of the Porchester squad marched none other than our Sally, armed with a pitchfork and full of valour.

They were at night confined to their quarters, some in wooden buildings erected in the outer court, some in the four towers of the inner Castle. Of these the largest, the keep, was divided into fourteen rooms, without counting the dungeons. Gloomy rooms they were, being lighted only by narrow loopholes.

The other towers were smaller ; in one—it was whispered with shuddering—there was a dissecting-room, used by the French surgeons who were prisoners, and by the English regimental surgeon. As for the men's quarters, it may be understood that these were not luxurious. Some of them had hammocks, but when the press grew thicker, straw was thrown upon the floor for those to sleep upon for whom hammock-room could not be found. Hard as was the lot of the Porchester prisoners, however, it was comfort compared with that of the men immured at Forton, where there was hardly room to stand in the exercise ground, and they lay at night as thick as herrings in a barrel ; or with those who were confined on the hulks, which were used as punishment ships, where the refractory and desperate were sent, and where half-rations brought them to reason and obedience. At Porchester the prisoners got at least plenty of fresh air, sunshine, and room to walk about. For the refractory, besides the hulks and half-rations, there was a black hole, and if a man tried to escape, the sentries had orders, after calling upon him to stand, to fire if he did not obey.

The prisoners, I have said, were mostly French sailors ; but there were a good many soldiers among them, those taken, namely, in the conquest of the French colonies. There were also hundreds of privateers' men, as good sailors as any in the Republican Navy. Among them were many Vendeans who had been concerned in the rising ; they thought to escape the penalty which overtook so many of their comrades by going on board a privateer, but, being taken prisoners, jumped, as one may say, out of the fire into the frying-pan. Among them also, at one time, were a thousand negroes, once slaves, but turned into soldiers by the French, and taken at the Island of St. Vincent. The cold weather, however, killed most of these poor fellows very quickly. Another company of soldiers were the fellows intended for the invasion of Ireland, and taken off the Irish coast ; a sturdy band of veterans they were. After the battle of Camperdown no fewer than one thousand eight hundred Dutch sailors were brought to the Castle ; but these gallant Hollanders, who had been dragged into the war without any wish on their part to fight for France, mostly volunteered into our service, and became good British sailors.

The earliest prisoners were zealous Republicans, especially those taken prisoners by Lord Howe after the 'First of June,' in 1794. These men used to show their sentiments by dancing and singing 'Ca Ira' and 'La Carmagnole' every night, and flinging their red caps in the air.

> ' Le Duc de York avait permis
> Que Dunkerque lui serait remis ;
> Mais il a mal conté,
> Grace à vos canoniers.
> Dansons la Carmagnole ;
> 　Vive le son,
> 　Vive le son—
> Dansons la Carmagnole—
> 　Vive le son
> 　Du canon.'

Such is the ignorance of the British soldier that the men understood not one word, and as they only laughed and were amused at these demonstrations, the zeal of these Republicans abated.

After the defeat of the Spanish fleet by Admiral Jervis off Cape St. Vincent, a great number of Spaniards were brought in, and these proved a very desperate lot indeed. It was a company of these fellows who laid a plot to escape, thinking to take one of the small vessels in the harbour and to get out to sea. They got some horseshoe files, ground them to a fine edge and a point, and fitted them to handles, so as to make excellent daggers. Armed with these they got into the dungeons under the Queen's Tower, and began to dig their way out. They were secured after a desperate fight, and sent on board the hulks.

Among the officers the most remarkable was a certain General Tate, formerly of the Irish Brigade, who was sent with a legion composed entirely of galley-slaves to invade the coast of Wales—a wild and desperate attempt, resolved upon, one would think, with the view of getting rid of the galley-slaves and effecting a diversion of troops to a distant part of the country. The ships were wrecked at a place called Fishguard, and the men mutinied and spread about the country to rob and plunder, until they were caught or shot down. Their commander was a fine old man, tall and erect, with long white hair, an hereditary enemy to Great Britain, but good company and a man of excellent manners.

There were other notable prisoners. The wretch Tallien, who murdered seven hundred Royalists at Quiberon, was here for a short time. The General Baraguay d'Hilliers was also here. Once there arrived a whole shipload of young ladies, taken on board a ship bound for the Isle of France, whither they were going in search of husbands. They were not detained long, and the ladies and gentry round about made their stay pleasant for them with dances and parties. One of them remained behind to marry an Englishman. There was also a certain black general, whose name I forget, but he had with him four wives; and there was a young fellow who, after six months in prison, fell ill, and was discovered to be a woman. Strange things happened among them. Thus one day, a certain French captain, who had been morose for a long time, mounted to the roof of the keep and threw himself off, being weary of his life. When they quarrelled, which was often, they fought duels with swords, for want of proper weapons, made out of bits of iron, filed and sharpened and tied to the ends of sticks. And there was one man who was continually escaping. He would climb down the wall at night unseen by the sentries; then he would seek shelter in the Forest of Bere, and live by depredation among the poultry-yards and farmhouses till he was caught and sent back. Once he made his way to London, and called at the house of M. Otto, who was the French Commissioner for the prisoners.

The daily life of the prisoners was wearisome and monotonous. Some of them had money sent by their friends, with which they would buy drink, tobacco, and clothes; most had none. They lounged away the hours talking idly; they gambled all day long, for what stakes I know not, but they were as eager on the games as if there were thousands of pounds depending on the result. They played dominoes, backgammon, and drafts; they smoked as much tobacco as they could procure; few of them—I speak of the common sort—knew how to read or write; their language was full of blasphemy and oaths. The soldiers for the most part had abandoned all religion, but the sailors retained their former faith. The happiest among them were those who had a trade and could work at it. The carpenter, tailor, shoemakers, cooks, and barbers, were always at work, and made considerable earnings. Besides the regular trades, there were arts by which large sums were made. The place in the summer was crowded with visitors, who came from all the country round—from Portsmouth, the Isle of Wight,

Southampton, Lymington, Faversham ; even from Winchester and Chichester — to gaze upon the prisoners. These people, after staring at the strange, wild creatures, unkempt and ragged, were easily persuaded to buy the pretty things which the more ingenious of them carved, such as toys, tobacco-stoppers, and nicknacks out of wood, the simpler things of soft deal, but the more expensive out of some chance piece of oak or pine-knot ; out of beef-bones they made models of ships, chessmen, draughts, dominoes, and card counters ; out of dried straws they braided little boxes, dinner-mats, and all kinds of pretty, useless things ; and some of them made thread-lace so beautifully that it was sold at a great price and carried all about the country, and all the lace-makers began to cry out, when the Government stopped that industry.

Two priests were allowed to go in and out among them, and to celebrate the papistical mass, which was done every morning in a ruined gallery called the Chapel. It was boarded, glass was put into the window, a door was provided, and an altar. Madam Claire came daily, and many of the Vendean and Breton sailors. The rest stayed away, even on Sundays, and many, if the priest spoke to them of religion, answered with blasphemy and execration. Why should a horrid atheism be joined to Republican principles ? Yet the United States of America and the Swiss States are not atheistical.

CHAPTER III.

THE FAMILY LUCK.

THE Arnolds—whose name was Arnault, but it has thus been Englished—came to Porchester early in the year 1794. Why they directed their steps to this village, I know not. They were saved, with many more, when the city of Toulon was taken by the French. Raymond, who was then fourteen years of age, has often described to me the terrible night when the French poured shot and shell upon the town, while the English fired the arsenal and destroyed those ships which they could not carry out. With his mother he was taken on board an English ship, being separated by the crowd from his father, who was unhappily left behind. On board the same ship was found his aunt, Madam Claire, called in religion Sister Angélique. How she got there she knew not, nor could she ever remember, her wits being scattered for the time with the terrors of the night, the awful flames, the roar of the cannon, and the bursting of shells. .When, however, she recovered her senses, it was found that she was still grasping the bag which contained the most precious of all the family treasures, namely, the Golden Rose, presented by a certain Pope, who lived I know not how long ago—it was when the Popes were at Avignon, instead of Rome—to one of the ladies of their house, then, and until the Revolution, one of the most illustrious houses in the South of France. With the Rose the Pope gave his blessing, with the promise, it was said—though how mere man, even the Pope of Rome, can presume to make such a promise one knows not—that so long as the Rose remained with the family, the line should never cease. Certainly the line hath never ceased for five hundred years and more, though after the death of Raymond's father he himself, a boy of thirteen, was the sole representative. As for the Rose itself, which is now in my possession and kept locked up, it is a strange thing to look at, being the imitation of a rose-bush about eighteen inches high in pure red gold. No one would guess, without being told, that it was intended for a rose-bush, for the trunk and branches are all straight and stiff, as much like a real rose-bush as a tree in a sampler is like a real tree. It is provided with leaves, also of gold, and with flowers and buds, which were set with all kinds of precious stones, small in size, but beautiful in colour, such as rubies, emeralds, sapphires, and many others whose names I know not. I suppose there is no other example in the whole of His Majesty's realms of such a Rose. I have heard that the King of Spain or the Emperor of Austria may possibly have one, but probably there is no other Holy Rose in the possession of a private family.

When they were landed at Portsmouth, these fugitives had nothing ; neither money, nor clothes, nor friends. One of them was a lady who knew nothing of the world, having been for the most of her life in a convent ; another was a lady whose anxiety for her husband was quickly driving her mad ; and the third was only a boy. A more pitiful party was never landed from France, not even counting that boatload of unfortunate émigrés which was found in Southampton Water one morning, starving and penniless, and almost naked. There was nothing by which these ladies could earn their bread, because they could do nothing. Yet they were richer than any of the rest, because they had with them the Golden Rose.

I know not exactly when they learned the truth about the head of their house thus left to the mercies of the Revolutionists, but it was after they landed at Portsmouth and before they went to

Porchester. The news was brought to them by an eye-witness. The Republican Army, masters of the city, made the whole of the remaining inhabitants prisoners. And they shot all those, including the Comte d'Eyragues, who were of rank and position. Against him, it was said, a certain man, who had been a dependent or humble friend, gave information, so that his fate was at once decided, and he was shot. And when this news arrived, his widow went out of her mind, and, unlike Madam Claire, who had only been scared, she never recovered.

'Ladies,' said the Vicar of Porchester, when he was first called to consider their case, 'there is no alternative. You must sell this precious relic.'

He addressed both ladies, but only one heard and understood him.

'Alas !' cried that one, 'if it were not for Raymond I would rather starve than part with it. And to let it go is to imperil the poor boy's life, since there is none other to continue the family.'

'You may send it to London,' said the Vicar, 'to be sold to some great nobleman as a wonderful curiosity. Or you may sell it to a merchant for the value of its gold and precious stones. Or, if you prefer, you might sell it little by little. Thus you might keep the Rose itself for a long time by selling the jewels of the flowers. See, some of the stones are large and valuable. Take one out, and let me sell it for your immediate wants. When the money is exhausted you can give me another, and so on. Perhaps, long before you come to an end, your fortunes will change ; the Republic will be overthrown, and the émigrés returned.'

'Alas !' she cried again. 'The jewels are a part of the Holy Rose, and they have been blessed by the Pope himself. Is it not the sin of sacrilege ?'

'On the contrary, madam,' the Vicar replied, smiling. 'I suppose that the blessing of the Pope has never before proved of so practical a value.'

I remember very well the day of their arrival, for the news had spread abroad that some French people were going to live in Mr. Phipps's cottage, and I went out to see them come. They were brought up in a boat from Portsmouth, and landed close to the water-gate of the Castle. (There were no prisoners in the Castle as yet.) The Vicar was with them, and led them through the Castle to the village. You may be sure we all stared, never thinking that we should behold on English ground so strange a creature as a nun. Yet here was one, dressed in a blue cloak and blue frock, with a white starched hood or cap. She carried a bag in her hand, and round her neck was a gold chain with a crucifix. On one side of her walked our Vicar, who, I suppose, had persuaded them to seek this asylum ; and on the other a lady richly dressed, though there were the stains of the voyage and rough weather upon her fine clothes. The nun was pale, and walked with her eyes downcast ; this lady tossed her head and laughed, talking without cessation. She laughed because she was out of her mind, having been driven mad, we learned, by terror and the loss of her husband; and she talked because she believed that her husband was still living, and that he was always with her day and night. This belief she maintained till her death, and certainly nothing happier could have befallen the poor lady. Very soon those who went to the house began to believe that the spirit of her husband was permitted to remain on earth for his wife's protection ; and though one may not be believed, I dare assert that the haunted house had no terrors for me, though a ghost in my own room would have driven me mad with fear. Behind the ladies walked a handsome boy, black-eyed and with black hair. Little did I think how that boy was to become the whole joy of my life.

There was never, I am certain, a household more frugal than this. The two ladies seemed to live altogether upon bread and salad, or upon bread dipped in oil ; while Madam Claire rigorously kept all the fasts of her Church (though none of the feasts), abstaining, on those days, from all food except that which is absolutely necessary. They kept fowls, the eggs of which were reserved for Raymond. They lived in a little cottage at three pounds a year. As for their clothes, Madam Claire mended them, washed and ironed them ; though sometimes Raymond was in need of boots and coats, when money must be found. Yet, with all this frugality, the stones of the Holy Rose slowly diminished ; its flowers began to assume a shabby and (so to speak) an autumnal aspect ; for the years went on, and the Republic was not overthrown, nor were the émigrés invited to return to their property.

When we became friends, which was very soon, the boy taught me his language, and I taught him mine. Which was the apter scholar I know not. He was three years older than I, but was never ashamed to play with a girl. When he had no work to do— either lessons for the Vicar, or work in the garden where they grew their salads—he would go with me, either to row down the creek among the men-o'-war in the harbour, or to ramble in the woods beyond Portsdown Hill. And thus we continued companions and friends, after we were grown out of boy and girl and before we became lovers—though I believe we were lovers from the beginning.

Raymond was not a bookish boy, nor did he take to the learning with which the Vicar would have willingly supplied him in ample quantities had he desired. But though he grew up a gentle young man, as a boy he excelled in all kinds of manly games, and was ready to wrestle, run, or leap with any of his own age, or to fight with any who called him French Frog, or Johnny Crapaud. Consequently he received the respect which is always paid to the possessor of courage. It is strange to note how boys will sometimes become enemies and rivals from the very first. This was the case with my Cousin Tom and Raymond. Tom was the stronger, but Raymond the more active. Tom spoke behind Raymond's back of French impudence, French presumption, and French brag ; but I never heard that he allowed himself those liberties before Raymond's face. And I well remember one 26th of July, which is Portsdown Fair, how, in the sports upon the Running Walks at the back of Richardson's Theatre, Raymond laid Tom fair and flat upon his back at wrestling, so that he limped away shaken all over and growling about foul play, though it was as fair a throw as was ever seen.

Later on it pleased Tom to describe himself as my wooer, which was ridiculous, because I never could have given a thought to Tom, even if Raymond had not been there before him. Who could endure the caresses of a man who was always longing to be where cocks are fought, badgers drawn, prize-fights fought, races run, and drink flowing ; whose clothes smelt of the stable, and whose language was that of grooms, hostlers, and jockeys ? It pleased him, too, in spite of the lesson taught him at Portsdown Fair, to affect a contempt for Raymond. He laughed scornfully when he spoke of him. 'One Englishman,' he said, 'is worth three Frenchmen. Everybody knows that. Wait, Molly, till I give him a basting.' Yet the day of that basting did not arrive. And I suppose that this threatening promise was made to none but myself, otherwise Raymond would have been told ; in which case it is certain the thing would have been brought to a head.

Very likely it made Tom happier to believe that he could administer that basting if he should choose. As you will see presently, the moment actually chosen by him for the purpose was unfortunate.

It was difficult for the émigrés and for their sons to find employment by which to make their livelihood. For though in this country every calling is open to all, so that many, even of our bishops and judges, have been poor boys to begin, yet a young man's choice is generally restricted by the circumstances of his birth and condition. Thus the son of the village carpenter succeeds his father, and the man who hath a good shop bequeaths it to his son. But if a young man aspires to a profession, he must be able to spend a great deal of money in order to learn its secrets, and to be received by some learned society as a member. Nothing can be done without money or interest. If he would be a farmer, he must be able to lay out money upon stock and implements ; if a tradesman, he must be first apprenticed and afterwards buy and stock his shop ; if he be a clergyman, he must be able to buy a living, unless he find a patron ; if he becomes a soldier, he must buy his commission ; if a sailor, he must bribe some one in place, or remain for ever a midshipman ; if he would find a Government office, even of the humblest kind, he must have interest to procure it for him, or money to buy it.

Some of them, therefore, became teachers, because teaching is the only kind of work which requires no money, apprenticeship, interest, or bribery. They taught their own language for the most part, or the accomplishments which they were best qualified to undertake, namely, dancing, music, deportment, drawing, and so forth. The more ingenious painted pictures or carved statues ; some composed music ; some carved in wood and ivory ; some became conjurers, ventriloquists, tumblers, or circus riders ; a good many became cooks or barbers ; some, I have heard, became gamblers by profession, and if they belonged to the better sort, played cards at clubs, if to the baser, held their tables at fairs and races. Some turned thieves and rogues, but these were few. A great many went home again as soon as it was safe, though they did not get back their lands. Some went to America, but I know not what they did there. Whatever they did, it was always considered as a makeshift against the day when they should return and be restored to their own property.

As for Raymond, it was necessary that he should work for his bread as soon as possible. Fortunately, though he loved not books, he was continually drawing and painting. It is an art by which some men live, either by teaching or selling their pictures.

'Let the boy,' said the Vicar, 'cultivate this gift, so that, perhaps, if the need still exists, it may provide him the means of an honourable livelihood until the day when you shall happily, under Providence, return to your own.'

In short, Raymond was put under a master at Gosport until the age of nineteen, when he had learned all that could be taught him. Then, because pupils were not to be found at Porchester, he went to Portsmouth, and began to teach to such of the young officers as wished to learn, the arts of drawing and painting, and making plans and maps, especially plans of fortifications.

But the time went on, and the successes of the Republican armies did not hold out much hope that the return of the Nobles would soon take place.

CHAPTER IV.

IN THE OTHER CAMP.

'Huzza, Molly!' cried my cousin, his face full of exultation. ''Tis now certain that we shall have peace. I have been drinking the health of Boney, whom I shall ever love for calling home all starving Frenchmen.'

'Will the émigrés go home, too, Tom?'

'Ay, they will all go. What? Do you think we shall suffer them to stay any longer, the ragged, greedy blood-suckers, when there are honest Britons out of work? Not so. They must pack.'

'Will their property be restored to them, then?'

'Nay, I know not! 'Tis thought at the tavern that something will be done for them, but I know not what. Well, Molly, so you will lose your fine lover.'

'Never mind my fine lover, Tom.'

'Nay, I mind him not a button!' Here he put one hand in his pocket, and with the other shook his cudgel playfully. 'Molly, he is a lucky lad. Another week and he would have had a basting. Ay, in another week at farthest I must have drubbed him.'

'Oh, Tom! how long has that drubbing been threatened? Nay, it were a pity, if Raymond must go, for him never to know your truly benevolent intentions. I will tell him this evening.'

'As you please, my girl; as you please,' he replied carelessly, and sauntered away, but returned back after a few steps. 'Molly,' he said, 'I think it would be kindest to let the poor man go in ignorance of what would have befallen him. What? He cannot help being a Frenchman.   Don't let him feel his misfortune more than is necessary.'

This was thoughtful of Tom.

' Then, Tom, I will not tell him.   But it is for your sake and to spare you, not him, the drubbing.   Oh, Tom, he would break every bone in your body ; but if you mean what you say, and are really not afraid of him, why not tell him what you have told me ?'

' Well, Molly, you can say what you like ; but you are not married yet, my girl.   You are not married yet.'

I did not tell Raymond, because I think it is wicked for a woman to set men a-fighting, though it is commonly done by village girls ; but I had no anxiety on the score of Tom's desire to baste anybody.   I might have felt some anxiety had I reflected that the ways of a man when in liquor cannot always be foretold.

Raymond thought little of Tom at this time.   The conditions of the peace left him, with the Royal Family of France and all the émigrés, out in the cold ; one cannot deny, though he is now an Englishman by choice, and contented to forget his native country, that he was then much cast down.

' For ten years,' he said, ' our lives have seemed an interruption ; we have been in parenthesis ; whatever we did, it was but as a stop-gap.   We have endured hardship patiently, because it would pass. Great Britain was fighting for us ; well, all that is over.   The Government has abandoned us ; the Revolution has succeeded ; there will be no more Kings or Nobles in France.'

Yes, peace was made, and the French Princes, the Royalists, and the French Nobles, who thought we should never lay down our arms until the old state of things was restored, found that they were abandoned.   To me, because I now took my ideas from Raymond, it seemed shameful, and I blushed for my country.   But one can now plainly see, that when an enterprise is found to be impossible, the honour of a country cannot be involved in prosecuting it any farther.   It took twelve years more of war for France to understand the miseries she had brought upon herself by driving away her Princes.   As soon as the opportunity arrived, Great Britain led them back again.

'Twas no great thing of a peace after the expenditure of so much blood and treasure.   England, we learned, was to keep certain possessions taken from the Dutch, and to give back those she had taken from the French.   But the strength of France was so enormously improved, Buonaparte being master in Spain, Italy,

Portugal, and I know not what beside, that everyone prophesied the breaking out, before long, of another and a more prolonged war. This, in fact, speedily happened, as everybody knows.

The general joy, however, was wonderful. So great was it in London, that the people fought and struggled for the honour of taking out the horses from the carriage of the French Ambassador —he was a certain Colonel Lauriston, of English ancestry, and yet a favourite with Buonaparte—and dragging it themselves with shouts and cheers. The City of London and every other town in the country were, we heard, illuminated at night with the lighting of bonfires, the firing of squibs, and the marching of mobs about the streets. At Portsmouth they received the intelligence with more moderate gratitude, because, although it is without doubt a grievous thing to consider the continual loss of so many gallant men, yet it must be remembered that a seaport flourishes in time of war, but languishes in time of peace. In time of war there happen every day arrivals and departures of ships and troops, the advance of prize money, the engagement of dockyard hands, the concourse of people to see the troops and the fleets, the fitting out and victualling of the vessels, all of which keep the worthy folk full of business, so that they quickly make their fortunes, build and buy houses, and retire to the country and a garden.

At Porchester the landlord of the tavern cursed the peace which would take from him all his custom. He, however, was the only man who did not hail the news with pleasure. As for the Castle, not only the prisoners, but the garrison as well—no soldier likes being converted into a prison warder—rejoiced. They made a great bonfire in the outer court—beautiful it was to see the keep and the walls and the church lit up at night by the red blaze of the flames ; soldiers and prisoners, arm-in-arm, danced round the fire, shouting and singing. There were casks of liquor sent in, I know not by whom, and the serving out of the drink greatly increased the general joy.

After this, and until the prisoners were all gone, it was truly wonderful to see the change. First of all the soldiers with the loaded muskets were removed from the walls, and there were no more sentries, except at the gates. Why should prisoners be watched who would certainly make no attempt to escape, now that the vessels which were to carry them home were preparing for them ? They were no longer enemies, but comrades, and it was strange to mark the transition from foe to friend. Our journals, we heard, in like manner ceased to abuse the First Consul, and began to find much to admire—the first time for nearly ten years —in the character of the French. Yet these prisoners had done nothing to make them our friends, which shows that Providence never designed that men should cut each other's throats, only because they speak different languages. And from this day until their departure the prisoners were allowed freely to go outside the Castle walls, a privilege which hitherto had been granted to few.

A strange wild crew they were who now trooped out of the Castle gates and swarmed in the village street. Some limped from old wounds, some had lost an arm, a leg, or an eye; nearly all were ragged and barefoot. They wore their hair hanging long and loose about their shoulders; some had monstrous great beards, and most wore long moustachios, which impart an air of great ferocity. Whether they were in rags or not, whatever their condition, one and all bore themselves with as much pride, and walked as gallantly, as if they were so many conquering heroes, and at the sight of a woman would toss up their chins, pull their moustachios, stick out their chests, and strut for all the world like a turkey-cock, and as if they were all able and willing to conquer the heart of every woman. They did no harm in the village that I heard of; they could not buy anything, because they had no money, and they were too proud to beg. One day, however, I saw a little company of them looking over our palings into the garden, where as yet there was but little blossom and the first pushing of the spring leaves. I thought that in their eyes I saw a yearning after certain herbs and roots which every Frenchman loves. It was long since these poor fellows had tasted onions, garlic, or any savoury herbs. I may confess that I called on the men and made them happy with as many strings of onions and other things as they could carry, a gift which, with the addition of a little oil and vinegar, sent them away completely happy.

They were now eager to get home again, although for many, Pierre told us, the exchange would be for the worse. 'The prison rations,' he said, 'are better than the fare which many of us will enjoy when we get home. In a campaign the soldiers have to fight on much less. Then if there is to be no more fighting, most of the army will be disbanded, and the men will betake themselves again to the plough or to their trades. But if a man goes for a soldier he forgets his trade, his hand and eye are out; then he will get bad wages with long hours, the condition of a slave—I call it nothing else—and none of the glory of war.' Pierre spoke of glory as if every private soldier who took part in a victory was to be remembered ever afterwards as an immortal hero. 'Oh! I deny not that there are some, even some Frenchmen, who love not war. Yet I confess that to them the peace is the most welcome news in the world. What! Is every soldier a hero? Does every man love the hard ground better than a soft bed? Is the roaring of artillery a pleasing sound for everyone? Not so; some men are by nature intended to drive quills, and weigh out spices, and dress the ladies' heads. There must be grocers and barbers as well as soldiers.'

'And what will you do, Pierre?' asked Raymond.

'I hope to remain in the army. But how long will the peace continue? Think you our great General is one who will be contented to remain quiet while a single country remains unconquered? He is another Alexander the Great; he marches from conquest to conquest; he is a Hannibal who knows no Capua. There are still two countries which dare to hold up their heads in defiance of him —Great Britain and Russia. He will humble both.'

'What! You look to overrun the world?'

'Consider,' he said, 'Prussia—Germany—Holland—Italy—these are at his feet. Spain is already in his grasp. Denmark—Norway —Sweden—all are within his reach. What is England—little England—against so mighty a combination? What is Russia with all her Cossacks? The peace is concluded in order that we may make more vessels to destroy your trade and take your fleets. When your ships are swept off the ocean, nothing remains except humble submission. Look, therefore, for another war as soon as we are ready, and prepare for the inevitable supremacy of France. Great Britain reduced, Buonaparte will then lead his victorious troops to Russia, which will offer nothing more than a show of resistance to his great army. When all the countries are his, and all the kings dethroned, there will be seen one vast Republic, with Paris for its capital, and Buonaparte for the First Consul. London, Constantinople, Rome, Vienna, and Moscow will be of no more importance than Marseilles and Lyons. All will be Paris.'

'Very good indeed,' said Raymond, 'and then your First Consul will, I suppose, sit down and take his rest?'

'No. There will remain the United States of America. India will be ours already by right of our conquest of Great Britain, and all the East will be ours because we shall have overrun Spain, Holland, and Turkey; also South America and Mexico. The United States will be the last to bow the neck. Buonaparte will fit out three great armaments, one to Canada, one to New York, and one to Baltimore. The Republicans of America will fight at first for their independence. Then they will be compelled to yield, and will join in the great confederacy, and from one end to the other the whole world will be part of the great French Republic.'

' There are still Persia, the Pacific Ocean, and China.'

''The Pacific will be ours because there will be no ships afloat but those which fly the French flag. Persia is but a mouthful. To conquer China will be but a military promenade.'

' And after this the reign of peace, I suppose ?'

Pierre sighed.

' Yes,' he said, ' when there will be nothing left to fight for, I suppose there will be peace. But by that time I shall perhaps have become a general of division, or very likely I shall be old and no longer fit for war. Oh,' his eyes kindled, ' think of the universal French Republic! No more Kings, no more priests, all men free and equal——'

' Why,' Raymond interrupted, ' as for Kings, the peace leaves them every man upon his throne ; and as for priests, Buonaparte's convention with the Pope brings them back to you. In place of your fine Republican principles you have got a military despotism ; it must be a grand thing when every man is free and equal to be drilled and kicked and cuffed into shape, in order to become a soldier.'

' Why,' said Pierre, ' I grant you that we did not expect the Concordat. Well, the women are too strong for us. But the men are emancipated ; they have got no religion left ; while, for your military despotism, how else can we establish our Universal Republic ? And what better use can you make of a man than to drill him and put him into the ranks? But wait till the conquest of the world is complete, and the reign of Universal Liberty begins.'

' I stand,' said Raymond, ' on the side of order, which means authority, rank, religion, and a monarchy.'

' And I,' said Pierre, ' on the side of Liberty, which means government by the people and the abolition of the privileged class. I am a son of the people, and you, my friend, are an aristo. Therefore we are in opposite camps.'

' Your Republic has her hands red with innocent blood, and her pockets full of gold which she has stolen. These are the first-fruits of government by the people.'

' We have made mistakes ; our men were mad at first. But we are now in our right senses, Raymond ; for every man equal rights and an equal chance, and the prizes to the strongest, and no man born without the fold of Universal Brotherhood. What can your old order show to compare with this ?'

His eyes glowed, and his dark cheek flushed. He would have said more, but refrained, because he would not pain his friend who belonged to the other side. When I think of Pierre I love to recall him as he stood there, brave and handsome. Ah, if all the children of the people were like him, then a Universal Republic might not be so dreadful a misfortune for the human race !

'Englishmen, at least, are free,' said Raymond. 'Shake hands, my brother. You shall go out and fight for your cause. Whether you win or whether you lose, you shall win honour and promotion. Captain Gavotte—Colonel Gavotte—General Gavotte—Field Marshal Gavotte.   I shall sit in peace at home, under the protection of the Union Jack—which may God protect !'

CHAPTER V.

TOM'S UNFORTUNATE MISTAKE.

IT was the evening after this conversation that my Cousin Tom made so unfortunate a mistake, and received a lesson so rude that it cured him for ever of speaking disrespectfully concerning the strength and courage of Frenchmen. The affair was partly due to me ; I do not say that it was my fault, because I should behave in exactly the same way again were it possible for such a thing to happen now.

My cousin rode into the village in the afternoon, as was his custom. Finding that there were no wagers being decided, cocks fought, or any other amusement going on at the tavern, he took a glass or two, and walked up the street to call upon me.

'Well, Molly,' he began, sitting down as if he intended to spend the afternoon with me, 'when does your Frenchman go ? Ha ! he is in luck to go so soon.'

'Tom,' I said, 'I forbid you ever again to mention the word Frenchman in my presence. Speak respectfully of a man who is your better, or go out of the house.'

'Suppose,' he said, 'that I will neither speak respectfully of him nor go out of the house ? What then, Miss Molly ? Respectfully of a beggarly Frenchman who teaches—actually teaches drawing to anybody he can get for a pupil ! Respectfully ! Molly, you make me sick. Give me a glass of your cowslip, cousin.'

'Well, Tom, I am not strong enough to turn you out; but I can leave you alone in the room.'

I turned to do so, but he sprang up and stood between me and the door.

'Now, Molly, let us understand one another. Send this fellow to the right-about'—he pronounced it, being a little disguised, rileabow; 'send him away, I say, and take a jolly Briton.'

'Let me pass, Tom.'

'No. Why, I always meant to marry you, my girl, and so I will. Do you think I will let you go for a sneakin' cowardly——' Here he held out his arms. 'Come and kiss me, Molly. There's only one that truly loves thee, and that is Tom Wilgress. Come, I say.'

At this I was frightened, there being no one in the house whom I could call. Fortunately, I thought of Sally, and, running to the window, I opened it and cried out to her to come quickly.

Tom instantly sank into a chair.

'Sally,' I said, 'I do not think I shall want you; but have you your rope's-end with you?'

'Ay, ay, miss,' she replied, shaking that weapon and looking curiously at Tom, whom she had never loved.

'I do not think,' I repeated, 'that we shall want the rope's-end. Are you afraid of my cousin, Sally?'

'Afraid! I should like to see any man among them all that I am afraid of.'

'Then wait at the door, Sally, until I call you or until he goes.'

'Now, Tom,' I went on, 'I am not without a protector, as you see. You may go. Why, you poor, blustering creature, you are afraid—yes, you are afraid to say the half in Raymond's presence that you have said to me. Fie! a coward, and try to wile a girl from her lover.'

'Well—I cannot fight a woman. You and your rope's-end,' he grumbled. 'Say what you like, Molly.'

'I will say no more to you. Sally, show him the rope's-end, if you please.' She held it up and nodded. 'Sally is as strong as any man, Tom, and I will ask her to lay that rope across your shoulders if you ever dare to come here again without my leave. Do you understand?'

'I am a coward, am I? I am afraid to say the half to Raymond, am I? Molly, suppose I say all this and more—suppose I thrash him and bring him on his knees?'

'Well, Tom, if you can do this you have no need to fear Sally and her rope's-end.'

He went away, making pretence of going slowly and of his own accord. Sally followed him to the garden gate, and reported that he had returned to the tavern, where I suppose that he spent the rest of the day smoking tobacco and drinking brandy and water or punch, in order to get that courage which we call Dutch.

In the interval between the signing of the peace and the return of the prisoners, Pierre spent his whole time in the company of Madam Claire and in her service. He was clever and ingenious with his fingers, always making and contriving things, so that the cottage furniture, which was scanty indeed, began to look as if it was all new.

On this day Tom remained at the tavern until late in the evening, and left it at eight o'clock, coming out of it, hat on head and riding-whip in hand, with intent to order his horse and ride home. Now, by bad luck he saw, or thought he saw, no other than his enemy Raymond coming slowly down the road, the night being clear and fine and a moon shining, so that it was well-nigh as bright as day. It was, in fact, Pierre returning to the Castle, but, dressed as he was, in a brown civilian coat, and being at all times like Raymond, it was not wonderful that, at a little distance, Tom should mistake him for Raymond. That he did not discover his mistake on getting to close quarters was due to the drink that was in him.

'Oh, Johnny Frenchman! Johnny Frog!' he cried. 'Stop, I say; you've got to reckon with me.'

Pierre stopped.

'Don't try to run away,' Tom continued. 'We have met at last, where there are no women to call upon.' Raymond, to be sure, never had asked the assistance of any woman; but that mattered nothing. 'Ha! would you run? Would you run?'

Pierre was standing still, certainly not attempting to run, and wondering what was the meaning of this angry gentleman dancing about before him in the road, brandishing his riding-whip, and calling him evidently insulting names.

'Ha!' said Tom, getting more courage, 'a pretty fool you will look when I have done with you; a very pretty fool.'

These words he strengthened in the usual way, and continued to shake his riding-whip.

Pierre still made no reply. The man was threatening him, that was certain from the use of gestures common to all languages; but he waited to brandish his riding-whip.

' French frog—Johnny Crapaud. I will flog you till you go on
your knees and swear that you'll never again dare to visit Molly.
Ha! 1 will teach you to interfere with a true-born Briton !'

He shook the whip in Pierre's face, and began to use the
language customary with those who are, or wish to appear, beyond
themselves with rage. It was, however, disconcerting that the
Frenchman made no reply, and showed no sign of submission.
For Pierre perceived that he had no choice but to fight, unless he
would tamely submit to be horsewhipped. Yet for the life of him
he could not understand why this man was attacking him. It
could not be for his money, because he had none ; nor for any
conduct of his which could give the man any pretext, because he
had never seen him before.

The French are not good at boxing, they do not practise fighting
with their fists as boys, they have no prize-fights, and in a street
quarrel I have heard that the knife is used where our people would
strip and fight it out. For this reason it is thought that they are
not so brave as the English, and it is sometimes thrown in their
teeth that they cannot hit out straight, and know not how to use
the left hand in a fight.

As for their bravery, we are foolish to impugn it, because we
have fought the French in many a field and in many a sea battle,
and we do ourselves a wrong when we lessen the valour of our
foes. Besides, it is very well known to all the world, whatever we
may say, that the French are a very brave and gallant nation.
Though they cannot box, they can fence ; though they do not
fight with fists, they can wrestle as well as any men in England.
And in their fights they have a certain trick which requires, I am
told, a vast amount of dexterity and agility, but is most effective
in astonishing and disconcerting an enemy who does not look for
it. Suppose, for instance, that a man went out to box in ignorance
of so common a trick as the catching of your adversary's head with
the left hand and pummelling his face with the right. With what
surprise and discomfiture would that manœuvre be followed ! Or,
again, imagine the surprise of an untaught man who stood up with
a master in wrestling, to receive one of those strokes which suddenly throw a man upon his back. Pierre, you see, was dexterous
in this French trick, of which Tom had never even heard.

The young Frenchman, therefore, perceiving that this was more
than a mere drunken insult and menace, assumed the watchful
attitude of one who intends to fight. He had nothing in his hand,
not even a walking-stick, and was, moreover, of slighter build and

less weight than his enemy.   But if Tom had been able to understand it, his attitude, something like that of a tiger about to spring,
his eyes fixed upon his adversary's face, his hands ready, his body
as if on springs, might have made him, even at the last moment,
hesitate.

With another oath Tom raised the whip and brought it down
upon Pierre's head.   Had the whip reached its destination there
would probably have been no need to say more about Pierre.   But
it did not, because he leaped aside and the blow fell harmless.   And
then an astonishing thing occurred.

The Frenchman did not strike his assailant with his fist, nor did
he close with him, nor did he try to wrench his whip from him,
nor did he curse and swear, nor did he go on his knees and cry for
mercy.   Any of these things might have been expected.   The last
thing that could have been expected was what happened.

The Frenchman, in fact, sprang into the air—Tom afterwards
swore that he leaped up twenty feet—and from that commanding
position administered upon Tom's right cheek, not a kick, or anything like a kick, but so shrewd a box with the flat of the left boot
that it fairly knocked him over.   He sprang to his feet again, but
again this astonishing Frenchman leaped up and gave him a second
blow on the left cheek with the flat of his right boot, which again
rolled him over.   This time he did not try to get up, nor did he
make the least resistance when his enemy seized the whip and
began to belabour him handsomely with it, in such sort that Tom
thought he was going to be murdered.   Presently, however, the
Frenchman left off, and threw away the whip.   Tom, taking heart,
sat up with astonishment in his face.   His enemy was standing
over him with folded arms.

'You kicked,' said Tom.   'Yah! you kicked.   You kicked your
man in the face.   Call that fair fighting?'

Pierre answered never a word.

'I say,' Tom repeated, 'that you kicked. Call that fair fighting?'

Pierre made no reply.   Then Tom reached for his hat, which
had been knocked off at the beginning, and for his whip, which
was beside him on the ground.   He put on his hat, and laid the
whip across his knees, but he did not get up.

'Very well—very well,' he said.   'I shall know what to expect
another time.   You don't play that trick twice.   No matter now.
My revenge will come.'

Still Pierre moved not.

'You think I care twopence because you bested me with your

tricks ? Well, I don't, then. Not I. Who would be ashamed of being knocked down by a kick on the head ? Well, all the country shall know about it. What ! Do you think I am afraid of you ? Promise not to kick, and come on.'

Although he vapoured in this way, he took care not to get up from the ground.

But Pierre made no reply, and after waiting a few minutes to see if his adversary was satisfied—to be sure he had every reason to express himself fully satisfied—he turned, and went on his way to the Castle gates.

Then Tom rose slowly, and, without brushing the mud and dirt of the road from his clothes, returned to the tavern, where the officers and gentlemen were sitting with lighted candles.

'Why, Tom,' said the Colonel, who was among them, 'what is the matter, man ? You have got a black eye.'

'Hang it,' said another, 'it seems to me that he has got two black eyes, and he has had a roll in the mud. What was it, my gallant Tom ? Did you mistake the handle of the door for your saddle ? or have you been fighting your horse in the stable ?'

'Landlord, a glass of brandy !' He waited till he had tossed off this restorative, and then sat down and took off his hat. 'Gentlemen,' he said solemnly, looking round him, and showing a face very beautifully coloured already, where the whip had fallen upon him, 'never offer to fight a Frenchman.'

'Why,' said the Colonel, ' what have we been doing for ten years and more ?'

'With cannons and guns it matters nothing ; or with swords and bayonets—I grant you that. But, gentlemen, never offer to fight a Frenchman with cudgel or fists, unless you know his tricks and are acquainted with his devilries.'

'As for fighting a Frenchman with your fists, that is impossible, because he cannot use them. And as for tricks and devilries, all war consists of them.'

'"Tis the disappointment,' said Tom, ' the disappointment that sticks.'

'It will be a devil of a black eye,' said the Colonel.

'You have a quarrel with a Frenchman,' Tom went on. 'You offer to fight him. What ! can you bestow upon a Frenchman a greater honour than to let him taste the quality of a British fist ? Instead of accepting your offer with gratitude, what does he do ? Gentlemen, what does he do ?'

He looked around for sympathy.

'What did he do, Tom ?'

'First, he pretended to accept. Then we began. I own that he took punishment like a man. Took it gamely, gentlemen. Wouldn't give in. We fought, man to man, for half an hour, or thereabouts, and I should hardly like to say how often he kissed the grass. Still, he wouldn't give in, and, as for me, so great was the pleasure I had in thrashing the Frenchman that I didn't care how long he went on.'

'Well ?'

'Well, gentlemen, the last time I knocked him down I thought he wasn't coming up to time. But he did. He sprang to his feet, jumped into the air like a wild cat, and kicked me—kicked me on the face with his boot so that I fell like a log. When I recovered he was gone.'

'That is very odd,' said one. 'Who was the Frenchman, Tom ?'

'Raymond Arnold, as he calls himself.'

'Gentlemen,' said my father, 'here is something we understand not. This young gentleman, almost an Englishman, is thoroughly versed in all manly sports. I cannot understand it. Kicked thee, Tom ? Kicked thee on the side of thy head? Besides, what quarrel hadst thou with Raymond ?'

'Why, Alderman, we need not discuss the question here, if you do not know.'

'I do know ; and I will have you to learn, sirrah '—my father at such moments as this spoke as becomes one who hath sat upon the judge's bench—'I will have you to learn, sirrah '—here he shook his forefinger—'that I will have no meddling in my household.'

'Very well,' said Tom ; 'then I will fasten another quarrel upon him. Oh, there are plenty of excuses. Kicked me in the head, he did.'

'As for the kicking business,' my father resumed, 'I should like to know what Raymond has to say. For, let me tell you, sir, you cut a very sorry figure. Your eyes are blacked ; there is a mark across your face which looks like the lash of a whip ; and you have been rolled in the mud. This looks as if there had been hard knocks, certainly, but not as if Raymond had got the worst of it. Landlord, go first to Madam Arnold's cottage, and ask if Mr. Raymond is there. If he is, tell him, with the compliments of this company, to step here for a few minutes. If he is not, try him at my house, where he mostly spends his evenings.'

'Bring him, bring him !' said Tom. 'Now you shall see what he

will say. Kicked me, he did, both sides of the head. Bring him,
bring him!'

In two or three minutes Raymond came back with the messenger.
Whatever was the severity of the late contest, he showed no signs
of punishment in the face, nor were his hands swollen, as happens
after a fight, nor were his clothes in any way rumpled or his hair
disordered.

The contrast between the two combatants was indeed most
striking.

'Raymond,' said my father, 'Tom Wilgress, whose face you seem
to have battered, is complaining that you do not fight fair.'

'He kicks,' said Tom.

'I do not fight fair? When have I shown that I do not fight
fair?'

'Why,' said my father, 'what have you been doing to him but
now?'

'Doing to him?—nothing. I have but just left your house,
Alderman, where your messenger found me.'

'But you have been fighting with Tom.'

'Don't deny it, man,' said Tom; 'don't wriggle out of it that
way.'

'I have not been fighting with Tom or with anyone.'

'This,' said Tom, 'is enough to make a man sick.'

'It is strange, gentlemen,' said my father. 'Do you assure us,
Raymond, that you have not fought Tom at all this evening?'

'Certainly not.'

'But look at the condition he is in. Can you deny that there
has been fighting?'

'It looks as if something had happened to him,' said Raymond.
'As for fighting, I know nothing of it. As for any quarrel, it has
been whispered to me that Tom has uttered threats which I dis-
regard. But if he wishes to fight I am at his service, with any
weapon he chooses—even with fists if he likes.'

'He kicks,' said Tom. 'I scorn to fight with a man who kicks.
A foul blow!'

One of the officers asked permission to look at Raymond's fist.

'Gentlemen,' he said, 'Mr. Arnold's statement is proved by the
condition of his hand. He has not fought; therefore, Tom, it
seems as if the drink had got into thy head. Go home to bed, and
to-morrow forget this foolishness.'

'Ay—ay, foolishness, was it? Well, after this, one may believe
anything. Look here, man'—he seized a candlestick and stood up.

'Do you deny your own handiwork?   Look at this black eye—and this—your own foul blow.'

'You are drunk, Tom,' said Raymond.

'I suppose, then, that I have not got a black eye.'

'You have two, Tom.'

Tom looked about for some backing, but found none, and retired, growling and threatening.

'He must have been more drunk than he appeared,' said one of the company.   'To-morrow he will have forgotten everything.'

But he did not, nor was he ever made to believe that he was not fighting Raymond, though the truth was many times told him.

Pierre related the history of Tom himself as the thing really occurred.   But as Tom continued to tell the tale, the Frenchman's leap into the air grew higher and higher, and the strength of that kick more stupendous, and the victorious character of his own fighting the more astonishing.

CHAPTER VI.

A TERRIBLE DISCOVERY.

I HAVE always been truly grateful that the terrible discovery we made concerning Pierre was in mercy deferred until the evening before his departure.   It is not in human nature, as you will shortly discover, to wish that it never had been made at all, because, though the discovery overwhelmed an innocent young man with shame and grief, what would afterwards have become of Raymond had the fact not been found out?

I love the memory of this brave young man; I commiserate his end; there is no one, I am sure, with a heart so stony as not to grieve that so brave a man should come to such an end.   But I am forbidden by every consideration of religion to look upon the events which followed as mere matters of chance, seeing to what important issues the discovery led.

Consider all the circumstances, and when you read what follows, confess that it was a truly dreadful discovery for all of us.   First of all, this young soldier owed his life to the nursing of Madam Claire; next, he attached himself to us, showing the liveliest gratitude and the most sincere affection, although we—that is, those of the Cottage—belonged to the class he had been brought up to hate and suspect, professing a creed which he had been taught to despise. In Madam he found a countrywoman with whom he could talk the language of his childhood, and hear over again the old stories of the Provence peasants. In her house, small though it was, he could escape from the rude companionship of the Castle, where among the prisoners there was nothing but gambling, betting, quarrelling, and drinking all day long. In her society—may I not say in mine also ?—he enjoyed, for the first time in his life, the society of gentlewomen. With Madam, he learned that a woman may be a gentlewoman, and yet not desire to trample on the poor, just as madam learned that a man may be a Republican and yet not be a tiger.

Perhaps, had he stayed longer with us, he would have discovered that the Christian religion he had been taught to deride had something to be said for it. Moreover, in Raymond he found one of his own age whom he loved, although they differed in almost every principle of government and of conduct. It was good for us to have this young man with us daily ; even the poor distracted woman grew to look for him, and talked with her husband in oracles—so we learned afterwards to consider them—about him. If it was good for us, it was surely good for him. Consider next, that, like most men, he regarded his father with respect ; not, perhaps, the respect with which Raymond remembered his brave and loyal father, but with that respect which belongs to a man of honourable record, though one of the humbler class.

'Our orders have come,' he came to tell us. 'To-morrow we embark ; the day after to-morrow we shall be in France again. After three years—well,' there is not much changed, I suppose. The streets will be the same and the barracks the same. I shall find some of my old comrades left, I dare say. Happy fellows ! They have gone up the ladder while I sit still.'

'Your turn will come next, Pierre.'

'This house, at least, I can never forget, nor the ladies who have shown so much kindness to a prisoner.'

'To our compatriot, Pierre,' said Madam.

'Send us letters sometimes,' I said. 'Let us follow your promotion, Pierre ; let us know when you distinguish yourself.'

He laughed ; but his eyes flashed. One could understand that he thought continually of getting an opportunity of distinction.

'Yes,' he said. 'If I get a chance ; if I am so happy as to do anything worthy to be recorded, I will write to you.'

'In two days you will be in France. The country which we are always fighting is so near, and yet it seems so far off. Why must we fight with France so continually?'

'How can you ask, Miss Molly? We respect and love each other so much that we do our best to maintain in each country the race of soldiers, without whom either would quickly become a race of slaves, so as to bring out all the virtues—courage, patriotism, endurance, invention and contrivances, watchfulness, obedience—everything. War turns a country lad into a hero; it teaches honour, good manners, and self-denial; it turns men of the same country into brothers, and makes them respect men of another country. Without war, what would become of the arts? Without war we should all be content to sit down, make love, eat and drink.'

'Thank you, Pierre,' I said, laughing.

Then, without thinking anything, I put the questions which led to the fatal discovery.

'What shall you do when you land, Pierre?'

'First,' he said, 'I must make my way to rejoin my regiment, wherever it may be, and report myself. As soon as I have done that I shall ask for leave, and then I shall go to see my father.'

I suppose it was not a very wonderful thing that we had never yet learned from him where his father lived and what was his calling. In the same way Pierre had not learned from any of us all the history of the family. He knew that Raymond's father was one of those who were shot at Toulon, after the taking of the town, and he knew that these two ladies with Raymond had been rescued from the flames of the burning city. That, I suppose, was all he knew.

'Where does he live, your father?'

'My father lives now on his estate. He bought it when it was confiscated as the property of a ci-devant. The house, I believe, was nearly destroyed by the Revolutionists. I have never seen it, because I was at school until, at fifteen, I was drafted into the army. I have often wondered how he got the money to buy the estate, because we were always so poor that sometimes there was not money enough for food.'

'What was his calling?'

'I hardly know. He is an ingenious man, who knows every-thing. He is a poet, and used to write songs and sing them himself in the café for money. Once he wrote an opera, music and all, which was played at the theatre. Sometimes he taught music, and sometimes dancing; sometimes he acted. Whatever he did, we were always just as poor—nothing made any difference. He was a son of the people, and he taught me from the first to hate the aristocrats and the Church.'

'Yes,' said Madam. 'It is now two generations since that education was begun. Fatal are its fruits.'

'Although he was so good an actor and singer, and could make people laugh, my father was not a happy man. As long as I can remember he was gloomy. Always he seemed to be brooding over things which have been set right now—the privileges of the nobility and the oppression of the people. When the Revolution came he was the first to rejoice. Ah! those were wonderful times.'

'They were truly wonderful,' said Madam.

'It was in 1794, the year before I went into the ranks, that he bought the estate. By what means he procured the money I know not. To be sure, they were cheap; the estates of the ci-devants.'

'Where is your father's estate?' asked Madam.

'There was a great town-house as well,' Pierre went on. 'Ma foi! It was not cheerful in that town-house, for the mob had destroyed all the furniture, and we had no money to buy more. The rooms were large, and at night were full of noises—rats, I suppose; ghosts, perhaps. My father used to wander about the dark rooms, and, naturally, this made him grow more gloomy. All his old friends had gone, I know not where. He seemed left quite alone. Then I was drawn for the army, and I have not seen my father since.'

'Where is the estate, Pierre?' asked Madam Claire again.

'It belonged to a family of tyrants. They had oppressed the country for a thousand years.'

'I should like to know the name of these tyrants,' said Madam.

Pierre laughed.

'My father always said so. Pardon me, ma mère. I have learned that he used to talk with extravagance; no doubt they were not tyrants at all. But they were Nobles—oh! of the noblest. The estate lies on the banks of the river Durance. There was a great Château there formerly; but it is now destroyed.'

'On the Durance?'

Madam sat upright full of interest.

'Yes; not many leagues from Aix, in Provence. There is a village beside the Château called Eyragues.'

This reply was like a shower of rain from a clear sky.

'Eyragues! Eyragues!' cried Madam, dropping her work. 'There is only one Château d'Eyragues.'

'They are talking, my dear,' said the poor mad lady to the spirit of her husband, ' of the Château—our Château of Eyragues. We shall go there again soon, shall we not? We spent many happy years at Eyragues. Well, my friend, if you wish it, Raymond shall go.'

'Young man!' Madam Claire's hands were trembling, her face flushed, and her voice agitated. 'I heard—but that cannot be—it cannot be! Yet I heard—— Young man, tell me who was your father? Why did he buy the place?'

'My father is what I have said—a man of the people, who hates aristos, Kings and priests. I know not why he bought it. The Château was destroyed by the people of Aix soon after the taking of Toulon, and the land was sold to the highest bidder.'

'Gavotte,' said Madam. 'I know not any Gavotte. Who could he be? There was no Gavotte in the village.'

'It is droll,' said Pierre, laughing. 'His name was not Gavotte at all. It was Leroy—Louis Leroy. They made him change it in the times when they were furiously Republican. Louis Leroy— that could not be endured ; so they called-him Scipio, Cato, or some such nonsense—it was their way in those days—and gave him the surname of Gavotte, which he still keeps.'

'Oh!' Madam Claire sank back in her chair. ' This is none other than the doing of Heaven itself,' she murmured, gazing upon the young man, who looked astonished, as well he might.

'Much more blood, my dear friend?' It was the voice of the Countess, talking with her dead husband. 'You say that there must be much more blood? It is terrible. But not again the blood of the innocent.'

'This is the hand of God,' said Madam Claire again.

'Why, ma mère——' Pierre began.

'Truly the hand of God.'

How can I describe the transformation of this meek, resigned, and patient nun into an inspired prophetess? Madam Claire sat upright, her eyes gazing before her as if she saw what we could not see. Suddenly she sprang to her feet, and with clasped hands she spoke words which, she declared afterwards, were put into her mouth.

'Unhappy boy!' she began. 'Oh, you know not—you have never known—what your father did. But the people of Aix knew ; and even the Revolutionists—his friends—fell from him.

There is not a man in the town fallen so low as to sit in his company, or to speak with him. Learn the shameful story, though the knowledge fill your heart with sorrow and even your head with shame. His name is Louis Leroy—named Louis by his father, but Leroy was the name of his mother. His father was the seigneur of that Château which is now his own ; and you—you who have been taught to hate your forefathers—you are that seigneur's grandson. I remember your father, he was a boy who refused to work ; they sent him away from the village, and he went to Aix, where he lived upon his wits and upon the money his half-brother would give him. Yes, his half-brother, who was none other than my murdered brother. And who murdered him ? Unhappy man ! it was your father. Oh, woe—woe—woe to Cain ! It was your father who denounced his own brother at Toulon. But for him he might have escaped. Louis Leroy, whom my brother had be-friended, spoke the word that sent him to his death, and now sits, his brother's blood upon his hands, in the place which he has bought for himself. Your father—alas, your father !'

'Madam,' I cried, 'for mercy's sake, spare him !' for the young man's face was terrible to behold.

She swayed backwards and forwards, and I thought that she would have fallen.

'The vengeance of Heaven never fails,' she said. 'For many years have I looked for news of this man. Once—twice—I knew not how, he has been struck. A third and more terrible blow will fall upon him—through his son—but I know not how. Yet he has done nothing—this poor boy—he is innocent ; he knows nothing ; and yet—and yet—oh, Molly, I am constrained to speak.'

'Oh, Madam !'

'Through his son—through his son —— Oh, unhappy man ! unhappy son !'

'Madam, for mercy's sake, say something to console him.'

She made no reply, her eyes still gazing upon something which we saw not.

Then she suddenly became again herself—soft-eyed, gentle—and tears ran down her cheeks.

'Pierre !' she said, holding out her hands. But he shrank back. 'My son whom I love ; for whom I have prayed. Oh, Pierre, what is it that you have told us ?' It seemed as if she knew not what she had said. 'Oh, I understand now the resemblance. You are Raymond's cousin.'

'My father,' Pierre said presently. 'My father—a murderer ?'

'Alas, it is true !'

'My father !'

'It is true, Pierre. Ask me no more. What! Did no one ever tell you of the Arnaults? Yet you have lived in our house at Aix—the old house, with the pilasters outside, and the carved woodwork within, and everywhere the arms of the Arnaults carved and painted.'

'Yes; I know of these; but I knew not that you—that Raymond—— I never thought that you were so great a family. I had no suspicion of my father's birth. I knew nothing. I was told that the Arnaults were tyrants who had committed detestable crimes. That was the way they talked in those days. All the Nobles had committed detestable crimes.'

'Alas! our crimes—what were they? Oh, Pierre, I would to Heaven that you had gone away before this dreadful thing had been discovered. I would to Heaven that you had never found it out at all, and so lived out your life in happy ignorance of this shameful story. There are things which Heaven will not suffer to be concealed. It is through me that you have found out the truth; forgive me, Pierre. Let us forgive each other and pray; oh, you cannot pray, child of the Revolution! Pierre——' he was so overwhelmed with shame, his cheek flushed, his lip quivering, his head bent, that she was filled with pity. 'Let us console each other. After the town was taken, I think my brother might have been killed, whether any witnesses were forced to speak against him or not. Yes, the evidence mattered little; he was the Comte d'Eyragues; he was one of those who brought the British troops into the city; yes, he must have been condemned.'

'But my father denounced him. And here——' he pointed to the Countess.

'She is the victim of that dreadful night which no one can ever forget who passed through it, and of the suspense when we waited anxiously for news of her husband, but heard none till we landed at Portsmouth and learned the truth.'

At this moment Raymond opened the door and burst into the room.

'Courage, Pierre!' he cried joyously, 'to-morrow you shall leave your prison. I wish thee joy, brother, promotion, and good fortune. When we go back to our own, if ever we do, I promise thee a hearty welcome, if it be only among the ruins of our old house.'

Pierre made no reply.

'You will write to me, will you not ? That is agreed. Tell me how everything is changed, and if it is true that there are no longer any men left to till the fields, but the women must do all the work. If you go to Aix, go and look for our house—everybody knows the Hôtel Arnault—tell me if it still stands.'

Still Pierre made no reply.

'Molly, have you nothing to give him, that he may remember you by ? You must find a keepsake for him. Pierre, it is the English custom for friends when they part to drink together. We will conform to the English custom.'

Thus far he talked without observing how Pierre stood, with hanging head, his eyes dropped, his cheek burning, the very picture and effigy of shame. Raymond laid a hand upon his shoulder.

'Come, comrade, let us two crack a bottle as the English use——'

But Pierre shrank away from him.

'Do not touch me,' he cried, 'do not dare to touch me. I am a man accursed.'

He seized his hat and rushed away.

'Why,' asked Raymond, in astonishment, 'what ails Pierre ?'

'We spoke,' said Madam Claire quietly, ' of the Revolution in which his father took a part, and we have shamed him.'

'They spoke,' echoed the mad woman, 'of the Revolution. He is a child of the Revclution, which devours everything, even her own children.'

CHAPTER VII.

THE DEPARTURE OF THE PRISONERS.

TWICE has it been my lot to witness the general departure of prisoners after the signing of peace between Great Britain and France, namely, in the year 1802 and the year 1814. As for their arrival, it seems now as if they were being brought in every day for nearly two-and-twenty years, so long, with the brief interval of one year, did this contest rage. Besides the general discharge there was a constant exchange of prisoners—chiefly, I believe, those who were sick and disabled, from serving again—by cartel. A general discharge is quite another thing ; for, immediately before such an event, the prison rules are relaxed, the prison becomes transformed into a palace of joy. There is nothing all day long, except singing, dancing, and drinking ; one would believe, to witness these extravagant rejoicings of the soldiers and sailors, that they were released for ever from all hardships of toil and service, and that the Reign of Plenty, Leisure, and Peace was immediately to begin.

'But Liberty,' said Raymond, 'is the dearest of all man's rights ; and, besides, at home they have their wives and sweethearts. Love, Molly, is not confined to this island of Great Britain.'

Those who made the greatest show of rejoicing were certainly the French ; the Spaniards, as they took their imprisonment sullenly, received the news of their release without outward emotion. No one, it is certain, can seriously wish to return to a country where they have the Inquisition. The Dutch, of whom many, as I have said, had volunteered for British service, heard the news of the peace with national phlegm ; the poor negroes, most of whom were dead and the rest fallen into a kind of stupid apathy, were unaffected ; the Vendean privateers with terror, thinking that General Hoche was still in their midst, ready to shoot them down.

The embarkation of so many prisoners was not effected in a single day. Some were sent across to Dunquerque ; some—those from Portsmouth and Porchester—to Dieppe ; those from Plymouth—some of whom were taken across in coasters—to Havre.

In the morning of the embarkation the narrow beach was crowded with those who came, like ourselves, to bid farewell, for we were not the only people who had friends among the prisoners. They came from Fareham, from the country round Southwick, from Cosham, from Titchbrook, and from Portsmouth and Gosport. There were sea-captains among them, come to see once more the prisoners they had made ; with them were army officers, country squires, and young fellows, the country Jessamys, like my cousin Tom, who had made friends among the French officers at horse-races, over the punchbowl, and at the cockpit. They came riding, brave in Hessian boots and padded shoulders. Among them were many ladies, and I think it is true, as was then alleged, that many a sore heart was left behind when the young French officers were released. But only to see the heartiness of the farewells, the happiness of those who went away, and the congratulations of those who sent them away, and how they shook hands, and came back, and then again shook hands, and swore to see each other again—'twould have moved the stoniest heart ! Who would have thought that yonder handsome officer, gallant in cocked hat, blue coat, and white pantaloons, amid the group of English ladies, to whom he was bidding farewell, was their hereditary enemy? Or who would believe that yonder gray-headed veteran, clasping the hand of a jovial Hampshire squire, had fought all his life against Great Britain? Or, again, could that little company, who had so often met at the cockpit, or at the bull-baiting. and who now were drinking together before they separated (my cousin Tom was one), become again deadly enemies? Alas! why should men fight when, if they would but be just to others and to themselves, there would be no need of any wars at all? Lastly, there were the rank and file, the privates and sailors, drinking about in friendship with our honest militiamen, as if the Reign of Peace was already come, instead of a short respite only.

I suppose there was never seen so various a collection of uniforms on this beach. Among them were the sailors of France, Holland, and Spain, alike with differences. Dress them exactly alike, if you will, but surely no one would ever take a Frenchman for a Hollander, or a Spaniard for a Frenchman. I know not what are the various uniforms of the Republican army, but here were grenadier hats of bearskin, round beavers, hats with the red cockade, cocked hats with gold lace, caps with a peak and high feather, the old three-corner hats, the common round hat with a red plume, the brass helmet, the red Republican cap, the blue thread cap, and a dozen others. And as for the coats and facings, they were of all colours, but mostly they seemed blue with drab facings. The French naval officers, in their blue jackets, red waistcoats, and blue pantaloons, looked more like soldiers than sailors. Some of the officers had been prisoners for five or six years, so that their uniform coats were worn threadbare, or even ragged, their epaulettes and gold lace tarnished, and their crimson seams faded. Yet they made a gallant show, and but for the absence of their swords looked as if they were dressed for a review. The common sort were barefoot—which was common in the Republican armies —and is no hardship to sailors. Some of them, having quite worn out their own clothes, wore the yellow suit provided by the British Government for the foreign prisoners.

Among the prisoners were their two priests. They, at least, were well pleased that the Reign of Atheism was over, and religion was once more established according to the will of the Pope.

Now, as we passed through the throng, the men all parted right and left, Madam saying a last word now to one and now to another of her friends, while even those who scoffed the loudest at religion, paid the lady the respect due to her virtues. She was an aristo, and they were citizens, equal, and of common brotherhood—at least, they said so : she a Christian and they atheists ; she a Royalist, and they Republicans ; yet not one among them but regarded her with gratitude.

She spoke to a young fellow in the dress of a common sailor, who looked as if he belonged to a better class, saying a few words of good wishes.

'Yes,' he replied bitterly, 'I go home. When last I saw the house it was in flames, when last I saw my father he was being dragged away to be shot ; my mother and sisters were guillotined in the Terror, and I escaped by going on board a privateer. What shall I find in the new France of which they speak so much ? They have left off murdering us ; I suppose they will even suffer me to carry a musket in the ranks.'

Apart from the groups of those who drank, and those who exchanged farewells, we found Pierre standing alone with gloomy looks.

'My son,' said Madam, 'we have come to bid you farewell.'

He raised his eyes heavily, but dropped them again. The sight of Madam was like the stroke of a whip.

'It is not so bad for you to look upon me as for me to hear your voice,' he said.

'Pierre, my son'—she held out her hand, but he refused to take it, not rudely, but as one who is unworthy—'Pierre, be patient. As for what has happened, I was constrained to tell you. Oh, I could not choose but tell you. Yet it was no sin or fault of yours, poor boy ! If any disaster befall you by act of God, accept it with resignation. It is for the sin of another. Count it as an atonement—for him. So if sufferings come to you—what do I say ? Alas ! I must be a prophetess, my son, because I know—yes, I know—that disaster will fall upon you, but I know not of what kind. Yet be assured that there is nothing ordered by Providence which can hurt your soul.'

'My soul !' cried Pierre impetuously. 'My soul ! What is it, my soul ?' He laughed in his Republican infidelity. 'What is it, and where is it ? It is my life that is ruined, do you understand ? You have taken away my honour—my pride—and my ambition. You have taken all that I had, and you bid me think of my soul.'

'When you go to the South—to Aix—you will see your father, Pierre. Fail not, I charge you, fail not to tell him that we have forgiven—yes, three of us have forgiven—the dead man, and the mad woman, and the religieuse—and the fourth—the son—does not know. Say that we all forgive him, and, for the sake of his son, we pray for him.'

Then Pierre, in the presence of the whole multitude—no British soldier would have done such a thing—fell upon his knees and kissed Madam's hands. When he rose his eyes were full of tears.

'Pierre,' I said, 'remember you have promised to send us a letter. Write to me, Pierre, if not to Raymond, will you not ?'

He shook his head sadly.

'If,' he said, 'there should happen anything worth telling you, anything by which you could think of me with pity as well as forgiveness, I would write.'

As you will hear presently, he kept this promise in the end.

Truly it was sorrowful to see the young man, so full of shame, who, but the day before, had been so full of joy and pride. Happy indeed is he whose father has lived an honourable life ! It is better to be the son of a good man than the son of a rich man.

'I have no right,' he said, ' to ask of you the least thing.'

'Ask what you please, Pierre.'

'Then, if it be possible, let not Raymond know. We have been friends, we have talked and laughed together, I have accepted from him a thousand gifts ; let him not know, if it can be avoided, that the man who—who now lives at Château d'Eyragues is my father.'

'We will not tell him. Raymond shall learn nothing from us that will trouble his friendship for you, Pierre.'

We kept our promise, but, had we broken it, how much misery we should have spared Raymond ! how different would have been the lot of Pierre !

'We will never tell him,' I repeated. 'Oh, Pierre ! We are so sorry—so sorry. Forget yesterday evening, and remember only the happy days you have spent with Raymond and with me.'

But then his turn came. The great ships' launches were drawn up, each rowed by a dozen sailors, and commanded by a midshipman, who steered. The last time these launches came up the harbour, in each boat stood a dozen marines, stationed in the bow and stern, armed with loaded muskets and fixed bayonets, while every sailor had his cutlass, and the boat was crammed with prisoners gloomy and downcast. Now the only arms on board consisted of the midshipman's dirk ; there were no marines, the sailors had no cutlasses, and they hailed the prisoners with cheers.

Pierre pressed my hand, and once more kissed Madam's fingers. Then he took his place. The rest of the boatload showed every outward sign of rejoicing ; Pierre alone sat in his place with hanging head.

'They are gone,' said my cousin Tom. He had been drinking, and his face was red. 'They are gone. Well, there were good men and true among them. Would that the rest of their nation would follow ! especially all—I say—who kick when they fight. Well—every man gets his turn.'

The launches kept coming and going day after day until the last prisoner was taken off the beach. Then the garrison was left in the Castle by itself.

When the militia regiments were presently disbanded and sent home, the Castle was quite empty. Then they sent boats from the Dockyard with men, who carried away the hammocks and the furniture, such as it was ; took down the wooden buildings, and carried away the timber ; pulled down the canteen, the blacksmiths' and carpenters' shops, burned the rubbish left behind by the prisoners, and left the Castle empty and deserted. We might climb the stairs of the keep to the top, passing all the silent chambers, where so many of them had slept; the chapel was stripped of its altar ; the stoves were taken out of the kitchens ; and the grass began to grow again in the court, which had been their place of resort and exercise. There were no traces left of the French occupants, except the names that they had carved on the stones, the half-finished carvings in wood and bone, which they left behind, and the rude tools which they had used. Once I found lying rusted in a dark chamber one of the daggers which they made for themselves with a file, sharpened and pointed, stuck in a piece of wood. Strange it was at first to wander in those empty courts, and to think of the monotonous time which the cruel war imposed upon those poor fellows.

'They are gone,' said Raymond. 'Well, let us hope that every man will find his mistress waiting faithfully for him. As for Pierre, who certainly had a bee in his bonnet, his only mistress is Madame la Guerre. He loved no other. She is horribly old ; covered with scars, hacked about with sword and spear, and riddled with shot. Yet he loves her. She is dressed in regimental flags, she gives her lovers crowns of laurel, which cost her nothing, titles which she invents, and a promise of immortality which she means to break. Poor Pierre ! We shall never see him again, but we may hear of him.'

CHAPTER VIII.

HE CANNOT CHOOSE BUT GO.

Thus began the peace, which it was hoped would be lasting, but which came to an end after a short twelve months. Porchester became once more the village out of the way, standing in no high-road, without travellers or stage-coaches. In its quiet streets there were no longer heard the voices of the soldiers at the tavern, or those of the prisoners on parole, or the nightly watch. There is never a hearty welcome to peace from those who prosper by war. I confess that when the boat came back with half its contents unsold, one was tempted to lament, with Sally, that war could not go on for ever. As for the towns of Portsmouth, Portsea, and Gosport, their condition threatened to become deplorable, because the dockyard was reduced, the militia sent home, and many thousands of sailors paid off. It has been said, by those who know Portsmouth well, that the petition, every Sunday morning, for peace in our time, meets with a response which is cold and without heart.

Now, however, all the talk was concerning France open to travellers after the years of Republican government. Not only did the prisoners go back, but the émigrés themselves, thinking that, although their estates were gone and their rank had no longer any value, it was better to live in one's native land than on a strange soil, began to flock back in great numbers. Great Britain had abandoned their cause; why should they any more stand apart from their own people? They went back trembling, lest they should find the guillotine erected to greet their return. But times had changed. The people had found out that even though there were neither kings nor nobles, their lives were not a whit easier and their work just as tedious. But the France to which they returned was very different from the France in which they had grown up, and the old order was clean gone with the old ideas.

Not only did the émigrés return, but crowds of English travellers flocked across the Channel to see Paris, which had been closed to them for ten years. They met, we are told, a most gracious welcome from the innkeepers, tradesmen, and all those with whom they spent their money.

Is it, then, wonderful that Raymond should grow restless, thus hearing continually of the country which, however much we might pretend to call him an Englishman, was really his native land?

'Molly,' he said, 'I am drawn and dragged as if by strong ropes towards the country. I feel that I must go across the Channel, even if I have to row myself over in an open boat and walk barefoot all the way to Paris. I must see Paris. I must see this brave army which hath overrun Europe.'

'But, Raymond, it would cost a great sum of money.'

'Yes, Molly,'—his face fell—'more money than we possess; therefore, I fear I must renounce the idea. Molly,' there were times when Raymond flashed into fire, and showed that a gentle exterior might cover a sleeping volcano, 'Molly, this village suits thy tender and gentle heart, but it is a poor life, only to endure the days that follow. The lot of Pierre, though the end may be a corpse with a bullet through the heart, seems sometimes better than this.'

This was no passing fancy or whim, but the desire grew upon him daily to see his native country, insomuch that he began to take little interest in anything else, and would be always reading or talking about France. It has been wisely observed of all émigrés that in secret they rejoiced at the wonderful triumphs of the French arms under Buonaparte—successes far surpassing any other in history, even under the great Turenne himself.

In a word, nothing would serve but that Raymond must go. He had but little money, and it was necessary that he should have enough for his expenses, though he was to travel cheaply. Therefore, the usual expedient was resorted to, and the rest of the small jewels taken from the Holy Rose.

He left us.

'There is no danger,' I said to Madam Claire. 'The country is peaceful, and he will be as safe as with us at home.'

'I know not, child,' she replied. 'When I think of France, I see nothing but maddened mobs rushing about the streets, bearing on their pikes the heads of innocent women and loyal men. Yes—yes —I know. All that is over. Yet I remember it.'

'The First Consul has turned all these mobs into soldiers.'

'And there is the man Gavotte. Suppose Raymond should fall into his hands.'

'Why, France is large. It is not likely that they will meet. And the man could not harm Raymond if he wished.'

'My dear,' she said, pointing to the Holy Rose, stripped and bare, 'all the jewels are now gone. There is nothing left but the trunk and the dead branches.'

He travelled with a passport which described him as Raymond

Arnold, British subject, and artist by profession. Had we carefully devised beforehand the method which would be most likely to lead to his destruction, we could not have hit upon a better plan. For, while France was most suspicious of British subjects, the passport described him as one, it concealed his nationality, altered his name, and gave him the profession which would most readily lend colour to suspicion, and support to the most groundless charges.

CHAPTER IX.

RAYMOND'S JOURNEY.

So Raymond left us, and for my own part I had no fears, none at all. Why should there be dangers in France more than in England ? In both countries there are thieves, murderers, and footpads. In both there are honest men. Those who consort with honest men do not generally encounter rogues. Raymond was not one of those who put themselves willingly in company where rogues are mostly found. We had letters from him. First a letter from Paris. He had seen the First Consul at a review of troops. ' He was, after all, only a little man,' Raymond wrote ; 'but he wore in his face the air of one accustomed to command.' At this time he was little more than thirty years of age, yet the foremost man in all Europe. 'Molly,' Raymond said, ' I confess that my heart glowed with admiration at the sight of this great commander and that of the brave troops whom he hath led to so many victories. They are not tall men, as you already know from the sight of the prisoners ; but they are full of spirit, and their marching is quicker than that of our own—the British troops. I forget not that here I am an Englishman travelling as a subject of His Majesty King George. I am staying at an hotel in the Rue St. Honoré, one of the principal streets in the town. The place is full of English visitors, and we all go about with our mouths wide open, looking at the wonders of Paris. I shall have plenty to tell you, dear, in the winter evenings. I have seen the place where the Bastille stood, and the great cathedrals of Notre Dame and St. Denis, and the palaces of the Louvre and Versailles ; above all, I have seen the prison of the Queen. The people are very lively and fond of spectacles and theatres, fairs and noise. I find that my French is antiquated, and there are many words and idioms used which are strange to me. But the Parisians talk a language of their own, which changes from day to day, and is always full of little terms and illusions, which no stranger or provincial can understand. Last night I went to the Théâtre des Variétés to hear a Vaudeville which contained a hundred good things, all of which I lost from not understanding the talk of the day. The ingenious author of the piece was this morning shown to me at a café. This happy man, who can make a whole theatre full of people laugh and forget their troubles, is himself one who is always laughing and singing.'

If I refrain from copying more of Raymond's letters, you must not suppose that they were short, or that they contained nothing but his adventures and observations. They were long letters, delightful to read, only there were some passages which in reading them aloud I was compelled to pass on in silence, because they were meant for no ear but mine. The things which a lover whispers to his sweetheart must not be told to anyone, though, indeed, I suppose all men say much the same things, since our language contains no more than a dozen words of endearment, so that they have no choice. Now, after Raymond had been in Paris about three weeks, he thought that he must begin his journey south.

He travelled by the stage-coach, which in France is called a diligence ; it is much slower than our flying coaches, while the roads are much worse than ours, being not only narrow, but also rendered dangerous by the deep ruts made by the heavy waggons. Before the Revolution they were kept in repair by forced labour. The roads being so bad, it is not wonderful that people travel no more than they are obliged. The diligence is, however, cheap, and as its progress is slow, one can see a good deal on the way. Thus Raymond saw the Palace of Fontainebleau, formerly inhabited by the Kings of France ; he visited also the old city of Dijon, once the capital of Burgundy ; the city of Lyons, which was destroyed by the Revolutionary army a little before they took Toulon, and many other places, all of which are set down in the map of France, which we now keep to show the children how great a traveller their father has been. He also made many drawings on the way, some of the women in their white caps, some of the peasants, some of churches and castles, but all these drawings were lost by an unexpected event, which I have presently to tell you.

At Lyons he left the stage-coach and took passage on one of the boats which go down the Rhone, and are called water coaches. They are crowded with people, and one sleeps on board, but the cabins are close, and there is not room for all to lie. Raymond found, however, that this mode of travel was vastly more pleasant than the coach with the dust and the noise. This journey terminated at a place called Arles, from which he wrote to me.

'I am at last,' he said, 'in my own country, among the people who use the language of my childhood. It is strange to hear them all talking as we love to talk in our cottage at Porchester. One seems back in England again. The people think it strange that an Englishman should know their tongue. I told them that I knew an English girl who knows the language and can speak it as well as myself. They are friendly to me, though they have the reputation of being quick-tempered and ready to strike. We stayed an hour or two at Avignon, where is an old broken bridge over the river, and in the town there are many remains of antiquity, with stone walls, and a great building once the palace of the Pope. At the town of Arles, where I write, there are Roman buildings ; a vast circus all of stone, where they used to have fights of gladiators, and where the people used to throng in order to witness the torture of Christian martyrs. . . . My dear, I am now within two days' journey of my birthplace. The nearer I draw, the more dearly do I remember it. The Château d'Eyragues stands upon a low cliff rising above the river Durance, which is wide and shallow, and subject to sudden floods. It is a large white house, with an ancient square tower at one end. The windows, which are small and high, are provided with green jalousies to keep out the sun. There is a broad veranda in front of the house ; on one side is a garden, and on the other side a farmyard, with turkeys, and fowls, and geese ; here are also the dogs and the stables, and here is a great pigeonhouse, with hundreds of pigeons flying about. It is the privilege of the Seigneur to keep pigeons, which eat up the corn of the farmers. Overhead is a sky always blue ; the hills are bare and treeless ; there are groves of gray olives, and the fields, which for the greater part of the year are dry and bare, are protected from the cold mistral wind by a kind of screen made of reeds. There are vines in the fields, and there are groves of mulberry-trees planted for the sake of the silkworms. It is, I confess, a country which few love save those who are born in it. The people are passionate, jealous, and headstrong ; they do nothing in cold blood ; they hate and love with equal ardour. My Molly, you love one of them. Will you be warned in time ?

'To-morrow I leave for the Rhone, and make for Aix, whence it is but a short journey to the village of Eyragues. How well I remember the last time I went to Aix ! We travelled in our great

gilt coach, hung upon springs, from the Château to our house. It
must have been early in the year 1793. My father was already
melancholy and a prey to gloomy forebodings. But he was the
Count d'Eyragues, and a grand Seigneur, and now his son is plain
Mr. Arnold, and a humble English traveller, who cannot afford
post-horses, but journeys in the panier with the common folk.
Adieu, my well-beloved ; I will write to thee again from Aix.'

A week later there came another endearing, delightful letter.

'I am at Aix,' he said. 'I am at last, and after a tedious journey
of three days, at Aix. The distance, which is not quite fifty miles,
or thereabouts, from Arles, would be covered on an English high-
road in a single day. Here, however, the roads are bad, the carriages heavy, and the horses weak and in poor condition. All the
best horses, I am told, have been taken for the cavalry. The road
is not, moreover, what you would call a high-road, but a cross-
country road, passing over a level plain through villages ; and the
coach, which is little better than a great clumsy basket, was filled
with farmers and small proprietors, talking of bad times and the
war. There was also a commis-voyageur, that is, a travelling clerk,
or rider, going, he told me, from Arles to Aix, and thence to
Toulon. He wanted to talk French to me, and was continually
expressing his astonishment to find that an Englishman should
wish to visit this part of the country at all ; and, secondly, that an
Englishman should be able to speak the Provençal language. I
told him I was often surprised myself, because, with the exception
of a single young lady of my acquaintance, there was probably no
one in England, apart from the émigrés, who could speak it like
myself.

'"Monsieur," said my commis-voyageur, "has the air of a Provençal. Oh ! quite the air of a Provençal. I have seen Englishmen. There are English prisoners at Marseilles ; and I have seen
English sailors at Bordeaux. Never did I see an Englishman who
resembled Monsieur." This gentleman is right, and he, for his
part, has the air of one who suspects me. Let him, however, suspect what he pleases. I have my passport. I am not a political
agent, and I am engaged in nothing that I wish to conceal. I
conversed freely with the people. Alas ! they are no longer Royalists. The events of the last ten years have turned their heads.
Though the wars have made them no richer, but have killed their
young men and laid the most terrible burdens upon the country—
it is certain that France has suffered far more than England—the
splendid successes of the French arms have turned their heads.

Nevertheless, everybody is afraid that war may break out again at any moment—in Paris they speak openly of speedily sweeping us from the seas—and prays that the peace may be lasting.

'I asked them about many things : the condition of the country, the change from the old order—I understand now that it can never return—the army, the state of religion, the cultivation of the fields —everything that one wants to know when returning to his native land after a long absence.

'"Decidedly," said my friend, the commis-voyageur, "Monsieur is curious. Monsieur probably proposes to write a book of travels."

'The road is lined for the greater part of the way with plane-trees, all bent over in the same direction and at the same height, by the mistral wind, just as on the King's bastion at Portsmouth the trees are all bent down by the wind from the sea. At this season Provence looks green and beautiful ; the planes are coming into leaf, the Arbre Judas, which grows in the gardens, is in full flower ; there is whitethorn in plenty ; the mulberries have not begun to lose their leaves ; while the cypresses, of which my people are so fond, and their gray olives, and even the long lines of reeds with which they shelter their fields from the mistral, look well behind the green maize. In two months the white road will be a foot deep in dust, the leaves by the roadside will be white with dust, and the mulberry-trees will be stripped of their foliage for the silkworms. As for flowers, there are few here compared with those in the English fields ; but there are some, especially when a canal for irrigation runs beside the road, crossed here and there by its passerelle—the little foot-bridge. There are few wayfarers along the road, and in the fields the workers are chiefly women.

' Our journey took three days, the sleeping accommodation in the villages being poor, but better than that in the boats. Here, at Aix, everything is good and comfortable.

'I have been sketching in the town ; I have made a drawing of our town house, which is an old house in a dark and narrow street. It stands round three sides of a court, in which are lilacs and fig-trees, and a fountain. I did not ask to whom the house now belongs, but I begged permission of the concierge to sketch it. There being no one at home, I was allowed to sit in the court and make my drawing. I have also sketched the cathedral and the church of St. John, where my ancestors lie buried. Happily, their tombs were not defaced by the Revolutionists.

'My dearest Molly, there remains to be seen only the old Château, and the place where my father died. Some day, perhaps, we may be able to erect a monument to him as well, though his body lies we know not where.

'To-morrow I walk to Eyragues, which is not more than ten miles from Aix. Shall I find the Château as we left it? But my father, who used to walk upon the terrace before the house, will be there no longer. I hope to write from Toulon. Farewell, my love, farewell!'

The letter reached us at the end of April. We waited patiently at first for the promised successor. None came the next week, and none the week after. Then I, for my part, began to grow impatient. Day by day I went out to meet the postboy from Fareham. Sometimes he turned at the road which leads to the Castle, and blew his horn at the Vicarage. But none for me. And the weeks passed by and nothing more was heard.

Now, by our calculations, the time for a letter to reach Porchester from Aix being eighteen days, if Raymond had arrived at Toulon about the middle of April, supposing that his business kept him there no more than two or three days, he would proceed to Marseilles, and thence make his way as rapidly as he could across France, and so home, and should arrive by the middle of May. That is the reason, I said, trying to assure myself, though I spent the nights in tears and prayers, why he has not written another letter, because he is posting homewards as speedily as he can travel, and comes as fast as any letter. He will be with us, therefore, about the middle of May.

The middle of May passed and he did not return, nor was there any letter from him.

Now, on the 18th of May in that year, a very grave step was taken by His Majesty the King. He declared war against France. Those who were in State secrets have since assured the world that this step was not taken without due consideration, and a full knowledge of its importance; and, further, that in declaring war, the King only anticipated the intentions of Buonaparte, whose only reason for deferring his declaration was that he might find time to build more ships.

Well, even though war was declared, Raymond was a man of peace who would be suffered to return. It was not likely that a war, which would not greatly move the hearts of the people, the causes for which lay in political reasons which they could not understand, would exasperate the French against a simple English traveller.

Letters, it is certain, sometimes miscarry; from the South of

France to Hampshire is, indeed, a terrible distance. Our traveller would come home before his letter, war or no war.

Thus passed seven weeks, and then we heard that Buonaparte, by an exercise of authority which was wholly without parallel in the history of nations, had ordered that all Englishmen travelling in France, even peaceful merchants and clergymen, should be detained. Among them, no doubt, was Raymond.

But other détenus, as they were called, wrote letters home, which were duly forwarded and received. Why did not Raymond write ?

It was through me—oh, through me, and none other—that he went away. I encouraged him to talk about his old home ; I fed the flame of desire to see it again. Had it not been for me he would have stayed at home, and now we should have been all happy together—safe and happy. But now—where was he ? In a French prison, in rags, like our French prisoners, with no money. How could we get to him ? How help him ? How know even where he was ?

'My child,' said Madam Claire, 'we are in the hands of Heaven. Do not reproach yourself. Raymond was filled with longing to see his native land again. Nay, what can have happened to him but detention with the other English travellers ?'

While I wept and wrung my hands, and Madam Claire consoled me, and we sought to find reasons for this long silence, it was strange to listen to the poor mad woman, laughing, and singing, and talking to her dead husband, chiefly about Raymond.

'The boy has grown tall, my friend,' she would say. 'The time comes when we must find a wife for him ; then, in our old age, we shall have our grandchildren round us. When he comes home he shall marry ; he will come now very soon.'

It seemed as if in some imperfect way she understood that her son was gone somewhere. Perhaps it was to comfort us that she kept repeating the words, 'He will come home soon ; he will come home soon.'

Alas ! the time soon arrived when those words were a mockery !

It was at the beginning of the tenth week that we received one more letter in that dear handwriting. But what a letter ! Oh, what a letter ! for it left us without one gleam of hope or comfort.

'I should meet my love in Heaven,' said Madam. Alas ! Heaven at nineteen seems so far away ; and to one whose heart is wholly given to an earthly passion, Heaven seems a joyless place. Sure I am that if when one is young the choice was offered of a

continuance of earthly joys, which we know, with youth and
health and plenty, or of the unknown heavenly joys, though we are
plainly told that mind cannot conceive, and tongue cannot tell their
raptures, we should, for the most part, prefer the former.

'Oh, this letter! Can I, now, think of it without a sinking of
the heart, and a wonder that the letter did not kill me on the spot ?
The postman stopped at our garden-gate ; 'twas a morning in June ;
the lilacs and laburnums were still out ; all the roses were in
blossom, and the sun was so warm that one was able already to sit
in the open air. At sight of the man my heart leaped up. He
had a letter for me, which he held up and laughed—for he knew
my impatience and anxiety—and I rushed to the gate and took it.
Yes, it was in my Raymond's handwriting. I left the postman to
get his money from Sally, and ran as fast as I could to the cottage,
my letter in my hand.

'A letter !' I cried. 'A letter from Raymond ! Oh, at last, at
last ; now we shall know !'

Then I tore open the seal and read it aloud.

'MY DEAREST MOLLY,

'This is the last letter you will ever receive from your
lover——'

His last letter ?

'Quick !' cried Madam ; 'read it quickly.'

'I am in prison at Toulon. I have but a few minutes given to
me for this letter, in which I should have said so much had I time.
My dear—my dear—I am about to die. Farewell. Try to forget
me, my poor heart. Oh, think of me as one who lived in thy heart
for a little and was then called away. I am to be guillotined for
an English spy in the very place where, ten years ago, they shot
my father. It is strange that my death should be like his, and in
the same way. I am not a spy, as you know ; but I have failed to
convince my judges. I was tried this very day, and I am to die to-
morrow morning amidst the execrations of the people. Is not this
a strange destiny for father and son ? Kiss my mother for me.
By the time this letter reaches you she will be already conversing
with the spirit of her son as well as that of her husband ; for, my
dear, where could my spirit rest if not near thee ! And if my
father's soul hath obtained this privilege, why not mine ? My
spirit can have no terrors for thee. I had much to tell ; but now
you will never hear what has happened to me, and why. I am
promised that this letter shall be sent to thee. To-morrow I am

to die. Farewell—farewell—farewell. Oh, Molly, my sweet girl, I kiss the place where I write thy name. Farewell, my dear. Farewell——'

I know not how I was able to read this letter aloud, for every word was like a dagger plunged into my heart. Oh ! a thousand daggers would have been better than this letter, so full of love and pity, and yet so terrible with its message.

Pass over this day. Think, if you can, how Madam fell upon her knees and prayed—not for herself, but for me ; think how I sat with dry eyes speechless ; think how my father came and wept ; think how all the time the poor mad lady laughed and sang as happy as the blackbird in the orchard, and repeated, like a parrot in a cage :

' He will come home soon ; he will come home soon.'

CHAPTER X.

IN THE TOWER.

IT was not until six months later, and under circumstances which will be related in their place, that we heard what happened after Raymond left Aix.

The village of Eyragues is about ten or twelve miles from Aix, along a dusty, white road, with plane-trees on either side or avenues of the spreading poplar, or when a village or a farmhouse is passed, cypresses and chestnuts.

It was late in the afternoon when he arrived at the place.

A low hill rises, steep on the south side, and on the west with a gentle slope. The village stands upon the slope, and on the top of the hill, where the cliff looks over the valley of the Durance, stood the Château. Here the valley is broad and the steam shallow, running over its gravel bed with a melodious ripple, as if it was the most innocent brook in the world, though no river is more dangerous, by reason of its sudden inundations. In the cliff overlooking the river there are caves, partly natural, partly artificial ; these are used as dwelling-houses by the poorer peasants and the shepherds, the entrances being closed with wood. The village itself consists of one sloping street, in the middle of which is the church, and beside it the presbytère, or vicarage ; opposite to the church, the village inn, with three shrubs in great green casks before the door, and the bunch of dry briar hanging over the door.

As Raymond drew nearer, approaching the village from the west, he remarked two or three things which seemed strange. There were no cattle in the meadows. Why, the meadows were formerly full of cattle. The bed of the river seemed to have grown broader than he remembered. When one revisits places, seen last in childhood, they generally look smaller. The buildings in the valley were roofless; the caves showed no sign of inhabitants.

He entered the street. There had been quite recently a dreadful fire, and most of the houses were destroyed wholly or in part. Those which had escaped were shut up. The village auberge had its bush above the door, and its three shrubs in green tubs in front ; but the door was closed, and the shrubs were dead.

And then he heard footsteps. At last then ! There was someone in the village. An old woman came out of a cottage beside the inn. She came hobbling upon two sticks, looking curiously at the stranger. She was bent with years, wrinkled, and decrepit. She advanced slowly. Suddenly she burst into a cackling kind of laugh not pleasant to hear.

'Ho, ho !' she cried. 'You are come at last. Oh ! I knew you would come some day. I told him that you would come.'

'Who am I, then ?'

'I knew very well that you would come. But I knew that you would not come before the proper time. Oh, everything in its place. First the inundation ; that carried away his cattle and destroyed his meadows. Next the burning ; that took away his village. What has he left to take ? There is only himself, or his son. Are you come for him, or shall you take his son ?'

Raymond remembered her now. But she was old when he had last seen her, ten years before—already an old woman, living with her grandchildren.

'I know you, Mother Vidal,' he said. 'Why, what, in Heaven's name, has happened ?'

'You are young again, M. le Comte. Those who come back from the dead do well to resume their youth. In heaven we shall all be young and beautiful. Hush ! He is horribly afraid. At sight of you I think he will drop down dead.'

'Who ?'

'Louis Leroy. Who else ?'

'Where are the people, then ?'

'They are gone. The war took some; the inundation took some ; the burning sent the rest away. The village is deserted. The people would stay no longer in a place accursed, lest something worse should befall them. But, as for me, I am old. Nothing can hurt me now.'

'Why is the place accursed?'

'Is it for you, M. le Comte, to ask such a question? The curé told him, when he went away, that the wrath of the bon Dieu was kindled against him. Go up the hill; you will find him at the Château.'

An empty and deserted village; the houses mostly burned down; nobody in the place. Here was a prospect of a pleasant night.

Raymond went on up the hill, and before long came to the top, on which the Château stood. Alas! the modern part of the house was destroyed, only the shell remaining, and beside it the ancient tower. The gardens were grown over; the farm buildings were in ruins; the great dovecot was empty. There were no signs of life about the place at all.

There was yet about half an hour of daylight, and Raymond sat down to make the most of it. He would have time to sketch the ruins, and he would then retrace his steps, and put up for the night at some auberge on the way to Aix.

The tower, however, was not uninhabited. Presently a man came forth from the great doorway.

He was dressed rather better than the peasants, but looked neglected, his chin unshaven, his hair without powder, his coat old and worn. When Raymond, who had taken off his hat and was working bareheaded, saw the man at the door he rose to salute him. To his amazement the proprietor of the tower, if the man was the proprietor, shrieked aloud and staggered.

Raymond ran to his assistance.

'Are you ill?' he asked.

The man made no reply, but his lips trembled. Raymond saw before him a man of forty-five, or perhaps fifty. His face was wolfish—the face of a man who lives alone and thinks continually of wickedness—yet the features might once have been fine.

'I am afraid,' said Raymond, 'that in this lonely place I have startled you. I am, however, only a harmless traveller, and I have taken the liberty of sketching this ruin, in which I have an interest.'

The man recovered a little.

'I am subject,' he said, biting his nails, 'to sudden fits of pain. You were saying, sir, that you are a traveller.'

'I am a traveller and an artist. It is my practice to make drawings of all the places which I visit.'

'An artist! It is strange. What is your name, sir?'

'My name is Arnold. Would you like to see my passport?'

'Not at all, sir. Arnold! What is your Christian name?'

'It is Raymond.'

'Then, sir,' said the man, speaking slowly, 'unless I am mistaken, your father's name was also Raymond. His full name was Raymond Arnault, Comte d'Eyragues. He was killed, I believe, at Toulon, after the capture of the city by the Revolutionary army.'

'All this, sir, is quite true, though I understand not how you know it.'

'I know it from the likeness you bear to your father, coupled with the fact that you bear his name——'

'Were you a friend of my father's?'

'Young man, your father was a great man. I was one of the canaille. He had no friendship for such as I.'

'An old woman in the village mentioned the name of Louis Leroy——'

'There is no Louis Leroy in this place. There has not been anyone of that name for many years,' he replied quickly.

'Well, sir,' said Raymond, 'I am Raymond Arnault. But I am now an Englishman, and have only come here in order to see the place where I was born. That is natural, is it not?'

'Quite natural. . I am the proprietor of the estates, such as they have become. A valuable possession, truly! The river has washed away my cattle and my meadows; a fire has destroyed my village the people have gone; the house is in ruins. A valuable possession, truly!'

'Is the old house in Aix also yours?'

'That is also mine. But I cannot let it, for they say that it is haunted. Then you do not know who bought this estate?'

'I have never learned.'

'Well, it matters nothing. Louis Leroy—I knew him well—has been dead, I think, for a long time. You were not in search of him? No? You do not know that it was he who denounced your father? Some sons might have sought revenge. You do not? That is well. Revenge is a foolish thing to desire. Better let him alone, even if he be still living.'

'The man shall never be sought by me. If I were to find him —if I had my fingers on his throat—I do not say.'

'Ah, your blood is Provençal—your hands would be at his throat! Yes, I think I see you. You have the Arnault face, and it is fierce when roused. Yes, you would make short work of Louis

Leroy if you had the chance. Ha, ha! he will do well to keep out of your way. That is quite certain—quite certain. Ha, ha!'

The man chuckled and rubbed his hands. The thought of Louis Leroy being throttled pleased him. He showed his teeth when he laughed, which made him look more like a wolf.

'Come,' he said; 'one of your family must not be sent away from this place. Share my dinner, and take what I can give you for a bed. Oh, it is not much—a poor meal and a simple pallet! But such as they are I offer them to you.'

Raymond accepted willingly. The man was not prepossessing to look at, but one must not judge by first impressions. Therefore, he followed his host, thinking himself lucky to get the chance of a supper and a bed.

His host led the way into the tower. The room into which the door—a great, massive door, set with big nails and provided with a solid lock—opened was a room with stone floor, stone walls, and a vaulted stone roof. A second door in the side opened upon spiral stairs leading to upper rooms. The room was furnished with two chairs and a table. There was a stove in it, and the smell of some cookery. His host lifted a saucepan from a fire of wood ashes.

'You are ready for your dinner? Good; then sit down.'

He poured out the contents of the saucepan into a dish, and set it on the table with a long loaf of bread, the salt, and a bottle of wine.

'It is a stew,' he said, 'of rabbits, rice, onions, and beans. Eat, Monsieur le Comte.'

Raymond was hungry, tired, and thirsty. He made accordingly an excellent meal, drinking freely of the black and strong Provence wine. His host ate and drank but little. When the first bottle was finished he brought out another, and encouraged his guest to talk, asking him a hundred questions, and appearing deeply interested in his replies; so that the young man freely spoke of himself—of his circumstances, and the conditions of his people; how his mother had lost her reason, and his father's sister had miraculously preserved the Holy Rose, on which they had subsisted until now; but that the jewels being by this time all sold, he was to become the support of the family.

'I understand,' said his host; 'they have now nothing left, so that if you were not to return they would starve.'

Raymond was also easily induced to show the drawings which he had made.

'Young man,' said his entertainer, biting his nails, 'you are going to Toulon, you say ? I can show you all the best spots for an artist. Do not forget to bring your portfolio of sketches with you. And upon my word'—he looked Raymond full in the face—'upon my word, young man, I feel as if your business was already completed, and you were standing where your father stood. It will be deeply interesting.'

It was then about ten o'clock. Raymond asked permission to go to bed.

'This way,' said his host, taking the candle and mounting the stairs. 'You will find nothing but a mattress and a blanket. Behold !'

There were two rooms on this floor, divided by a partition wall. The one into which Raymond was shown was lighted by a single narrow window, barred with iron and without glass. A mattress lay in a corner ; there was no other furniture in it.

'You remember the place, without doubt ; formerly it was a store-room ; the accommodation is simple.'

'Thank you,' said Raymond ; 'it will serve me very well.'

'I sleep in the next room. There is no other occupant of the tower. It is silent here at night when one is alone. There are ghosts, I am told, especially of your father. But I never see him. He was denounced, you know, by Louis Leroy, who was his half-brother. Ha ! if you had your fingers upon his throat ! Good night and good repose, Monsieur le Comte.'

Raymond quickly undressed, and threw himself upon the mattress. In a few minutes he was asleep.

In the middle of the night he had a dream. He dreamed that he woke up suddenly ; the moon was shining through the bars of the window so as to send some light to the room. Then he saw, lying quite still and having no desire to move, the door between the two rooms slowly open. He was not in the least afraid, being in a dream, but he wondered what was going to happen. Then he saw his host standing at the open door. He had taken off boots and coat. For a few moments he stood as if uncertain. Then he began to move slowly and cautiously toward the mattress. Raymond saw that he had a knife in his hand. But he was not in the least afraid, because he was in a dream ; the man proposed to murder him, perhaps. That was interesting and curious. How would he be prevented ?

Suddenly the murderer sprang back, throwing up his arms, and with a moan of terror rushed from the room. And in the middle of the room, just where the moonlight fell, Raymond saw, in this strange dream, the figure of his father. This did not surprise him either. But he was glad that the murderer had been stayed in his purpose, and he wondered what he would say about it in the morning.

When Raymond woke up the sun was already high ; he rose quickly and dressed. His host was up before him. Strange to say, he had quite forgotten his curious dream.

CHAPTER XI.

THE KISS OF JUDAS.

RAYMOND forgot, I say, his dream of the man with a knife. Had he remembered it, he would have been ashamed of it, so friendly was his entertainer. He led him about the place, showed him how the greatest inundation ever known in the history of the Durance River had destroyed his cattle, overthrown his farmhouses, and covered his meadows with stones and gravel. ' But this,' he said, always biting his nails, ' might have happened to anyone. If your father were living, it would have happened just the same.'

' I suppose it would,' said Raymond.

Then the man led his guest through the village.

' When you were a child,' he said, ' the village was full of people. There were five hundred souls in this place. Here was the tavern where they drank ; here was the church where they went to mass ; under these trees the lads played at bowls on Sunday morning ; many a time have I seen your parents watching the villagers on their way home after mass ; in the evening they danced here.'

' You know the place, then ? You are a native of the village ?'

' I have been here on business. They plundered your house at Aix ; then they came on here and sacked the Château. The books and pictures they burned and trampled under foot, the furniture they broke up, but the plate they carried off. However, the estate remained, and the village ; now there is nothing. Then came the inundation ; then these young men had to go to war ; when the village was burned down there were not fifty people left. And now they are gone, and there is nobody except myself and an old woman who is mad. But all this would have happened whether your father was shot or no—would it not ?'

' I suppose it would,' said Raymond. ' One cannot think that the wrath of Heaven for my father's murder would fall upon innocent folk.'

'No—no. It would fall on the head of Louis Leroy. Ah! if your fingers were once about his throat! However, the man is dead.'

The man was very friendly, and yet Raymond was ill at ease with him, and he had a trick of glancing suspiciously about him as if he was afraid of something, which made Raymond uncomfortable.

He was so friendly that he accompanied Raymond back to Aix, and from Aix to Toulon, where he said that he had business. He was so very friendly that he followed the young man about everywhere, and seemed unwilling to suffer him out of his sight.

At Toulon he acted as guide, and led Raymond to the spot where his father suffered death.

'Here, beneath these trees,' he said, 'sat the Commissioners, Fréron, young Robespierre, and the others. Eh! they are all dead now. They sat in chairs; the prisoners were brought here to be tried. Oh, they were all aristocrats, and they had no chance. Among them were a few poor devils who were servants. They were shot, to deter others from serving Royalists. Some of them were ladies—oh, I assure you, beautiful ladies, but all pale and trembling with terror. Well, they had not long to wait. Some of them were mere children, some old men, some were young men, like your father. Some of them wept and lamented, especially the servants, when they saw that there would be no favour shown to any, but every man and woman must be taken impartially and placed in front of the soldiers; but most bore themselves proudly, like your father. Young man, there never was anyone prouder than your father. I, who was standing by, remember the contempt with which he regarded his judges.'

'What did he say to the witness, his half-brother?'

'He said—nothing,' the man replied with hesitation; 'what could he say?'

'Did he curse him?'

'He did not.'

'What has the lot of that man been since that day?'

'He had nothing to lose; therefore, if he is a poor man now, he is no worse off than he was before.'

'But he is dead, you say?'

'Louis Leroy has been dead for a long time.'

'Had he children of his own?'

'He had one son only.'

'Perhaps, then,' said Raymond, 'Heaven will strike him in the person of his son.'

'Here,' the man continued, 'each man stood to take his trial. On this spot stood the witnesses, when there were any. In your father's case there was one only ; but he was enough. Here stood the prisoner when his turn came to be shot ; here stood the file of soldiers. Oh, it was a day of vengeance for the Revolution.'

Raymond took off his hat reverently before the spot where his father had perished.

'Very likely,' continued his guide, 'your father might have escaped but for the man Leroy, who first caused him to be arrested —perhaps you did not know that—and then gave evidence against him. There were several thousands left in Toulon when the English went away. There were not more than eight or nine hundred shot. Very likely he would have escaped. As for that man Leroy,' he went on, 'you would like to have your fingers on his throat, would you not ?'

'If I had,' said Raymond hoarsely, 'I would kill him here— where my father died.'

'Ah ! he is dead now. That is fortunate for him. He lived in great fear, because misfortune always fell upon him—just as it has upon me. But the thing he never thought upon, the danger he least expected, was the return of the Count's son. What should he do if he were living now ?' There never could be eyes more full of meaning and suspicion than this man's. 'What should he do ?'

'I care not ; what does it matter ?'

'He would protect himself, would he not ?'

'I suppose so. Now leave me, if you please. I wish to be alone.'

The guide obeyed ; that is to say, he withdrew a little. But he watched. Meanwhile Raymond tried to people the scene, now a peaceful market-place, full of stalls and market women, with the prisoners, soldiers, and commissioners of that day of massacre. Then he took out his sketch-book and made a drawing of the Place.

When he had finished his drawing he remembered the Quai, where he had stood with his mother all through that fearful night, the shells hissing and bursting in the air, the flames of the arsenal making it as light as day. It was easy to find the place. From the Place d'Armes a street leads straight to the spot. The sight was very different now. The harbour was full of men-of-war, frigates, and all kinds of war vessels, a sight which might have filled an English sailor's heart with joy, giving rich promise of prizes. The Quai itself was covered with all kinds of ship's gear. There was the sound of hammering and the running to and fro of men. For an outbreak of war with England was again imminent, and the work of the dockyards was carried on night and day.

Raymond looked about him, trying to remember, which was in vain, where they had been standing.

Then he took out his sketch-book again, and began to sketch. Behind him at a little distance a gend'arme watched him. Beside the gend'arme stood Raymond's host and friend whispering furtively.

When he had completed this little drawing he rose, and began to wander about the town, glad to be alone. His work was done. He had seen his ancestral home, shattered and ruined ; he had. visited the old church at Aix where the bones of his forefathers were buried ; he had seen the great house which had been their town residence ; he had stood upon the spot where his father was shot, and upon the Quai, whence he was dragged with his mother by the English sailors ; now there remained nothing more but to go home.

He wandered about the town, thinking of these things, and of his journey home, and of his sweetheart. Presently, he found himself at the fortifications. Without any thought of danger he sat down before a gate and began to sketch it. There was nothing especially interesting about the building, yet he made a drawing of it.

He did not observe that the gend'arme who had watched him making his sketch on the Quai had followed him, and was still watching him at a distance. When he had drawn the gateway, he walked out of the town, having no object but to wander about aimlessly until the evening. On the following day he would begin his homeward journey.

Outside the town, half-way up the hill on the western side, there stands an outpost or fort, which, when the British troops held the town, was also held by them, and called Gibraltar, because it was considered impregnable. It commands the town, and from its bastions a fine view is obtained of the harbour, the arsenals, the town, and the fortifications. This fort was taken by Buonaparte. It was the first act by which he distinguished himself ; and, once taken, the capture of the town was rendered easy.

Raymond, following a winding path, presently found himself within the bastion. He looked over the rampart and found that it commanded a beautiful view of Toulon Harbour, which, with the dockyard, the walls, and the town, lay stretched out at his feet. Again he drew forth his book and began to sketch the view before him. Presently he heard footsteps approaching, but he thought nothing of them, and went on with his work.

'I arrest you in the name of the Republic.'

A heavy hand was laid upon his shoulder. Raymond sprang to his feet. It was a gend'arme ; behind the gend'arme were a dozen soldiers.

'Why do you arrest me ?'

'I arrest you as an English spy, detected in the act of making a plan of the fortifications.'

Raymond laughed. The man pointed to his sketch, on which some parts of the walls were already drawn.

'Come with me,' he said.

Raymond obeyed. Resistance, indeed, would have been impossible. The man took from him his sketch-book, and laid his hand upon his shoulder.

The soldiers followed. When they were within the town a crowd began to gather, and presently ominous cries were uttered : 'English spy ! English spy ! Death to spies !'

Then the crowd pressed closer, and cried the louder. Fists were shaken in Raymond's face ; voices were raised crying for immediate justice. 'A la lanterne !' The crowd grew larger, and the cries louder and more threatening.

There is no rage more unreasonable, swifter, and more uncontrollable than the rage of a mob. Raymond would have been torn to pieces but for the soldiers who had accompanied his capture, and now surrounded the prisoner, and acted as a guard.

At last he was within the prison walls and in safety for the moment. Outside, the mob raged and shouted ; it was a warlike mob, composed chiefly of sailors and soldiers, whom the very word 'spy' maddens. They would have liked nothing better than to have the English spy thrown out to them.

When Raymond found himself stripped of everything, and thrust roughly into a cell, he consoled himself by thinking that a charge so absurd could not be maintained. He should be released the next day.

He was mistaken.

In the morning he was taken before a magistrate.

On the table were laid the sketches taken from his portfolio, his drawing pencils, his passport, his pocket-book, and his purse.

The prisoner, asked to give an account of himself, stated that he was an English subject named Raymond Arnold; that he was an artist by profession; and that he was travelling for his pleasure in France.

On further examination he confessed that his name was Raymond Arnault, and that he was a French subject by birth, and the son of the ci-devant Comte d'Eyragues, condemned to death for treason. He also confessed that he taught the young officers of the British navy the art of drawing plans of fortifications; he declared that he had no other motive in visiting this part of France but the natural curiosity of seeing once more his birthplace, and the place where his father died; also that he was actuated in making these sketches by no other motive than the desire of preserving alive his recollections of these scenes.

His preliminary examination was short; now it was completed, he was taken back to prison.

Two days afterwards he was again taken before the magistrate, who asked him a great number of questions as to the object of his journey, and the various places he had visited. His note-book was produced, and he was asked why certain facts had been set down, and for what reason he had shown so great a curiosity as to the condition of the country. Raymond replied as well as he could, explaining that these notes were nothing but the simple observations of a traveller. His answers were taken down without comment. He then requested permission to send a letter to the British Ambassador at Paris. This request was at once refused, on the ground that he was not a British subject.

On the third examination, the magistrate, who was not hostile or unnecessarily harsh, pointed out to the prisoner that his case was one in which the penalty, should he be found guilty, was nothing short of death; that the aspect of the case was most serious; that the relations between France and England were already strained; and that should war unhappily break out before his trial, it would probably go hard with him. Therefore, he exhorted him to confess everything, including the secret instructions given him by the British Government, and the nature of the information he had collected.

Finding that the prisoner remained obdurate, the magistrate ordered him to be taken back to prison.

He was forbidden to write any letters, or to communicate with the outer world at all. An ordinary criminal may get this indulgence, but not a spy. More than this, he was treated by the gaolers with every indignity they had the power to inflict upon him, the men letting him understand daily that they would enjoy nothing so much as to murder a British spy.

'I could not understand,' he told us afterwards, 'I could never understand all that time, how such a suspicion could possibly fall upon me. Nor was it till I heard the speech of the advocate for the prosecution, and the evidence, that I was able to see the weight of the suspicions against me.'

CHAPTER XII.

THE TRIAL.

IF the time had been tranquil, I suppose that Raymond would have been immediately released. But the air was filled with rumours and suspicions ; the dockyard of Toulon was active ; ships were being fitted out ; there was talk of nothing but war. Therefore the most innocent action, such as the drawing of a gateway, or a sketch of the Quai, was liable to be exaggerated into the action of an English spy. Added to this was the fact, now known to all, that the prisoner was not a British, but a French subject ; that he was travelling under an assumed name ; and that he was the son of one who had been instrumental in bringing the British troops into Toulon.

He was brought to trial three weeks after his arrest, having been kept all this time in close confinement, except for his examination by the magistrate. In accordance with French custom, he was in ignorance of the evidence, if any, on which the charge against him was to be supported ; but he knew that he was accused of being a spy in the service of the British Government.

I suppose that, innocent or guilty, there cannot be a more terrible thing for a man than to stand a trial on a capital charge, and more especially on such a charge as this, where a hostile feeling against the prisoner is sure to exist.

When Raymond found himself in the great Hall of Justice, placed in the prisoners' box, he was at first confused and in a manner overwhelmed. The tribunal, as it is called, was occupied by three judges. On the right of the tribunal sat the jury, on the left was the prisoner, guarded on both sides by gend'armes. The advocate for the prisoner stood immediately before his client, so that he could communicate, and the counsel for the prosecution was on the opposite side. A large table below the tribunal was occupied by clerks, and the great body of the hall was crowded with spectators. The windows were so placed that their full light fell upon the features of the prisoner, so that no change of countenance could escape the eyes of judge or jury.

The clerk first read the indictment.

It was to the effect that Raymond Arnault, born at the Château d'Eyragues, only son of the late Raymond Arnault, commonly called Comte d'Eyragues, who was shot for treason to the Republic, was a spy, engaged by the British Government to collect information as to the condition of the country, make plans of fortresses, learn the state of the arsenals, the number, armaments, etc., of ships fitted out or building, with all other facts and information which might be useful to the British Government and prejudicial to the Republic.

The indictment read, the President began the trial by putting questions to the prisoner. These were nothing more than those already put by the magistrate in his examinations. They made the prisoner give his name, his age, and occupation ; they inquired into the reasons which made him undertake the journey, and why he travelled under a false name ; why he made sketches ; why he made certain entries in his note-book ; why he asked questions everywhere.

'You travelled from Lyons to Arles in a water-coach,' said the President, 'and from Arles to Aix by diligence. On the way you conversed with the other passengers.'

'I did. I was pleased, after ten years, to talk with Frenchmen again.'

'You asked questions of everybody.'

'If I did it was out of pure curiosity. The questions were such as to call for no information that might not be published to all the world.'

'What ? You inquired into the condition of the army ; you asked if the country was not drained of fighting men ; you asked if the women were obliged to do all the work in the fields ; you inquired whether the people were good Republicans, or whether they wanted the Bourbons back again ; you call these questions such as might be published ?'

'I repeat,' said Raymond, 'that the questions I asked were solely out of curiosity.'

It appears that in France the judges examine and cross-examine a prisoner before the witnesses are called, and that they have thus the power to make him criminate himself, which is contrary to our custom.

When the question was finished, Raymond having to repeat a dozen times his solemn denial that he was engaged and paid by the British Government, the witnesses were called.

'I was curious,' said Raymond, ' to see who these witnesses might be, and you may judge of my astonishment when the first witness was no other than my host of Eyragues, and that he was none other than the man Louis Leroy himself ; and then I understood all.'

Yes, the man who had received and entertained him, who had given him advice, and accompanied him to Toulon, was no other than the man Louis Leroy.

'My name,' he said in answer to the President, 'is now Scipio Gavotte ; before the Revolution it was Louis Leroy. I am a proprietor. On the 20th of April last I observed the prisoner walking about the ruins of Eyragues, a village which has been burned and is now abandoned. He was making sketches. I accosted him, and inquired his name and business. I gave him dinner and a bed in my own house. He began by saying that he was an Englishman, but on my discovering that he spoke Provençal, and had the air of a native of this country, he confessed that he was by birth a Provençal, and that he was travelling under an assumed name under protection of a British passport. I began, therefore, to suspect something, and accompanied him to Aix, where I found him making sketches of the walls, and to Toulon, where he began, trusting to his passport, to make plans of the Quai and harbour and drawings of the ships. I gave him no warning, but communicated the facts to a gend'arme, who watched him and arrested him. The prisoner seemed to me a man of great intelligence, and showed himself most curious in respect of everything connected with the condition of the country.'

He had nothing more to say, but the counsel for the defence asked him two or three questions.

'Are you,' he asked, ' the same Louis Leroy on whose evidence the prisoner's father was shot on December 19th, 1793 ?'

'I am the same man.'

'You gave that evidence knowing that it would cause his death ?'

'Certainly.'

'You were his half-brother, I think?'

'I was.'

'And you purchased his confiscated estate?'

'I did.'

'Did you reveal these facts to the prisoner?'

'I did not.'

'Did you give the information which led to his arrest in the hope of getting him out of the way?'

'I gave the information for the good of the Republic.'   ·

The next witness was the commis-voyageur who had travelled with the prisoner in the diligence between Arles and Aix. This person deposed that his suspicions were aroused by observing the prisoner, who professed to be an Englishman, conversing with the country people in their own language; whereas the ignorance of Englishmen, even in French—a language known and universally spoken by every other civilized nation—was notorious. He further stated that, on listening to the conversation, he found that the young man was asking the people questions concerning their political opinions, their views as to the Republic, the state of their industries, and the drain of young men by the recent wars. Finally, he declared that he had seen the prisoner from time to time making notes and drawings in a little book which he carried. He identified the book, which was handed to him for the purpose, and pointed out—partly with indignation and partly as a proof of the truth of his statement—that among the drawings was one representing himself in an attitude grossly insulting. In fact, Raymond had drawn a picture of this man eating his breakfast like a hog.

The counsel for the defence refused to ask any questions of this witness, and desired to confirm his testimony. All that he had stated was true.

The next witness called was the gend'arme who had followed and watched Raymond. He swore that he saw him sitting on the Quai drawing the ships; that he followed him and watched him while he made a sketch of the Porte de Marseilles; that he again followed him, and found him in the act of making a plan of the fortifications.

Counsel for the defence asked this witness whether the prisoner had made any attempt at concealment. Witness replied that he had not.

'Did he not openly seat himself on the Quai and make the drawings before the eyes of all present?'

'He did.'

'Did he show any embarrassment or terror when you arrested him ?'

'He did not. He laughed.'

There were no other witnesses except the note-book and the sketch-book.

Then the prisoner's counsel rose to make his speech.

He began by relating, from the prisoner's point of view, the history of his life. He was born in this part of France, and was fourteen years of age when he was taken from Toulon by the British fleet, on the capture of the city ; that he was carried, with his mother and aunt, to Portsmouth, where they were landed ; and that he had lived in a small village near to that town, and that, finding it necessary to adopt some profession in order to make a livelihood, he had become a teacher of drawing and painting. To this he added the art of fortification and drawing plans, and his pupils were chiefly young officers of the navy.

'Gentlemen of the jury,' he went on, 'consider, if you please, that this humble and obscure person was absolutely unknown to anybody connected with the British Government. He has never spoken to an official person ; he is ignorant of politics. But it is not difficult to understand one feeling which survived in his breast, after ten years of exile, namely, love of France and the desire to see again his native country. It was to gratify this desire, and with no other object whatever, that he made this journey. Why, then, did he assume the name and procure the passport of a British subject ? It was in order to escape questioning about his origin and family. Like all émigrés, he was uncertain of the reception he would meet, as the son of an aristocrat, and of one sentenced to death and executed for treason towards the Republic. But, gentlemen, it was not an assumed name ; it was the name by which he was commonly known in England—the Anglicized form of his own name. As for the questions which he asked of everybody, I confess that I see nothing in them but such as would be prompted by the natural curiosity of one returning to his country after ten years—and those ten years the most momentous and the most glorious in the whole history of the country. Gentlemen, there is his note-book ; read it, I beg of you, with unprejudiced eyes. There is nothing in the notes, I submit, which would be of the least advantage for a foreign country to know. Then there remain the sketches. Gentlemen of the jury, examine these for yourselves. There are the ruined Château where the prisoner was born ; the house in Aix which belonged to his ancestors ; here is the Place d'Armes of this town ; here is a sketch of the busy and crowded Quai, with the ships and harbour; here is a drawing of the Porte de Marseilles ; and here is the unfinished drawing which caused his arrest. Gentlemen, the gend'arme who arrested him states that it was a plan of the fortifications. I submit that it is nothing of the kind. It would have been, when finished, a drawing of the view from the bastion on which he stood, showing the town, with the harbour, arsenal, and the walls. I can find in these drawings nothing that can disprove the prisoner's own statements. Add to this that there was not found upon him a single document of a suspicious character, unless the pencil portrait of a young lady is suspicious ; that the prisoner was but poorly supplied with money ; that his movements were open for all to see ; and that every statement of his which could be proved has been tested and found true. There is one other point, gentlemen, that I would press upon you. The British held this town for several months. Do you think it possible that they should have gone away without taking a plan of the fortifications with them ? Do you think it likely that they should have sent this young man on an errand so useless and so dangerous ? Would anyone be so foolish as to accept such a mission ?'

With these words the counsel sat down. So clear and reasonable was the defence that Raymond would probably have been acquitted, but for a most untoward accident. There was heard from the street outside a great shouting and roaring of men, and an usher brought a note to the President, who read it, and after handing it to his brother judges, gave it to the counsel for the prosecution ; evidently something had happened of importance, for he sprang to his feet, and began a speech of the most furious kind.

'I rise,' he said, ' to demand justice upon a traitor to the Republic—the son of a traitor. Was he ignorant when he left England that the King of Great Britain had already resolved on war ? Was he ignorant that war was to be declared immediately ? Yes, gentlemen of the jury, immediately. War has been declared. The news has just reached this town. The huzzas of the crowd which you have just heard demonstrate the spirit with which we have received this news. Already the fleets which are to humble the pride of our enemies are preparing in our harbours ; already our brave sailors are exulting in the approaching downfall of the enemy of freedom and justice.

'Gentlemen, let us not be revengeful, but let us be just. Consider the circumstances. It is natural that the enemy should wish to learn everything possible concerning our armaments and the state of the country. Since, then, it is natural to expect that English spies are among us in disguise as innocent travellers, what sort of person would Pitt select for a spy in this country? First, it is absolutely necessary for him to know the language. But in Provence our common people do not speak French, but the Langue d'Oc. Probably there is not one living Briton who knows that language. Some there may be who have read the Troubadours, and know the tongue spoken in the Middle Ages, but for the common talk of the peasantry, the patois, there needs a man who was born and brought up among them. Such a man he found in the prisoner. He is an émigré. His father was shot for treasonable correspondence with the British. The title and the estates which might have been his are lost to him. It is the Revolution which has ruined him. Therefore, he hates the Revolution, and regards the success of our arms with envy and disgust. He had lived so long in his native country before his exile, that he can never forget the language of its people—in fact, he was already fourteen when he was taken away by a British ship. On the other hand, he has been so long in England that he can now speak English perfectly, and pass himself off for an Englishman. While in this country, in appearance and in language he can appear, if he please, as an honest Provençal.

'There is, again, another circumstance in favour of the selection of this young man. He is an artist. That is to say, he can draw, paint, and plan—especially plan. In England, his residence, when not employed in service of this kind, is Portsmouth, which is to Great Britain what Toulon is to France. There he enjoys the society of the British officers, to whom he teaches the art of making plans and drawings—of what? Of fortifications. So that we have in this young man all that combine to form the perfect spy. Given the conditions of his birth and his education, and we might predict beforehand what would be his work. Poor, like all émigrés; filled with hatred to the Revolution; eager for revenge on account of his lost wealth and rank; an Englishman one day, a Provençal the next; intelligent, well educated, a draughtsman, and, perhaps—it is in the blood of Provence—brave. Behold the spy of Pitt! Behold the tool of the British Government! Yet a willing instrument, and, therefore, one which must be rendered useless for any future work, as an example and a discouragement.'

'All this time,' Raymond tells me, 'while the advocate thun-

dered, and even I myself began to feel that after all I must be a
secret messenger of the British Government, I was filled with that
strange feeling that the issue of the trial concerned some other
man.   Until the moment when I wrote the letter to you, which I
thought would be my last, I was callous to an extent which I cannot now understand.   For certainly no man ever had an escape
such as mine.'

The jury, without hesitation, gave their verdict—the prisoner
was guilty.   Then the President sentenced Raymond to death, and
he was taken away.

Outside the court there was such a crowd as had never been seen
before, yelling death to the English spy, and demanding that he
should be given up to them.

.. Amid a storm of execrations he was taken back to his cell in
safety.

'Even then,' said Raymond, 'in the midst of the savage faces,
and with the certain prospect of death, I was insensible.   It was
as if I was playing a part, and that the principal part, of a play.'

What it was that supported him through this time of trouble, I
know not ; but, remembering Raymond's dream at the Château
and the strange events which followed, and his mother's constant
companionship with her dead husband, and the assurance which she
received as to her son's safety, I have formed a judgment which
nothing can shake.

At last the prisoner was safely lodged in his cell, the key turned
and the mob dispersed, hungering for the moment when he should
be brought forth to be beheaded in their sight.

CHAPTER XIII.

AT HOME.

It was in the second week of June, when Raymond, as we judged,
had been already dead for three weeks, that we received his last
letter.   Indeed, I cannot bear to think even now or to speak of
that terrible time, in which nothing could bring consolation, not
even weeping.   Raymond was dead.   Then was all the sun taken
from the heavens, and the warmth from the air, and the joy from
my life.   There were others who mourned for Raymond besides
myself ; but we women who lose our lovers are selfish, and we
think not of any others.

It is good for those who mourn and refuse to be comforted, that they should be forced by necessity into thinking of other things. It was about the end of October that I was compelled to turn away my thoughts from my own sorrows. I have said that with the arrival of peace and the paying off of the ships, the profits of our boat greatly diminished. This decrease grew worse as ship after ship was paid off and none were put into commission except to relieve the regular West India and Mediterranean Fleets. Many days during the summer of that year the boat returned with half her cargo unsold. If this was the case in the summer, when we looked to make our chief harvest, what was to be expected from the winter? Day after day passed, and not enough business done to pay even the wages of Sally and her father. More than this ; there was no longer any demand for our dried sloe leaves, and Portsmouth herbalists bought no more of our drugs.

I regarded this change at first without the least concern. Was it likely that the daughter of a substantial merchant should be rendered anxious by so small a matter? Besides, this was the most delightful season in my life, being in the first six months of my engagement, and, naturally, I thought all day long of Raymond.

In winter, we have little to sell except potatoes, onions, and cabbages. This winter it appeared that no one wanted to buy our things at all, because there were so many who sold and so few to buy. Thus it is with a seaport town. A long war gives rise to many new trades. Where there was one shop there are seen, after a few brisk years, ten ; where there was one market-garden there are ten. Then Raymond went away. Was it likely that I should concern myself about the boat when I had to prepare for his departure ? Whose hands but mine prepared his linen and packed his trunk ?

In the spring a great misfortune fell upon us. I mean, a misfortune apart from the dreadful letter of Raymond's. War was declared, and we thought to recover our losses, the dockyards being busy day and night, the harbour full of vessels in commission, and Spithead and the Solent crowded with ships waiting for convoy. The promise of April was beautiful. Never were trees thicker with blossom. Then there came a hard frost one night which did dreadful damage, and after this a cold east wind which destroyed whatever escaped the frost. After the east wind, the weather grew suddenly hot, and then came swarms of caterpillars, the like of which I have never seen before or since. They stripped the currant, gooseberry and raspberry bushes of leaf and fruit ; they left not a single strawberry; they ate up our asparagus, our young peas, our beans, and our lettuces. They left us nothing. It was like the plague of locusts which fell upon the land of Egypt, and ate up every herb of the land and all the fruit of the trees.

And now there was no use for the boat to go down the harbour, because there was nothing to put into her.

Very soon, naturally, the day came when I had no more money to pay even the wages, and none for the housekeeping. Note that, like all the world, in the prosperous times we had kept a good table, and my father had taken his punch nightly, as if the fat times were going to last. I declare that I had no suspicion at all of the truth. My poor father had always spoken of himself as a substantial merchant. It was thus that he qualified himself. Everybody regarded him as a merchant, who had retired with what is considered a substantial fortune. To be sure, I had never seen any evidence of that fortune; but there was no need to draw upon it, seeing that the garden provided amply for the needs of the house, and, besides, is a daughter to suspect her father of exaggeration? However, there was now nothing to be done but to inform my father of the circumstances, namely, that we had nothing hardly to sell and no money for wages. For a garden must be kept up. If labourers are not continually employed upon it, how is anything to be made out of it?

Nothing ever surprised me more than the effect of my communication, for my father first turned pale and then red. He then rose, and softly shut the door.

'My child,' he said, and there his voice stuck. 'My child,' he began again, and a second time he was fain to stop and gasp. 'Molly'—this time he made an effort and succeeded—'I feared that this was coming, but I would not worry you. What are we to do? What in the wide world shall we do?'

'Why, sir,' I said, 'if you will find the money to tide us over this bad season, I doubt not that we shall do very well, seeing that the war has begun again and times are brisk.'

'Find the money, child? I find the money? Molly,' he whispered, 'listen, child: I have no money. Yes, you all think me a man of substance, but I am not. Molly, your father is a man of straw—a man of straw, child. He is worth nothing.'

He rose from his chair, and walked about the room, beating his hands together. All his consequence vanished, and he now seemed to become suddenly thin.

'I have no money, Molly.'

'But I thought——'

'Yes, yes, I know. Why did I retire from the City, the only place where a man can find true happiness? Why did I come to this miserable village? Child, because I had no choice—because I was a bankrupt, and my creditors, after they had taken all I had, suffered me to withdraw unmolested. So I came here, and—Molly—'tis hard for a man who has been Alderman and Warden of his Company, and lived respected, to go among other men and own that he is bankrupt—bankrupt.'

'Oh, sir!' I cried, 'forgive me for ignorantly opening up the past. I could not know——'

'Say no more, Molly, say no more. Let us consider. There is a little purse ; let us hope it may be enough. Perhaps our friends may not learn the truth, if this will serve till next year.' He opened his desk and took out a purse containing fifty sovereigns. 'If this will serve, Molly. It is not my money, but your own, saved by me.'

You now understand how I was dragged out of my trouble by necessity. We had fifty pounds for all our stock ; we had to make it serve for six months and more, supposing that we did no trade for that time. But the potatoes and the cauliflowers turned out well, and in the end we pulled through, though with desperate shifts at home, so that no one suspected of the Alderman that he was not, as he always pretended, a substantial merchant.

I then discovered, having my eyes opened again, as I said, by necessity, that the two ladies at the Cottage were threatened with straits as dreadful as our own, or more, because, with a great garden and no rent to pay, it goes hard if one cannot live ; but these two ladies had nothing at all, except the mere hollow trunk of thin gold, from which the jewels of the Rose had all been taken. And now they must sell even that.

'My dear,' said Madam, 'since it hath pleased Heaven to call away our boy, for whom we broke up this Holy Relic, the possession of which, we were taught to believe, secured the continuation of our house, I see no reason why the gold should not follow the jewels, and all be sold. When we have spent the money there will be nothing. But we are in hands which never fail.'

'Oh, Madam!' I cried, 'you and the Countess shall come and live with us. We will all live together, and talk about Raymond every day.'

They did come to live with us, but, as you shall see, under happier conditions than we looked for.

The Vicar took away the Rose, and brought them money for it. Never was any man more taken with a work of art than the Vicar with the Rose. He loved to look upon it ; he would make it the text for a discourse upon the Popes of Avignon ; upon the early Protestants of Provençe ; upon the arts of the Middle Ages, and upon a thousand things. Yet, when he took it away, wrapped in flannel, he showed no sign of grief, but rather of satisfaction, a thing difficult to understand.

When it was gone, one felt as if the blessing of the Pope had departed from the place ; strange that we, who are Protestants, and should not value the Pope's blessing a farthing, should believe in a superstition which associated the extinction of the house with the loss of the Rose. Yet Raymond was dead, and the Holy Rose was gone. That could not be denied, and Raymond was the last of the Arnaults.

There are many strange and surprising things in this story. It is wonderful to remember how, in the wisdom of Providence, the son of the man Leroy, ignorant of his father's crime, should have been brought to the village where his father's victims lived ; it is wonderful to think that his life was saved by none other than the sister of the man whom his father had murdered ; that he should become a friend of that man's son ; and that he should discover the truth in so sudden and unexpected a manner, on the very eve of his departure.

Remember next how Pierre prayed that we would not tell Raymond, and how, through that very ignorance, Raymond was brought mysteriously to the house of his father's murderer, and received his hospitality ; how he was lured on by him in apparent security to encounter the most dreadful risk ; and how the same man who denounced the father also bore false witness against the son. Who that considers can doubt the Providential guidance of these things ?

For my own part, I remember also the dream which Raymond had in the tower of the Château ; and I see in all these things together, and in those which followed, the vengeance of God.

The world is, however, full of those who scoff at such interpretations, and foolishly boast that they believe no more than they can see. Well, for my own part, I believe not only in what I see, but also in the things which even a woman's mind may gather and conclude, from the things seen, concerning things unseen.

For instance, was it for nothing that all this time the poor mad-woman talked and laughed, always happy, always with smiles and songs, with her dead husband? She knew in a dim and uncertain way that Raymond was gone away. She even knew that he was gone to Aix, to Eyragues, and to Toulon. She talked about him at those places, wondering what he was doing, and so forth. From her husband's replies she learned that all was well with her son—which we knew, alas! was not true ; but one may surely deceive a mother on this point—and that he would return home safe and well. How could he return home who was lying dead somewhere among the graves of the criminals? Well, I am now going to tell you exactly what did come to pass, and show what little faith we possessed, who knew that the dead Count was always with his wife day and night, yet could not be brought to believe his most solemn and repeated assurances.

CHAPTER XIV.

THE RELEASE.

RAYMOND sat in his cell, saved from the yelling mob, which wanted to have him delivered into their hands. Why, he thought, had his guards been overpowered it would have been all over, and quickly. Now, those execrations and those furious yells would have to be faced again.

It was six o'clock when they brought him back. The Governor of the prison followed him into his cell.

'I have to inform you,' he said coldly, 'that your sentence is to be carried into effect without delay. You will be executed to-morrow morning, at daybreak. Expect no commutation of the sentence.'

Raymond bowed.

'If there is any request you have to make, you can do so now.'

'I should like to send a letter of farewell to—to a certain English girl whom I was to have married.'

'You can write the letter. Confine yourself solely to the facts, and to a brief farewell. It will be read, and, if it contains nothing treasonable, it will be forwarded. Have you any other request to make ?'

'I should like,' said Raymond, 'if this request can be granted, my sketch of the Château d'Eyragues to be enclosed in the letter.'

'If it is not a drawing of a place of arms, and conveys no information, it shall be enclosed in your letter.'

'I thank you, M. le Directeur.   There is no other request that I have to make.'

'Will you see a priest?—no?   It is sometimes the case that a condemned criminal likes to make a confession or statement.   You shall have a candle to enable you to do so, if you wish.'

'I have nothing more to add,' said Raymond, 'to the statement I made in Court.'

The Governor left him, and they presently sent the writing materials ; the turnkey standing over Raymond while he wrote the letter, which you have already seen.   The letter must have been despatched that very evening, otherwise, as you will discover immediately, it would not have been sent at all.

His dinner, or supper, was brought to him at seven o'clock.   It was a sumptuous meal for a prison, consisting of soup, a roast chicken, and a bottle of good wine.   But it was to be his last, and people are naturally kind to a man who is about to die.

His last !   Astonishing to relate, he devoured it with great appetite and heartiness, as if it was to be succeeded by thousands. When he had finished it, he endeavoured to compose his mind to the meditation and prayer in which he intended to pass the night.

'Either,' he says now, 'I am naturally insensible to religion, which I am loth to believe—indeed, I am sure I am not so cold a wretch—or I was sustained by some inward assurance, because, though my end was so imminent that every minute seemed to bring me closer to the axe, I could not so clearly face the situation as to question my conscience and confess my sins before Heaven ; but continually my thoughts turned towards you, my dear, and my mother, and this quiet village.   Nay, though I knew that my dinner would be the last I should ever take, I devoured it with appetite, and only wished there had been twice as much.   In vain I said to myself that in twelve hours or so I should be in the presence of my Judge, and my body would be lying a senseless, headless log ; my thoughts were turned earthwards, and wholly directed to thee, my sweetheart.'

I do not blame him in this ; nor do I think that he was insensible to religion ; because I am well assured that, as he was sustained at the trial, and as he heard the execrations of the people without alarm, so he was now miraculously kept from the despair which would otherwise have laid hold upon his soul.

Surely, a more solemn time there can never be in a man's life than the last night of it ; especially if he knows that he is to die the next day, and if he be in such a condition of mental strength as to understand it. There are so many wretched criminals hanged every year that we think nothing of the anguish, the terror, the remorse of their last night upon the earth. Of some, I know, it is reported that they drink away their terrors, and go to the fatal tree stupid with liquor ; and of others, that they sleep through the whole night, apparently careless of their coming end.

It was about ten o'clock that Raymond was interrupted by foot-steps outside his door, and the turning of the key in the lock.

He started to his feet. Was he—the thought made his heart stand still—to be taken out in the night and thrown to the mob ?

'I thank you, M. le Directeur '—Raymond started because he thought he knew the voice—'and I will not trouble you to wait. My orders are to put certain questions to the prisoner alone. Leave one of your men outside the cell, and he can conduct me to the door. Good-night, M. le Directeur.'

The door was thrown open and an officer entered wearing a military cloak thrown over his shoulders, and covering half his face. He shut the door carefully, put the lamp he had taken from the turnkey upon the table, and threw back the cloak.

'Heavens, it is Pierre !'

'Hush !' It was none other than Pierre Gavotte, but no longer in rags. Pierre Gavotte, Lieutenant of the Forty-ninth, in uniform. 'Hush ! There is no time to spare.'

'My friend, you are come to say farewell. I did not expect to see a friendly face again before I died.'

'I come with an order from the General-Commandant to put certain questions to the English spy. Well, here I am.'

He threw out his arms, and laughed as if he had kept an appoint-ment to an evening's amusement.

'And your questions ?'

'My first question——' he hesitated. 'Raymond, do you know —have they told you—who I am ?'

'Why, you are my old friend and enemy, Pierre Gavotte. Who else should you be ?'

The name had escaped him at the trial ; in the discovery that Leroy and the witness were the same, Raymond paid no attention to his assumed name. This was a happy accident, if anything can be called an accident in the course of this history, so manifestly Providential.

He held out his hand. Pierre hesitated a moment. Then he took it.

'Yes,' he said. 'Yes, we can shake hands now.'

'It has been impossible,' he explained, 'for me to have access to you until now. I discovered a week ago the name of the so-called English spy, and I knew that it must be no other than you. Oh! my friend, you a spy? I have been considering and devising. Now I have completed my plan.'

'Your plan?'

'Certainly; my plan. Why not? What is the good of having friends if they do nothing for you? You are to escape, Raymond.'

'Escape? Why, Pierre, who is to take me through these stone walls? There is no time, either. I am to die at daybreak.'

'Everything is arranged if you will do exactly what I order. Will you promise that? I give you freedom, Raymond, if you will act by my orders. It is for Molly's sake,' he added.

'I promise.'

'Then change your clothes with me. Quick; time presses.'

'Change with you? Why, what will you do? Pierre, I understand you now. You think that we are so much alike that I have only to walk out in your uniform, and I shall pass for you.'

'That is, my friend, exactly my plan. That is, you have guessed a part of it. But as you would infallibly be found out if you went on parade, that is not all my plan.'

'And what about yourself?'

Pierre laughed. ·

'I had to make two plans; one for you, and one for me. What do I do, when you are gone? My man outside—whom I have bribed—returns for me, and lets me out by the Governor's private entrance when he is asleep. I go home to my barracks quietly. No one will ever suspect me, and presently I get a letter from you telling me that you have arrived in safety.'

All this was pure fiction.

'Are you quite sure, Pierre, that you are safe?'

'My dear friend,' he replied earnestly, 'I am as sure of my future as I am of your escape, if you will do exactly as I order you. There can be no doubt whatever of my future.'

Again he laughed, and looked so careless and light-hearted that one could not choose but believe him.

'A Field-Marshal's bâton—or——'

'That, or the other fate common to soldiers,' said Pierre.

'Quick, now ; undress and change. Think of Molly, not of my future.'

'You are now complete,' he said, five minutes afterwards. 'Upon my word, Raymond, you make a pretty lieutenant. But stand upright ; swing your shoulders. You civilians never understand a military walk ; clank your heels, rattle your sword, look at the turnkeys at the gate as an officer looks at his men, without fear and with authority ; but keep your face in shade. When you leave the cell, follow the turnkey without a word. Do you understand so far ?'

'Yes ; so far.'

'Very well. Outside the prison is a sentry who will call for the word. It is "Espion Anglais." Turn to the right, and walk straight along the street until you come to a little wine-shop with the sign of the "Bleating Lamb." Enter this shop, and without saying a word walk through it and up the stairs to the room above. Do you understand all this ?'

'Perfectly. Shall I wait there for you ?'

'No. You will there find a young lady. You will obey her. Now, my friend, farewell.'

'We shall meet again.'

'Perhaps. I do not know. Farewell. If—say rather, when you get home in safety, give this note to Miss Molly, and '—he pulled off the gold lace knot that hung from the sword-handle— 'give her this as well. Tell her it is the badge of my honour that I give her. She will explain what that means. Now, farewell, Raymond.'

'Farewell, Pierre.' They clasped hands for the last time, and looked each into the other's face. At the last moment a doubt crossed Raymond's mind. 'You are quite sure—perfectly sure, Pierre, that you are in no danger whatever ?'

'Perfectly sure,' he replied ; 'I know perfectly well where I shall be to-morrow morning. There is a thing concerning myself that Molly knows, and Madam Claire. When you get home, ask them to tell you. I shall not mind your knowing it then. Forgive me, friend ; it is the only secret that I have kept from you, and even this I only discovered the day before I came away from Porchester. Go now.'

He kissed him, French fashion, on both cheeks.

It all happened exactly as Pierre had arranged. The turnkeys glanced a moment at the officer, and let him out. The sentry demanded the word and suffered him to pass. He was a free man once more. In the Place d'Armes, through which his way led, stood the guillotine, tall and slender, which was set up to take off his head; the workmen were still engaged upon the scaffold. Presently he came to the wine-shop with the sign of the 'Bleating Lamb,' its doors open. Raymond walked through it unchallenged and up the stairs, all this exactly in accordance with his instructions.

When I received Pierre's letter he had been dead for nearly six months, so long did it take Raymond to effect his escape from the country. 'I promised,' he said, 'to write to you if ever I had the chance of doing something worthy. The chance has come, but not in the way you thought and I hoped. I have set Raymond free. The guilt of my father is atoned, and the life of your lover is saved for you. What more could I desire or expect? Let Madam Claire know that I was not ungrateful or forgetful. If, as she thinks, there is another life beyond the grave—my grave will be among the criminals and the outcasts—perhaps the sin of my father will not follow me there. Farewell, and be happy.'

'So, Monsieur'—this was the young lady who was to meet Raymond—'I have expected you for two hours. Dieu! you are exactly like Pierre Gavotte. Are you brothers, by accident? Strange accidents happen off the stage as well as upon it. Well, I promised that I would ask no questions, but you must do exactly what I order you. Very well, then. Oh, I know who you are, because I was in the Court to-day and saw the trial! What? You are no more a spy than I am, and you would have been acquitted but for the news of the war, which turned their heads. You played with great dignity the part of hero in the last act but one. Believe me, sir, it is only gentlemen who preserve their dignity at such moments. I understand good playing. You looked as if you were so strong in your innocence that you would not show any anxiety or irritation, even when the procureur was thundering for justice.' She rattled on without pause or stop, being a pretty little black-eyed girl, well formed but slender. 'Understand, then, Monsieur, that I am an actress. We trust our lives to each other—I to you, because this is a job which the First Consul would regard with severe displeasure. But you are innocent: first, because you look so; next, because you say so; and, lastly, because Pierre Gavotte —who is the soul of honour—says so. Therefore, I am pleased to protect innocence. On the stage I am frequently innocent myself,

and therefore I know what it is to want protection. Now, listen
and obey. In the next room you will find the dress of a laquais.
Go and put it on. First, however'—she took a pair of scissors and
cut off his hair, which was tied behind, and cropped the rest so as
to hang over his ear, as is the way with the common folk—'There
—now change your dress. You are a Provençal ; you speak French
badly ; with me you talk in your own language ; you are a little
lame—let me see you walk—no, this is the way that lame men walk.
You are also a little deaf, and you put up your hand to your ear,
like this—turn your head a little, and open your mouth, and say
'Hein !' So ; you are an apt pupil. Remember to be respectful
to your mistress, who will sometimes scold you ; above all, study
the manners of servants. We are to start to-morrow for Marseilles ;
you will, perhaps, be able to pass over to Spain, but you must not
run risks. After Marseilles, I am going north to Burgundy, where
we shall be near the frontier, and you may get across in safety.'

'I understand everything.'

'As for your papers, I have them. They will be found perfectly
regular. All this, Monsieur, I do for you at the request of
Lieutenant Gavotte, who is, it seems, your friend. I hope that no
suspicion will fall upon him.'

'He declares that he is in .no danger whatever,' said Raymond.

'He is not my lover. Do not think that. All other men make
love to me if they can ; but Pierre does better. He has protected
me from those who delight to insult an actress. If we were found
out, Monsieur my servant who is lame and deaf, remember we
should all three have an opportunity of looking into the basket
which Madame la Guillotine keeps for her friends.'

'I assure you, Mademoiselle, that when I left Pierre he was
laughing at the danger.'

'That is bad,' she said, shaking her head. 'Men must not laugh
when they go into danger. It brings bad luck.'

The occupant of the condemned cell remained undisturbed ; nor
did the turnkey come to let him out by the Governor's private
entrance. He was left there all night long.

Very early in the morning, before daybreak, he was aroused by
two of the gaolers. They brought candles, and informed him that
in two hours he would be executed ; the time being fixed early to
avoid a conflict with the crowd, who would certainly attempt to
tear him in pieces.

They asked him if he wanted anything; he might have coffee if he chose, or brandy, or tobacco.

The prisoner wanted nothing except a cup of coffee, which they brought him. Shortly before six o'clock they came again, and led him to the room where criminals are prepared for the scaffold, their hands tied behind them, and their hair cut.

Then a very unexpected thing happened. The prisoner remarked, when they began to tie his hands:

'Monsieur le Directeur, these ceremonies are useless. The execution will not take place this morning.'

The Governor made no reply, and they went on with the toilette.

'The execution, I repeat, Monsieur le Directeur, cannot take place.'

'Why not?'

'Because the prisoner has escaped!'

'Escaped? The prisoner has escaped? Then who are you?'

'The prisoner has escaped, I repeat. He is now, if he is prudent, concealed so securely that you will not be able to find him, though you search every house in France. As for me, you would observe, if the light was stronger, that I am not the prisoner, though I am said to resemble him. I am, on the other hand, an officer of the Forty-ninth Regiment of the Line.'

'Is it possible?' cried the Governor. 'An officer? What does this mean?'

'If you doubt my word, lead me to the guillotine. But if you desire to prove the truth of my words, call in any man of that regiment and ask him who I am.'

'But you brought me a letter from the Commandant.'

'It was a forgery. I forged the signature.'

'But—how did the prisoner escape?'

'He went out of the prison dressed in my uniform. I gave him, besides, the password.'

'Where is he now, then?' asked the Governor stupidly.

'Why, if he is a wise man he will, certainly, keep that a secret.'

'If the thing be as you say,' said the Governor, 'you have yourself, Monsieur, committed a most serious crime. What! you, an officer in the army, to release an English spy?'

'That is true. I have committed a very serious crime, indeed. It is so serious that I might just as well have suffered the execution to go on. Meanwhile, I must ask you to take me back to the cell, and to acquaint my Colonel immediately with what has happened.'

There was a great crowd upon the Place d'Armes, where the guillotine was standing on a scaffold ready to embrace her victim. A military guard was stationed round the scaffold to keep off the crowd. Early as it was, the square was crowded with people, chiefly soldiers and sailors, who were in great spirits at the prospect of seeing the head taken off an English spy—an agent of perfidious Albion. They sang songs, and played rough jokes upon each other. Among them were the country people, who had brought in their fruit and vegetables for the market, and a few servants who were out thus early to see the execution as well as to do the day's marketing.

The criminal was late. The time crept along. Decidedly it was very late. Had anything happened? Were they going to pardon him at the last moment? Had he confessed his guilt and revealed the whole of the English plots? Would it not be well to storm the prison as the Bastille had been stormed, and to seize the spy whether he had confessed or not?

Presently, men came and began to take down the scaffold, and it was understood that there would be no execution that day, because the prisoner had escaped.

The town was searched; house by house, room by room. At the gates no one in the least corresponding to him had passed. The prisoner must be somewhere in the town. Good. When found he should be torn to pieces by the people. But he was not found.

Three days afterwards, however, there was a most exciting spectacle in the Place d'Armes; a sight such as had not been witnessed since December, 1793—a military execution.

Everybody now knew that Lieutenant Gavotte, of the Forty-ninth Regiment, had effected the escape of the English spy. It was whispered by those who know everything that a great plot had been discovered in which many of the French officers themselves were implicated. None, however, except the Colonel, knew for certain why he had done this thing. In his trial he simply said that the so-called English spy was an innocent man whose story was true; that he had been kind to himself when a prisoner in England; and that, therefore, he had assisted him to escape.

His Colonel went, at the prisoner's request, to see him. I know not what passed between them, but on his return the Colonel was greatly agitated, and openly declared that no braver officer ever existed than Lieutenant Gavotte, and no better man.

They brought him out to die between six and seven in the morning. First they tore away his epaulettes, then his cuffs, and then his facings. He was no longer an officer ; he was no longer a soldier. But his face showed no sense of shame or fear.

Among the spectators was a man who, to see the show, had been sitting under the tiers all night long. He was a restless man, who moved and fidgeted continually, and bit his nails ; his eyes were red ; he spoke to no one.

When they led out the young man he nodded his head.

'Good,' he said. 'First the flood, then the fire. The property is first destroyed, and then the son.'

When they set Pierre in his place this man nodded his head again.

'Good,' he said. 'On that spot died the Count.'

They offered to tie a handkerchief round the prisoner's eyes, but he refused, and stood with folded arms.

'Good,' said the spectator again. 'Thus the Count refused to be bound.'

Then at the word they fired, and Pierre Gavotte fell dead.

'Thus fell the Count,' said the spectator. He walked slowly from his place and stood beside the dead body. 'This is mine,' he said ; 'I am his father.'

CHAPTER XV.

CONCLUSION.

THERE is one more chapter to write, and my story, which I am never tired of telling, will be finished. In the years to come it will be told by my children, and by my children's children—nay, among my descendants, so sure I am that my story will never be forgotten, so wonderful it is and strange.

Raymond was dead ; he had been guillotined : his letter told us this : only the poor mad woman assured us (speaking through the spirit of her husband) that he was safe, and this we would not believe.

Raymond was not dead ; you have heard by what a miracle he was saved ; hear now how he came home to us.

It was on Christmas Eve. First, there was a great surprise for us, unexpected and astonishing. But not the greatest surprise of all.

A sad Christmas Eve. The time was between six and seven. I was sitting beside Madam Claire, on a stool before the fire. There was no candle, because these poor ladies could only afford candles when Madam Claire was working. And to-night she was doing nothing.

To Frenchwomen the feast of Christmas is not so great an occasion for festivity as that of the New Year, when they exchange presents and make merry. But Madam Claire had lived ten years with us and understood our Christmas rejoicing. Alas! there was little joy for us this year, we thought, and there would be little in the years to come.

As we sat there, in silence, my head in Madam's lap, the waits came to sing before our door, the lusty cobbler leading. They sang 'When shepherds watched their flocks by night,' and 'Let nothing you dismay,' with fiddle and harp to accompany. I believe the cobbler sang his loudest and lustiest, out of pure sympathy, because he knew that we were in trouble.

'Last Christmas——' I began, but could say no more.

'Patience, child, patience!' said Madam. 'The Lord knows what is best, even for two humble women. Though Raymond will never come to us, we shall go to him.'

'My friend'—it was the poor, mad lady, talking to her dead husband—'it is time for Raymond to come home. I thought I heard his footsteps; we have missed our boy——'

She looked about the room, as if expecting to see him sitting among us.

'Claire, my sister, when Raymond comes we will make a feast for him. There shall be a dance and a supper for the villagers. Raymond will come home to-day. My husband! Thou art always ready to make us happy. To-day, Claire; to-day.' She laughed with a gentle satisfaction. 'We cannot keep the boy always at home, can we? That is impossible. But he has not forgotten his mother. He is coming home to-day—to-day!'

One should have been accustomed to such words as these, but they went to our hearts; so great was the mockery between our grief and the poor creature's happiness.

Then there came a single footstep along the road. I knew it for the Vicar's, and it stopped at the cottage door.

He came in, bearing in his arms something most carefully swathed and wrapped.

'Ladies,' he bowed to all of us together, 'at this time of the year it is the custom in England, as you doubtless know, to exchange with each other those good wishes of Christian folk one to other, which are based upon the Event which the Church will to-morrow commemorate. I wish for this household a merry——'

'Nay, sir,' I said, 'can we have merry hearts, this Christmas or any Christmas?'

'A merry Christmas,' he said stoutly, 'and a happy New Year. Ay, the merriest Christmas and the happiest New Year that Heaven can bestow——'

Was his Reverence in his right mind?

'It is also,' he went on, 'the godly custom among us to make presents one to the other, at this season, in token of our mutual affection, and in gratitude to the Giver of all good things. Therefore, Madam, I have ventured to bring with me my offering. It is this.'

He placed the parcel upon the table, and began to unroll the coverings.

'What!' he looked at me with a kind of fierceness quite unusual in his character—'what! do you think that I could look on unmoved at the afflictions of this innocent family?' (I declare that I never thought anything of the kind.) 'You think that I could suffer them to break up and destroy, for the sake of a few miserable guineas, so priceless a relic as the Golden Rose, given to this family five hundred years ago? Never! Learn, Madam '—he bowed again to Madam Claire—' that I have been the holder, not the buyer or the seller, of the jewels belonging to this precious monument of ancient (though mistaken and corrupt) religion. I have now replaced every stone in its proper setting—you will not find one missing—and I give you back complete, just as when it was hallowed by the Pope at Avignon, your Holy Rose.'

He threw off the coverings, and behold it—the gems sparkling and the gold branches glowing in the firelight; every jewel replaced, and the Rose as complete as ever; and most beautiful it looked, with its flowers all of precious stones.

'Pardon me,' he said, 'the deception which I have practised. I was determined to save the Rose, and without my little falsehood (which may Heaven forgive!) you would not have taken the money.'

'We must bring out the Holy Rose because Raymond comes home to-day,' said the mad lady.

'Sir!' cried Madam Claire. 'Oh, sir, this is too much!'

She burst into sobbing and weeping and fell upon her knees at the table, throwing her arms round the Rose. I never knew before how much she loved it.

'It is one thing to restore to you the Rose,' said the Vicar ; ' it is another to give you back the dead. Heaven alone can do that. Yet there was a legend, a tradition, a superstitious belief concerning this Rose, was there not ? The House should never want heirs so long as the Rose remained in its possession. Why, it has never left your hands except to be, as we may say, repaired.'

'Alas !' said Madam, ' the tradition has proved false. It was, I fear, a human and earthly tradition, not warranted by the blessing of the Pope, which must have been intended for some other than the lady to whom he made the gift.'

'Perhaps. Yet sometimes—nay. I know not——'

Here he hesitated, and looked from Madam to me, and from me to Madam, as one who has something to communicate, but doubts how to say it or what he should say. What could he have to say ?

'Poor Molly !' he said at length, laying his hand upon my head. ' Poor child ! thou hast had a grievous time of trial. Hast thou faith enough to believe that there may still be happiness in store for thee ?'

I shook my head. There was no more happiness possible for me.

'Strange !' he said, still with that hesitation. ' 'Twas an old legend, it seems a foolish legend. How can the blessing of a mere man have such merit ? We may not believe it. Yet—— Sometimes we are deceived, and idle words prove true. It hath happened that things which seemed impossible have happened. Wherefore, Molly, let us hope—let us hope. But why connect such things as may happen with the Pope ?'

I think we ought to have guessed something at these words. But Raymond was dead. We cannot expect the dead to be raised to life. And, besides, I was thinking of Madam, who was weeping and praying and praising God upon her knees ; being carried quite out of herself, as I had never seen her before, except when she spoke like a prophetess to Pierre.

'Molly,' said the Vicar, ' the ways of Providence are wonderful ; we cannot try to fathom them. If sorrow falls upon us, we must learn to be resigned ; if joy comes, we must be grateful. My dear, how shall I tell thee what has happened ?'

'Is it some new misfortune ?' I asked. ' Has my father——'

'Nay, it is no misfortune. And yet thou must summon up all

thy courage to hear the news which came to me this afternoon. Listen, then ; and if I do not tell thee all at once, it is because I fear for thy reason. Thy father, child, knows the news, and he is already—but I anticipate. Sally knows, and she comes with him in a few minutes. But I must speak slowly. Her father knows, because he brought him in the boat. But I am going too quickly.'

'Who has come in the boat—my father ?'

'No, Molly, no ; not thy father. I fear, child, that I have broken the news too abruptly—let me begin again. If, I say, resignation is the duty of the sorrowful, a grateful heart, which is also the duty of the joyful, must be shown in a spirit that is tranquil and self-contained. Be tranquil and self-contained ; and now, my dear, I have this day received a letter—this afternoon only—followed by the boat from the harbour with—with—the potatoes and onions and—and—the woman whom they call Porchester Sal——'

Was the Vicar going off his head ? What could he mean ?

He was not, however, permitted to prepare my mind any more, for at that moment a man came running down the road, and the door burst open.

It was my cousin Tom.

'I hear the footstep of my boy,' said the Countess.

'Molly !' he cried. 'A Ghost ! A Ghost ! I have seen a Ghost !'

His wild eyes and pale cheeks showed at least that he was horribly frightened. His hat had fallen off, and the whip which he generally carried had been dropped somewhere in the road.

'Molly ! A real Ghost ! When I saw him I said : "Who's afraid of a Ghost ?" That's what I said. "Who's afraid of a Ghost ? You'd like to kick me again, would you ?" And with that I gave him one with my whip. Would you believe it ? My whip was knocked out of my hand, and I got a one-two with his fists—— Well, any man may be afraid of a Ghost, and I ran away.'

'A Ghost, Tom ?'

'Molly, you remember that story about the fight and the kick in the face, don't you ? I used to say that I had him down and was laying on with a will. That wasn't true, Molly. I dare say I should have had him down in another round—no—no—he will haunt me—it wasn't true at all. I never had him down, and he would never have gone down, because he began it ; but he did kick me.'

'Tom, that was Pierre Gavotte, not Raymond at all.'

'Ah ! all of a tale ; stick to it. Oh ! Lord—here he is again !'
Sally rushed in before him.

'Miss Molly ! Miss Molly ! I brought him up the harbour in the boat. We picked him up at Point. Here he is ! Here he is ! Not a bit of a Frenchman, though he is dressed in a blue sack and a cloth cap. Oh ! here he is !'

Oh ! Heavens ; can I ever forget that moment ? 'Twas Raymond himself ! Raymond, strong and well, his arms stretched out for me. When he let me go, I saw that the Vicar and my father were shaking hands, and the tears were in their eyes. But Madam Claire was still on her knees, her head in her hands. And so we stood in silence until she rose and solemnly kissed her nephew.

'My friend,' said Raymond's mother to her dead husband, 'I knew that your words come always true. You said that Raymond would come home to-day. We will have a feast to welcome the boy's return. And the villagers shall dance.'

'It is,' said Madam Claire, 'the Blessing of the Holy Rose.'

THE LAST MASS.

I.

EXACTLY a Year before the Coming of the Spanish Armada (which they blasphemously call'd the Invincible) there happen'd in a remote Country Village an Event which can hardly be accounted as other than a Miracle. It is very well known that the Purpose of Miracles was to Establish the Kingdom of Christ; and that Accomplisht, it is thought by some (but not by Papists) that no more were permitted. Yet (which we cannot but acknowledge) when we pray for Grace and Succour, we ask for the continual Miraculous Interposition of the Providential Hand. And when the Mouth of an old Woman is open'd, and she is permitted to Foretell Things about to Happen, before ever they are Suspected (save perhaps by those deep in the Counsels of Sovereigns), what can we call it but Miraculous, unless we attribute it to the Pow'r of Witchcraft? No one, for certain, ever thought the Lady Katharine to be a Witch, seeing that she was not only a Black Nun, but also formerly Abbess of her Convent, and always Faithful and Obedient to her Order. We are now taught that all Orders of Monks and Nuns are Fond and Superstitious Inventions, but we are not taught that Nuns are Witches.

You shall hear exactly what Lady Katharine Predicted, and in what Words. For what Purpose the Future was Reveal'd to her I know not, nor shall I inquire into Things too deep for a Woman —or even for the most Learned of Divines—to find out. If it be Objected that it was the Bounden Duty of those who heard the Prophecy Straightway to Inform the Sheriff of the County, so that the Matter might be brought before the Queen's Most Excellent Highness, I have to reply that although the Coming of the Spanish Armada was indeed foretold to us in Clear Language, Plain to Understand, the Prophecy was like unto those Oracles recorded in History, inasmuch as its Full Interpretation only became Visible after its Fulfilment. This is, methinks, the Custom observed even by the Sacred Prophets : they Proclaim the Coming Woes, but never Name the Day or Hour, else would the Guilty (being warn'd) take Care to Get out of the Way, and so the Thunder-Bolts would Fall Harmless, and thus the Prophecy remain Unfulfill'd. What, indeed, could the Maidens of Jerusalem do, after the Prophet had gone about the City announcing its Overthrow, except pray that the Hand of the Lord might be Stay'd, so that they at least and their Children might be Spar'd ?

Nay, just as sometimes happen'd to the Delphic Priestess, our Prophetess, as you shall see, prov'd to have been Herself in part Deceiv'd. Though she knew Something, she did not know All. Though she could see Beforehand the Coming Battle, she prov'd to be mistaken as to the Victors. Praise be to GOD, the Victors were not the Queen's Enemies, but her own Brave Soldiers !

The Miracle cannot be in any way Explain'd. No one knew or suspected so early, in our Part of the Country, the Designs of the Spanish King. No one in our Parts could possibly know them. Why, I have been credibly inform'd that it was not until November of that Year that the First News of the Armada reach'd the Queen Herself. I do not say that we are more than commonly cut off from News, but that no News of the Kind could have reach'd the Lady Katharine. As regards the Hearing of News in General, indeed, I think that we are as commodiously situated as in any Part of the Country, except London. Our Ships bring Intelligence from every Part : from Northumberland, for instance, and from Durham, whither they sail for Coal ; from the Low Countries, whither they go with Wool and come back with Cloth ; from France and Spain, whence they return Laden with Wines of all Kinds, as Malmsey, Sack, Sherris, Mountain, and good Bordeaux ; from Norway, whither they go for Timber ; and from the Baltic Sea and Muscovy, whence come Amber and Peltry of all Kinds, such as Sable, Ermine, and Miniver. Some there are who have sail'd from Lynn to the Mediterranean Sea and the Levant, escaping the Pirates of the Moorish Coast. Our Ships also bring us News from London, whither they go as to the Market of the World, seeing that there is Nothing which is not to be had as abundantly at that great Port as in Rome of old or in Venice of later Times. So that when News is stirring we presently hear it, and you will see that it was not many Weeks after the Court learned the Preparations of the Spaniard before our People also heard and were talking of them.   But to learn News quickly, after others, is different from learning it before all others, by way of Prophecy.   And this is what we learn'd.

We live in the Village of Burnham St. Clement, which, as everybody knows, is close to the ancient Port of Wells-by-the-Sea, on the Coast of Norfolk. Wells is not so rich and thriving a Place as Great Yarmouth or as Lynn, but there are many Tall Vessels which sail up and down its Winding Creek and Anchor alongside the Quay.   And in the Town there are many Fair Houses belonging to the Merchants and Adventurers, and in them many strange things may be seen, brought from Foreign Parts, and one can see and converse with the Captains and Mates of the Ships, and hear Stories of Foreign Folk and their Ways, and of the dangers which those must dare who make their Livelihood upon the Ocean.

Burnham Hall is but half a mile from the Port of Wells : from the Roof one can even see the Masts of the Ships as well as the Tower of the Church.   The House is of Stone and very Stately. It was built by my Grandfather in the Time of Henry the Eighth, in Place of a House of Timber and Plaster which formerly stood there : by Permission of the King it is Embattled, and hath a Moat, but I doubt how long the House could stand a Siege against Artillery.

The Time was Eight o' the Clock in the Evening of the 20th of July, in the Year of Grace 1587, and the Sun nigh unto his Setting. At this Time of Day there is often a Hush or Stillness in the Air, as if most Things were resting.   Yet from the Orchard was heard the Note of a Thrush : the Pigeons cooed in the Dove-Cot : from the Farm-Yard came the Satisfied Clucking of the Hens : the Honey-Bees Dron'd as they flew Home heavily : the Peacocks dragg'd their long Tails across the Grass : the Hounds lay sleeping in the Sun : over the low Hedge we could see the Gentle Deer lying under the Oaks in the Park : all the Summer Flowers were blooming, the Honeysuckle in the Hedge, the Roses on their long Stems, the Sweet-Peas, the Mignonette, the great Red Lily, the Jasmin, the Stocks and Pinks and Sweet-Williams, so that there was hardly a single Foot of Ground in the Flower Beds but had its Blossoms.   Our Winter in Norfolk is cold, and in Spring the Winds blow long from the East and the Icy North : but in no Part of the Kingdom is the Summer sweeter than in Norfolk.

Two Young Men, in their Doublets, and Bareheaded, were playing Bowls upon the Grass : these were Will Hayes and my brother Roger. Beneath the great Walnut-Tree sat my Father Sir Francis, and Sir Anthony, Parson of the Parish. Between them was a Dish of Strawberries. They were both well stricken in Years and Gray-Beards. As for Sir Anthony, he was a Learned Divine able to read Greek and Hebrew, and a Maintainer of the Protestant Faith—such as few could be found in Country Places, where so many Changed by Order of Queen Mary and Queen Elizabeth from Protestant to Catholick and Back again to save their Benefice. My Father, as everybody knows, was a Justice of the Peace much feared by Rogues, Deer-slayers, Vagabonds, Witches, and other Evil doers. They talk'd gravely, and of things too high for the Understanding of Women. It was truly a Time full of Danger, with Traitors at Home and Enemies abroad. Queen Mary was Executed in this Year : and many there were who Rag'd furiously about that Dread Deed. It was known that Frenchman and Spaniard alike, with the Pope behind, desir'd Nothing so much as to set Loose the Dogs of War in this Kingdom, while even in the Universities there were Many who long'd for the Restoration of the Ancient Faith. What do I say ? Are there not still Traitors at Home and Enemies Abroad ? Yea ; and always will be. Wherefore let us still be Ready, and send forth our Lads to singe the Spaniard's Beard, and to snatch from him at the Cannon's Mouth and from his Ports on the Caribbean Sea his great Galeasses and his Carracks full of Treasure.

There stood leaning over the Sun-Dial on the Terrace two Girls, of whom I was one, and Alice Hayes the other. Like the two Young Men, we were nearly of the same age, and if Roger was betroth'd to Alice, then was I for my Part Promis'd to her Brother Will. We stood beside the Sun-Dial, I say, and watch'd our Lovers at their Game. Oh, Happy Time, when a Maiden hath given up all her Heart, and is her Lover's Slave, though still he Choose to call her Queen and Mistress ! A Modest Maiden may, I hope, take Delight in the Comeliness of her Lover without Blame. Two more Comely Lads than Will and Roger could nowhere else be seen. Alas ! that one of them should be no more ! He dyed for Queen and Religion : therefore we ought not to mourn : yet he was taken from the Girl he loved : therefore she goeth still in Sadness.

It was for Coolness' sake that the Young Men play'd in their Doublets, and their Cloaks and Caps lay upon the Grass. Will always had plain Camlet for his Doublet and green Taffeta for his Cloak, but Roger, like a London Gallant, went more Brave in Violet Silk, his Cloak Garnished with Velvet Guards and Bugles.

A Young Man must needs go Fine if only to do Honour unto his Mistress—yet not to put his whole Estate upon his Back. Who would love one who neglects to set off his Face and Figure with such Attire as becomes his Rank and Station? For my own part I desire to see a Young Man Fine with French Hosen, Starched Ruff, Feathered Cap of Velvet, Shirt of Lawn, Doublet Slashed and Laced, Cloak Lined and Laced and Hung with Tassels of Gold and Silver. Let him show to the World by his Brave Attire the Stout Heart that Beats Beneath. What? Doth the Gallant King of the Farm-Yard hide his Splendid Plumes? Not so; the Braver he is, the more he Displays his Purple Feathers to the Sun.

While we looked on, and the Lads laugh'd and made Bets upon the Game, we became aware that Lady Katharine was walking on the Terrace. She came forth every Day to take the Air in the Garden. It was nothing Unusual to Meet her; but this Evening I shiver'd when I saw her, and caught Alice by the Hand. She went slowly, looking toward us, but as one who saw no one; and she was follow'd at due Distance by her Three Nuns.

No one, I am sure—not even, speaking with all Respect, the Queen herself—could move with more Dignity than Lady Katharine. She was call'd the Abbess; but as there are no longer any Convents, I give the name by which she was Christen'd and the Style to which she was born. She was tall and erect, though now near Eighty Years of Age; her Nose was hooked like the Beak of an Eagle; her Chin was Long; her Lips were Firm; her Eyes under Thick Red Eyebrows were as Keen as any Hawk's, but they were full of Wrath. I have never (but once) seen Lady Katharine when her Eyes were not full of Wrath. They were Gray in Colour, I believe, but I am not sure, because no one Dared to look her Steadily in the Eyes. Such, however, was the Effect of her Red eyebrows and her Wrathful Look that they seem'd Bloodshot. She was Wrathful because she had been Deprived of her Convent and her Spiritual Rank; for Fifty Years she Nourish'd Rage therefor, and daily Prophecy'd to her Nuns the Woes and Punishments which should Fall upon the Land. It is a Terrible Thing for a Woman to Nurse this Passion of Wrath: a Man may Fight his Enemy, and so an End; here there was no Enemy, but a Thing done Fifty Years before. And a private Gentlewoman can do nothing but sit with Clinched Hands and Flaming Eyes, and sometimes fly out into Fiery Speech. It is only a Queen who can Punish her Enemies. Wherefore it especially Behooves a Woman to Forgive all who wrong her, lest she spend her Life (and Lose her Soul) in Longing for Revenge.

Some there are who Praise the Past, and would Praise it even if it were the Past before the Flood, or the Past before the Coming of Joshua, or the Past of King Herod. These Men speak of the Godly Monks and the Meek Nuns, now Dispersed. Here was not only a Nun but an Abbess. But as for the Grace of Meekness or Humility, one might look in vain for it. My Father was blam'd by some for suffering her to remain in his House, but she was his Mother's Sister, and it is well known that those who were driven forth when the Houses were dissolved were permitted to remain with their Friends, even though it was notorious that they pray'd daily for the Restoration of the Old Religion. She wore the Habit Proper to an Abbess of her Order ; and was the last who wore that Habit in this Country. Therefore I describe it particularly. It consisted of a black Tunic or Gown reaching to the Feet with a Border of Ermine : the Sleeves were tight and long, and at the Wrists there was a white Edge. Over the black Gown was a white Surplice reaching to the Ermine : over that a short black Surplice. For Head Dress she wore a white linen Hood, very full, and tied under the Chin. It was low over the Forehead, and hid the Hair. Over all she wore a black Mantle with gray Fur. Round her Waist was a Cord with the triple knot of Charity, Poverty, and Obedience.

Round her Neck was a Chain of Gold with a Crucifix. Behind her, at the Distance of six Feet or so, walked the three Ancient Dames, her Nuns and Servants. They too were still dressed in their Benedictine Robes. By Living long together they had grown to resemble each other so that one hardly knew which was Sister Claire, Sister Angela, or Sister Clementina. They were as old as their Mistress ; their Shrivell'd Faces wore Something the Look of Sheep, and when the Abbess spoke they Trembled and Huddled together. These poor old Ladies had been turn'd out of the Convent with Lady Katharine, but there was no Wrath in their Faces, rather a Desire to Rest and be at Peace.

She walk'd along the Terrace and presently stopp'd. When she stopp'd the Old Nuns began to tremble and crept close together. But she did not stop in Order to admonish them. On the contrary, which was a strange thing of her to do, she stopped to look at the Players. Mostly she regarded no one in the Garden. Then she beckoned to them ; and they left their Bowls and walked across the Grass, wondering, and stood before her, Will's Hand on Roger's

Shoulder. As for us, we drew near as well. And my Father arose and followed the Boys. But Sir Anthony moved not. For such as himself the Popish Woman would have none but Words of Wrath.

'So,' she said, addressing Will. She had a Deep Man's Voice, which made her the more Terrible. 'So, Sirrah ; by thy Face thou shouldest be Grandson to Sir Humphrey Hayes, Robber of the Church. I play'd with him when we were Children together, before he despoil'd the Sanctuaries and grew Rich upon the Lands and Beeves of Holy Church.'

'Madam,' said Will, 'I am the Grandson of Sir Humphrey who is dead, and the Son of Sir Humphrey who is alive.'

'They shall not prosper who despoil the Church,' she said, speaking slowly. 'Thy Grandsire is dead. They shall be accursed. They shall be cut off, they and theirs.'

'By your Leave, Madam,' said Will, 'some of those who despoiled the Church have since done, methinks, indifferently Well. As for my Grandsire, he was long past Threescore Years and Ten when he died.'

'Silence, Sirrah !' She raised the Goldheaded Stick which she carried and pointed it to the Western Sky, now red and flaming. 'Behold !' she said. 'The Sky is full of Blood. I hear the Groans of Dying Men : I see a Great and Terrible Slaughter : there is a mighty Battle upon the Ocean : the tall Ships are crushed like Egg Shells, and sink to the Bottom of the Deep with all their Armaments : the Waves are Red : those who went forth to Fight are Drowning in the Flood : never before was there such a Battle : never in Days to come shall be such another : the Arm of the Lord is outstretched : the Mighty are scattered. After the Roaring of the Cannon, the Weeping of the Women : after the Weeping of the Women, Punishment—yea, the Torture of the Flames for those who have led the People astray. After their Punishment the Ancient Faith shall be restored : then shall those who thought to grow fat upon the Lands of the Church be driven forth homeless and Beggars to wander upon the Roads. Woe ! Woe ! Woe ! to the Mothers and the Children in that day ! Death to the young Men ! Woe to the Maidens !'

'Madam,' said Will calmly, 'we who wait upon the Lord and are His Servants fear not any Evils.'

The Abbess made no Sign of hearing him.

'I see,' she said, still gazing into the Sky—'I see the Bones of one who thought to go Home and wed his Bride : this is his Marriage Bed among the Seaweed : the Crabs crawl about his

Ribs : the Fishes eat out his Eyes : the Tides roll him hither and thither.'

'Madam,' said Will again, calmly, 'we who are in the Hands of the Lord fear not any of these Evils.'

'Fools ! Fools ! ye lean upon a Reed, and it shall Pierce your Hands.' Then she rais'd her Stick again. 'Death and Ruin for the Enemies of the Church ! Death and Ruin for those who have despoil'd the Holy Shrines ! The Avenger cometh—lo ! the Avenger cometh quickly.'

Her Nuns, all Huddled close together, cross'd themselves. Alice caught my Hand, and we trembled and shook.

The Abbess slowly lower'd her Stick, and turn'd and walk'd away, followed by her Attendants, who shook in their Limbs as if the Curse was pronounced upon themselves.

The Sun was down by this Time : a Thunder Cloud rolled up which hid the Splendour of the West : it grew darker than it is wont to be at this Season : an Owl screeched from the Ivy.

'Cheer up, Lads,' said my Father, who alone had heard her unmoved. 'This is not the first Time by many that my Lady hath prophecy'd Death and Disaster. Before the Pilgrimage of Grace —as I have heard : before the Rebellion of the Ketts : before the Death of King Edward—many Times hath she uprais'd her Voice in this Fashion. I have never heard that any were hurt—whatever she may have said.'

'Sir,' I said, 'by your Leave : great Disasters followed her Words then. What new Disaster is to follow this new and terrible Forecast ?'

It was Sir Anthony who answered, gravely, having now joined us:

' Those who are assur'd that they hold the true Catholick Faith need fear nothing. Since it hath been prov'd abundantly that the only true Catholick Doctrine is that of our own Church, we are, as Master Will truly said, in the Lord's Hand. Therefore let us fear nothing. The Times are truly full of Trouble : there will be Wars, and many of our Young Men may fall. Yet be of Good Cheer all, as those who are on the Lord's Side, though Owls may screech and Nuns predict Confusion.'

As he spoke, the Owl screech'd again, and the first Drops fell of the coming Shower, and the Thunder roll'd and rumbled.

'Sweetheart !' cried Will, catching my Hand, ' why so pale and white ? The Thunder is the Cannon with which we shall salute our Enemies. Let us meet our Fate, whatever happens, with Stout Heart and Steady Eye.'

'Words, Words,' said my Father. 'Let the poor mad Woman rave. Now, Lads, let us within. Nell shall Pop a Posset upon us, and Alice shall Sing us a Song, before we go to Bed.'

II.

THE Abbess came to this House—the House of her Sister's Husband—in the Year 1539, when, with her Nuns, she was turn'd out of her Convent of Benedictine Sisters at Binstead. 'Twas the Year when the Great Religious Houses were made to Follow the Small, and All together were Overwhelm'd in One Destruction. It was thirty Years before I was born, yet have I talk'd with old Men who Remember'd very well this Great Event, and to their Dying Day they could never Understand how this Great Destruction could have been peacefully carried out.

There was then, to be sure, a most Masterful King who would have his Will in everything: he had also Masterful Ministers under him who carried out his Bidding. But still the Affections of the People must have been already turn'd away from the Monks, or there must have been a Rising everywhere. Not here and there one Convent suppress'd, but everywhere, over the Whole Country —Six Hundred and More—with Thousands of Monks and Nuns driven forth : a Hundred Hospitals, a Hundred Colleges, and I know not how many Hundreds of Chantries—of which there is not now left a single one. What befell the Priests and Monks is not known. Some, I believe, fell into a low Way of Life, and became mere Vagabonds and Rogues. Some, being of rustical Origin, return'd to their People, and once more Steer'd the Plough —a Wholesome Discipline, though the Flesh might Rebel. I have never heard how these became afterwards Disposed towards the Protestant Faith. They would, methinks, regard it with half-hearted Loyalty. As for the Nuns, they, in our Part of the Country, mostly took Ship and sail'd across to the Low Countries, where they were admitted into other Convents, and looked for Rest, but I fear found none, by Reason of the Wars of Religion. Some of them, especially those who belong'd to Substantial Families, return'd to their Friends, and were by them Maintain'd until their Death, no one asking whether a harmless Woman read her Prayers in Latin or in English, from a Missal or the Book of Common Prayer.

The Convent of Binstead would have been held in Greater

Respect had it not been for its Rich and Illustrious Neighbour of Walsingham. The Sisters possess'd a Priceless Treasure (as it was then deemed) in the Arm of St. Philip. There are still living Country People who will tell you how Miracles were worked at Binstead as well as at Walsingham, the Arm of St. Philip being strong to heal the Sick, sovereign in Cases of Rheumatism. The Walls are now pulled down, and their Stones have been used for Farm Buildings : the Chapel itself, the Refectory, the Dormitory, are all Destroyed : Nothing remains but a few Stone Walls of what is said to have been the Kitchen, and the broad Moat which guarded it on all Sides. The last Abbess of Binstead, the Lady Katharine, was but twenty-eight Years of Age, though ten Years Novice and Nun and six Years Abbess, at the Time of the Suppression of the Religious Houses. Though so young, she ruled her House with Authority, strictly Enforcing the Rules of the Order, so that the Sisters Trembled daily lest they should incur her Displeasure, and receive those Punishments by which Obedience is enforc'd in such Houses, where I cannot but think little Things are magnify'd, and a Broken Rule, even one of no Consequence, becomes a Great Sin. The Visitors of the King could find no Fault at all with this House ; but, like the rest, it must needs go.

On the Day when they must Depart, the Sisters, Sixteen in Number, came forth Weeping from the Chapel where they had Held their Last Service. These Walls had Shelter'd them from the Dangers of the World : some of them had grown Old in the House and look'd to lay their Bones in the Convent Burying-Ground : some were of Middle Age, who never Thought to leave the House : some were Young, and yet had no other Hope but to Continue where they were until they should Exchange the Black Frock of their Order for the White Robe of the Angels. Therefore they came forth Weeping. They knew not, besides, whither they would go, or what would become of them, or where they should find Friends. By the Order of the Abbess, however, they chang'd their Wailing into Singing, and with the Chanting of Psalms they walked to Wells, where Thirteen of them said Farewell to the Rest and went on Board Ship, and so to the Low Countries. But how they fared there I know not and have never heard. Long since, doubtless, their Troubles have ceased.

The three youngest remained with the Abbess, who took them to her Sister's House at Burnham St. Clement. Here they had their own Chambers set apart for them, in which they lived and took their Meals. The Chapel was also given to them, in which they might Worship after their own Fashion, and so might keep up in their Chambers the Convent Rules, as they still wore the Dress of their Order. And just as before they never went beyond the Walls of their Convent, so now they never pass'd outside the Garden. In a Word, there was a little Convent of four Benedictine Nuns establish'd within a Protestant Household, whose Master was a Justice of the Peace, yet tolerated this Breaking of the Law. The Abbess from the first Day of the Dissolution looked for some signal Punishment which should fall from Heaven upon the King or the Country. Herod, for Instance, was Devoured of Worms for his Blasphemies : for the Sins of David a Pestilence raged among his People. So should it be with King Henry. And after he was gone the old Order would be Restored, save for the Glories of the Shrines which were scatter'd and destroyed. (So Nehemiah rebuilt the Temple, but could not Restore the Gold and Silver Vessels and the Carved Work.) No Punishment, as the Years went on, fell upon King or People. It is true that King Henry dyed some ten Years after the Suppression of the Houses. But then he was arrived at a good Age, and we must all die. And his Son, who succeeded him, was a Protestant, who dyed in his Youth —on Account of his Protestantism, said the Papists. Then Queen Mary came to the Throne, and for a While it seem'd as if the Roman Catholick Religion was Restored for Good. Then the Abbess, Lady Katharine, with her three Sisters, rode to Binstead, purposing to return to their House. Alas! it was already destroy'd. The Country Folk had Broken down the Wood Work and carry'd off the Stones. No Human Creature could live among the Ruins. Therefore the Sisters rode back to Burnham St. Clement, and continued to abide there.

Queen Mary dyed, and Queen Elizabeth succeeded.

The Abbess once more fell to looking for the Judgment of Heaven upon the Country. Surely for all that hath been granted to us, the Gracious Mercies and the Crowning Victories, we should be prepar'd to Acknowledge the Blessing of the Lord and His Approbation of the Protestant Faith.

Lady Katharine was old when first I remember her. As long as she lived afterwards no change fell upon her. She was always Lofty in her Spirit, always Terrible in her Eyes, and always Wrathful. So look'd, I suppose, Judith : so Jael, the Wife of Heber the Kenite : so Deborah : so Boadicea. Mostly Lady Katharine sat in her own Chamber, her three Women standing around her : she took her Meals alone : she walk'd about the

Garden followed by the three Sisters, all in Silence. They, however, were certainly not Wrathful, nor did they ever Prophesy Disaster. On the contrary, they were as Happy as Women who are old can expect to be : nay, they were Happier than we who have the Protestant Light can ever be, because they were Convinced that their Salvation was Assured to them by their Profession and by the Power of the Church. Their only Care was not to incur the Displeasure of the Abbess, of whom, old as they were, they still stood in as much Dread as a young Maid who fears to be whipped for Carelessness : in the Presence of the Abbess they were Mute as Mice. But when, as sometimes Happened, they were permitted or ordered to leave her Presence, they would run and play and laugh like unto Children. They were also like Children in their Simple Contentment with small Things, and in their Readiness to Laugh and be amused with Toys, and in their Fear of being Punish'd. Sometimes one would be in Disgrace, though of this the others did not speak. After the Abbess died—in what Manner you shall hear—the Sisters told me how hard was her Discipline, so that for Little Things they were put upon Bread and Water : their Warm Clothing was taken from them : they had to say more Prayers : they had to Kneel in Corners—I know not what Indignities they did not endure. But with me, from my Childhood, they would Play as if they were Children too, and they knew many Stories about Saints and Miracles, which I now understand to have been Fables, but which then pleased me mightily. When I hear Talk of Nunneries, I think of these poor old Women, so Simple and so Childish. And when I hear Talk of an Abbess, I think of a tall old Woman with a Hooked Nose and Fierce Eyes and a Man's Voice.

III.

I was, to be sure, thrown into a most Dreadful Fear by this Prophecy, despite of Will's Courage. Such a Prediction, utter'd by a Woman, hath in it Something much more Terrible than if it were Pronounc'd by a man. We of Norfolk are quick to consider any old Woman as a Witch ; and if any poor Old Rustical Creature who desires it can command Magic Power, why not a Stately Lady of Gentle Birth, like the Lady Katharine ?

Why, it was but three or four Years before this that they Burned at Lynn Regis an old Woman—her Name was Mother Gobley—because of her Abominable Witchcraft. With Egg Shells and

Water she Compass'd the Shipwreck of a Noble Vessel and the Cruel Deaths of Fourteen Brave Sailors. If such Mischief be permitted, I say, to a Miserable Old Woman like her, even at the Cost of her Immortal Soul, what would not be accorded to such as Lady Katharine if she Sought it?

'As for Battles,' said Will, 'the World is full of them, and always shall be. They are Fighting in the Low Countries: they are Fighting in France; there is never any Peace upon the West Indian Seas: and as for Spain, is not Drake gone forth to destroy as many of the Spaniard's Ships as he can? Sweetheart, it needs no Witch to see Blood in the Red Sky and to hear the Groans of Dying Men. Courage! Perhaps War will not come hither.'

It was in August—only a few Weeks later—that certain good News made us forget our Fears, and put the Prophecy for a while clean out of our minds.

Will brought us the News. It was on the last Day of our Harvest, the Day of the Horkey Load, when the Last Waggon is driven Home, adorn'd, according to our Country Custom, with Flags and Ribbons, very splendid, and perch'd atop, a Kern Baby. We were in the very Middle of the Feast. When the Waggon drew near to the House my Father went out to meet it, followed by Myself and all the Maids. He carry'd a great Horn fill'd with Ale. When the Waggon stopp'd, the Men all took Hands and shouted, 'Largesse!' 'Largesse!' after which the Horn was passed about, and one who had a Trumpet blew it. After the Passage of the Horn from Hand to Hand, the Men sat down to a Feast of Beef and Pudding with more Ale: nowhere are the Rustics better at the Drinking of Ale than in our Norfolk; and if they Drink too much, it is but a Headache the next Morning, and so no more Mischief. As soon as the Men were at their Work, the Lord of the Harvest, as they call a Fellow dressed Fantastically, began to run about the Tables, singing:

> 'So Drink, Boys, Drink,
> And See you Do not Spill:
> For if you Do, you Shall Drink Twice;
> It is your Master's Will.'

Now, while they were thus making Merry, we heard the Clattering of Hoofs, and Will rode into the midst of us, his Handsome Face so full of Joy that we knew at the first Sight of him that he had Good News to Tell.

'Good News, Sir Francis!' he cry'd unto my Father. 'Rare News, Roger!' Here he threw himself from his Horse, and toss'd the Reins to one of the Varlets. 'I come from Wells, and am carrying the News to my Father. Up, Men, shout for the Queen, and toss your Caps, and drink her Health, and Confusion to her Enemies !'

Our Honest Lads needed no Second Invitation. With one Consent they sprang to their Feet and threw up their Caps, and drank with Zeal. Both Drinking and Shouting were very much to their Taste.

Then Will began his Story.

'I come from Wells,' he said, 'whither the News hath been Brought by John Eldred, Master Mariner of the Ship *Good Intent*, from London, laden with Wine and other Goods. He reports that the Day before he dropped down the River Thames there arrived Francis Drake himself from Plymouth, bringing to the Queen the most excellent News that he had enter'd the Spanish Port of Cadiz, and under the Enemy's Nose, look you, there Fired and Sunk no fewer than Thirty Ships, great and small, without Damage to his own Fleet.'

'That is good,' said my Father. 'Thirty Ships cannot be built in a day.'

'But they may be borrow'd or bought,' said Sir Anthony, who was present. 'Go on, Will. Is there more ? Thirty Ships will not destroy the Spanish Kingdom. Is there more ?'

'There is Much More,' Will reply'd. 'For when he left Cadiz, Drake sail'd along the Coast and Destroyed a Hundred more Ships.'

'That is Brave News indeed,' said my Father.

'It is Brave News,' said Sir Anthony. 'But I would rather have Heard that Drake had Captur'd one of the King's Treasure Ships. It is in the West, in the West, that the Spaniard must be struck. A Hundred and Fifty Ships will not destroy the Spanish Kingdom. But I grant you that it is Brave News.'

'They are Ringing the Bells at Wells,' said Will. 'You can hear them. Listen !'

'Nay,' said Sir Anthony, 'we will not be behindhand,' and commanded the Ringers to be set to Work.

'A Hundred and Thirty Vessels !' said my Father. ''Tis a splendid Fleet destroy'd.'

'Why,' said Will, 'I doubt if from all our Ports we could get together so vast a Fleet. A Hundred and Thirty Ships ! With all his Treasure, yea, and back'd by the Pope himself, I doubt if the King of Spain will recover this Blow in his Lifetime. Well,

it seems that we are Safe at Last. Without Ships, what can he
do ? Will he Cross the Flood like Moses or like Joshua ?'

'The longer Time we have,' said my Father, 'the better for us.
Let us not forget that though the King of Spain may Die, the
Pope doth never Die. Therefore, we have an Enemy who, until
he himself is Overthrown, will never cease to Conspire against us.'

'Yet, Sir, with Submission,' said Will, 'one Fears the Pope less
than one Fears the King of Spain. The Pope is but a Priest.'

'Fear him therefore the More,' said Sir Anthony.

Well, so we talk'd and gave Thanks to God for this signal Mercy,
and for a Time I wholly forgot the Prophecy of Evil, and lived in
a Fool's Paradise, and thought of nothing but of Will and of happy
Love.   Yet, as Afterwards I remember'd, there were many
Warnings which should have Shaken my Confidence. I know that
under the new Religion we are Taught not to Regard these Warnings (yet the Country People are slow to give them up) : but
certain it is that all this Autumn I saw Shooting Stars (particularly
in November) : there was an Eclipse of the Sun : the Moon
showed in September of a Bloody Hue : I continually heard the
Screech-Owl, the Croaking Raven, and the Chattering Pie : the
Dogs Howled : I had Fearful Dreams : there were Strange Sounds
at Night. All this was not for Nothing, as you will presently
Understand. But being Young and Happy, I pay'd no Heed.

I know not if Lady Katharine heard this News. In those Days
I avoided her : it seem'd to me that her Eyes were Growing
Fiercer : she Mutter'd as she Walk'd : and once I saw her Stop
short on the Terrace and Throw up her eyes to Heaven, crying
aloud in her deep Man's Voice, 'O Lord ! how long ?' The three
Ancient Nuns behind her Caught each other by the Hand and
huddled together, trembling and shaking for Fear.

IV.

It was a Christmas Day—None Other—the Day when Peace and
Good-Will should Reign among Men—that our Peace was rudely
interrupted. We awoke in the Morning and arose long before
Daybreak, expecting Nothing more than a Day of Feasting and
Rejoicing, with Twelve more Days to Follow, all of Mirth and
Joy. Well : Feasting there was. As for the Rejoicing—but you
shall hear.

In the Morning all my Father's Tenants and the Servants

gather'd about Eight of the Clock in the Hall. Here we met them, and after Christmas Greetings— all the Old Customs did not perish when the Religion was changed—the Black Jack went Round full of Strong October instead of Small Ale, and the Men sat down to the great Christmas Sausage with Toast and Cheese. There had been a Bowl of Lamb's Wool the Night before, and some of them had drunk deeply thereat, so that their Heads were Heavy ; yet at the Morning Draught they seem'd to be refresh'd suddenly and Ready for More.

After Breakfast we all went together to Church. 'Twas a still Morning, the Snow falling, and the Ditches frozen over. Such a Christmas Morning one loves, when the World seems Hushed and Awed by the Tremendous Event of the Night. In every Church, methinks, on that Morning, is a Manger ; every Star is the Star of Bethlehem ; the Way of Walsingham, as the People still call the Milky Way, points to the Church in every Parish. In this Night, they say, the Cock awoke and crow'd, 'Christ is Born.' Then the Raven awoke and croak'd, 'When ?' And the Crow reply'd, 'This Night.' And the Ox ask'd, 'Where ?' And the Sheep reply'd, 'In Bethlehem.'

My Father led the Way, and after him I walked with my Brother and all the People after, save the Maids, who were wanted by the Cook to dress and serve the Christmas Feast. That, to be sure, was ready long before, with its Store of Christmas Pye, Shrid Pye, Plum Pudding, and Plum Porridge ; its Beef and Turkeys—none so good as those from Norfolk ; its Capons, Fat Geese, and Manchets.

After the Service Sir Anthony gave a Weighty Discourse on the Superstition of those who Worship the Mother and Babe instead of the Holy Trinity, and reminded us of the Fond Practices which were finally renounced when the Queen's Grace ascended the Throne : how they would set a Wooden Child dress'd up on the Altar, while the Boys and Girls danc'd before it, and the Priests shouted : how on St. Stephen's Day they gallop'd the Horses into a Sweat, hoping thus to keep them well for the next Year ; how on St. John's Day the Priests consecrated Wine and sold it for the Making of Manchets to keep off Storms—nay, we have some of these Manchets still. And how on Childermas the Priests beat one another, which, Sir Anthony said, was the only Righteous Custom of all. Many there were in that Church who could remember when the Mass was set up again under Queen Mary, whose Husband, the King of Spain, was never weary of contriving and conspiring for

the Overthrow of the Protestant Faith. Many there were also
who remember'd the Martyrs of Norwich. Therefore Sir Anthony
bade us never forget that we might be call'd upon, one and all, to
testify for the Truth in like Manner, even to the Horrible Agony
of the Stake.

Sermon over, the People flock'd out, and we follow'd. But in
the Porch, waiting for Speech with Sir Francis, was none other
than Sir Humphrey Hayes, and with him Will and two or three
Grave Merchants of Wells. So Sir Humphrey went into the
Church and talk'd for the Space of ten Minutes, and then they
came forth. My Father, instead of walking through the People,
who were waiting in two Lines for us to pass, mounted the Steps
of the old Church Cross, where he stood looking mighty Grave, so
that all the World could tell that he had News to tell. Sir
Humphrey remained in the Porch with Sir Anthony and the
Merchants.

Then my Father spoke.

' My Friends,' he say'd, ' here is News which is likely to be a Mar-
Feast. Yet needs must that I tell you. It is such News as I had
hoped never to hear in my Lifetime. Yet, since it has been
threaten'd long, surely the Sooner it happens the Better, while we
have Stomach for the Fight. You all know how the King of
Spain, once the Consort of Queen Mary, doth continually devise
Mischief to this Country. That has long been known. Nor will
anything, we are convinc'd, assuage his Hellish Malice and Rage
Insatiable. Briefly, then, he now Aims at Nothing short of the
Subjugation of this Realm, the Enslaving of us all, and the Overthrow of our Free Religion. Doubtless he hath been more than
commonly Enraged by the Great Havoc wrought among his Ships
by our Brave Commander Francis Drake. Wherefore, having few
Ships of his own, he hath bought or borrow'd from Venice, Genoa,
and other Ports so great a Fleet as was never before gotten together, which he is now fitting out with Guns and Men and Muni-
ments of War, intending to launch it against this Country as soon
as the Winter is over. Nay, it is not so vast but what, with the
Blessing of the Lord, we shall know how to meet it. But every
Man who can handle a Pike and carry a Harquebus will be wanted.
Wherefore you will go Home to your Christmas Fare with the
Knowledge that you must shortly Fight for your Liberties and
your Religion. Keep the Feast joyfully, in the Firm Trust that
the Lord will protect His Servants.

' My Lads,' he continu'd, ' I know that you will all play the Part

of Men, seeing what is before you if you Play that of Cowards.
Every Seaport will, according to its Means, contribute a Ship or
more towards the Fleet which the Queen will raise to meet this
great Expedition. There is talk of Ten Ships or more from the
City of London. Wells is but a small Port, but we will do our
Part, and if we get Volunteers we will, with the Blessing of God,
send one Tall Ship, well armed and equipped, to strike a Blow for
Freedom and for Faith. My Lads '—here he raised his hat—' God
save the Queen! Who volunteers ?'

Roger and Will sprang forward the first, drawing their Swords
with a Shout. Then one of the Village Lads—'twas a mere Stable
Boy—stepped forth and lugged off his Hat and pulled his Fore-
lock. ' May it Please your Honour to take me,' he said. And then
another and another—oh, Brave Lads of Burnham !—till from our
Little Village alone there were a Dozen at least. My Heart swells
with Pride when I think of those Brave Lads. They had plodded
in the Fields all their Days, with Plough and Flail, and Hook and
Sickle : they had no more Knowledge of War than comes from a
Wrestling Match and a Bout with Quarter Staff : and now they
were Soldiers going forth to fight upon the Ocean. They went
because Roger led the way : our Brave English will go anywhere
if they are led.

' Gentlemen,' said my Father to the Merchants, 'here are our
Lads. If every Village does as well, we shall be well sped. Roger,
bring your Troop to the Hall. Sir Humphrey, you will Feast with
me this Day, and to-morrow we will take such Order as the Queen
in Council hath directed.'

So with a Shout the Men followed, headed by Roger, and with
him Will, walking with Drawn Swords : and not a Lad among
them but held up his Head and straighten'd his Back as if he was
Marching to Battle. Nay, the Ancient Men, who would stay at
Home, also straighten'd their Backs and stuck out their Legs, as if
they too felt the Glow of War, and would Fain go forth to Fight.
And the Boys cheer'd and ran beside the Troop of Volunteers and
envied them. As for the Women, some Wept, but not aloud ; and
some there were whose Cheeks were pale : and one, at least, among
them would Fain have been alone in her Chamber to fall upon her
Knees and Weep and Pray.

Never, I declare, was Christmas kept with more Lusty Cheer or
greater Rejoicing. One would have thought, from the Way that
these Brave Fellows Feasted and Laugh'd and Sang, that the
Prospect of Fighting was the most Joyful Thing in the Whole

World. The Heavy Country Lads show'd themselves suddenly Nimble-witted : those who only Yesterday would have sat Mum all the Evening over a Tankard of Ale and a Crab, now Sang and Joked, and were as Merry as so many Players at the Fair. Even Sir Anthony himself, who, if King Philip won the Victory, would assuredly meet the Fate of St. Bilney on Mousehold Heath—even Sir Anthony, I say, Laugh'd and Crack'd his Fingers at the Jests of the Lord of Misrule.

They feasted all the Day. My Father sat in his great Arm-Chair : Sir Humphrey sat beside him : after the Christmas Antics a Bowl of Punch was brought, and some sang Songs : and the Talk fell upon War and Battles and the Brave Deeds of English Men in Days gone by. Presently the Village Lads went away, singing noisily Outside, and the Maids went to Bed, and we were alone, the Red Light of the Logs for Candles. Then we fell to more serious Talk. While we talk'd we heard the Voices of the Abbess and the three Sisters from the Chapel. They were singing a Triumphal Psalm. It was doubtless the Psalm appointed for the Office of the Day : yet to me it seemed as if they were Singing for the Overthrow of the English Armaments, and my Heart fell, thinking of the Prophecy, and there rose before me in the Embers a Shape which seemed to be the Skeleton of my Lover rolled about by the Waves at the Bottom of the Sea. The deep Man's Voice of Lady Katharine rose Loud above the Quaverings of the three Ancient Sisters.

The Others seemed not to hear.

'There are no Sailors,' said Sir Anthony, 'like the English Sailors, for Courage and for Holding on. The Dutch are Good, but the English are Best. There are none who can Handle a Ship like an Englishman. God grant we meet them on the Ocean !'

Alas ! it was on the Ocean that Lady Katharine's Battle was to be fought ; when the Ships should be Crush'd like Egg Shells, and sink down to the Bottom of the Deep with their Gallant Freight of Brave Hearts.

V.

The Ship furnish'd by the Merchants of Wells for the Service of the Queen was named the *Mere Honour :* she was a Stout and Serviceable Craft and a Swift Sailer : she carry'd Sixteen Guns,

and was three Hundred Tons Burden : as for her Complement of
Men, I know not how many she carry'd, with Sailors and Volunteers. They were Fighting Men all, Tall and Resolute Fellows,
with Half a Dozen young Gentlemen of Family such as Will and
Roger, and while the Ship was making Ready with her Equipment,
not only of Provisions and Water, but also of Arms, such as Board-
ing Pikes, Grappling Irons, Harquebuses, and Cutlasses, there were
Martial Exercises every Day for the Volunteers, who were taught
to Board a Ship, to Repel Boarders, to handle their Weapons, and
all the Time you never saw Young Men so Gay and Cheerful.
They went to their Exercises with Songs, as if they were going to
a Wedding or a Feast. As for us, we look'd on, but I promise you
without Joke and Laughter : and because we would be doing
Something towards the Good Work, we made a great Standard for
the Ship, all of Silk, with the Royal Arms embroider'd thereon,
and a very fine Flag it was. Sailors love their Ship to be adorn'd,
like a Woman, with Ribbons and fine Colours.

At last all was ready, and our Brave Lads must sail. I say
Nothing of the Fond and Tender Farewells of those who had
Lovers among 'em. There was not one, I am sure, of the Girls
who would keep her Sweetheart Ignobly Tied to her Apron
String, while the others went forth to Fight for their Country :
yet of Tears there were Many, with Dismal Forebodings and
Prayers, both secret and public. Alas ! it seems better to be a
Man and go forth to fight, even to meet Wounds or Death, than
to be a Woman and to stay at Home.

It was a Morning Early in February when the *Mere Honour*
sail'd away. The Day was fine, with a South-easterly Breeze, and
the Sun Shining. We were all gather'd upon the Quay to see the
Ship set Sail. Guns were fired : Trumpets play'd : Drums were
beat. On the High Poop stood the Gentlemen waving their Caps
—the most Comely among them all my Brother and my Lover.
The Waist and Forecastle were Crowded with the Volunteers, who
also wav'd their Caps and shouted. The Yards were mann'd by
the Sailors : and on the Quay were all the People of the Town,
and Hundreds from the Country, as far as Hunstanton on one
Side and Clay on the other, to see the Sight. The Ship was Hung
with long Streamers and waving Pennons, and our great Flag
Floated Bravely from the Poop. Then the Anchor was weigh'd
and the Sails unfurl'd, and the Ship mov'd slowly down the Creek,
and so out into the Open Sea. To the Last I saw the two Lads
standing beside our Flag, with Caps doff'd in Farewell to their

Sweethearts. Well : it was not until we could see them no longer that we fell to Weeping.

There they go,' said Sir Humphrey, 'for a Shipload of as Gallant Fellows as one would wish to have in the Queen's Navy. Some there are among them who will never come back, I doubt. Well, God speed the Ship !'

' Old Friend,' said my Father, ' your Son is on Board her, and so is mine. If we were sending them to certain Death, would we keep them at Home ? God Knows that they would not Stay. Many a Brave Lad shall meet with a Watery Grave. In the End we hope 'twill be no Worse for him.'

We rode Home ; but all that Day I seem'd to hear the Voice of Lady Katharine saying, ' I see his white bones lying among the Seaweed beneath the Waves ; the Fishes have eaten out his Eyes, and the Tide Rolls him hither and thither.'

VI.

ALL that Year, until the Sea-Fight was over, the Country was full of Rumours and Alarms. Everybody knew by this Time that the King of Spain had gotten together a vast great Army, with Ships innumerable. The Pope had renew'd his Bill of Excommunication against the Queen : that matter'd no more than the Barking òf a Dog ; but he also supply'd King Philip with Vast Sums of Money. For our Part, not only were the Fleets fitted out with Expedition, but every Man in the Country became a Soldier, the Catholicks being as eager in the Cause as the Protestants, though the Catholick Gentlemen were not allow'd to have a Command (but Lord Howard of Effingham, the High Admiral, my Kinsman, was himself a Catholick). I know not what Forces were collected, but it was said that wherever the Spaniard might Attempt to Land, there within two Days an Army of Twenty Thousand Men could be gather'd together to meet him. All this is Matter of History known to all the World. It is also very well known that the English Fleet, consisting of a Hundred and Fifty Ships with Fifteen Thousand Men, was ready in the Spring to meet the Armada on the Sea, though there were twice that number of Spaniards, with Ships twice as big as the little English Craft.

As for our Boys, I had one Letter from Will. That dear Letter have I always kept. It is the only Letter that I have ever had in all my Life. This is what he said :

'SWEETHEART,—Our Good Ship the *Mere Honour* is now cruising off the Coast of Flanders, and I promise you the Duke of Parma keeps Snug Ashore, and only Peeps out to See if we are Out of Sight. 'Tis said that he has Innumerable Flat-Boats and Twenty Thousand Men with whom to invade our Island. Well: we boast not. We are Commanded by Lord Henry Seymour. Two Score Ships we be; our Friends the Dutchmen have promised three Score more: with Drake and Hawkins at Plymouth are other three Score or even a greater Number. We know not yet what Force will come against us: 'tis said that the King of Spain designs to imitate King William the Conqueror, but with a Larger Fleet and a Greater Army: he is, by the Latest News to Hand when we sailed out of the Port of London, levying Troops everywhere: hiring and buying Ships at Venice, Genoa, Naples, and Sicily, not to speak of his own Ports. I boast not, I say again, but every Man of us is Resolute. My Dear, I long for the Sight of thy most sweet Face once more. Forget not, whatever happens, that I love thee. As for Roger, he is the most proper Man of our Company, and the lightest-hearted. If he hath not Written to thy Father or to Alice, let this Letter send them News of him. Most of our Lads were down with Seasickness, but that is past, and now there is not one but can walk about and Exercise with the Rest. I knew not before that a Sailor's Life was so Merry. We are never plagu'd with Thoughts of the Harvest: we have no Hay to cut, or Corn to reap: we care little whether the Sun shines or not: we are not Troubl'd with Rumours such as continually disquiet our Folk at Home: we have no Trouble for Money: we Fear not Poverty: there is little Sickness at Sea save when the Voyage has been long and the Provisions are mouldy: and as for Tempest, Shipwreck, or the Enemy, no one at Sea regards these Dangers. I talk as a Sailor, for indeed when one is on Board, although a Volunteer only, one begins to become a Sailor and to Speak and Think like one. They said in London that the Spanish Fleet would certainly Sail in the Spring. It is now April, wherefore we may shortly look for Hot Work. Farewell, Sweetheart.

'From your loving

'W. H.'

The Spring pass'd and the Summer follow'd: then we heard—'twas in June—that the Armada had set Sail from the Tagus. Next we heard that it had met with Gales in the Bay of Biscay, and was Dispers'd and Scatter'd. At the News we had a Thanksgiving Service in the Church. But presently it appear'd that though the Fleet was scatter'd by a Storm, little Harm was done, and then for a Space we had no more news, but waited with Beating Hearts.

VII.

ALL that Summer the Air was Thick with Rumours. The Spaniards, we heard one Day, had landed: another Day, Drake's Fleet was sunk and himself kill'd: the Queen had fled: the Camp at Tilbury had been broken up. There was nothing too monstrous to be whispered or to be believ'd. All was idle Gossip, the Effect of Fear and Uncertainty. How could the People escape Fear and Uncertainty, when in every Village all the Men who could bear Arms were daily train'd, and all were under Orders to repair, on the Signal made, to such and such a Rendezvous, and on every Hill along the South Coast—I say not along our Eastern Shores—there was a Watch by Day and Night, and a Beacon Pile ready to be Fir'd should the Spanish Fleet be Discern'd upon the Horizon? Let these Rumours pass: what I have to tell was not the Effect of Fear.

Everybody knows now that the Armada was first seen on the 21st Day of July: on Tuesday, the 23rd, the Fighting Began, and was Continued, the Spaniards every Day getting into worse Troubles, until the last Day of the Month, when they had no more Stomach for the Fight, and resolved to Fly Northwards, which they did, a Part of the English Fleet in Pursuit, until they had no more Ammunition and were compell'd to stop. But the Hand of the Lord was heavy upon them, and the Tempests Overwhelm'd them, so that in the End out of all that Great Fleet, that Invincible Armada, the Spanish Admiral brought Home barely Fifty Ships, and out of Thirty Thousand Men not half return'd.

Now on Tuesday Evening, the Day when the Fighting began, the Lady Katharine spoke to me again. (Note that she had not spoken to any of us for a whole Year, namely, since the Evening when she saw the Skies red with Blood, and foretold the Battle.) She came forth, as before, to take the Air in the Evening, follow'd by her Nuns. According to her wont, she Walk'd Slowly along the Terrace, looking before her as if she saw Nothing. But her Lips moved. She was Agitated. Suddenly she Stopp'd as one who is call'd, or who hears Something. I, who was sitting beside my

Father in the Garden, saw that her Face Changed Suddenly. Tears rose in those Hard Eyes: her Lips Trembled.

Then she Beckon'd to me.

'Child,' she said softly, 'come hither. Listen!'—for I obey'd and stood before her. 'Listen! The Day of the Lord hath come at last. Listen! You can hear the Roaring of the Cannon and the Shrieks of the Wounded Men; the Ships are dash'd together, and they Break like Egg Shells, and Sink with their Guns to the Bottom of the Deep. The Day of the Lord hath come! The Day of the Lord hath come! Let us within—to sing Praises—to sing Praises—to sing Praises.'

So without a Word more she turn'd and walk'd back to the House, follow'd by the Nuns, and so to the Chapel, where until Midnight I heard their Voices Singing Psalms of Praise, while I spent the Night in Tears and Prayers.

After this I saw her no more for nearly a Fortnight. But I have learn'd since that she was all the Time as one possess'd with a Spirit. She Spoke to the Sisters as if she was the Spectator of the Fight: she told them how here a Tall Ship was Sinking, and here Another was in Flames, and how one blew up, and how the Fire-Ships in the Dead of Night spread Destruction and Dismay. She rested not nor had any Sleep by Night: she took no Food: and broke out Continually into Praise and Thanksgiving for the Destruction of Heretics and those who had Despoil'd the Holy Sanctuaries.

It was on the Last Day of July (when the Spanish Fleet was sailing Northwards in full flight) that this Ecstasy of Spirit left her suddenly. Then she Clasp'd her Hands, Solemnly Thanked God, took some Food, and fell Asleep, continuing to Sleep like a Child for a Whole Night and Most of the following Day. In the Evening of that Day, when she Awoke, the Sisters saw that she was Chang'd: for she was now Meek and Gentle: she Spoke to them as a Sister, not as their Abbess: she ask'd Humbly for Food, and when she had taken it and read a few Prayers from her Book, she fell asleep again. And so also the next Day, and the next, being always Gentle when she awoke, and falling to Sleep again quickly.

Now on the Night of Saturday, the 4th of August, I could not Sleep for the Great Trouble of my Mind. Reports had reach'd us that the Fleets had met: a Ship from London brought the News that there had been Heavy Fighting: there were other Rumours, which I pass over: my Father was more than Commonly Grave:

I had heard him saying to Sir Anthony that the Last Stand Might, after all, have to be made upon the Dykes of Holland, if our own Land were to be Conquer'd by the Papists. Therefore I could not Sleep, but lay awake thinking that if Will were Dead his Spirit might perhaps be Permitted to Whisper Consolation to me. I even cry'd aloud to him at Midnight while the Church Clock was striking the Hour: I say that I sat up in Bed and held out my Arms and cry'd: 'Will! Will! Will! come to me, O Dead Spirit of my Dead Lover!' He came not. There was no Sound or Sigh, no Voice or Appearance at all. Yet now I knew—or thought I knew—that he was surely Dead, since she who foretold his Death was also permitted to Hear the Roaring of the Guns and to Witness afar off the Sinking of the Ships.

Two Hours and more pass'd thus in Wakefulness and in Weeping. Then, while the First Light of the Day was just Showing in the Sky, I heard Footsteps Outside, and my Door was open'd, and one of the Sisters came running in. 'Twas Sister Clementina, the Youngest (though she was already Seventy-six).

'Awake!' she cried—'oh! awake and come Quickly. The Abbess calls you. Dress Quickly, and come.'

She helped me to Dress, and I Hurry'd away with her—a Dreadful Fear in my Heart—to the Chamber where no one had been permitted to Enter for Fifty Years.

The Daylight was quickly growing stronger. The Abbess sat in her Bed propp'd up by Pillows. She was dying: anyone, even a Girl who had never looked on Death, could Perceive that Immediately. The Face, as happens often to Dying People, was Young again, and it was Beautiful. Her Eyes were Soft and Kind.

'My Dear,' she said—she called me my Dear—'thou wilt do me a Service. These Sisters of Mine are Old and Weak, but thou art Young and Strong. Hasten therefore. Take Horse and ride to the Meals beyond Wells: ride over the Meals to the Sea-Shore. There is a Fisherman's Hut. Bid the old Fisherman mount the Horse, and do thou sit behind him and come back. Tell him that I am Dying; but I cannot Die until I have Heard the Holy Mass again. Tell him that the Day of the Lord hath come; He hath Blown with His Breath, and His Enemies are scatter'd. The Holy Faith hath Come Again.'

I marvell'd at these Words, but I lost no Time. The Stable Boys were all asleep: I Saddled a Horse and rode forth. The Town of Wells was Fast Asleep; I Rode through it and out upon the Sand-Hills that we call the Meals. It is a Wild and Deserted

Place; the Wild Fowl Fly about it all the Year round: nobody comes with Hawk or Dog for them: the Rabbits swarm among the Sand and Swamps: if there be any Fishermen's Huts, there are no Fishing-Boats; the Going is dangerous for Horses on account of the Holes made by the Rabbits.

By this Time it was broad Daylight. Presently from a Sand-Hill a little higher than the Rest I discern'd in the Distance a Hut standing alone very near the Shore. It was a rude Hut form'd by an old Boat turn'd Bottom upwards, and placed on Supports, the whole Cover'd with Black Pitch. As I drew near the Hut I saw an Ancient Man in a rough Fisherman's Dress, with long white Hair and Beard, standing at the Door, as if waiting.

'I am ready,' he said. 'I was waiting for the Message.'

I have never learn'd what he meant, or how he knew I was Coming.

He Mounted, however, and I behind him, and so we Rode slowly away, but on the Journey he said no Single Word. I, however, understood by this Time what this Meant. He was no Fisherman, which anyone could understand by his Speech: and if the Lady Katharine sent for him because she would Fain Hear the Mass once more, he must be a Catholick Priest.

At the Entrance of the Park—Lo! a Marvel. Sometimes I think I must have Dream'd this Thing. But no; I cannot have Dream'd it. Besides, there was living until a Year or two ago the Sister Clementina (she died at the Age of ninety-five), who could Testify to the Truth of what I tell.

I had left a Dying Woman waiting for the Priest before her Soul could leave her Body. She was too Weak to stand; she spoke Feebly. Now—could one believe one's Eyes ?—she was Standing at the Entrance of the Park, erect and strong, without even her Stick ; she was Dress'd in her Full Habit as a Benedictine Abbess: in her Hands she bore Reverently Something—I know not what —wrapp'd in Silk and Cloth of Gold. Behind her stood the Three Sisters bearing Vestments and Vessels of Gold. Then the Priest dismounted, and the Sisters clothed him with some of the Vestments. And then, the Priest going first, they walk'd in Procession, carrying their Sacred Things, towards the Church, which stands outside the Park. I follow'd, Watching and Wondering. They sang, as they went, that Psalm which begins *Exurgat Deus.* It is the Sixty-eighth Psalm, and is Appointed for the Thirteenth Day of the Month. It is a Psalm of Thanksgiving and Praise : ' Let God Arise, and let His Enemies be Scatter'd '—why, they were already Scatter'd, she thought. 'Kings with their Armies did Flee'—the poor Lady thought that Queen Elizabeth with her Armies was in Flight. 'The Lord hath said, I will bring my People again'—they were the People from Rome. 'Sing therefore as unto God, O ye Kingdoms of the Earth ; oh ! sing Praises unto the Lord.'

Then they reach'd the Church Door, which was open—who had Open'd it ?—nay, I know not—and they Walked in, still singing, and so to the Table, which stood, as is our Custom, unfurnish'd save with a Red Cloth Covering or Pall ; but upon this Table they placed these Vessels and so made it into an Altar for their Mass.

The Sun was now High in the Heavens, and shone through the East Window (which is Splendid with Colour'd Glass) upon the Abbess and the three Sisters, who Knelt together upon the Steps before the Communion Table, making their White Cassocks look as if they were Cloth of Gold, and Painting their White Faces a rosy red.

There was never, sure, a Stranger Service than this Mass in the Early Morning, sung by the Old Priest to the Four Old Nuns in the Parish Church, now handed over to Protestant Use. I look'd on, unnoticed, while the Priest went through the Service, sometimes putting on and sometimes taking off his Vestments, sometimes praying in Silence. Then I beheld for the first Time the Elevation of the Host. It was Strange to think that until Forty Years Agone they held this Service every Sunday in the Church, and had so held it since the Church was built.

At last the Mass was said.

The Abbess was on her Knees, bow'd down almost to the Ground ; the Sisters beside her were in Like Manner humbly bow'd and kneeling ; the Priest knelt in Silence before the Altar ; upon it glitter'd the Cups and Vessels of the Service, and the Thing, whatever it was, which the Abbess had carry'd wrapt in Cloth of Gold.

Then as I watch'd, standing beside a Pillar, I saw the Lady Katharine suddenly Sink Forward. I cry'd out and ran to lift her up ; the Sisters sprang to their Feet ; the Priest stopp'd his Prayers, and we lifted her up.

But she was dead. And oh ! how Sweet a Face was that upon which we gazed ! All the Pride and Wrath were gone out of it : a Sweet Pale Face, full of Meekness and Piety ; the Face with which, Sixty Years before, she had taken her Vows.

She was dead. First the Sisters began to Tremble and to Weep ;

then they recover'd their Wits, and set themselves, refusing my Help, to Carry the Dead Body of the Abbess back to her Chamber.

No one had seen the Procession on its Way : no one saw its Return : as. for the Priest, I know not what became of him, nor did I ever learn.

At Eight o' the Clock that Morning the Sexton went to open the Church Door. He found it open. Also—this was his Story —he found upon the Communion Table a Human Bone, which he had thrown into a newly opened Grave. Nothing more. When I told my Father what had happen'd, he said that the Bone could have been none other than the Famous Arm of St. Philip, which had once belong'd to Binstead Abbey.

Now while we talk'd of this strange Event I heard a Footstep outside the Hall—a Footstep which I knew. "'Tis Will !' I cried ; ' 'tis Will !' and would have run to meet him, but the Door open'd, and he stood before us.

He was Alone, and he Hung his Head.

'Will !' cried my Father, 'what Cheer, my Lad ?'

He Hung his Head lower, and the Tears stood in his Eyes. In his Hand he bore a Sword. Alas! I knew whose Sword it was.

'First, Man,' said my Father, 'what of the Enemy ?'

'They are Dispers'd and Scatter'd. Half their Fleet is Sunk or Taken ; the Rest are in Flight. We Pursu'd them until we had no more Powder. We were Order'd to Return, each Ship to her own Port, and to be in Readiness. But it is Finish'd. They will not try to Invade us again.'

'God save the Queen !' said my Father solemnly.

'I have brought you his Sword,' said Will, without more Words. 'He was Kill'd in the last Day's Fighting by a Musket Shot when we Boarded and Took the *San Matteo*. We bury'd him at Sea.'

So the Prophecy of Lady Katharine came True. There was the Great Sea-Fight : there was the Sinking of the Ships : there was the Mighty Slaughter : and of the two Young Men who stood before me one was to Lie at the Bottom of the Deep as she Foretold. It was my Brother—my Brave and Gallant Brother. Wherefore Alice goeth still in Sadness and Mourning, and hath Refused to Marry, saying that her Husband indeed Liveth, and in Heaven is waiting still for her.

THE INNER HOUSE.

PROLOGUE.

AT THE ROYAL INSTITUTION.

'Professor !' cried the Director, rushing to meet their guest and lecturer as the door was thrown open, and the great man appeared, calm and composed, as if there was nothing more in the wind than an ordinary Scientific Discourse. 'You are always welcome, my friend, always welcome '—the two enthusiasts for science wrung hands—'and never more welcome than to-night. Then the great Mystery is to be solved at last. The Theatre is crammed with people. What does it mean ? You must tell me before you go in.'

The Physicist smiled.

'I came to a conviction that I was on the true line five years ago,' he said. 'It is only within the last six months that I have demonstrated the thing to a certainty. I will tell you, my friend,' he whispered, ' before we go in.'

Then he advanced and shook hands with the President.

'Whatever the importance of your Discovery, Professor,' said the President, ' we are fully sensible of the honour you have done us in bringing it before an English audience first of all, and especially before an audience of the Royal Institution.'

'Ja, Ja, Herr President. But I give my Discovery to all the world at this same hour. As for myself, I announce it to my very good friends of the Royal Institution. Why not to my other very good friends of the Royal Society ? Because it is á thing which belongs to the whole world, and not to scientific men only.'

It was in the Library of the Royal Institution. The President and Council of the Institution were gathered together to receive their illustrious lecturer, and every face was touched with interrogation and anxiety. What was this Great Discovery?

For six months there had appeared, from time to time, mysterious telegrams in the papers, all connected with this industrious Professor's laboratory. Nothing definite, nothing certain : it was whispered that a new discovery, soon about to be announced, would entirely change the relations of man to man ; of nation to nation. Those who professed to be in the secret suggested that it might alter all governments and abolish all laws. Why they said that I know not, because certainly nobody was admitted to the laboratory, and the Professor had no confidant. This big-headed man, with the enormous bald forehead and the big glasses on his fat nose—it was long and broad as well as fat—kept his own counsel. Yet, in some way, people were perfectly certain that something wonderful was coming. So, when Roger Bacon made his gunpowder, the monks might have whispered to each other, only from the smell which came through the keyhole, that now the Devil would be at last met upon his own ground. The telegrams were continued with exasperating pertinacity, until over the whole civilized world the eyes of all who loved science were turned upon that modest laboratory in the little University of Ganzweltweisst am Rhein. What was coming from it? One does not go so far as to say that all interest in contemporary business, politics, art, and letters ceased ; but it is quite certain that every morning and every evening, when everybody opened his paper, his first thought was to look for news from Ganzweltweisst am Rhein.

But the days passed by, and no news came. This was especially hard on the leader-writers, who were one and all waiting, each man longing to have a cut in with the subject before anybody else got it. But it was good for the people who write letters to the papers, because they had so many opportunities of suggestion and surmise. And so the leader-writers got something to talk about after all. For some suggested that Prof. Schwarzbaum had found out a way to make food artificially, by chemically compounding nitrogens, phosphates, and so forth. And these philosophers built a magnificent Palace of Imagination, in which dwelt a glorified mankind no longer occupied in endless toil for the sake of providing meat and drink for themselves and families, but all engaged in the pursuit of knowledge, and in Art of all kinds, such as Fiction, Poetry, Painting, Music, Acting, and so forth, getting out of Life such a wealth of emotion, pleasure, and culture as the world had never before imagined. Others there were who thought that the great Discovery might be a method of instantaneous transmission of matter from place to place; so that, as by the electric wire one can send a message, so by some kind of electric method one could send a human body from any one part of the world to any other in a moment. This suggestion offered a fine field for the imagination; and there was a novel written on this subject which had a great success, until the Discovery itself was announced. Others, again, thought that the new Discovery meant some great and wonderful development of the Destructive Art; so that the whole of an army might be blown into countless fragments by the touch of a button, the discharge of a spring, the fall of a hammer. This took the fancy hugely, and it was pleasant to read the imaginary developments of history as influenced by this Discovery. But it seemed certain that the learned Professor would keep it for the use of his own country. So that there was no longer any room to doubt that, if this was the nature of the Discovery, the whole of the habitable world must inevitably fall under the Teutonic yoke, and an Empire of Armed Peace would set in, the like of which had never before been witnessed upon the globe. On the whole, the prospect was received everywhere, except in France and Russia, with resignation. Even the United States remembered that they had already many millions of Germans among them; and that the new Empire, though it would give certainly all the places to these Germans, would also save them a great many Elections, and therefore a good deal of trouble, and would relieve the national conscience—long grievously oppressed in this particular—of truckling to the Irish Vote. Dynamiters and anarchists, however, were despondent, and Socialists regarded each other with an ever-deepening gloom. This particular Theory of the great Discovery met, in fact, with universal credence over the whole civilized globe.

From the great man himself there came no sign. Enterprising interviewers failed to get speech with him. Scientific men wrote to him, but got no real information in reply. And the minds of men grew more and more agitated. Some great change was considered certain—but what?

One morning—it was the morning of Thursday, June 20th, 1896—there appeared an advertisement in the papers. By the telegrams it was discovered that a similar advertisement had been published in every great city all over the world. That of the London papers differed from others in one important respect—in this, namely : Professor Schwarzbaum would himself, without any delay, read before a London audience a Paper which should reveal his new Discovery. There was not, however, the least hint in the announcement of the nature of this Discovery.

'Yes,' said the Physicist, speaking slowly, 'I have given the particulars to my friends over the whole earth ; and, as London is still the centre of the world, I resolved that I would myself communicate it to the English.'

'But what is it ?—what is it ?' asked the President.

'The Discovery,' the Professor continued, 'is to be announced at the same moment all over the world, so that none of the newspapers shall have an unfair start. It is now close upon nine o'clock by London time. In Paris it is ten minutes past nine : in Berlin it is six minutes before ten : at St. Petersburg it is eleven o'clock : at New York it is four o'clock in the afternoon. Very good. When the clock in your theatre points to nine exactly, at that moment everywhere the same Paper will be read.'

In fact, at that moment the clock began to strike. The President led the way to the Theatre, followed by the Council. The Director remained behind with the Lecturer of the evening.

'My friend,' said Professor Schwarzbaum, 'my subject is nothing less'—he laid his finger upon the Director's arm— 'nothing less than "The Prolongation of the Vital Energy." '

'What ! The Prolongation of the Vital Energy ? Do you know what that means ?' The Director turned pale. 'Are we to understand——'

'Come,' said the Professor, 'we must not waste the time.'

Then the Director, startled and pale, took his German brother by the arm and led him into the Theatre, murmuring, 'Prolongation . . . Prolongation . . . Prolongation . . . of the Vital—the Vital—Energy !'

The Theatre was crowded. There was not a vacant seat : there was no more standing room on the stairs : the very doors of the gallery were thronged : the great staircase was thronged with those who could not get in, but waited to get the first news. Nay, outside the Institution, Albemarle Street was crowded with people waiting to hear what this great thing might be which all the world had waited six months to hear. Within the Theatre, what an audience ! For the first time in English history no re-

spect at all had been paid to rank : the people gathered in the
Theatre were all that the great City could boast that was distinguished in science, art, and letters.   Those present were the
men who moved the world.   Among them, naturally, a sprinkling
of the men who are born to the best things of the world, and
are sometimes told that they help to move it.   There were
ladies among the company, too : ladies well known in scientific
and literary circles ; with certain great ladies led by curiosity.
On the left-hand side of the Theatre, for instance, close to the
door, sat two very great ladies indeed—one of them the Countess
of Thordisá, and the other her only daughter, the Lady Mildred
Carera.   Leaning against the pillar beside them stood a young
man of singularly handsome appearance, tall and commanding of
stature.

'To you, Dr. Linister,' said the Countess, 'I suppose everything
that the Professor has to tell us will be already well known ?'

'That,' said Dr. Linister, 'would be too much to expect.'

'For me,' her Ladyship went on delicately, 'I love to catch
Science on the wing—on the wing—in her lighter moods, when she
has something really popular to tell.'

Dr. Linister bowed.   Then his eyes met those of the beautiful
girl sitting below him, and he leaned and whispered :

'I looked for you everywhere last night.   You had led me to
understand——'

'We went nowhere, after all.   Mamma fancied she had a bad
cold.'

'Then this evening.   May I be quite—quite sure ?' ·

His voice dropped, and his fingers met hers beneath the fan.
She drew them away quickly with a blush.

'Yes,' she whispered, 'you may find me to-night at Lady
Chatterton's or Lady Ingleby's.'

From which you can understand that this young Dr. Linister
was quite a man in society.   He was young : he had already a
great reputation for Biological research ; he was the only son of a
fashionable physician ; and he would be very rich.   Therefore, in
the season, Harry Linister was *of* the season.

On most of the faces present there sat an expression of anxiety,
and even fear.   What was this new thing ?   Was the world really
going to be turned upside down ?   And when the West End was
so very comfortable and its position so very well assured !   But
there were a few present who rubbed their hands at the thought of
a great upturn of everything.   Up with the scum first ; when that

had been ladled overboard a new arrangement would be possible, to
the advantage of those who rubbed their hands.

When the clock struck nine, a dead silence fell upon the Theatre ;
not a breath was heard ; not a cough ; not the rustle of a dress.
Their faces were pale with expectancy ; their lips were parted ;
their very breathing seemed arrested.

Then the President and the Council walked in and took their
places.

'Ladies and Gentlemen,' said the President shortly, 'the learned
Professor will himself communicate to you the subject and title of
his Paper, and we may be certain beforehand that his subject and
matter will adorn the motto of the Society—*Illustrans commoda
vitæ.*'

Then Dr. Schwarzbaum stood at the table before them all, and
looked round the room.   Lady Mildred glanced at the young man,
Harry Linister.   He was staring at the German like the rest,
speechless.   She sighed.   Women did not in those days like love-
making to be forgotten or interrupted by anything, certainly not
by science.

The learned German carried a small bundle of papers, which he
laid on the table.   He carefully and slowly adjusted his spectacles.
Then he drew from his pocket a small leathern case.   Then he
looked round the room and smiled.   That is to say, his lips were
covered with a full beard, so that the sweetness of the smile was
mostly lost ; but it was observed under and behind the beard.   The
mere ghost of a smile ; yet a benevolent ghost.

The Lecturer began, somewhat in copybook fashion, to remind
his audience that everything in Nature is born, grows slowly to
maturity, enjoys a brief period of full force and strength, then
decays, and finally dies.   The tree of life is first a green sapling,
and last a white and leafless trunk.   He expatiated at some length
on the growth of the young life.   He pointed out that methods
had been discovered to hinder that growth, turn it into unnatural
forms, even to stop and destroy it altogether.   He showed how the
body is gradually strengthened in all its parts ; he showed, for his
unscientific hearers, how the various parts of the structure assume
strength.   All this was familiar to most of his audience.   Next he
proceeded to dwell upon the period of full maturity of bodily and
mental strength, which, in a man, should last from twenty-five to
sixty, and even beyond that time.   The decay of the bodily, and
even of the mental organs, may have already set in, even when mind
and body seem the most vigorous.   At this period of the discussion

most of the audience were beginning to flag in their attention. Was such a gathering as this assembled only to hear a discussion on the growth and decay of the faculties? But the Director, who knew what was coming, sat bolt upright, expectant. It was strange, the people said afterwards, that no one should have suspected what was coming. There was to be, everybody knew, a great announcement. That was certain. Destruction, Locomotion, Food, Transmission of Thought, Substitution of Speech for Writing—all these things, as has been seen, had been suggested. But no one even guessed the real nature of the Discovery. And now, with the exception of the people who always pretend to have known all along, to have been favoured with the Great Man's Confidence, to have guessed the thing from the outset, no one had the least suspicion.

Therefore, when the Professor suddenly stopped short, after a prolix description of wasting power and wearied organs, and held up an admonitory finger, everybody jumped, because now the Secret was to be divulged. They had come to hear a great Secret.

'What is this Decay?' he asked. 'What is it? Why does it begin? What laws regulate it? What check can we place upon it? How can we prevent it? How can we stay its progress? Can Science, which has done so much to make Life happy—which has found out so many things by which Man's brief span is crowded with delightful emotions—can Science do no more? Cannot Science add to these gifts that more precious gift of all—the lengthening of that brief span?'

Here everybody gasped.

'I ask,' the speaker went on, 'whether Science cannot put off that day which closes the eyes and turns the body into a senseless lump? Consider: we are no sooner arrived at the goal of our ambitions than we have to go away; we are no sooner at the plenitude of our wisdom and knowledge, than we have to lay down all that we have learned and go away—nay, we cannot even transmit to others our accumulations of knowledge. They are lost. We are no sooner happy with those we love, than we have to leave them. We collect but cannot enjoy; we inherit—it is but for a day; we learn, but we have no time to use our learning; we love—it is but for an hour; we pass our youth in hope, our manhood in effort, and we die before we are old; we are strong, but our strength passes like a dream; we are beautiful, but our beauty perishes in a single day. Cannot, I ask again—cannot Science prolong the Vital Force, and stay the destroying hand of Decay?'

At this point a wonderful passion seized upon many of the people present. For some sprang to their feet and lifted hands and shouted: some wept aloud: some clasped each other by the hand: there were lovers among the crowd who fell openly into each other's arms: there were men of learning who hugged imaginary books and looked up with wild eyes: there were girls who smiled, thinking that their beauty might last longer than a day: there were women down whose cheeks rolled the tears of sorrow for their vanished beauty: there were old men who heard and trembled.

One of them spoke—out of all this crowd only one found words. It was an old statesman; an old man eloquent. He rose with shaking limbs.

'Sir,' he cried, his voice still sonorous, 'give me back my manhood!'

The Professor continued, regardless:

'Suppose,' he said, 'that Science had found out the way, not to restore what is lost, but to arrest further loss; not to give back what is gone—you might as well try to restore a leg that has been cut off—but to prevent further loss. Consider this for a moment, I pray you. Those who search into Nature's secrets might, if this were done for them, carry on their investigations far beyond any point which had yet been reached: those who cultivate Art might attain to a greater skill of hand and truth of sight than has ever yet been seen: those who study human nature might multiply their observations: those who love might have a longer time for their passion: men who are strong might remain strong: women who are beautiful might remain beautiful——'

'Sir,' cried again the old man eloquent, 'give me back my manhood!'

The Lecturer made no reply, but went on:

'The rich might have a time—a sensible length of time—in which to enjoy their wealth: the young might remain young: the old might grow no older: the feeble might not become more feeble—all for a prolonged time. As for those whose lives could never become anything but a burden to themselves and to the rest of the world—the crippled, the criminal, the poor, the imbecile, the incompetent, the stupid and the frivolous—they would live out their allotted lives and die. It would be for the salt of the earth, for the flower of mankind, for the men strong of intellect and endowed above the common herd, that Science would reserve this precious gift.'

'Give me back my manhood!' cried again the old man eloquent.

But he was not alone. For they all sprang to their feet together

and cried aloud, shrieking, weeping, stretching forth hands, 'Give
—give—give!' But the Director, who knew that what was asked
for would be given, sat silent and self-possessed.

The Speaker motioned them all to sit down again.

'I would not,' he said, 'limit this great gift to those alone whose
intellect leads the world. I would extend it to all who help to
make life beautiful and happy: to lovely women'—here the men
heaved a sigh so deep, so simultaneous, that it fell upon the ear
like the voice of thanksgiving from a Cathedral choir—'to those
who love only the empty show and pleasures and vainglories of
life'—here many smiled, especially of the younger sort—'even to
some of those who desire nothing of life but love and song and
dalliance and laughter.' Again the younger sort smiled, and tried
to look as if they had no connection at all with that band. 'I would
extend this gift, I repeat, to all who can themselves be happy in the
sunshine and the light, and to all who can make the happiness of
others. Then, again, consider. When you have enjoyed those things
for awhile: when your life has been prolonged, so that you have
enjoyed all that you desire in full measure and running over: when
not two or three years have passed, but perhaps two or three centuries, you would then, of your own accord, put aside the aid of
Science and suffer your body to fall into the decay which awaits all
living matter. Contented and resigned, you would sink into the
tomb, not satiated with the joys of life, but satisfied to have had
your share. There would be no terror in death, since it would take
none but those who could say, "I have had enough." That day
would surely come to everyone. There is nothing—not research
and discovery, not the beauty of Nature, not love and pleasure, not
art, not flowers and sunshine and perpetual youth—of which we
should not in time grow weary. Science cannot alter the Laws of
Nature. Of all things there must be an end. But she can prolong:
she can avert: she can . . . . . Yes, my friends. This is my Discovery: this is my Gift to Humanity: this is the fruit, the outcome
of my life: for me this great thing has been reserved. Science can
arrest Decay. She can make you live—live on—live for centuries
—nay, I know not—why not?—she can, if you foolishly desire it,
make you live for ever.'

Now, when these words were spoken there fell a deep silence
upon the crowd. No one spoke: no one looked up: they were
awed: they could not realize what it meant that would be given
them: they were suddenly relieved of a great terror, the constant
dread that lies in man's heart, ever present, though we conceal it—

the dread of Death ; but they could not, in a moment, understand that it was given.

But the Director sprang to his feet, and grasped his brother physicist by the hand :

'Of all the sons of Science,' he said solemnly, 'thou shalt be proclaimed the first and best.'

The assembly heard these words, but made no sign. There was no applause—not a murmur, not a voice. They were stricken dumb with wonder and with awe. They were going to live—to live on—to live for centuries—nay, why not ?—to live for ever !

'You all know,' the Professor continued, 'how at a dinner a single glass of champagne revives the spirits, looses the tongue, and brings activity to the brain. The guests were weary: they were in decay: the Champagne arrests that decay. My discovery is of another kind of Champagne, which acts with a more lasting effect. It strengthens the nerves, hardens the muscles, quickens the blood, and brings activity to the digestion. With new strength of the body returns new strength to the mind : mind and body are one.' He paused a moment. Then he gave the leathern case into the hands of the Director. 'This is my Gift, I say. I give to my brother full particulars and the history of the invention. I seek no profit for myself. It is your own. This day a new epoch begins for humanity. We shall not die, but live. Accident, fire, lightning, may kill us. Against these things we cannot guard. But old age shall no more fall upon us : decay shall no more rob us of our life and strength : and death shall be voluntary. This is a great change. I know not if I have done aright. That is for you to determine. See that you use this gift aright.'

Then, before the people had understood the last words, the speaker stepped out of the Theatre and was gone.

But the Director of the Royal Institution stood in his place, and in his hand was the leathern case containing the GIFT OF . LIFE.

The Countess of Thordisá, who had been asleep throughout the lecture, woke up when it was finished.

'How deeply interesting !' she sighed. 'This it is, to catch Science on the wing.' Then she looked round. 'Mildred, dear,' she said, 'has Dr. Linister gone to find the carriage ? Dear me ! what a commotion ! And at the Royal Institution, of all places in the world !'

'I think, Mamma,' said Lady Mildred coldly, 'that we had better get someone else to find the carriage. Dr. Linister is over there. He is better engaged.'

He was : he was among his brother physicists : they were eagerly asking questions and crowding round the Director. And the Theatre seemed filled with mad people, who surged and crowded and pushed.

'Come, Mamma,' said Lady Mildred, pale, but with a red spot on either cheek, 'we will leave them to fight it out.'

Science had beaten love. She did not meet Harry Linister again that night. And when they met again, long years afterwards, he passed her by with eyes that showed he had clean forgotten her existence, unaltered though she was in face and form.

CHAPTER I.

THE SUPPER-BELL.

WHEN the big bell, in the Tower of the House of Life, struck the hour of seven, the other bells began to chime as they had done every day at this hour for I know not how many years. Very likely in the Library, where we still keep a great collection of perfectly use-less books, there is preserved some History which may speak of these Bells, and of the builders of the House. When these chimes began, the swifts and jackdaws which live in the Tower began to fly about with a great show of hurry, as if there was barely time for supper, though, as it was yet only the month of July, the sun would not be setting for an hour or more.

We have long since ceased to preach to the people: otherwise, we might make them learn a great deal from the animal world. They live, for instance, from day to day ; not only are their lives miser-ably short, but they are always hungry, always fighting, always quarrelling, always fierce in their loves and their jealousies. Watch-ing the swifts, for instance, which we may do nearly all day long, we ought to congratulate ourselves on our own leisurely order, the adequate provision for food made by the Wisdom of the College, the assurance of preservation also established by that Wisdom, and our freedom from haste and anxiety, as from the emotions of love, hatred, jealousy, and rivalry. But the time has gone by for that kind of exhortation.

Thus, our people, who at this hour crowded the great Square, showed in their faces, their attitudes, and their movements, the calm that reigned in their souls. Some were lying on the grass ; some were sitting on the benches ; some were strolling : they were for the most part alone : if not alone—because habit often survives when the original cause of the habit is gone—then in pairs.

In the old unhappy days there would have been restless activity —a hurrying to and fro : there would have been laughter and talking—everybody would have been talking : there would have been young men eagerly courting the favours of young women, looking on them with longing eyes, ready to fight for them, each for the girl he loved ; thinking each of the girl he loved as of a goddess or an angel—all perfection. The girls themselves ardently desired this foolish worship. Again, formerly there would have been old men and old women looking with melancholy eyes on the scenes they were about to quit, and lamenting the days of their strength and their youth. And formerly there would have been among the crowd beggars and paupers : there would have been some masters and some servants ; some noble and some bourgeois : there would have been every conceivable difference in age, rank, strength, intellect, and distinction.

Again, formerly there would have been the most insolent differences in costume. Some of the men used to wear broadcloth, sleek and smooth, with glossy hats, and gloves, and flowers at their button-hole ; while beside them crawled the wretched half-clad objects pretending to sell matches, but in reality begging for their bread. · And some of the women used to flaunt in dainty and expensive stuffs, setting off their supposed charms (which were mostly made by the dressmaker's art) with the curves and colours of their drapery. And beside them would be crawling the wretched creatures to whom in the summer, when the days were hot and fine, the Park was their only home, and rusty black their only wear.

Now, no activity at all : no hurrying, no laughing, not even any talking. That might have struck a visitor as one of the most remarkable results of our system. No foolish talking. As for their dress, it was all alike. The men wore blue flannel jackets and trousers, with a flannel shirt and a flat blue cap : for the working hours they had a rougher dress. The women wore a costume in gray, made of a stuff called beige. It is a useful stuff, because it wears well ; it is soft and yet warm, and cannot be objected to by any of them on the score of ugliness. What mutinies! what secret conspiracies ! what mad revolts! had to be faced before the women could be made to understand that Socialism—the only form of Society which can now be accepted—must be logical and complete. What is one woman more than another that she should separate herself from her sisters by her dress! Therefore, since their subjugation they all wear a gray beige frock, with a jacket of the same, and a flat gray cap, like the men's, under which they are made to gather up their hair.

This scene, indeed—the gathering of the People before the supper-bell—is one of which I never tire. I look at all the eager, hurrying swifts in the air, I remember the Past; and I think of the Present when I gaze upon the great multitude, in which no one regardeth his neighbour, none speaks to none. There are no individual aims, but all is pure, unadulterated Socialism, with—not far distant—the Ultimate Triumph of Science!

I desire to relate the exact circumstances connected with certain recent events. It is generally known that they caused one deplorable Death—one of our own Society, although not a Physician of the House. I shall have to explain, before I begin the narrative, certain points in our internal management which may differ from the customs adopted elsewhere. We of the Later Era visit each other so seldom that differences may easily grow up. Indeed, considering the terrible dangers of travel—how, if one walks, there are the perils of unfiltered water, damp beds, sprained ankles, byrsitis of the knee, chills from frosts and showers; or, if one gets into a wheeled vehicle, the wheels may fall off, or the carriage may be overturned in a ditch. . . . But why pursue the subject? I repeat, therefore, that I must speak of the community and its order, but that as briefly as may be.

The Rebels have been driven forth from the Pale of Humanity to wander where they please. In a few years they will be released —if that has not already happened—by Death from the diseases and sufferings which will fall upon them. Then we shall remember them no more. The centuries will roll by, and they shall be forgotten; the very mounds of earth which once marked the place of their burial will be level with the ground around them. But the House and the Glory of the House will continue.

Thus perish all the enemies of Science!

The City of Canterbury, as it was rebuilt when Socialism was finally established, has in its centre a great Square, Park, or Garden, the central breathing place and relaxation ground of the City. Each side is exactly half a mile in length. The Garden, thus occupying an area of a fourth of a square mile, is planted with every kind of ornamental tree, and laid out in flower-beds, winding walks, serpentine rivers, lakes, cascades, bridges, grottoes, summer-houses, lawns, and everything that can help to make the place attractive. During the summer it is thronged every evening with the people. On its west side has been erected an enormous Palace of glass, low in height, but stretching far away to the west, covering an immense area. Here the heat is artificially maintained at temperatures varying with the season and the plants that are in cultivation. In winter, frost, bad weather, and in rain, it forms a place of recreation and rest. Here grow all kinds of fruit-trees, with all kinds of vegetables, flowers, and plants. All the year round it furnishes, in quantities, sufficient for all our wants, an endless supply of fruit; so that we have a supply of some during the whole year, as grapes, bananas, and oranges; others for at least half the year, as peaches, strawberries, and so forth; while of the commoner vegetables, as peas, beans, and the like, there is now no season, but they are grown continuously. In the old times we were dependent upon the changes and chances of a capricious and variable climate. Now, not only has the erection of these vast houses made us independent of summer and winter, but the placing of much grass and corn land under glass has also assured our crops and secured us from the danger of famine. This is by no means one of the least advantages of modern civilization.

On the South side of the Square stands our Public Hall. The building has not, like the House of Life, any architectural beauty—why should we aim at beauty, when efficiency is our sole object? The House of Life was designed and erected when men thought perpetually of beauty, working from their admiration of beauty in woman and in nature to beauty in things which they made with their own hands, setting beauty above usefulness; even thinking it necessary, when usefulness had been attained, to add adornment, as when they added a Tower to the House of Life, yet did nothing with their Tower and did not want it.

The Public Hall is built of red brick: it resembles a row of houses each with a gable to the street. There is for each a broad plain door with a simple porch, below; and above, a broad plain window, twenty feet wide, divided into four compartments or divisions, the whole set in a framework of wood. The appearance of the Hall is, therefore, remarkably plain. There are thirty-one of these gables, each forty feet wide; so that the whole length of the Hall is twelve hundred and forty feet, or nearly a quarter of a mile.

Within, the roof of each of these gables covers a Hall separated from its neighbours by plain columns. They are all alike, except that the middle Hall, set apart for the College, has a gallery originally intended for an orchestra, now never used. In the central Hall one table alone is placed; in all the others there are four, every Hall accommodating eight hundred people and every table two hundred. The length of each Hall is the same—namely, two hundred and fifty feet. The Hall is lit by one large window at each end. There are no carvings, sculptures, or other ornaments in the building. At the back is an extensive range of buildings, all of brick, built in small compartments, and fire-proof: they contain the kitchens, granaries, *abattoirs*, larders, cellars, dairies, still-rooms, pantries, curing-houses, ovens, breweries, and all the other offices and chambers required for the daily pro-visioning of a city with twenty-four thousand inhabitants.

On the East side of the Square there are two great groups of buildings. That nearest to the Public Hall contains, in a series of buildings which communicate with one another, the Library, the Museum, the Armoury, the Model-room, and the Picture Gallery. The last is a building as old as the House. They were, when these events began, open to the whole Community, though they were never visited by any even out of idle curiosity. The inquisitive spirit is dead. For myself, I am not anxious to see the people acquire, or revive, the habit of reading and inquiring. It might be argued that the study of history might make them contrast the present with the past, and shudder at the lot of their forefathers. But I am going to show that this study may produce quite the opposite effect. Or, there is the study of science. How should this help the People? They have the College always studying and investigating for their benefit the secrets of medical science, which alone concerns their happiness. They might learn how to make machines: but machinery requires steam, explosives, electricity, and other uncontrolled and dangerous forces. Many thousands of lives were formerly lost in the making and management of these machines, and we do very well without them. They might, it is true, read the books which tell of the people in former times. But why read works which are filled with the Presence of Death, the Shortness of Life, and the intensity of passions which we have almost forgotten? You shall see what comes of these studies which seem so innocent.

I say, therefore, that I never had any wish to see the people flocking into the Library. For the same reason—that a study and contemplation of things past might unsettle or disturb the tranquillity of their minds—I have never wished to see them in the Museum, the Armoury, or any other part of our Collections. And since the events of which I have to tell, we have enclosed these buildings and added them to the College, so that the people can no longer enter them even if they wished.

The Curator of the Museum was an aged man, one of the few old men left—in the old days he had held a title of some kind. He was placed there because he was old and much broken, and could do no work. Therefore he was told to keep the glass cases free from dust and to sweep the floors every morning. At the time of the Great Discovery he had been an Earl or Viscount—I know not what—and by some accident he escaped the Great Slaughter, when it was resolved to kill all the old men and women in order to reduce the population to the number which the land would support. I believe that he hid himself, and was secretly fed by some man who had formerly been his groom, and still preserved some remains of what he called attachment and duty, until such time as the executions were over. Then he ventured forth again, and so great was the horror of the recent massacre, with the recollection of the prayers and shrieks of the victims, that he was allowed to continue alive. The old man was troubled with an asthma which hardly permitted him an hour of repose, and was incurable. This would have made his life intolerable, except that to live—only to live, in any pain and misery—is always better than to die.

For the last few years the old man had had a companion in the Museum. This was a girl—the only girl in our Community—who called him—I know not why; perhaps because the relationship really existed—Grandfather, and lived with him. She it was who dusted the cases and swept the floors. She found some means of relieving the old man's asthma, and all day long—would that I had discovered the fact, or suspected whither it would lead the wretched girl!—she read the books of the Library, and studied the contents of the cases, and talked to the old man, making him tell her everything that belonged to the past. All she cared for was the Past: all that she studied was to understand more and more—how men lived then, and what they thought, and what they talked.

She was about eighteen years of age; but, indeed, we thought her still a child. I know not how many years had elapsed since any in the City were children, because it is a vain thing to keep account of the years: if anything happens to distinguish them, it must be something disastrous, because we have now arrived almost at the last stage possible to man. It only remains for us to discover, not only how to prevent disease, but how to annihilate it. Since, then, there is only one step left to take in advance, every other event which can happen must be in the nature of a calamity, and therefore may be forgotten.

I have said that Christine called the old man her grandfather. We have long, long since agreed to forget old ties of blood. How can father and son, mother and daughter, brother and sister continue for hundreds of years, and when all remain fixed at the same age, to keep up the old relationship? The maternal love dies out with us—it is now but seldom called into existence—when the child can run about. Why not? The animals, from whom we learn so much, desert their offspring when they can feed themselves; our mothers cease to care for their children when they are old enough to be the charge of the Community. Therefore Christine's mother cheerfully suffered the child to leave her as soon as she was old enough to sit in the Public Hall. Her grandfather—if indeed he was her grandfather—obtained permission to have the child with him. So she remained in the quiet Museum. We never imagined or suspected, however, that the old man, who was eighty at the time of the Great Discovery, remembered everything that took place when he was young, and talked with the girl all day long about the Past.

I do not know who was Christine's father. It matters not now; and, indeed, he never claimed his daughter. One smiles to think of the importance formerly attached to fathers. We no longer work for their support. We are no longer dependent upon their assistance: the father does nothing for the son, nor the son for the father. Five hundred years ago, say—or a thousand years ago—the father carried a baby in his arms. What then? My own father—I believe he is my own father, but on this point I may be mistaken—I saw yesterday taking his turn in the hayfield. He seemed distressed with the heat and fatigue of it. Why not? It makes no difference to me. He is, though not so young, still as strong and as able-bodied as myself. Christine was called into existence by the sanction of the College when one of the Community was struck dead by lightning. It was my brother, I believe. The terrible event filled us all with consternation. However, the population having thus been diminished by one, it was resolved that the loss should be repaired. There was precedent. A great many years previously, owing to a man being killed by the fall of a hayrick—all hayricks are now made low—another birth had been allowed. That was a boy.

Let us now return to our Square. On the same side are the buildings of the College. Here are the Anatomical collections; the store-house of Materia Medica; and the residences of the Arch Physician, the Suffragan, the Fellows of the College or Associate Physicians, and the Assistants or Experimenters. The buildings are plain and fire-proof. The College has its own private gardens, which are large and filled with trees. Here the Physicians walk and meditate, undisturbed by the outer world. Here is also their Library.

On the North side of the Square stands the great and venerable HOUSE OF LIFE, the Glory of the City, the Pride of the whole Country.

It is very ancient: formerly there were many such splendid monuments standing in the country; now this alone remains. It was built in the dim, distant ages, when men believed things now forgotten: it was designed for the celebration of certain ceremonies or functions; their nature and meaning may, I dare say, be ascertained by any who cares to waste time in an inquiry so useless. The edifice itself could not possibly be built in these times: first, because we have no artificers capable of rearing such a pile; and next, because we have not among us anyone capable of conceiving it, or drawing the design of it. Nay, we have none who could execute the carved stone-work.

I do not say this with humility, but with satisfaction. For, if we contemplate the building, we must acknowledge that, though it is, as I have said, the Glory of the City, and though it is vast in proportions, imposing by its grandeur, and splendid in its work, yet most of it is perfectly useless. What need of the tall columns to support a roof which might very well have been one-fourth the present height? Why build the Tower at all? What is the good of the carved work? We of the New Era build in brick, which is fire-proof; we put up structures which are no larger than are wanted; we waste no labour, because we grudge the time which must be spent in necessary work, over things unnecessary. Besides, we are no longer tortured by the feverish anxiety to do something —anything—by which we may be remembered when the short span of life is past. Death to us is a thing which may happen by accident, but not from old age or by disease. Why should men toil and trouble in order to be remembered? All things are equal; why should one man try to do something better than another—or what another cannot do—or what is useless when it is done? Sculptures, pictures, Art of any kind, will not add a single ear of corn to the general stock, or a single glass of wine, or a yard of flannel. Therefore we need not regret the decay of Art.

As everybody knows, however, the HOUSE is the chief Laboratory of the whole country. It is here that the Great Secret is preserved; it is known to the Arch Physician and to his Suffragan alone. No other man in the country knows by what process is compounded that potent liquid which arrests decay and prolongs life, apparently without any bound or limit. I say without any bound or limit. There certainly are croakers, who maintain that at some future time—it may be this very year, it may be a thousand years hence—the compound will lose its power, and so we—all of us, even the College—must then inevitably begin to decay, and after a few short years perish and sink into the silent grave. The very thought causes a horror too dreadful for words; the limbs tremble, the teeth chatter. But others declare that there is no fear whatever of this result, and that the only dread is lest the whole College should suddenly be struck by lightning, and so the Secret be lost. For though none other than the Arch Physician and his Suffragan knew, until recently, the Secret, the whole Society—the Fellows or Assistant Physicians—knew where the Secret was kept in writing, just as it was communicated by the Discoverer. The Fellows of the College all assist in the production of this precious liquid, which is made only in the HOUSE OF LIFE. But none of them, until, as I said, recently, knew whether they were working for the Arcanum itself, or on some experiment conducted for the Arch Physician. Even if one guessed, he would not dare to communicate his suspicions even to a Brother-Fellow, being forbidden, under the most awful of all penalties, that of Death itself, to divulge the experiments and processes that he is ordered to carry out.

It is needless to say that if we are proud of the HOUSE, we are equally proud of the City. There was formerly an old Canterbury, of which pictures exist in the Library. The streets of that town were narrow and winding; the houses were irregular in height, size and style. There were close courts, not six feet broad, in which no air could circulate, and where fevers and other disorders were bred. Some houses, again, stood in stately gardens, while others had none at all; and the owners of the gardens kept them closed. But we can easily understand what might have happened when private property was recognised, and laws protected the so-called rights of owners. Now that there is no property, there are no laws. There are also no crimes, because there is no incentive to jealousy, rapine, or double-dealing. Where there is no crime, there is that condition of Innocence which our ancestors so eagerly desired, and sought by means which were perfectly certain to fail.

How different is the Canterbury of the present! First, like all modern towns, it is limited in size; there are in it twenty-four thousand inhabitants, neither more nor less. Round its great central Square or Garden are the public buildings. The streets, which branch off at right angles, are all of the same width, the same length, and the same appearance. They are planted with trees. The houses are built of red brick, each house containing four rooms on the ground floor—namely, two on either side the door—and four on the first-floor, with a bath-room. The rooms are vaulted with brick, so that there is no fear of fire. Every room has its own occupant; and as all the rooms are of the same size, and are all furnished in the same way, with the same regard to comfort and warmth, there is really no ground for complaint or jealousies. The occupants also, who have the same meals in the same Hall every day, cannot complain of inequalities, any more than they can accuse each other of gluttonous living. In the matter of clothes, again, it was at first expected that the grave difficulties with the women as to uniformity of fashion and of material would continue to trouble us. But with the decay of those emotions which formerly caused so much trouble, since the men have ceased to court the women, and the women have ceased to desire men's admiration, there has been no opposition. All of them now are clad alike: gray is found the most convenient colour; soft beige the most convenient material.

The same beautiful equality rules the hours and methods of work. Five hours a day are found ample, and everybody takes his time at every kind of work, the men's work being kept separate from that given to the women. I confess that the work is not performed with as much zeal as one could wish; but think of the old times, when one had to work eight, ten, and even eighteen hours a day, in order to earn a poor and miserable subsistence! What zeal could they have put into their work? How different is this glorious equality in all things from the ancient anomalies and injustices of class and rank, wealth and poverty! Why, formerly, the chief pursuit of man was the pursuit of money. And now there is no money at all; and our wealth lies in our barns and garners.

I must be forgiven if I dwell upon these contrasts. The history which has to be told—how an attempt was actually made to destroy this Eden, and to substitute in its place the old condition of things —fills me with such indignation that I am constrained to speak.

Consider, for one other thing, the former condition of the world. It was filled with diseases. People were not in any way protected. They were allowed to live as they pleased. Consequently, they all committed excesses and all contracted disease. Some drank too much ; some ate too much ; some took no exercise ; some took too little ; some lay in bed too long ; some went to bed too late ; some suffered themselves to fall into violent rages, into remorse, into despair ; some loved inordinately ; thousands worked too hard. All ran after Jack-o'-Lanterns continually ; for, before one there was dangled the hope of promotion ; before another, that of glory ; before another, that of distinction, fame, or praise ; before another, that of wealth ; before another, the chance of retiring to rest and meditate during the brief remainder of his life—miserably short even in its whole length. Then diseases fell upon them, and they died.

We have now prevented all new diseases, though we cannot wholly cure those which have so long existed. Rheumatism, gout, fevers, arise no more, though of gout and other maladies there are hereditary cases. And since there are no longer any old men among us, there are none of the maladies to which old age is liable. No more pain, no more suffering, no more anxiety, no more Death (except by accident) in the world. Yet some of them would return to the old miseries ; and for what?—for what ? You shall hear.

When the Chimes began, the people turned their faces with one consent towards the Public Hall, and a smile of satisfaction spread over all their faces. They were going to Supper—the principal event of the day. At the same moment a Procession issued from the iron gates of the College. First marched our Warder, or Porter, John Lax, bearing a halberd ; next came an Assistant, carrying a cushion, on which were the Keys of Gold, symbolical of the Gate of Life ; then came another, bearing our banner, with the Labarum or symbol of Life ; the Assistants followed, in ancient garb of cap and gown ; then came the twelve Fellows or Physicians of the College, in scarlet gowns and flat fur-lined caps ; after them, I myself—Samuel Grout, M.D., Suffragan—followed. Last, there marched the first Person in the Realm—none other than the Arch Physician Himself, Dr. Henry Linister, in lawn sleeves, a black silk gown and a scarlet hood. Four Bedells closed the Procession.

For, with us, the only deviation from equality absolute is made in the case of the College. We are a Caste apart ; we keep mankind alive and free from pain. This is our work ; this occupies all our thoughts ; we are, therefore, held in honour, and excused the ordinary work which the others must daily perform. And behold the difference between ancient and modern times ! For, formerly, those who were held in honour and had high office in this always sacred HOUSE were aged and white-haired men, who arrived at this distinction but a year or two before they had to die. But we of the Holy College are as stalwart, as strong, and as young as any man in the Hall. And so have we been for hundreds of years ; and so we mean to continue.

In the Public Hall, we take our meals apart in our own Hall ; yet the food is the same for all. Life is the common possession ; it is maintained for all by the same process ; here must be no difference. Let all, therefore, eat and drink alike.

When I consider, I repeat, the universal happiness, I am carried away, first, with a burning indignation that any should be so mad as to mar this happiness. They have failed. But they cost us, as you shall hear, much trouble, and caused the lamentable death of a most zealous and able officer.

Among the last to enter the gates were the girl Christine and her grandfather, who walked slowly, coughing all the way.

' Come, grandad,' she said, as we passed her, ' take my arm. You will be better after your supper. Lean on me.'

There was in her face so remarkable a light that I wonder now that no suspicion or distrust possessed us. I call it light, for I can compare it to nothing else. The easy, comfortable life our people led, and the absence of all exciting work, the decay of reading and the abandonment of art, had left their faces placid to look upon, but dull. They were certainly dull . They moved heavily ; if they lifted their eyes, they wanted the light that flashed from Christine's. It was a childish face, still—full of softness ; no one would ever believe that a creature so slight in form, so gentle to look upon, whose eyes were so soft, whose cheeks were like the untouched bloom of a ripe peach, whose half-parted lips were so rosy, was already harbouring thoughts so abominable and already conceiving an enterprise so wicked.

We do not suspect, in this our new World. As we have no property to defend, no one is a thief ; as everybody has as much of everything as he wants, no one tries to get more ; we fear not Death, and therefore need no religion ; we have no private ambitions to gratify, and no private ends to attain. Therefore, we have long since ceased to be suspicious. Least of all should we have been suspicious of Christine. Why, but a year or two ago she was a little newly-born babe, whom the Holy College crowded to see, as a new thing. And yet—was it possible that one so young should be so corrupt?

'Suffragan,' said the Arch Physician to me at supper, 'I begin to think that your Triumph of Science must be really complete.'

'Why, Physician?'

'Because, day after day, that child leads the old man by the hand, places him in his seat, and ministers, after the old forgotten fashion, to his slightest wants, and no one pays her the slightest heed.'

'Why should they?'

'A child—a beautiful child! A feeble old man! One who ministers to another. Suffragan, the Past is indeed far, far away. But I knew not until now that it was so utterly lost. Childhood and Age and the offices of Love! And these things are wholly unheeded. Grout, you are indeed a great man!'

He spoke in the mocking tone which was usual with him; so that we never knew exactly whether he was in earnest or not. But I think that on this occasion he was in earnest. No one but a very great man—none smaller than Samuel Grout—myself—could have accomplished this miracle upon the minds of the People. They did not minister one to the other. Why should they? Everybody could eat his own ration without any help. Offices of Love? These to pass unheeded? What did the Arch Physician mean?

CHAPTER II.

GROUT, SUFFRAGAN.

IT always pleases me, from my place at the College table, which is raised two feet above the rest, to contemplate the multitude whom it is our duty and our pleasure to keep in contentment and in health. It is a daily joy to watch them flocking, as you have seen them flock, to their meals. The heart glows to think of what we have done. I see the faces of all light up with satisfaction at the prospect of the food; it is the only thing that moves them. Yes; we have reduced life to its simplest form. Here is true happiness. Nothing to hope; nothing to fear—except accident; a little work for the common preservation; a body of wise men always devising measures for the common good; food plentiful and varied;

gardens for repose and recreation, both summer and winter; warmth; shelter; and the entire absence of all emotions. Why, the very faces of the People are growing alike; one face for the men, and another for the women; perhaps, in the far-off future, the face of the man will approach nearer and nearer to that of the woman, and so all will be at last exactly alike, and the individual will exist, indeed, no more. Then there will be from first to last among the whole multitude neither distinction nor difference.

It is a face which fills one with contentment, though it will be many centuries before it approaches completeness. It is a smooth face, there are no lines on it; it is a grave face, the lips seldom smile, and never laugh; the eyes are heavy, and move slowly; there has already been achieved, though the change has been very gradual, the complete banishment of that expression which has been preserved in every one of the ancient portraits, which may be usefully studied for purposes of contrast. Whatever the emotion attempted to be portrayed, and even when the face was supposed to be at rest, there was always behind, visible to the eye, an expression of anxiety or eagerness. Some kind of pain always lies upon those old faces, even upon the youngest. How could it be otherwise? On the morrow they would be dead. They had to crowd into a few days whatever they could grasp of life.

As I sit there and watch our People at dinner, I see with satisfaction that the old pain has gone out of their faces. They have lived so long that they have forgotten Death. They live so easily that they are contented with life: we have reduced existence to the simplest. They eat and drink—it is their only pleasure: they work—it is a necessity for health and existence. But their work takes them no longer than till noontide: they lie in the sun: they sit in the shade: they sleep. If they had once any knowledge, it is now forgotten: their old ambitions, their old desires, all are forgotten. They sleep and eat: they work and rest. To rest and to eat are pleasures which they never desire to end. To live for ever: to eat and drink for ever: this is now their only hope. And this has been accomplished for them by the Holy College. Science has justified herself: this is the outcome of man's long search for generations into the secrets of Nature. We, who have carried on this search, have at length succeeded in stripping humanity of all those things which formerly made existence intolerable to him. He lives, he eats, he sleeps. Perhaps—I know not, but of this we sometimes talk in the College—I say, perhaps —we may succeed in making some kind of artificial food, as we compound the great Arcanum, with simple ingredients and without labour : we may also extend the duration of sleep. We may thus still further simplify existence. Man in the end—as I propose to make and mould the People—will sleep until Nature calls upon him to awake and eat. He will then eat, drink, and sleep again, while the years roll by : he will lie heedless of all : he will be heedless of the seasons, heedless of the centuries. Time will have no meaning for him—a breathing, living, inarticulate mass will be all that is left of the active, eager, chattering Man of the Past.

This may be done in the future, when yonder laboratory, which we call the House of Life, shall yield the secrets of Nature deeper and deeper still. At present we have arrived at this point. The chief pleasure of life is to eat and to drink. We have taught the People so much : of all the tastes which formerly gratified man, this alone remains. We provide them daily with a sufficiency and variety of food : there are so many kinds of food, and the combinations are so endless, that practically the choice of our cooks is unlimited. Good food, varied food, well-cooked food, with drink also varied and pure, and the best that can be made, make our public meals a daily joy. We have learned to make all kinds of wine from the grapes in our hothouses : it is so abundant that every day, all the year round, the People may call for a ration of what they please. We make also beer of every kind, cider, perry, and mead. The gratification of the sense of taste helps to remove the incentive to restlessness or discontent. The minds of most are occupied by no other thought than that of the last feast and the next : if they were to revolt, where would they find their next meal ? At the outset we had, I confess, grave difficulties. There was not in existence any Holy College. We drifted without object or purpose. For a long time the old ambitions remained : the old passions were continued : the old ideas of private property prevailed : the old inequalities were kept up. Presently there arose from those who had no property the demand for a more equal share : the cry was fiercely resisted : then there followed civil war for a space, till both sides were horrified by the bloodshed that followed. Time also was on the side of them who rebelled. I was one, because at the time when the whole nation was admitted to a patricipation in the great Arcanum, I was myself a young man of nineteen, employed as a washer of bottles in Dr. Linister's laboratory, and therefore, according to the ideas of the time, a very humble person. Time helped us in an unexpected way. Property was in the hands of single individuals. Formerly they died and were succeeded by their sons : now the sons grew tired of waiting. How much longer were their fathers, who grew no older, to keep all the wealth to themselves ? Therefore, the civil war having come to an end, with no result except a barren peace, the revolutionary party was presently joined by all but the holders of property, and the State took over to itself the whole wealth—that is to say, the whole land : there is no other wealth. Since that time there has been no private property. For since it was clearly unjust to take away from the father in order to give it to the son, with no limitation as to the time of enjoyment, everything followed the land— great houses, which were allowed to fall into ruin : pictures and works of art, libraries, jewels, which are in Museums : and money, which, however, ceased to be of value as soon as there was nothing which could be bought.

As for me, I was so fortunate as to perceive—Dr. Linister daily impressed it upon me—that of all occupations, that of Physicist would very quickly become the most important. I therefore remained in my employment, worked, read, experimented, and learned all that my master had to teach me. The other professions, indeed, fell into decay more speedily than some of us expected. There could be no more lawyers when there was no more property. Even libel, which was formerly the cause of many actions, became harmless when a man could not be injured ; and, besides, it is impossible to libel any man when there are no longer any rules of conduct except the one duty of work, which is done in the eyes of all and cannot be shirked. And how could Religion survive the removal of Death to some possible remote future ? They tried, it is true, to keep up the pretence of it, and many, especially women, clung to the old forms of faith for I know not how long : with the great mass, religion ceased to have any influence as soon as life was assured. As for Art, Learning, Science—other than that of Physics, Biology, and Medicine—all gradually decayed and died away. And the old foolish pursuit of Literature, which once occupied so many, and was even held in a kind of honour—the writing of histories, poems, dramas, novels, essays on human life— this also decayed and died, because men ceased to be anxious about their past or their future, and were at last contented to dwell in the present.

Another and a most important change, which may be noted, was the gradual decline and disappearance of the passion called Love. This was once a curious and inexplicable yearning—so much is certain—of two young people towards each other, so that they were never content unless they were together, and longed to live apart from the rest of the world, each trying to make the other happier. At least, this is as I read history. For my own part, as I was constantly occupied with Science, I never felt this passion ; or if I did, then I have quite forgotten it. Now, at the outset, people who were in love rejoiced beyond measure that their happiness would last so long. They began, so long as the words had any meaning, to call each other Angels, Goddesses, Divinely Fair, possessed of every perfect gift, with other extravagancies, at the mere recollection of which we should now blush. Presently they grew tired of each other : they no longer lived apart from the rest of the world. They separated : or, if they continued to walk together, it was from force of habit. Some still continue thus to sit side by side. No new connections were formed. People ceased desiring to make others happy, because the State began to provide for everybody's happiness. The whole essence of the old society was a fight. Everybody fought for existence. Everybody trampled on the weaker. If a man loved a woman, he fought for her as well as for himself. Love ? Why, when the true principle of life is recognised—the right of every individual to his or her share —and that an equal share, in everything — and when the con- tinuance of life is assured—what room is there for love ? The very fact of the public life—the constant companionship, the open mingling of women with men, and this for year after year—the same women with the same men—has destroyed the mystery which formerly hung about womanhood, and was in itself the principal cause of love.

It is gone, therefore, and with it the most disturbing element of life. Without love, without ambition, without suffering, without religion, without quarrelling, without private rights, without rank or class, life is calm, gentle, undisturbed. Therefore, they all sit down to supper in peace and contentment, every man's mind intent upon nothing but the bill of fare.

This evening, directed by the observation of the Arch Physician, I turned my eyes upon the girl Christine, who sat beside her grand- father. I observed, first — but the fact inspired me with no suspicion—that she was no longer a child, but a woman grown : and I began to wonder when she would come with the rest for the Arcanum. Most women, when births were common among us, used to come at about five-and-twenty ; that is to say, in the first year or two of full womanhood, before their worse enemies—where there were two women, in the old days, there were two enemies—

could say that they had begun to fall off. If you look round our table, you will see very few women older than twenty-four, and very few men older than thirty. There were many women at this table who might, perhaps, have been called beautiful in the old times ; though now the men had ceased to think of beauty, and the women had ceased to desire admiration. Yet, if regular features, large eyes, small mouths, a great quantity of hair, and a rounded figure are beautiful, then there were many at the table who might have been called beautiful. But the girl Christine— I observed the fact with scientific interest—was so different from the other women, that she seemed another kind of creature.

Her eyes were soft : there is no scientific term to express this softness of youth—one observes it especially in the young of the *cervus* kind. There was also a curious softness on her cheek, as if something would be rubbed away if one touched it. And her voice differed from that of her elder sisters : it was curiously gentle, and full of that quality which may be remarked in the wood-dove when she pairs in spring. They used to call it tenderness ; but, since the thing itself disappeared, the word has naturally fallen out of use.

Now, I might have observed with suspicion, whereas I only remarked it as something strange, that the company among which Christine and the old man sat were curiously stirred and uneasy. They were disturbed out of their habitual tranquillity because the girl was discoursing to them. She was telling them what she had learned about the Past.

'Oh,' I heard her say, 'it was a beautiful time ! Why did they ever suffer it to perish ? Do you mean that you actually remember nothing of it ?'

They looked at each other sheepishly.

'There were soldiers—men were soldiers : they went out to fight, with bands of music and the shouts of the people. There were whole armies of soldiers—thousands of them. They dressed in beautiful glittering clothes. Do you forget that ?'

One of the men murmured, hazily, that there *were* soldiers.

'And there were sailors, who went upon the sea in great ships. Jack Carera '—she turned to one of them—'you are a sailor, too. You ought to remember.'

'I remember the sailors very well indeed,' said this young man readily.

I always had my doubts about the wisdom of admitting our sailors among the People. We have a few ships for the carriage

of those things which as yet we have not succeeded in growing
for ourselves : these are manned by a few hundred sailors who
long ago volunteered, and have gone on ever since. They are a
brave race, ready to face the most terrible dangers of tempest and
shipwreck ; but they are also a dangerous, restless, talkative,
questioning tribe. They have, in fact, preserved almost as much
independence as the College itself. They are now confined to their
own port of Sheerness.

Then the girl began to tell some pestilent story of love and
shipwreck and rescue : and at hearing it, some of them looked
puzzled and some pained ; but the sailor listened with all his ears.

'Where did you get that from, Christine ?'

'Where I get everything—from the old Library. Come and
read it in the book, Jack.'

'I am not much hand at reading. But some day, perhaps after
the next voyage, Christine.'

The girl poured out a glass of claret for the old man. Then she
went on telling them stories ; but most of her neighbours seemed
neither to hear nor to comprehend. Only the sailor-man listened
and nodded. Then she laughed out loud.

At this sound, so strange, so unexpected, everybody within hearing jumped. Her table was in the Hall next to our own, so that
we heard the laugh quite plainly.

The Arch Physician looked round approvingly.

'How many years since we heard a good, honest *young* laugh,
Suffragan ? Give us more children, and soften our hearts for us.
But, no : the heart you want is the hard, crusted, selfish heart.
See ! No one asks why she laughed. They are all eating again
now, just as if nothing had happened. Happy, enviable People !'

Presently he turned to me and remarked, in his lofty manner, as
if he was above all the world :

'You cannot explain, Suffragan, why, at an unexpected touch, a
sound, a voice, a trifle, the memory may be suddenly awakened to
things long, long past by and forgotten. Do you know what that
laugh caused me to remember ? I cannot explain why, nor can
you. It recalled the evening of the Great Discovery—not the
Discovery itself, but quite another thing. I went there more to
meet a girl than to hear what the German had to say. As to that,
I expected very little. To meet that girl seemed of far more importance. I meant to make love to her—love, Suffragan—a thing
which you can never understand—real, genuine love ! I meant to
marry her. . Well, I did meet her ; and I arranged for a con-

venient place where we could meet again after the Lecture. Then came the Discovery; and I was carried away, body and soul, and forgot the girl and love and everything in the stupefaction of this most wonderful Discovery, of which we have made, between us, such admirable use.'

You never knew whether the Arch Physician was in earnest or not. Truly, we had made a most beautiful use of the Discovery; but it was not in the way that Dr. Linister would have chosen.

'All this remembered just because a girl laughed! Suffragan, Science cannot explain all.'

I shall never pretend to deny that Dr. Linister's powers as a physicist were of the first order, nor that his Discoveries warranted his election to the Headship of the College. Yet, something was due, perhaps, to his tall and commanding figure, and to the look of authority which reigned naturally on his face, and to the way in which he always stepped into the first rank. He was always the Chief, long before the College of Physicians assumed the whole authority, in everything that he joined. He opposed the extinction of property, and would have had everybody win what he could, and keep it as long as he would: he opposed the Massacre of the Old: he was opposed, in short, to the majority of the College. Yet he was our Chief. His voice was clear, and what he said always produced its effect, though it did not upset my solid majority, or thwart the Grand Advance of the Triumph of Science. As for me, my position has been won by sheer work and merit. My figure is not commanding; I am short-sighted and dark-visaged: my voice is rough; and as for manners, I have nothing to do with them. But in Science there is but one second to Linister—and that is Grout.

When the supper came to an end, we rose and marched back to the College in the same state and order with which we had arrived. As for the people, some of them went out into the Garden; some remained in the Hall. It was then nine o'clock, and twilight. Some went straight to their own rooms, where they would smoke tobacco—an old habit allowed by the College on account of its soothing and sedative influence—before going to bed. By ten o'clock everybody would be in bed and asleep. What more beautiful proof of the advance of Science than the fact that the whole of the twenty-four thousand people who formed the population of Canterbury dropped off to sleep the moment they laid their heads upon the pillow? This it is to have learned the proper quantities and kinds of food: the proper amount of bodily exercise and work : and the complete subjugation of all the ancient forces of unrest and disquiet. To be sure, we were all, with one or two exceptions, in the very prime and flower of early manhood and womanhood. It would be hard, indeed, if a young man of thirty should not sleep well.

I was presently joined in the garden of the College by the Arch Physician.

'Grout,' he said, 'let us sit and talk. My mind is disturbed. It is always disturbed when the memory of the Past is forced upon me.'

'The Evil Past,' I said.

'If you please—the Evil Past. The question is, whether it was not infinitely more tolerable for mankind than the Evil Present ?'

We argued out the point. But it was one on which we could never agree. For he remained saturated with the old ideas of private property and individualism. He maintained that there are no Rights of Man at all, except his Right to what he can get and what he can keep. He even went so far as to say that the true use of the Great Discovery should have been to cause the incompetent, the idle, the hereditarily corrupt, and the vicious, to die painlessly.

'As to those who were left,' he said, 'I would have taught them the selfishness of staying too long. When they had taken time for work and play and society and love, they should have been exhorted to go away of their own accord, and to make room for their children. Then we should have had always the due succession of father and son, mother and daughter : always age and manhood and childhood : and always the world advancing by the efforts of those who would have time to work for an appreciable period. Instead, we have——'—he waved his hand.

I was going to reply, when suddenly a voice, light, clear, and sweet, broke upon our astonished ears. 'Twas the voice of a woman, and she was singing. At first I hardly listened, because I knew that it could be none other than the child Christine, whom, indeed, I had often heard singing. It is natural, I believe, for children to sing. But the Arch Physician listened, first with wonder, and then with every sign of amazement. How could he be concerned by the voice of a child singing silly verses ? Then I heard the last lines of her song, which she sang, I admit, with great vigour :

> 'Oh ! Love is worth the whole broad earth :
> Oh ! Love is worth the whole broad earth :
> Give that, you give us all !'

'Grout!' cried the Arch Physician in tones of the deepest agitation, 'I choke—I am stifled. Listen! They are words that I wrote—I myself wrote—with my own hand—long, long ago in the Past. I wrote them for a girl—the girl I told you of at dinner. I loved her. I thought never again to feel as I felt then. Yet, the memory of that feeling has come back to me. Is it possible? Can some things never die? Can we administer no drug that will destroy memory? For the earth reeled beneath my feet again, and my senses reeled, and I would once more—yes, I would once more have given all the world—yes, life—even life—only to call that woman mine for a year—a month—a day—an hour!'

The Arch Physician made this astonishing confession in a broken and agitated voice. Then he rushed away, and left me alone in the summer-house.

The singer could certainly have been none other than the girl Christine. How should she get hold of Dr. Linister's love-song? Strange! She had disturbed our peace at supper by laughing, and she had agitated the Arch Physician himself to such a degree as I should have believed impossible by singing a foolish old song. When I went to bed there came into my mind some of the old idle talk about witches, and I even dreamed that we were burning a witch who was filling our minds with disturbing thoughts.

CHAPTER III.

CHRISTINE AT HOME.

WHEN the girl Christine walked through the loitering crowd outside the Hall, some of the people looked after her with wondering eyes.

'Strange!' said a woman. 'She laughed! She laughed!'

'Ay,' said another, 'we have forgotten how to laugh. But we used to laugh, before——'—she broke off with a sigh.

'And she sings,' said a third; 'I have heard her sing like a lark in the Museum.'

'Once,' said the first woman, 'we used to sing as well as laugh. I remember, we used to sing. She makes us remember the old days.'

'The bad old days'—it was one of the Assistant Physicians who admonished her—'the times when nothing was certain, not even life, from day to day. It should bring you increased happiness to think sometimes of those old times.'

The first woman who had spoken was one whom men would have called beautiful in those old times, when their heads were turned by such a thing as a woman's face. She was pale of cheek and had black eyes, which, in those days of passion and jealousy, might have flashed like lightning. Now they were dull. She was shapely of limb and figure too, with an ample cheek and a full mouth. Formerly, in the days of love and rage, those limbs would have been lithe and active ; now they were heavy and slow. Heaviness of movement and of eyes sensibly grows upon our people. I welcome every indication of advance towards the Perfect Type of Humanity which will do nothing but lie down, breathe, eat, and sleep.

'Yes,' she replied, with a deep sigh. ' Nothing was certain. The bad old times when people died. But there was love, and we danced and sang and laughed.' She sighed again and walked away alone, slowly, hanging her head.

The girl passed through them, leading the old man by the hand.

I know very well, now, that we ought to have been suspicious. What meant the gleam and sparkle of her eyes, when all other eyes were dull ? What meant the parting of her lips, and the smile which always lay upon them, when no one else smiled at all ? Why did she carry her head erect, when the rest walked with hanging heads ? Why, again, did she sing, when no one else sang ? Why did she move as if her limbs were on springs, when all the rest went slowly and heavily ? These signs meant mischief. I took them for the natural accompaniments of youth. They meant more than youth : they meant dangerous curiosity : they meant— presently—Purpose. How should one of the People dare to have a Purpose unknown to the Sacred College ? You shall hear.

All that followed was, in fact, due to our own blindness. We should long before have shut up every avenue which might lead the curious to the study of the Past : we should have closed the Museum and the Library altogether. We did not, because we lived in the supposition that the more the old times were investigated the more the people would be satisfied with the Present. When, indeed, one looks at the pictures of battle, murder, cruelty, and all kinds of passion ; when one reads the old books, full of foolishness which can only be excused on the plea of a life too short to have a right comprehension of anything, it is amazing that the scene does not strike the observer with a kind of horror. When, which is seldom, I carry my own memory back to the old times and see myself before I went to the Laboratory, boy-of-all-work to a Brewery, ordered here and there, working all day long with no other prospect than to be a servant for a short span of life and then to die ; when I remember the people among whom I lived, poor, starving, dependent from day to day on the chance of work, or, at best, from week to week ; when I think of the misery from which these poor people have been rescued, I cannot find within me a spark of sympathy for the misguided wretches who voluntarily exchanged their calm and happy Present for the tumult and anxiety of the Past. However, we are not all reasonable, as you shall hear.

It was already twilight outside, and in the Museum there was only light enough to see that a few persons were assembled in the Great Hall. Christine placed her grandfather in a high-backed wooden chair, in which he spent most of his time, clutching at the arms and fighting with his asthma. Then she turned up the electric light. It showed a large, rather lofty room, oblong in shape : old arms were arranged round the walls : great glass cases stood about, filled with a collection of all kinds of things preserved from the old times. There were illustrations of their arts —now entirely useless : such as the jewels they wore, set in bracelets and necklaces : their gloves, fans, rings, umbrellas, pictures, and statuary. Then there were cases filled with the old implements of writing—paper, inkstands, pens, and so forth—the people have long since left off writing : there were boxes full of coins with which they bought things, and for which they sold their freedom : there were things with which they played games—many of them dangerous ones—and whiled away the tedium of their short lives : there were models of the ships in which they went to sea ; also models of all kinds of engines and machines which slaves—they were nearly all slaves—made for the purpose of getting more money for their masters : there were also crowns, coronets and mitres, which formerly belonged to people who possessed what they called rank : there were the praying books which were formerly used every day in great buildings like the House of Life : there were specimens of legal documents on parchment, by the drawing up of which, when law existed, a great many people procured a contemptible existence : there were also models, with figures of the people in them, of Parliament Houses, Churches, and Courts of Justice : there were life-size models of soldiers in uniform, when men were of understanding so contemptible as to be tempted to risk life—even life—in exchange for a gold-laced coat !

But then our ancestors were indescribably foolish. There were musical instruments of all kinds—I have always been glad that music fell so soon into disuse. It is impossible to cultivate contentment while music is practised. Besides the ordinary weapons —sword, pike, and javelin—there were all kinds of horrible inventions, such as vast cannons, torpedo boats, dynamite shells, and so forth, for the destruction of towns, ships, and armour. It is a great and splendid Collection, but it ought to have been long, long before transferred to the custody of the Holy College.

The girl looked inquiringly at her visitors, counting them all. There were ten—namely, five men and five women. Like all the people, they were young—the men about thirty, the women about twenty-two or twenty-three. The men were dressed in their blue flannels, with a flat cap of the same material : the women in their gray beige, short frock, the flat gray cap under which their hair was gathered, gray stockings and heavy shoes. The dress was, in fact, invented by myself for both sexes : it has many advantages. First, there is always plenty of the stuff to be had : next, both flannel and beige are soft, warm, and healthy textures : with such a dress there is no possibility of distinction or of superiority : and, lastly, with such a dress the women have lost all power of setting forth their attractions so as to charm the men with new fashions, crafty subtleties of dress, provocations of the troublesome passion of love in the shape of jewels, ribbons, gloves, and the like. No one wears gloves : all the women's hands are hard ; and although they are still young and their faces are unchanged, their eyes are dull and hard. I am pleased to think that there is no more foolishness of love among us.

The people were standing or sitting about, not together, but separately—each by himself or herself. This tendency to solitary habits is a most healthy indication of the advance of humanity. Self-preservation is the first Law—separate and solitary existence is the last condition—of mankind. They were silent and regardless of each other. Their attitudes showed the listlessness of their minds.

'I am glad you are here,' said Christine. 'You promised you would not fail me. And yet, though you promised, I feared that at the last moment you might change your minds. I was afraid that you would rather not be disturbed in the even current of your thoughts.'

'Why disturb our minds ?' asked one—a woman. 'We were at peace before you began to talk of the Past. We had almost for-

gotten it. And it is so long ago '—her voice sank to a murmur—
'so long ago.'

They all echoed :

'It is so long ago—so long ago !'

'Oh !' cried the girl, ' you call this to be at peace ! Why, if you
were so many stones in the garden you could not be more truly at
peace. To work : to rest : to eat : to sleep :—you will call that
Life ! And yet you can remember—if you please—the time when
you were full of activity and hope.'

' If to remember is to regret, why should we invite the pain of
regret ? We cannot have the old life except with the old conditions : the short life and the——'

' If I could remember—if I had ever belonged to the Past,' the
girl interrupted quickly—'oh ! I would remember every moment
—I would live every day of the old life over and over again. But
I can do nothing—nothing—but read of the splendid Past and
look forward to such a future as your own. Alas ! why was I born
at all, since I was born into such a world as this ? Why was I
called into existence when all the things of which I read every
day have passed away ? And what remains in their place ?'

' We have Life,' said one of the men, but not confidently.

'Life ! Yes—and what a life ! Oh, what a life ! Well, we
waste time. Listen now—and if you can, for once forget the present and recall the past. Do not stay to think how great a gulf
lies between : do not count the years—indeed, you cannot.
Whether they are one hundred or five hundred they do not know,
even at the Holy College itself. I am sure it will make you
happier—'twill console and comfort you—in this our life of
desperate monotony, only to remember—to recall—how you used
to live.'

They answered with a look of blank bewilderment.

' It is so long ago—so long ago,' said one of them again.

' Look around you. Here are all the things that used to be your
own. Let them help you to remember. Here are the arms that
the men carried when they went out to fight ; here are the jewels
that the women wore. Think of your dress in the days when you
were allowed to dress, and we did not all wear frocks of gray beige
as if all women were exactly alike. Will that not help ?'

They looked about them helplessly. No ; they did not yet
remember ; their dull eyes were filled with a kind of anxious
wonder, as might be seen in one rudely awakened out of sleep.
They looked at the things in the great room, but that seemed to

bring nothing back to their minds. The Present was round them like a net which they could neither cut through nor see through; it was a veil around them through which they could not pass. It had been so long with them; it was so unchanging; for so long they had had nothing to expect; for so long, therefore, they had not cared to look back. The Holy College had produced, in fact, what it had proposed and designed. The minds of the people had become quiescent. And to think that so beautiful a state of things should be destroyed by a girl—the only child in the Community!

'Will it help,' said the girl, 'if we turn down the light a little? So. Now we are almost in darkness, but for the moonlight through the window. In the old times, when you were children, I have read that you loved to sit together and to tell stories. Let us tell each other stories.'

Nobody replied. But the young man called Jack took Christine's hand and held it.

'Let us try,' said the girl again. 'I will tell you a story. Long ago there were people called gentlefolk. Grandad here was a gentleman. I have read about them in the old books. I wonder if any of you remember those people. They were exempt from work; the lower sort worked for them; they led a life of ease; they made their own work for themselves. Some of the men fought for their country—it was in the old time, you know, when men still fought; some worked for their country; some worked for the welfare of those who worked for bread; some only amused themselves, some were profligates, and did wicked things. . . .'

She paused; no one responded.

'The women had no work to do at all. They only occupied themselves in making everybody happy; they were treated with the greatest respect; they were not allowed to do anything at all that could be done for them; they played and sang; they painted and embroidered; they knew foreign languages; they constantly inspired the men to do great things, even if they should be killed.'

Here all shuddered and trembled. Christine made haste to change the subject.

'They wore beautiful dresses—think—dresses of silk and satin, embroidered with gold, trimmed with lace; they had necklaces, bracelets, and rings; their hands were white, and they wore long gloves to their elbows; they dressed their hair as they pleased. Some wore it long, like this.' She pulled off her flat cap, and threw back her long tresses, and quickly turned up the light. She was transformed! The women started and gasped. 'Take off your

caps!' she ordered.   They obeyed, and at sight of the flowing locks
that fell upon their shoulders, curling, rippling, flowing, their eyes
brightened, but only for a moment.

'Yes,' said the girl, 'they wore their beautiful hair as they
pleased. Oh!'—she gathered in her hands the flowing tresses of
one—'you have such long and beautiful hair! It is a shame—it is
a shame to hide it. Think of the lovely dresses to match this
beauty of the hair!'

'Oh!' cried the women, 'we remember the dresses. We
remember them now. Why make us remember them? It is so
long ago—so long ago—and we can never wear them any more.'

'Nay; but you have the same beauty,' said Christine. 'That at
least remains; you have preserved your youth and your beauty.'

'Of what good are our faces to us,' said another woman, 'with
such a dress as this? Men no longer look upon our beauty.'

'Let us be,' said the woman who had spoken first. 'There can
be no change for us. Why disturb our minds? The Present is
horrible. But we have ceased to care much for anything; we do
our day's work every day—all the same hours of work; we wear
the same dress—to every woman the same dress; we eat and drink
the same food—to every one the same; we are happy because we
have got all we can get, and we expect no more: we never talk—
why should we talk? When you laughed to-day it was like an
earthquake.' Her words were strong, but her manner of speech
was a monotone. This way of speaking grows upon us; it is the
easiest; I watch the indications with interest. From rapid talk to
slow talk; from animated talk to monotony; the next step will be
to silence absolute. 'There is no change for us,' she repeated,
'neither in summer nor in winter. We have preserved our youth,
but we have lost all the things which the youthful used to desire;
we thought to preserve our beauty. What is the good of beauty
with such a dress and such a life? Why should we make ourselves
miserable in remembering any of the things we used to desire?'

'Oh!' cried the girl, clasping her hands. 'To me there is no
pleasure possible but in learning all about the past. I read the old
books; I look at the old pictures; I play the old music; I sing the
old songs. But it is not enough. I know how you were dressed—
not all alike in gray beige frocks, but in lovely silk and beautiful
embroidered stuffs. I will show you presently how you dressed.
I know how you danced and played games and acted most beautiful
plays, and I have read stories about you; I know that you were
always dissatisfied, and wanting something or other. The stories

are full of discontent; nobody ever sits down satisfied except one pair. There is always one pair, and they fall in Love—in Love,' she repeated. 'What is that, I wonder?' Then she went on again: 'They only want one thing then, and the story-books are all about how they got it after wonderful adventures. There are no adventures now. The books tell us all this. But I want more. I want to know more; I want to see the old stories with my own eyes; I want to see you in your old dresses, talking in your own old way. The books cannot tell me how you talked and how you looked. I am sure it was not as you talk now—because you never talk.'

'There is no reason why we should talk. All the old desires have ceased to be. We no longer want anything or expect anything.'

'Come. I shall do my best to bring the Past back to you. First, I have learned who you were. That is why I have called you together. In the old times you all belonged to gentlefolk.'

This announcement produced no effect at all. They listened with lack-lustre looks. They had entirely forgotten that there were ever such distinctions as gentle and simple.

'You will remember presently,' said Christine, not discouraged. 'I have found out in the ancient Rolls your names and your families.'

'Names and families,' said one of the men, 'are gone long ago. Christine, what is the good of reviving the memory of things that can never be restored?'

But the man named Jack Carera, the sailor of whom I have already spoken, stepped forward. I have said that the sailors were a dangerous class, on account of their independence and their good meaning.

'Tell us,' he said, 'about our families. Why I, for one, have never forgotten that I was once a gentleman. It is hard to tell now, because they have made us all alike; but for many, many years—I know not how many—we who had been gentlemen consorted together.'

'You shall again,' said Christine, 'if you please. Listen, then. First, my grandfather. He was called Sir Arthur Farrance, and he was called a Baronet. To be a Baronet was, in those days, something greatly desired by many people. A man, in the old books, was said to enjoy the title of Baronet. But I know not why one man was so raised above another.'

'Heugh! Heugh! Heugh!' coughed the old man. 'I remember that. Why, what is there to remember except the old times? I was a Baronet—the fifth Baronet. My country place was in Sussex, and my town address was White's and the Travellers'.'

'Yes,' Christine nodded. 'My grandfather's memory is tenacious ; he forgets nothing of the things that happened when he was young. I have learned a great deal from him. He seems to have known all your grandmothers, for instance, and speaks of them as if he had loved them all.'

'I did—I did,' said the old man. 'I loved them every one.'

The girl turned to the women before her—the dull-eyed, heavy-headed women, all in the gray dresses exactly alike ; but their gray flat caps had been thrown off, and they looked disturbed, moved out of the common languor.

'Now I will tell you who you were formerly. You '—she pointed to the nearest—'were the Lady Mildred Carera, only daughter of the Earl of Thordisá. Your father and mother survived the Discovery, but were killed in the Great Massacre Year, when nearly all the old were put to death. You were a great beauty in your time, and when the Discovery was announced you were in your second season. People wondered who would win you. But those who pretended to know talked of a young scientific Professor.'

The woman heard as if she was trying to understand a foreign language. This was, in fact, a language without meaning to her. As yet she caught nothing.

'You,' said Christine, turning to the next, 'were Dorothy Oliphant ; you were also young, beautiful, and an heiress ; you, like Lady Mildred, had all the men at your feet. I don't know what that means, but the books say so. Then the Discovery came, and love-making, whatever that was, seems to have gone out of fashion.'

The second woman heard this information with lack-lustre eyes. What did it matter ?

'You,' Christine turned to a third and to a fourth and fifth— 'you were Rosie Lorrayne ; you, Adela Dupré ; you, Susie Campbell. You were all in Society ; you were all young and beautiful and happy. Now for the men.' She turned to them. The sailor, named Jack, gazed upon her with eyes of admiration. The other men, startled at first by the apparition of the tresses, had relapsed into listlessness. They hardly looked up as she addressed them.

First she pointed to the sailor.

'Your name——'

'I remember my name,' he said. 'I have not forgotten so much as our friends. Sailors talk more with each other, and remember. I am named John Carera, and I was formerly first cousin to Lady Mildred. Cousin'—he held out his hand—'have you forgotten your cousin? We used to play together in the old times. You promised to marry me when you should grow up.'

Lady Mildred gave him her hand.

'It is so long ago—so long ago,' she murmured; but her eyes were troubled. She had begun to remember the things put away and forgotten for so long.

'You,' Christine turned to another, 'were Geoffrey Heron. You were Captain in a Cavalry Regiment. You will remember that presently, and a great deal more. You,' she turned to another, 'were Laurence De Heyn, and you were a young lawyer, intending to be a Judge. You will remember that in time. You,' she turned to another, 'were Jack Culliford; and you were a Private Secretary, intending to go into Parliament, and to rise perhaps to be Prime Minister. And you,' she turned to the last, 'were Arnold Buckland, already a Poet of Society. You will all remember these things before long. Lastly, you all belonged to the people who were born rich, and never used to have any care or anxiety about their daily bread. Nor did you ever do any work, unless you chose.'

'It is so long ago,' said Lady Mildred—her face was brighter now—'that we have forgotten even that there ever were gentle-folks.'

'It is not strange,' said Christine, 'that you should have forgotten it. Why should you remember anything? We are only a herd, one with another: one not greater, and one not less, than another. Now that you know your names again and remember clearly—because I have told you'—she repeated the information for fear they should again forget—'who and what you were, each of you—you will go on to remember more.'

'Oh! what good? What good?' asked Lady Mildred.

'Because it will rouse you from your lethargy,' said the girl im-petuously. 'Oh! you sit in silence day after day: you walk alone: you ought to be together as you used to be, talking, playing. See! I have read the books: your lives were full of excitement. It makes my heart beat only to read how the men went out to fight, daring everything, for the sake of the women they loved.'

'The men love us no longer,' said Lady Mildred.

'If the brave men fell——'

But here all faces, except the sailor's, turned pale, and they shuddered. Christine did not finish the sentence. She, too, shuddered.

In the old times I remember how, being then errand-boy in the Brewery, I used to listen, in the Whitechapel Road, to the men who, every Sunday morning and evening, used to tell us that religion was a mockery and a snare, invented by the so-called priests for their own selfish ends, so that they might be kept in sloth and at their ease. There was no need now for these orators. The old religion was clean dead and forgotten. When men ceased to expect Death, what need was there to keep up any interest in the future world, if there should be any? But the bare mention of the dreadful thing is still enough to make all cheeks turn pale. Every year, the farther off Death recedes, the more terrible he looks. Therefore they all shuddered.

Among the musical instruments in the Museum there stands one, a square wooden box on legs, with wires inside it. There are many other musical instruments, the use of all (as I thought) forgotten. Very soon after the Great Discovery people ceased to care for music. For my own part, I have never been able to understand how the touching of chords and the striking of hammers on wires can produce any effect at all upon the mind except that of irritation. We preserve trumpets for the processions of the College because mere noise awes people, and because trumpets make more noise with less trouble than the human voice. But with music, such as it used to be, we have now nothing to do at all. I have been told that people were formerly greatly moved by music, so that every kind of emotion was produced in their minds merely by listening to a man or woman playing some instrument. It must have been so, because Christine, merely by playing the old music to the company, was able to bring back their minds to the long-forgotten Past. But it must be remembered that she had disturbed their minds first.

She sat down, then, before this box, and she began to play upon it, watching the people meanwhile. She played the music of their own time—indeed, there has been none written since. It was a kind of witchery. First the sailor named Jack sprang to his feet and began to walk up and down the room with wild gestures and strange looks. Then the rest, one by one, grew restless : they looked about them : they left their chairs and began to look at each other, and at the things in the cases: the Past was coming slowly into sight. I have heard how men at sea perceive an island far away, but like a cloud on the horizon : how the cloud grows larger and assumes outline: how this grows clearer and larger still, until before the ship reaches the harbour and drops her anchor, the cliffs and the woods, and even the single trees on the hill-sides, are clearly visible.

Thus the listeners gradually began to see the Past again. Now, to feel these old times again, one must go back to them and become once more part of them. It is possible, because we are still of the age when we left them. Therefore, this little company, who had left the old time when they were still young, began to look again as they had then looked. Their eyes brightened, their cheeks flushed: their limbs became elastic: their heads were thrown back: the faces of the women grew soft, and those of the men strong: on all alike there fell once more the look of restless expectancy and of unsatisfied yearning which belonged to all ages in the old time.

Presently they began to murmur, I know not what: and then to whisper to each other with gentle sighs. Then the girls—they were really girls again—caught each other by the hand, and panted and sighed again. And at last they fell upon each other's necks and kissed. As for the men, they now stood erect and firm, but for the most part they gazed upon the girls with wonder and admiration unspeakable. So great was the power of witchery possessed by this insignificant girl.

Christine looked on and laughed gently. Then she suddenly changed her music, and began to play a March, loud and triumphant. And as she played she spoke:

'When the brave soldiers came home from battle and from victory, it was right that the people should all go forth to meet them. The music played for them: the children strewed roses under their feet: the bells were set ringing: the crowds cheered them: the women wept and laughed at the same time, and waved them welcome. Nothing could be too good for the men who fought for their country. Listen! I found the song of the Victors' Return in an old book. I wonder if you remember it. I think it is a very simple little thing.'

Then she sang. She had a strong, clear voice—they had heard her singing before—no one sang in the whole City except this child, and already it had been observed that her singing made men restless. I do not deny the fulness and richness of her voice ; but the words she sang—Dr. Linister's words, they were—are mere foolishness :

> 'With flying flag, with beat of drum,
>   Oh ! brave and gallant show !
> In rags and tatters home they come—
>   We love them better, so.

With sun-burnt cheeks and wounds and scars :—
  Yet still their swords are bright :
Oh ! welcome, welcome from the wars,
  Brave lads who fought the fight !

'The girls they laugh, the girls they cry,
  "What shall their guerdon be ?—
Alas ! that some must fall and die !—
  Bring forth our gauds to see.
'Twere all too slight, give what we might."
  Up spoke a soldier tall,
"Oh ! Love is worth the whole broad earth :
Oh ! Love is worth the whole broad earth :
  Give that, you give us all !"'

'Do you remember the song ?' Christine asked.

They shook their heads. Yet it seemed familiar. They remembered some such songs.

'Geoffrey Heron,' said the girl, turning to one of the men, 'you were Captain Heron in the old days. You remember that you were in the army.'

'Was I ?' He started. 'No : yes. I remember : I was Captain Heron. We rode out of Portsmouth Dockyard Gates when we came home—all that were left of us. The women were waiting on the Hard outside, and they laughed and cried, and caught our hands, and ran beside the horses. Our ranks were thin, for we had been pretty well knocked about. I remember now. Yes—yes, I was— I was Captain Heron.'

'Go into that room. You will find your old uniform. Take off the blue flannels, and show us how you looked when you were in uniform.'

As if it was nothing at all unusual, the man rose and obeyed. It was observed that he now carried himself differently. He stood erect, with shoulders squared, head up, and limbs straight. They all obeyed whatever this girl ordered them to do.

Christine began to play again. She played another March, but always loud and triumphant.

When the soldier came back, he was dressed in the uniform which he had worn in the time of the Great Discovery, when they left off taking account of time.

'Oh !' cried Christine, springing to her feet. 'See ! See ! Here is a soldier ! Here is a man who has fought !'

He stood before them dressed in a scarlet tunic and a white helmet : a red sash hung across him, and on his breast were medals. At sight of him, the girl called Dorothy Oliphant changed countenance: all caught their breath. The aspect of the man carried them, indeed, back to the old, old time.

'Welcome home, Captain Heron,' said Christine. 'We have followed your campaign day by day.'

'We are home again,' the soldier replied gravely. 'Unfortunately, we have left a good many of our regiment behind.'

'Behind ? You mean—they—are—dead.' Christine shuddered. The others shuddered. Even Captain Heron himself for a moment turned pale. But he was again in the Past, and the honour of his regiment was in his hands.

'You have fought with other men,' said Christine. 'Let me look in your face. Yes—it is changed. You have the look of the fighting men in the old pictures. You look as if you mean to have something, whatever it is, whether other men want it or not. Oh ! you have fought with men. It is wonderful! Perhaps you have even killed men. Were you dreadfully afraid ?'

Captain Heron started and flushed.

'Afraid ?' he asked. 'Afraid ?'

'Oh !' Christine clapped her hands. 'I wanted to see that look. It is the look of a man in sudden wrath. Forgive me ! It is terrible to see a man thus moved. No, Captain Heron, no ! I understand. An officer in your regiment could be afraid of nothing.'

She sat down, still looking at him.

'I have seen a soldier,' she said. Then she sprang to her feet. 'Now,' she cried, 'it is our turn. Come with me, you ladies, and you—gentlemen—go into that room. For one night we will put on the dresses you used to wear. Come !'

They obeyed. There was nothing that they would not have done, so completely had she bewitched them. How long since they had been addressed as ladies and gentlemen !

'Come,' she said, in a room whither she led the women, 'look about, and choose what you please. But we must make haste.'

There was a great pile of dainty dresses laid out for them to choose—dresses in silk and all kinds of delicate stuffs, with embroidery, lace, ribbons, jewels, chains, rings, bracelets, gloves, fans, shoes—everything that the folly of the past time required to make rich women seem as if they were not the same as their poorer sisters.

They turned over the dresses, and cried out with admiration. Then they hastened to tear off their ugly gray frocks, and began to dress.

But the girl called Dorothy Oliphant sank into a chair.

' Oh ! he has forgotten me ! he has forgotten me ! Who am I that he should remember me after all these years ?'

'Why,' said Christine, 'how should he remember ? What matters that you have the same face ? Think of your dull look and your heavy eyes : think of the dowdy dress and the ugly cap. Wait till you have put on a pretty frock and have dressed your hair : here is a chain of pearls which will look pretty in your hair ; here is a sweet coloured silk. I am sure it will fit you. Oh ! it is a shame—it is a shame that we have to dress so. Never mind. Now I have found out the old dresses, we will have many evenings together. We will go back to the Past. He will remember you, Dorothy dear. Oh ! how could you give them up ? How *could* you give up your lovely dresses ?'

' We were made to give them up because there were not enough beautiful dresses to go round. They said that no woman must be dressed better than another. So they invented—it was Dr. Grout, the Suffragan, who did it— the gray dress for the women and the blue flannel for the men. And I had almost forgotten that there were such things. Christine, my head is swimming. My heart is beating. I have not felt my heart beating for I know not how long. Oh ! will Geoffrey remember me when I am dressed ?'

'Quick ! Of course he will. Let me dress you. Oh ! I often come here in the daytime and dress up, and pretend that it is the Past again. You shall come with me. But I want to hear you talk as you used to talk, and to see you dance as you used to dance. Then I shall understand it all.'

When they returned, the men were waiting for them. Their blue flannels were exchanged for black cloth clothes, which it had been the custom of those who called themselves gentlemen to wear in the evening. In ancient times this was their absurd custom, kept up in order to mark the difference between a gentleman and one of the lower class. If you had no dress-coat, you were not a gentleman. How could men ever tolerate, for a single day, the existence of such a social difference ? As for me, in the part of London where I lived, called Whitechapel, there were no dress-coats. The change, however, seemed to have transformed them. Their · faces had an eager look, as if they wanted something. Of course, in the old times everybody always wanted something : you can see it in the pictures ; the faces are never at rest ; in the portraits, the eyes are always seeking for something ; nowhere is there visible the least sign of contentment. These unfortunate men had acquired, with their old clothes, something of the old restlessness.

Christine laughed aloud and clapped her hands.

The women did not laugh. They saluted the men, who bowed with a certain coldness. The manners of the Past were coming back to them swiftly, but the old ease was not recovered for the first quarter of an hour. Then Captain Heron, who had changed his uniform for civilian dress, suddenly flushed and stepped forward, whispering :

'Dorothy ! you have forgotten me ?'

Dorothy smiled softly, and gave him her hand with a quick sigh. No, she had not forgotten him.

'Dance !' said Christine. 'I want to see you dance. I will play for you.'

She played a piece of music called a Waltz. When this kind of music used to be played—I mean in the houses of (so-called) ladies, not those of the People—the young men and women caught each other round the waist and twirled round. They had many foolish customs, but none more foolish, I should suppose, than this. I have never seen the thing done, because all this foolishness was forgotten as soon as we settled down to the enjoyment of the Great Discovery. When, therefore, Christine began this music, they looked at each other for a few moments, and then, inspired by memory, they fell into each other's arms and began their dance.

She played for them for a quarter of an hour. While the rest danced, the young man Jack stood beside the piano, as if he was chained to the spot. She had bewitched them all, but none so much as this man. He therefore gazed upon the girl with an admiration which certainly belonged to the old time. Indeed, I have never been able to understand how the Past could be so suddenly assumed. To admire—actually to admire—a woman, knowing all the time—it is impossible to conceal the fact—-that she is your inferior, that she is inferior in strength and intellect ! Well, I have already called them unfortunate men : I can say no more. How can people admire things below themselves ? When she had played for a quarter of an hour or so, this young man called upon her to stop. The dancers stopped too, panting, their eyes full of light, their cheeks flushed and their lips parted.

'Oh !' Dorothy sighed. 'I never thought to feel such happiness again. I could dance on for ever.'

'With me ?' murmured Geoffrey. 'I was praying that the last round might never stop. With me ?'

' With you,' she whispered.

'Come !' cried the young man Jack. 'It is too bad. Christine must dance. Play for us, Cousin Mildred, and I will give her a lesson.'

Mildred laughed. Then she started at the unwonted sound. The others laughed to hear it, and the walls of the Museum echoed with the laughter of girls. The old man sat up in his chair and looked around.

'I thought I was at Philippe's, in Paris,' he said. 'I thought we were having a supper after the theatre. There was Ninette, and there was Madeleine—and—and——'

He looked about him bewildered. Then he dropped his head and went to sleep again. When he was neither eating nor battling for his breath, he was always sleeping.

'I am your cousin, Jack,' said Mildred. 'But I had long forgotten it. And as for playing—but I will try. Perhaps the old touch will return.'

It did. She played with far greater skill and power than the self-taught Christine ; but not (as they have said since) with greater sweetness.

Then Jack took Christine and gave her a first lesson. It lasted nearly half an hour.

'Oh !' cried the girl, when Lady Mildred stopped. 'I feel as if I had been floating round in a dream. Was I a stupid pupil, Jack ?'

'You were the aptest pupil that dancing master ever had.'

'I know now,' she said, with panting breath and flushed cheeks, ' what dancing means. It is wonderful that the feet should answer to the music. Surely you must have loved dancing ?'

'We did,' the girls replied ; 'we did. There was no greater pleasure in the world.'

' Why did you give it up ?'

They looked at each other.

'After the Great Discovery,' said Dorothy Oliphant, ' we were so happy to get rid of the terrors of old age, and the loss of our beauty, and everything, that at first we thought of nothing else. When we tried to dance again, something had gone out of it. The men were not the same. Perhaps we were not the same. Everything languished after that. There was no longer any enjoyment. We ceased to dance because we found no pleasure in dancing.'

'But now you do ?' said Christine.

'To-night we do, because you have filled our hearts with the old thoughts. To get out of the dull, dull round—why is it that we never felt it dull till to-night ?   Oh ! so long as we can remember the old thoughts, let us continue to dance and to play and to sing. If the old thoughts cease to come back to us '—she looked at Geoffrey—'let us fall back into our dulness, like the men and women round us.'

'It was to please me first,' said Christine. 'You were so very kind as to come here to please me, because I can have no recollection at all of the Past, and I was curious to understand what I read. Come again—to please yourselves. Oh ! I have learned so much—so very much more than I ever expected. There are so many, many things that I did not dream of. But let us always dance,' she said—'let us always dance—let me always feel every time you come as if there was nothing in the world but sweet music calling me, and I was spinning round and round, but always in some place far better and sweeter than this.'

'Yes,' Lady Mildred said gravely. 'Thus it was we used to feel.'

'And I have seen you as you were—gentlemen and gentlewomen together. Oh, it is beautiful ! Come every night. Let us never cease to change the dismal Present for the sunny Past. But there is one thing—one thing that I cannot understand.'

'What is that ?' asked Lady Mildred.

'In the old books there is always, as I said before, a young man in love with a girl. What is it—Love ?' The girls sighed and cast down their eyes. 'Was it possible for a man so to love a girl as to desire nothing in the world but to have her love, and even to throw away his life—actually his very life—his very life—for her sake ?'

'Dorothy,' said Geoffrey, taking both her hands—'was it possible ? Oh ! was it possible ?'

Dorothy burst into tears.

'It *was* possible !' she cried ; 'but, oh ! it is not possible any longer.'

'Let us pretend,' said Geoffrey—'let us dream that it is possible.'

'Even to throw away your life—to die—actually your life ?' asked Christine. 'To die ? To exist no longer ? To abandon life—for the sake of another person ?'

A sudden change passed over all their faces. The light died out of their eyes ; the smile died on their lips ; the softness vanished from the ladies' faces ; the men hung their heads. All their gallantry left them. And Geoffrey let Mildred's hands slip from his holding. The thought of Death brought them back to the Present.

'No,' said Lady Mildred sadly, and with changed voice. 'Such things are no longer possible. Formerly, men despised death because it was certain to come, in a few years at best ; and why not, therefore, to-morrow ? But we cannot brave death any more. We live each for himself. This is the only safety; there is only the law of self-preservation. All are alike ; we cannot love each other any more, because we are all alike. No woman is better. than another in any man's eyes, because we are all dressed the same, and we are all the same. What more do we want ?' she said harshly. 'There is no change for us ; we go from bed to work, from work to rest and food, and so to bed again. What more can we want? We are all equals ; we are all the same ; there are no more gentlewomen. Let us put on our gray frocks and our flat caps again, and hide our hair and go home to bed.'

'Yes, yes,' cried Christine ; 'but you will come again. You will come again, and we will make every night a Play and Pretence of the beautiful—the lovely Past. When we lay aside the gray frocks, and let down our hair, we shall go back to the old time—the dear old time.'

The young man named Jack remained behind when the others were gone. 'If it were possible,' he said, 'for a man to give up everything—even his life—for a woman, in the old times, when life was a rich and glorious possession—how much more ought he not to be willing to lay it down, now that it has been made a worthless weed !'

'I have never felt so happy '—the girl was thinking of something else—'I have never dreamed that I could feel so happy. Now I know what I have always longed for—to dance round and round for ever, forgetting all but the joy of the music and the dance. But, oh ! Jack,' her face turned pale again, 'how could they ever have been happy, even while they waltzed, knowing that every minute brought them nearer and nearer to the dreadful end ?'

'I don't know. Christine, if I were you, I would never mention that ugly topic again, except when we are not dressed up and acting. How lovely they looked—all of them ! But none of them to compare with the sweetest rosebud of the garden.'

He took her hand and kissed it, and then left her alone with the old man in the great Museum.

CHAPTER IV.

WHAT IS LOVE?

IT would be idle to dwell upon the repetition of such scenes as those described in the last chapter. These unhappy persons continued to meet day after day in the Museum ; after changing their lawful garments for the fantastic habits worn before the Great Discovery, they lost themselves nightly in the imagination of the Past. They presently found others among the People, who had also been gentlewomen and gentlemen in the old days, and brought them also into the company ; so that there were now, every evening, some thirty gathered together. Nay, they even procured food and made suppers for themselves, contrary to the practice of common meals enjoined by the Holy College ; they gloried in being a company apart from the rest ; and because they remembered the past, they had the audacity to give themselves, but only among themselves, airs of superiority. In the daytime they wore the common dress, and were like the rest of the People. The thing grew, however. Every evening they recalled more of the long-vanished customs and modes of thought—one remembering this and the other that little detail—until almost every particular of the ancient life had returned to them. Then a strange thing happened. For though the Present offered still—and this they never denied—its calm, unchanging face, with no disasters to trouble and no certain and miserable end to dread ; with no anxieties, cares, and miseries ; with no ambitions and no struggles ; they fell to yearning after the old things : they grew to loathe the Present : they could hardly sit with patience in the Public Hall ; they went to their day's work with ill-concealed disgust. Yet, so apathetic had the people grown, that nothing of this was observed ; so careless and so unsuspicious were we ourselves, that though the singing and playing grew louder and continued longer every evening, none of us suspected anything. Singing, in my ears, was no more than an unmeaning noise ; that the girl in the Museum should sing and play seemed foolish ; but, then, children are foolish. They like to make a great noise.

One afternoon—it was some weeks since this dangerous fooling began—the cause of the whole, the girl Christine, was in the Museum alone. She had a book in her hand, and was reading in it. First she read a few lines, and then paused and meditated awhile. Then she read again, and laughed gently to herself. And then she read, and changed colour. And again she read, and knitted her brows as one who considers but cannot understand.

The place was quite deserted, save for her grandfather, who sat in his great chair, propped up with pillows and fast asleep. He had passed a bad night with his miserable asthma; in the morning, as often happens with this disease, he found himself able to breathe again, and was now, therefore, taking a good spell of sleep. His long white hair fell down upon his shoulders, his wrinkled old cheek showed a thousand crows' feet and lines innumerable; he looked a very, very old man. Yet he was no more than seventy-five or so, in the language of the Past. He belonged formerly to those who lived upon the labour of others, and devoured their substance. Now, but for his asthma, which even the College cannot cure, he should have been as perfectly happy as the rest of the People. The sunshine which warmed his old limbs fell full upon his chair; so that he seemed, of all the rare and curious objects in that collection, the rarest and most curious. The old armour on the wall, the trophies of arms, the glass vases containing all the things of the Past, were not so rare and curious as this old man—the only old man left among us. I daily, for my own part, contemplated the old man with a singular satisfaction. He was, I thought, a standing lesson to the People—one daily set before their eyes. Here was the sole surviving specimen of what in the Past was the best that the men and women could expect—namely, to be spared until the age of seventy-five, and then to linger on afflicted with miserable diseases and, slowly or swiftly, to be tortured to death. Beholding that spectacle, I argued, all the people ought to rub their hands in complacency and gratitude. But our people had long ceased to reason or reflect. The lesson was consequently thrown away upon them. Nay, when this girl began her destructive career, those whom she dragged into her toils only considered this old man because he would still be talking, as all old men used to talk, about the days of his youth, for the purpose of increasing their knowledge of the Past, and filling their foolish souls with yearning after the bad old times.

While Christine read and pondered, the door of the Museum opened. The young man called Jack stood there gazing upon her. She had thrown off her cap, and her long brown curls lay over her shoulders. She had a red rose in the bosom of her gray dress, and she had tied a crimson scarf round her waist. Jack (suffer me to use the foolishness of their language—of course his name was John) closed the door silently.

'Christine,' he whispered.

She started, and let her book fall. Then she gave him her hand, which he raised to his lips. (Again I must ask leave to report a great deal of foolishness.)

'It is the sweet old fashion,' he said. 'It is my homage to my lady.'

They were now so far gone in folly that she accepted this act as if it was one natural and becoming.

'I have been reading,' she said, 'a book full of extracts—all about love. I have never understood what love is. If I ask Dorothy, she looks at Geoffrey Heron and sighs. If I ask him, he tells me that he cannot be my servant to teach me, because he is already sworn to another. What does this mean? Have the old times come back again, so that men once more call themselves slaves of love? Yet what does it mean?'

'Tell me,' said Jack, 'what you have been reading.'

'Listen, then. Oh, it is the strangest extravagance! What did men mean when they could gravely write down, and expect to be read, such things as—

> ' "I do love you more than words can wield the matter—
> Dearer than eyesight, space and liberty ;
> Beyond what can be valued, rich or rare."

"Dearer than eyesight, space, and liberty." Did they really mean that?'

'They meant more : they meant dearer than life itself!' said Jack slowly. 'Only it was stupid always to say the same thing.'

'Well, then, listen to this :

> ' " Had I no eyes but ears, my ears would love
> That inward beauty and invisible :
> Or, were I deaf, thy outward parts would move
> Each part in me that were but sensible :
> Though neither eyes nor ears, to hear nor see,
> Yet should I be in love, by touching thee."

Now, Jack, what can that mean? Was anything more absurd?'

'Read another extract, Christine.'

'Here is a passage more difficult than any other :

> ' " Love looks not with the eyes, but with the mind ;
> And therefore is wing'd Cupid painted blind :
> Nor hath Love's mind of any judgment taste ;
> Wings and no eyes, figure unheedy haste :
> And therefore is Love said to be a child,
> Because in choice he is so oft beguiled."

Tell me, if you can, what this means.   But perhaps you were never in love, Jack, in the old times.'

'Romeo was in love before he met Juliet,' said Jack.   'I, too, have been reading the old books, you see, Child.   I remember— but how can I tell you ?   I cannot speak like the poet.   Yet I remember—I remember.'   He looked round the room.   'It is only here,' he murmured, 'that one can clearly remember.   Here are the very things which used to surround our daily life.   And here are youth and age.   They were always with us in the old time— youth and age.   Youth with love before, and age with love behind. Always we knew that as that old man, so should we become.   The chief joys of life belonged to youth : we knew very well that un- less we snatched them then, we should never have them.   To age we gave respect ; because age, we thought, had wisdom : but to us —to us—who were young, age cried unceasingly :

> "Gather your rosebuds while ye may."

If I could tell only you !   Christine ! come with me, into the Picture Gallery.   My words are weak, but the poets and the painters speak for us.   Come.   We shall find something there that will speak for me what I have not words to say for myself.'

Nothing in the whole world—I have maintained this in the College over and over again—has done so much harm to Humanity as Art.   In a world of common-sense which deals with nothing but fact and actuality, Art can have no place.   Why imitate what we see around us ?   Artists cheated the world : they pretended to imitate, and they distorted or they exaggerated.   They put a light into the sky that never was there : they filled the human face with yearning after things impossible : they put thoughts into the heart which had no business there : they made woman into a god- dess, and made love—simple love—a form of worship : they ex- aggerated every joy : they created a heaven which could not exist. I have seen their pictures, and I know it.   Why—why did we not destroy all works of Art long ago—or, at least, why did we not enclose the Gallery, with the Museum, within the College wall ?

The Picture Gallery is a long room with ancient stone walls : statuary is arranged along the central line, and the pictures line the walls.

The young man led the girl into the gallery and looked around him.   Presently he stopped at a figure in white marble.   It re- presented a woman, hands clasped, gazing upwards.   Anatomically, I must say, the figure is fairly correct.

'See,' he said, 'when in the olden times our sculptors desired to depict the Higher Life—which we have lost or thrown away for awhile—they carved the marble image of a woman. Her form represented perfect beauty : her face represented perfect purity ; the perfect soul must be wedded to the perfect body, otherwise there can be no perfection of Humanity. This is the Ideal Woman : look in her face : look at the curves of her form : look at the carriage of her head : such a woman it was whom men used to love.'

'But were women once like this ? Could they look so ? Had they such sweet and tender faces ? This figure makes me ashamed.'

'When men were in love, Christine, the woman that each man loved became in his mind such as this. He worshipped in his mistress the highest form of life that he could conceive. Some men were gross ; their ideals were low : some were noble ; then their ideals were high. Always there were among mankind some men who were continually trying to raise the ideal : always, the mass of men were keeping the ideal low.'

'Were the women ashamed to receive such worship ? Because they must have known what they were in cold reality.'

'Perhaps to the nobler sort,' said the young man, ' to be thought so good, lifted up their hearts and kept them at that high level. But indeed I know not. Remember that when men wrote the words that you think extravagant, they were filled and wholly possessed with the image of the Perfect Woman. Nay, the nobler and stronger their nature, the more they were filled with that Vision. The deeper their love for any woman, the higher they placed her on the Altar of their worship.'

'And if another man should try to take that woman from them——'

'They would kill that other man,' said Jack, with a fierce gleam in his eye which made the girl shudder. Yet she respected him for it.

'If another man should come between us now, Christine, I would . . . Nay, dear, forgive my rude words. What has jealousy to do with you ?'

She dropped her eyes and blushed, and in all her limbs she trembled. This young man made her afraid. And yet—she knew not why—it made her happy, only to be afraid of him.

'Let us see some of the pictures,' said Jack.

There were many hundreds of them. They represented I know

not what: scenes of the old life in the old time. I dare say everything was there, with all the exaggerations which pleased the painters and cheated the senses of those who looked on. Fair women were painted fairer than women could ever be : their eyes were larger, softer, fuller of thought ; their cheeks more tender ; their limbs more comely.

There were battle scenes : the young man led the girl past them. There were scenes from history — kings laying down crowns : traitors receiving sentence : and so forth : he passed them by. There were groups of nymphs : portraits of fair women : groups of girls dancing : girls at play : girls laughing : girls bathing : he passed them by. Presently he stopped before three panels side by side, representing a simple allegory of the old time. In the first picture, two, a young man and a girl, walked hand-in-hand beside a stream. The water danced and rippled in the sunlight : behind them was an orchard full of blossom : flowers sprang up at their feet—the flowers of spring. And they walked hand-in-hand, gazing in each other's eyes. The second picture showed a man in middle age returning home from work : beside him walked his boys : in the porch the mother sat with her daughters spinning at the wheel. The stream was now a full, majestic river : the trees were loaded with fruit not yet ripe : the fields were covered with corn, green still, but waving with light and shade under the summer sky : in the distance, passing away, was a heavy thundercloud. In the third panel an old pair stood beside a great river, looking out upon the ocean. Again they were hand-in-hand. The sun was setting in great splendour across the sea : the reapers were carrying their harvest home with songs and dances. And the old people still gazed in each other's face, just as they had done fifty years ago.

'See, Christine !' said Jack. 'In the first panel, this pair think of nothing but of each other. Presently they will have other thoughts. The stream beside which they wander is the Stream of Life. It widens as it goes. While they walk along its banks, the river grows broader and deeper. This means that as they grow older they grow wiser and learn more. So they go on continually, until they come to the mouth of the river, where it loses itself in the ocean of—what our friends tremble so much as to name. Tell me, is there terror, or doubt, or anxiety on their faces now that they have come to the end ?'

'No : their faces are entirely happy.'

'This you do not understand. Christine, if you were sure that in the end you would be as happy as that old woman at the end, would you be content to begin with the beginning? Would you play the part of that girl, and walk—with me—along the Stream of Life?'

He took her hand, but she made no reply, save that her eyes filled with tears. Presently she murmured :

'They are always happy—at the beginning and at the end. Did they know at the beginning that there would be an end?'

'They knew : everybody knew : the very children knew almost from infancy the great Law of Nature, that for everything there is the allotted end. They knew it.'

'And yet they were always happy. I cannot understand it.'

'We have destroyed that happiness,' said the young man. 'Love cannot exist when there is no longer end, or change, or anything to hope or fear—no mystery, nothing to hope or fear. What is a woman outside the Museum in the eyes of the College? She is only the half of humanity, subject to disease and requiring food at intervals. She no longer attracts men by the sacred mystery of her beauty. She is not even permitted any longer to make herself beautiful by her dress : nor is she allowed to create the feeling of mystery and the unknown by seclusion. She lives in the open, like the rest. We all live together : we know what each one says and thinks and does : nay, most of us have left off thinking and talking altogether.'

But Christine was hardly listening : she could not understand this talk. She was looking at the pictures.

'Oh !' she said, 'they look so happy. There is such a beautiful contentment in their eyes : they love each other so, that they think of nothing but their love. They have forgotten the end.'

'Nay ; but look at the end.'

'They are happy still, although the river flows into the Ocean. How can they be happy?'

'You shall learn more, Christine. You have seen enough to understand that the talk of the Physicians about the miseries of the old time is mischievous nonsense, with which they have fooled us into slavery.'

'Oh ! if they heard you——'

'Let them hear,' he replied sternly. 'I hope, before long, we may make them hear. Christine, you can restore the old love by your own example. You alone have nothing to remember and nothing to unlearn. As for the rest of us, we have old habits to forget and prejudices to overcome before we can get back to the Past.'

Then he led her to another picture.

The scene was a green village churchyard, standing amid trees—yews and oaks—and round a gray old church. Six strong men bore a bier piled with flowers towards an open grave, newly dug. Beside the grave stood one in a white robe, carrying a book. Behind the bier followed, hand-in-hand, a weeping company of men, women, and children. But he who walked first wept not.

'Oh!' cried Christine. 'He is dead! He is dead!'

She burst into tears.

'Nay,' said Jack. 'It is the wife who is dead. The husband lives still. See, he follows with tottering step. His grandchild leads him as you lead your grandfather. And they are all weeping except him. Why does he alone not weep? He has been married for fifty years and more : all his life has been shared by the love and sympathy of the woman—the dead woman. She is dead, my dear '—he repeated these words, taking the girl's hands—'she is dead, and he sheds no tears. Why not? Look at his face. Is it unhappy? Tell me, Christine, do you read the sorrow of hopelessness in that old man's face ?'

'No—no,' she said. 'He is grave, but he is not unhappy. Yet here is Death, with all the terrible things that we read of in the books—the deep pit, the body to be lowered in the grave—oh !'

She shuddered and turned her head.

'As I read his face,' said Jack, 'I see hope and consolation.'

'Why is there a man in white ?'

'I will tell you sometime. Meanwhile, observe that the old man is happy, though his wife is dead, and though he knows that to-morrow his turn will come, and a grave will be dug for him beside his wife, and he also will be laid among the cold clay-clods, as cold, as senseless as them, there to lie while the great world rolls round and round. He knows this, I say, and yet he is not unhappy.'

'What does it mean, Jack ?'

'I will tell you—soon.'

'We who are sailors,' this young man continued, 'are not like the rest of the world. We are always exposed to danger : we are not afraid to speak of Death : and though we have taken advantage (as we thought) of the Great Discovery, we have never forgotten the Past or the old ideas. We have to think for ourselves, which makes us independent. There is no Holy College on board ship, and no sacred Physician ventures his precious life upon a

rolling deck.   When we come ashore, we look round and see things.
Then we go on board again and talk, in the night watches below
the stars.   I think the Holy College would be pleased if they could
sometimes hear our talk.   Christine, there is no happiness left in
the world except among those whom the Great Discovery cannot
save from the dangers of a storm.   When you spoke to me my
heart leaped up, because I saw—what as yet you do not see.   The
others were too sluggish to remember, until you had dragged
their thoughts into the old channels.   But there was no need to
drag me.   For I remember always, and I only pretended until the
others should come with me.'

Christine only heard half of this, for she was looking at the
picture of the village funeral again.

'Oh ! how could men be happy with such an end before them ?'
she cried.   'I cannot understand it.   To be torn away : to be laid
in a box : to be put away deep under ground, there to lie for ever
—oh !' She trembled again.   'And not to be unhappy !'

'Look round the room, Christine.   Read the faces.   Here are
portraits of men and women.   Some of them are eager : some are
calm : none are unhappy for thinking of the end.   Here is a
battlefield.   The dead and wounded are lying about the ground :
look at this troop of horsemen charging.   Is there any terror in
their faces ?   What do they care about the men who have fallen ?
Their duty is to fight.   See here again.   It is a dying girl.   What
do you read in her face ?   I see no fear, but a sweet joy of resignation.   Here is a man led forth to execution.   There is no fear
in his face.'

'I could never bear to be alone in this room, because Death is
everywhere, and no one seems to regard it.'

'Christine, did you never hear, by any chance, from your grandfather, why people were not afraid ?'

'No ; he cannot bear to speak of such a thing.   He trembles
and shakes if it is even mentioned.   They all do, except you.'

'What does he tell you ?'

'He talks of the time when he was young.   It was long before
the Great Discovery.   Oh ! he is very old.   He was always going
to feasts and dances.   He had a great many friends, and some of
them used to sing and dance in theatres.   They were all very fond
of suppers after the theatre, and there was a great deal of singing
and laughing.   They used to drive about in carriages, and they
went to races.   I do not understand, very well, the pleasure of his
life.'

'Ah !' said Jack, 'he has forgotten the really important part of it.'

They were at a part of the gallery where there was a door of strong oak, studded with big square nails, under an arch of carved stone.

'Have you ever been into this place ?' he asked.

'Once I went in. But there is a dreadful tomb in it, with carved skulls and the figure of a dead man. So I ran away.'

'Come in with me. You shall not be frightened.'

He turned the great iron handle, and pushed open the heavy door.

The room was lofty, with a pointed roof : it was lit by long narrow windows, filled with painted glass. There were seats of carved wood, with carved canopies on either side : there was the figure of a brass eagle, with a great book upon it : and under the three lights of the window at the end was a table covered with a cloth which hung in rags and tatters, and was covered with dust. It was, in fact, an ancient Chapel, shut up and suffered to fall into decay.

'This,' said the young man, 'is the Chapel where, in the old time, they came to worship. They also worshipped in the great place that is now the House of Life. But here some of them worshipped also, though with less splendour.'

'Did they,' asked the girl, 'worship the Beautiful Woman of their dreams ?'

'No ; not the Beautiful Woman. They worshipped her, outside. In this Chapel they worshipped the Maker of Perfect Man and Perfect Woman. Come in with me, and I will tell you something of what it meant.'

*   *   *   *   *

It was two hours and more before they came out of the Chapel. The girl's eyes were full of tears, and tears lay upon his cheeks.

'My dear—my love,' said Jack, 'I have tried to show you how the old true love was nourished and sustained. It would not have lived but for the short duration of its life : it was the heritage of each generation, to be passed on unto the next. Only on one con- dition was it possible. It is a condition which you have been taught to believe horrible beyond the power of words. I have tried to show you that it was not horrible : my love—my sweet —fresh as the maidens who in the old time blossomed and flowered, and presently—fulfilled that condition—the only woman among us who is young in heart—let us agree to love—we two—

after the old fashion, under the old conditions. Do not shiver, dear. There is the old faith to sustain us. You shall go to sea with me. Perhaps we shall be cast away and drowned : perhaps we shall contract some unknown disease and die. We shall presently lie down to sleep, and awake again in each other's arms once more, in a new life which we cannot now comprehend. Everything must have an end. Human life must have an end, or it becomes horrible, monstrous, selfish. The life beyond will be glorified beyond all our hopes and beyond all our imagination. My dear, are you afraid ?'

She laid her head upon his shoulder.

'Oh! Jack, with you I am afraid of nothing. I should not be afraid to die this very moment, if we died together. Is it really true? Can we love now as men loved women long ago? Oh! can you love me so? I am so weak and small a creature—so weak and foolish. I would die with you, Jack—both together, taking each other by the hand : and oh! if you were to die first, I could not live after. I must then die too. My head is swimming—my heart is beating—lay your arm about me. Oh! love, my love— I have never lived before. Oh! welcome Life—and welcome Death, so that we may never—never more be parted !'

CHAPTER V.

THE OPEN DOOR.

It was in this way that the whole trouble began. There was an inquisitive girl foolishly allowed to grow up in this ancient Museum and among the old books, who developed a morbid curiosity for the Past, of which the books and pictures and collections taught her something ; yet, not all she wished to learn. She was unconsciously aided by the old man, who had been approaching his second childhood even at the time of the Great Discovery, and whose memory now continually carried him backwards to the days of his youth, without the least recollection of the great intervals between. Lastly, there had come to the town, in the pursuit of his business, a sailor, restless and discontented, as is the case with all his class ; questioning and independent ; impatient of authority, and curiously unable to forget the old times. The sailor and the girl, between them, at first instigated and pushed on the whole business : they were joined, no doubt, by many others ; but these two were the first leaders. The Chief Culprit of all—the nominal Leader—but you shall presently hear what kind of excuse could be made for him by himself. As for those whom they dragged reluctantly out of the tranquillity of oblivion, they were at first wholly drawn from the class which, at the outset, gave us so much trouble—the so-called gentle class—who desired nothing so much as to continue to live under the old conditions ; namely, by the labour of others. It wanted, for these people, only the revival of memory to produce the revival of discontent. When their minds were once more filled with the thought of the things they had lost —the leadership, the land, the wealth ; and with the memory of the arts which they had formerly loved—music, painting, letters ; and with the actual sight, once more restored to them, of their old amusements—their dancing, their society, their singing, their games : and when the foolish old idol—Love—was once more trotted out, like an old-fashioned Guy Fawkes, decked in his silly old rainbow tints : when, night after night, they actually began to play, act, and to pretend these things—what could possibly follow but revolt, with subsequent punishment and expulsion? You shall hear. Of course they would have been punished with expulsion, had not—but everything in its place.

Five or six weeks after the first evening, which I have described at full length, the Museum was again occupied by the same company, increased by a good many more. The women came in more readily, being sooner caught with the bait of fine dress, which had such an attraction for them that the mere sight of it caused them to forget everything that had been done for them—their present tranquillity, their freedom from agitation and anxiety—and carried them back to the old time, when they wore, indeed, those dainty dresses. What they endured, besides, they do not so readily remember. But the dresses carried back their minds to the society which once filled up the whole worthless lives of these poor creatures. I say, therefore, that it was easier to attract the women than the men. For the latter, no bait at all corresponding in power could be discovered. The company assembled were engaged in much the same sort of make-believe and play-acting as on the first evening. They were dressed in the old fashion : they danced, they sang, they talked and laughed—actually they talked and laughed—though what there is, from any view of life, to laugh about, I never could understand. Laughing, however, belonged to the old manners, and they had now completely recovered the old manners : anything, however foolish, which belonged to that time would have been welcomed by them. So they laughed : for the same reason, they were full of animation ; and the old, old, unhappy emotion which I had thought blotted out for ever—restlessness—had either broken out among them or was well simulated. They were all young, save for the old man who sat in his chair coughing, and sometimes talking. Christine had dressed him in a velvet coat, which gave him great dignity, and made him look as if he was taking part in the play. I say not that the acting was not very good—of the kind. Acting of any kind could never have served any useful purpose, even in the Past. Perhaps a company of beautiful women, beautifully dressed, and of gallant men—I talk their own foolish language—amusing themselves in this way may have given pleasure to some, but not to those among whom I was born. In the days when these things were done every night at one part of the town, in another part the men were drinking, if they had any money, and the women and children were starving. And much they concerned themselves about dancing and laughing ! Laughing, indeed ! My part of the town was where they starved. There was mighty little laughing among us, I can promise you.

In their masquerading they had naturally, as if it was a part of the life they represented, assumed, as I have said, the old expression of eagerness, as if there was always something wanting. And yet, I say, they laughed with each other. In the unreasonable, illogical way of the Past, although everybody always wanted everything for himself, and tried to overreach his neighbour, it was the custom to pretend that nobody wanted anything ; but that everybody trusted his friend, and that everybody lived for the sole purpose of helping other people. Therefore, they shook hands continually, and grinned at each other when they met, as if they were pleased to meet and . . . Well, the hypocrisies of the Past were as ridiculous as its selfishness was base.

But three of the party sat apart in the Picture Gallery. They were Christine and the two cousins, Mildred and Jack Carera. They were talking seriously and gravely.

'It comes then,' said Jack, 'to this : that to all of us the Present has grown to be utterly hateful, and to one or two of us intolerable.'

'Intolerable !' the other two repeated.

'We are resolved, for our own selves at least, that we will have no more of it, if we can help it. Are we not ? But, Cousin Mildred, let us remember that we are only three. Perhaps, among our friends in the Museum, there may be half a dozen more who have learned to feel as strongly as ourselves. Is half a dozen a Party large enough to effect a Revolution? Remember, it is useless to think of remonstrance or petition with the College. No King, Council, or Parliament in the Past was ever half so autocratic as the College of Physicians.

'I used to read,' he went on, 'ages ago, about the Domination of Priests. I don't think any Rule of Priests was ever half so intolerant or so thorough as the Rule of the Physicians. They have not only deprived us of the Right of Thought, but also of the Power of Thought. The poor people cannot think. It is a truly desperate state of things. A few years more and we, too, shall sink into the same awful slough——'

'Some of us were in it already, but Christine pulled us out,' said Mildred.

'Shall we ever get another chance of getting out?' Jack asked. 'I think not.'

'Well, Jack, go on.'

'As for these evening meetings of ours; you may be very sure that they will be found out before long, and that they will be stopped. Do you think that Grout—Grout!—will suffer his beloved invention of the common dress to be trampled on? Do you imagine that Grout will suffer the revival of the old forms of society?'

'Oh!' Christine replied. 'If we could convert Dr. Grout!'

'Another danger,' said Jack, 'is, that we may all get tired of these meetings. You see, they are not the real thing. Formerly, the evening followed the day : it was the feast after the fight. Where is now the fight? And all the dancing, courting, pretty speeches, and tender looks, meant only the fore-words of Love in earnest. Now, are we ready again for Love in earnest? Can the men once more worship the women upon whom they have gazed so long unmoved? If so, we must brave the College and face the consequences. I know of two people only who are at present so much in earnest as to brave the College. They are Christine and myself.'

He took the girl's hand and kissed it.

'You may add one more, Jack,' said Mildred. 'If you go away with Christine, take me with you. For the Present is more intolerable than any possible Future.'

'That makes three, then. There may be more. Geoffrey and Dorothy are never tired of whispering and billing. Perhaps they, too, are strong enough to throw off the old terrors and to join us. But we shall see.'

' I think,' said Mildred, ' it might depend partly on how the case is put before them.   If you made them see very clearly the miseries of their present life, and made them yearn ardently for the things which they have only just remembered, some of them might follow, at all costs.   But for most, the College and what it holds would prove too much.'

' Yet you yourself—and Christine.——'

' As for me, it seems as if I remember more than anybody because I think of the sorrows of the Past.   I cannot tell now how I ever came to forget those sorrows.   And they are now grown so dear to me, that for the very fear of losing them again, I would give up the Gift of the College and go with you.   As for Christine, she has never known at all the dread which they now pretend used to fill all our minds and poisoned all our lives.   How, then, should she hesitate ?   Besides, she loves you, Jack—and that is enough.'

' Quite enough,' said Christine, smiling.

'If you remember everything,' Jack went on gravely, ' you remember, Mildred, that there was something in life besides play and society.   In a corner of your father's park, for instance, there was an old gray building, with a small tower and a peal of bells. The place stood in a square enclosure, in which were an old broken cross, an ancient yew-tree, two or three head-stones, and the graves of buried villagers.   You remember that place, Mildred ?   You and I have often played in that ground : in week-days we have prowled about the old building and read the monuments on the walls ; on Sundays we used to sit there with all the people.   Do you remember ?'

Mildred clasped her hands.

' How could I ever forget ?' she cried.   ' How could any of us forget ?'

' Because Grout robbed you of your memory, my cousin.   He could not rob mine.'

' Alas !' she lamented, ' how can we ever get that back again ?'

' By memory, Mildred.   It will come back presently.   Think of that, and you will be less afraid to come with us.   If that was able to comfort the world formerly when the world was full of life and joy and needed so little comfort, what should it not do for you now, when the world is so dull and dismal, and the Awful Present is so long that it seems never to have had a beginning, just as it promises never to have an end. Courage, Cousin Mildred.'

'And now,' he went on, after a pause, 'for my plan. My ship is bound for any port to which the College may despatch her. She must sail in about four or five weeks. I shall take you both on board. Christine will be my wife—you shall be our companion. Perhaps one or two more may go with us. We shall take certain things that we shall want. I can procure all these without the least suspicion, and we shall sail to an island of which I know, where the air is always warm and the soil is fruitful. There the sailors shall land us and shall sail away, unless they please to join us. And there we will live out our allotted lives, without asking anything of the College. The revival of that lost part of your memory, Mildred, will serve you in place of what they could have given you. You agree ? Well, that is settled then. Let us go back.'

But, as you shall see, this plan was never carried out.

When all went away that evening, Mildred remained behind.

'Christine,' she said, 'I have something to tell you. Take me somewhere—to some dark place—where we can whisper.'

One might as well have talked at the top of his voice, just where they were, for any chance of being heard. But guilt made the woman tremble.

'Come into the Picture Gallery,' said Christine, leading the way. 'No one can hear what we say there. My dear, in the old days when people were going to conspire they always began by going to dark galleries, vaults, and secret places. This is quite delightful. I feel like a conspirator.'

'Don't laugh at me, dear,' said Mildred ; 'for indeed when you have heard what I have to say, you will feel very much more like a conspirator.'

The room was in darkness, but for the moonlight which poured in through the windows of one side, and made queer work with the pictures on which it fell. At the end the moonlight shone through the door, hardly ever used, which led from the gallery into the Garden of the College beyond.

'What is that ?'

Mildred caught Christine by the hand.

'It is the door leading into the College Gardens. How came it open?'

'Have you a key ?'

'I suppose there is a key on the old rusty bunch hanging up in the Museum, but I do not know—I have never tried the keys. Who could have opened it ?'

Christine walked down the gallery hastily, Mildred following. The door was standing wide open.

'Who has done this?' asked Christine again. 'I cannot tell who could have opened the door, or why. It has never been opened before.'

Mildred shuddered.

'It is thrown open for some mischief,' she said: 'we shall find out soon enough by whom.'

Then they looked out through the door into the Garden of the College. The door faced a semicircular lawn run wild with rank grass never shorn: behind the lawn were trees: and the moonlight lay on all.

Suddenly the girls caught hands and shrank back into the doorway. For a tall form emerged from the trees and appeared upon the lawn, where he walked with hanging head and hands clasped behind his back.

'It is the Arch Physician!' Christine whispered.

'It is Harry Linister,' Mildred murmured.

Then they retreated within and shut the door noiselessly. But they could not lock or fasten it.

'I can see that part of the Garden from a window in the Library,' said Christine. 'He walks there every morning and every evening. He is always alone. He always hangs his head, and he always looks fit to cry for trouble. What is the good of being Arch Physician if you cannot have things done as you want?'

'My dear,' said Mildred, 'I am afraid you do not quite understand. In the old days—I mean not quite the dear old days, but in the time when people still discussed things and we had not been robbed of memory and of understanding—it was very well known that the Arch Physician was outvoted in the College by Grout and his Party.'

'By Dr. Grout?'

'My dear, Grout was never a Doctor. He only calls himself Doctor. I remember when Grout was an ignorant man taken into Professor Linister's Laboratory to wash up the pots and bottles. He was thin, just as he is now—a short, dark, and sour-faced man, with bright eyes. Oh! a clever man, I dare say. But ignorant, and full of hatred for the class of culture and refinement. It was Grout who led the Party which took away land and wealth from individuals and transferred all to the State. It was Grout who ordered the massacre of the Old. It was Grout who invented the horrible cruelty of the Common Dress. It was Grout who made the College what it is—not what it was meant to be. It was originally the Guardian of Life and Health. It has become the Tyrant of the People. It has destroyed everything—everything that makes life possible—and it tells the People to be happy because they live. It is Grout—Grout!—who has done this. Not the Arch Physician. Not Harry Linister.'

'Why do you say "Harry Linister," Mildred?'

'My dear, I think that of all women living I have the greatest cause to hate the Great Discovery, because it robbed me of my lover.'

'Tell me how, dear.'

'I told you, Christine, that the revival of the Past was the revival of sorrows that I would never again forget. Listen, then, and I will tell you what they were. When the Great Discovery was announced, Harry Linister was already a man well known in Science, Christine ; but he was also well known in Society as well. Science did not prevent him from falling in love. And he fell in love with—me. Yes—with me. We met that fatal evening at the Royal Institution, and we arranged, before the Lecture, where we should meet after the Lecture. My dear, I knew very well what he was going to say; and—oh, my poor heart !—how happy I was to think of it ! There was nobody in London more clever, more handsome, and more promising than Harry. He was rich, if that mattered anything to me : he was already a Fellow of the Royal Society, for some great discoveries he had made : everybody said that a splendid career was before him—and he loved me, Christine.'

'Well ?'

'Well : the news of the Great Discovery carried him out of himself. He forgot his love—and me—and everything. When his eyes fell upon me again, I know not how long after, I was in the hideous Common Dress, and he no more recognised me than a stranger would recognise one out of a herd of sheep.'

'How could he forget ? Do you think that Jack could ever forget me ?'

'I am sure he will not, at any rate. Now, Christine, I am going to try something serious. I am going to try to convert the Arch Physician himself !'

'Mildred !'

'Why not ? He is still a man, I suppose. Nobody ever thought that Grout was a man. But Harry Linister was once a man, and should be still. And if he have a memory as well as eyes, why—

14

then . . .' she sighed. 'But that would be too much, indeed, to hope.'

'What if you win him, Mildred ?'

'Why, child, he used to love me. Is not that enough ? Besides, he *knows the Great Secret.* If we have him with us, we have also with us all the people whom we can shake, push, or prick out of their present miserable apathy. Why did we ever agree to the stupid work day by day ? We began by fighting for the wealth, and those who survived enjoyed it. Why did we not go on fighting ? Why did we consent to wear this hideous dress ? Why did we consent to be robbed of our intelligence, and to be reduced to the condition of sheep ? All because the College had the Great Secret, and they made the People think that to forego that one advantage was worse than all other evils that could happen to them. It was Grout—the villainy of Grout—that did it. Now, if we can by any persuasion draw the Arch Physician over to ourselves, we win the cause for all those who join us, because they will lose nothing.'

'How will you win him, Mildred ?'

'Child, you are young: you do not know the history of Dalilah ; of the Sirens ; of Circe ; of Cleopatra ; of Vivien ; of a thousand Fair Ladies who have witched away the senses of great men, so that they have become as wax in the hands of their conquerors. Poor Harry ! His heart was not always as hard as stone : nor was it always as heavy as lead. I would witch him, if I could, for his own happiness—poor lad !—and for mine as well. Let him only come with us, bringing the precious Secret, and we are safe !'

It has been observed that many hard things were said concerning me—Grout—and that I have, nevertheless, written them down. First, the things are all true, and I rejoice to think of the part that I have always played in the conduct of the People since the Great Discovery enabled me to obtain a share in that conduct. Next, it may be asked how I became possessed of this information. That you shall presently understand.

All that I have done in my public capacity—as for private life, I never had any, except that one goes into a private room for sleep —has been for the Advancement of Humanity. In order to effect this advance with the greater ease, I found it necessary to get rid of useless hands—therefore the Old were sacrificed : to adopt one common standard in everything ; so that there should be the same hours of work for all ; the same food both in quantity and quality ;

the same dress ; and the same housing. As by far the greater number belong to what were formerly known as the lower classes, everything has been a gain for them. Now, a gain for the majority is a gain for Humanity. As for the abolition of disturbing emotions, such as Love, Jealousy, Ambition, Study, Learning, and the like, the loss of them is, of course, pure gain. In short, I willingly set down all that may be or has been said against myself, being quite satisfied to let the truth speak for itself. I have now to tell of the Daring Attempt made upon the Fidelity of the Chief—the Arch Physician Himself.

CHAPTER VI.

THE ARCH PHYSICIAN.

THE Arch Physician generally walked in the College Gardens for an hour or so every forenoon. They are very large and spacious Gardens, including plantations of trees, orchards, ferneries, lawns, flower-beds, and shrubberies. In one corner is a certain portion which, having been left entirely alone by the gardeners, has long since become like a tangled coppice, rather than a garden, covered with oaks and elms and all kinds of trees, and overgrown with thick underwoods. It was in this wild and secluded part that Dr. Linister daily walked. It lay conveniently at the back of his own residence, and adjoining the Museum and Picture Gallery. No one came here except himself, and but for the beaten path which his footsteps had made in their daily walk, the place would have become entirely overgrown. As it was, there were thick growths of holly and of yew: tall hawthorn trees, wild roses spreading about among brambles: ferns grew tall in the shade, and under the great trees there was a deep shadow even on the brightest day. In this neglected wood there were creatures of all kinds—rabbits, squirrels, snakes, moles, badgers, weasels, and stoats. There were also birds of all kinds in the wood, and in the stream that ran through the place there were otters. In this solitary place Dr. Linister walked every day and meditated. The wildness and the solitude pleased and soothed him. I have already explained that he had always, from the outset, been most strongly opposed to the policy of the majority, and that he was never free from a certain melancholy. Perhaps he meditated on the world as he would have made it, had he been able to have his own way.

I have heard that much was said among the Rebels about my conduct during these events, as wanting in Gratitude. In the first place, if it is at all necessary for me to defend my conduct, let me point out that my duty to the Authority of the House must come before everything—certainly before the claims of private gratitude. In the second place, I owe no gratitude at all to Dr. Linister, or to anybody. I have made myself. Whatever I have done, alone I have done it, and unaided. Dr. Linister, it is very true, received me into his laboratory as bottle-washer and servant. Very good. He paid me my wages, and I did his work for him. Much room for gratitude there. He looked for the proper discharge of the work, and I looked for the regular payment of the wages. Where does the gratitude come in? He next taught me the elements of the science. To be sure : he wanted the simpler part of his experiments conducted by a skilled, not an ignorant, hand. Therefore, he taught me those elements. The better skilled the hand, the more he could depend upon the successful conduct of his research. Therefore, when he found that he could depend upon my eye and hand, he taught me more, and encouraged me to work on my own account, and gave me the best books to read. Very good. All for his own purposes.

What happened next? Presently, Grout the Bottle-washer became so important in the laboratory that he became Grout the Assistant, or Demonstrator ; and another Bottle-washer was appointed—a worthy creature who still performs that useful Function, and desires nothing more than to wash the bottles truly and thoroughly. Next, Grout became known outside the laboratory : many interesting and important discoveries were made by Grout ; then Grout became too big a man to be any longer Dr. Linister's Assistant : he had his own laboratory ; Grout entered upon his own field of research. This was a practical field, and one in which he quickly surpassed all others.

Remember that Dr. Linister never claimed, or looked for, gratitude. He was much too wise a man. On all occasions when it was becoming in him, he spoke in the highest terms of his former Assistant's scientific achievements.

There was, in fact, no question of Gratitude at all.

As for personal friendship, the association of years, the bond of union, or work in common—these are mere phrases, the worn-out old phrases of the vanished Past. Besides, there never was any personal friendship. Quite the contrary. Dr. Linister was never able to forget that in the old time I had been the servant and he the master. Where equality has been so long established, the continual reminder of former inequality is galling.

Dr. Linister, indeed, was always antipathetic from the beginning. Except over a research, we could have nothing in common. In the old days he was what they called a gentleman ; he was also a scholar ; he used to play music, and write verses : he would act and dance and sing, and do all kinds of things ; he was one of those men who always wanted to do everything that other men can do, and to do it as well as other men could do it. So that, though he was a great scientific worker, he spent half his day at his club, or at his sports, or in Society ; that is to say, with the women—and mostly, I think, among the games and amusements of the women. There was every day, I remember, a great running to and fro of page-boys with notes from them ; and he was always ready to leave any, even the most important work, just to run after a woman's caprice.

As for me, I never had any school education at all : I never had anything to do with Society : the sight of a woman always filled me with contempt for the man who could waste time in running after a creature who knew no science, never cared for any, and was so wont to disfigure her natural figure by the way she crowded on her misshapen clothes that no one could guess what it was like beneath them. As for music, art, and the rest of it, I never asked so much as what they meant. After I began to make my way, I had the laboratory for work, play, and all.

When, again, it came to the time when the Property question became acute, and we attempted to solve it by a Civil War, although Dr. Linister adhered to his determination not to leave his laboratory, his sympathies were always with individualism. Nay, he never disguised his opinion, but was accustomed regularly to set it forth at our Council meetings in the House of Life—that the abolition of property and the establishment of the perfect Socialism were the greatest blows ever inflicted upon civilization. It is not, however, civilization which the College advances, but Science— which is a very different thing—and the Scientific End of Humanity. The gradual extinction of all the emotions—love, jealousy, ambi- tion, rivalry—Dr. Linister maintained, made life so poor a thing that painless extinction would be the very best thing possible for the whole race. It is useless to point out, to one so prejudiced, the enormous advantage gained in securing constant tranquillity of mind. He was even, sometimes, an advocate for the revival of fighting—fighting, the old barbarous way of settling disputes, in which lives were thrown away by thousands on a single field. Nor would he ever agree with the majority of the House that the only End of Humanity is mere existence, at which Science should always aim, prolonged without exertion, thought, care, or emotion of any kind.

In fact, according to the contention of my followers and myself, the Triumph of Science is as follows : The Philosopher finds a creature, extremely short-lived at the best, liable to every kind of disease and suffering from external causes, torn to pieces from within by all kinds of conflicting emotions ; a creature most eager and insatiate of appetite, fiery and impetuous, quarrelsome and murderous, most difficult to drive or lead, guided only by its own selfish desires, tormented by intellectual doubts and questions which can never be answered. The Philosopher works upon this creature until he has moulded it into another so different, that no one would perceive any likeness to the original creature. The new creature is immortal ; it is free from disease or the possibility of disease ; it has no emotions, no desires, and no intellectual restlessness. It breathes, eats, sleeps.

Such is my idea of Science Triumphant. It was never Dr. Linister's.

In manners, the Arch Physician preserved the old manners of courtesy and deference which were the fashion when he was brought up. His special work had been for many years the study of the so-called incurable diseases, such as asthma, gout, rheumatism, and so forth. For my own part, my mind, since I became Suffragan, has always been occupied with Administration, having steadily in view the Triumph of Science. I have, with this intention, made the Social Equality real and complete from every point : I have also endeavoured to simplify labour, to enlarge the production and the distribution of food by mechanical means, and thus to decrease the necessity for thought, contrivance, and the exercise of ingenuity. Most of our work is so subdivided that no one understands more than the little part of it which occupies him for four hours every day. Workmen who know the whole process are impossible. They ask ; they inquire ; they want to improve : when their daily task is but a bit of mechanical drudgery, they do it without thought and they come away. Since labour is necessary, let it be as mechanical as possible, so that the head may not be in the least concerned with the work of the hand. In this—my view of things—the Arch Physician could never be brought to acquiesce. Had he been able to have his own way, the whole of my magnificent scheme would have been long ago destroyed and rendered impossible. I suppose it was this impossibility of having his own way which afflicted him with so profound a melancholy. His face was always sad, because he could never reconcile himself to the doctrine of human equality, without which the Perfection of Man is impossible.

It will be seen, in short, that the Arch Physician and myself held hardly a single view in common. But he had been elected to his post, and I to mine. We shared between us the Great Secret : and if my views prevailed in our Council, it was due either to my own power of impressing my views upon my colleagues, or to the truth and justice of those views.

But as to gratitude, there was no room or cause for any.

As, then, Dr. Linister walked to and fro upon the open space outside the Picture Gallery, his hands behind him, his head hanging, and his thought I know not where, he became conscious of something that was out of the usual order. When one lives as we live, one day following another, each like the one which went before, little departures from the accustomed order disturb the mind. For many, many years the Doctor had not given a thought to the Picture Gallery or to the door. Yet, because it stood open, and he had been accustomed to see it closed, he was disturbed, and presently lifted his head and discovered the cause.

The door stood open. Why ? What was the door ? Then he remembered what it was, and whither it led. It opened into the ancient Picture Gallery, the very existence of which he had forgotten, though every day he saw the door and the building itself. The Picture Gallery ! It was full of the pictures painted in the few years before the Great Discovery : that is to say, it was full of the life which he had long ago lived—nay, he lived it still. As he stood hesitating without the door, that life came back to him with a strange yearning and sinking of the heart. He had never, you see, ceased to regret it, nor had he ever forgotten it. And now he was tempted to look upon it again. As well might a monk in the old times look upon a picture of fair women years after he had forsworn love.

He hesitated, his knees trembling, for merely thinking what was within. Then he yielded to the temptation, and went into the Gallery.

The morning sun streamed through the windows and lay upon the floor ; the motes danced in the sunshine ; the Gallery was quite empty ; but on the walls hung, one above the other, five or six in each row, the pictures of the Past. In some the pigments were faded : crimson was pale pink ; green was gray ; red was brown ; but the figures were there, and the Life which he had lost once more flashed upon his brain. He saw the women whom once he had loved so much ; they were lying on soft couches, gazing upon him with eyes which made his heart to beat and his whole frame to tremble ; they were dancing ; they were in boats, dressed in dainty summer costume ; they were playing lawn-tennis ; they were in drawing-rooms, on horseback, on lawns, in gardens ; they were being wooed by their lovers. What more ? They were painted in fancy costumes, ancient costumes, and even with no costume at all. And the more he looked, the more his cheek glowed and his heart beat. Where had they gone—the women of his youth ?

Suddenly, he heard the tinkling of a musical instrument. It was a thing they used to call a zither. He started, as one awakened out of a dream. Then he heard a voice singing. And it sang the same song he had heard that night five or six weeks ago—his own song :

> ' The girls they laugh, the girls they cry,
>   " What shall their guerdon be ?—
> Alas ! that some must fall and die !—
>   Bring forth our gauds to see,
> 'Twere all too slight, give what we might."
>   Up spake a soldier tall,
> " Oh ! Love is worth the whole broad earth :
> Oh ! Love is worth the whole broad earth :
>   Give that, you give us all." '

This time, however, it was another voice—a fuller and richer voice—which sang those words.

Dr. Linister started again when the voice began. He changed colour, and his cheek grew pale.

'Heavens !' he murmured. 'Are there phantoms in the air ? What does it mean ? This is the second time—my own song—the foolish old song—my own air—the foolish, tinkling air that they used to like ! And the voice—I remember the voice—whose voice is it ? I remember the voice—whose voice is it ?'

He looked round him again, at the pictures, as if to find among them the face he sought. The pictures showed all the life of the Past ; the ballroom with the dancers ; the sports of the field ; the drive in the afternoon, the ride in the morning ; the bevy of girls ; the soldiers and the sailors ; the streets crowded with people ; the vile slums and the picturesque blackguardism of the City—but not the face he wanted. Then he left off looking for the singer, and began to think of the faces before him.

'On every face,' he said, 'there is unsatisfied desire. Yet they are the happier for that very dissatisfaction. Yes—they are the happier.' He paused before a painted group of street children ; some were playing over the gutter ; some were sitting on doorsteps, carrying babies as big as themselves ; one was sucking a piece of orange-peel picked up on the pavement ; one was gnawing a crust. They were all ragged and half-starved. 'Yet,' said the Arch Physician, ' they are happy. But we have no children now. In those days they could paint and draw—and we have lost the Art. Great Heavens !' he cried impatiently, ' we have lost every Art. Cruel ! cruel !' Then from within there broke upon his ears a strain of music. It was so long since he had heard any music, that at first it took away his breath. Wonderful that a mere sound such as that of music should produce such an effect upon a man of science ! ' Oh !' he sighed heavily, ' we have even thrown away that ! Yet—where—where does the music come from ? Who plays it ?'

While he listened, carried away by the pictures and by the music and by his own thoughts to the Past, his mind full of the Past, it did not surprise him in the least that there came out from the door between the Gallery and the Museum—a young lady belonging absolutely to the Past. There was no touch of the Present about her at all. She did not wear the regulation dress ; she did not wear the flat cap.

'It is,' said Dr. Linister, 'the Face that belongs to the Voice. I know it now. Where did I see it last ? To whom does it belong ?'

She stood for a few moments in the sunshine. Behind her was a great picture all crimson and purple, a mass of flaming colour, before which her tall and slight figure, dressed in a delicate stuff of soft creamy colour, stood clearly outlined. The front of the dress —at least that part which covered the throat to the waist—was of some warmer colour ; there were flowers at her left shoulder ; her hair was braided tightly round her head : round her neck was a ribbon with something hanging from it ; she wore brown gloves, and carried a straw hat dangling in her hand. It was, perhaps, the sunshine which made her eyes so bright, her cheek so glowing, her rosy lips so quivering.

She stood there, looking straight down the Hall, as if she saw no one.

Dr. Linister gazed and turned pale ; his cheeks were so white that you might have thought him about to faint; he reeled and trembled.

'Good God!' he murmured, falling back upon the interjection of the Past, 'we have lost the Beauty of women! Oh! Fools! Fools! We have thrown all away—all—and for what?'

Then the girl came swiftly down the Hall towards him. A smile of welcome was on her lips; a blush upon her cheek: her eyes looked up and dropped again, and again looked up and once more dropped.

Then she stopped before him and held out both her hands.

'Harry Linister!' she cried, as if surprised, and with a little laugh, 'how long is it since last we met?'

CHAPTER VII.

THE FIDELITY OF JOHN LAX.

THAT morning, while I was in my private laboratory, idly turning over certain Notes on experiments conducted for the artificial manufacture of food, I was interrupted by a knock at the door.

My visitor was the Porter of the House of Life, our most trusted servant, John Lax. His duty it was to sleep in the House—his chamber being that ancient room over the South Porch—to inspect the furnaces and laboratories after the work of the day was closed, and at all times to keep an eye upon the Fabric itself, so that it should in no way fall out of repair. His orders were also to kill any strangers who might try to force their way into the House on any pretence whatever.

He was a stout, sturdy fellow, vigorous and strong, though the Great Discovery had found him nearly forty years of age: his hair, though his head had gone bald on the top, was still thick on the sides, and gave him a terrifying appearance under his cap of scarlet and gold. He carried a great halberd as a wand of office, and his coat and cap matched each other for colour and for gold embroidery. Save as representing the authority of the House and College, I would never have allowed such a splendid appearance to anyone.

'What have you come to tell me, John?' I asked.

I may explain that I had always found John Lax useful in keeping me informed as to the internal condition of the College and its Assistants—what was said and debated—what opinions were advanced, by what men, and so forth.

'In the College itself, Suffragan,' he said, 'and in the House, things are mighty dull and quiet. Blessed if a little Discontent or a Mutiny, or something, wouldn't be worth having, just to shake up the lot. There's not even a grumbler left. A little rising and a few heads broken, and we should settle down again, quiet and contented again.'

'Don't talk like a fool, John.'

'Well, Suffragan, you like to hear all that goes on. I wonder what you'll say to what I'm going to tell you now ?'

'Go on, John. What is it ?'

'It's irregular, Suffragan ; but your Honour is above the Law ; and, before beginning a long story—mind you, a most important story it is——'

'What is it about ? Who's in it ?'

'Lots of the People are in it. They don't count. He's in it, now—come.'

'He ?'

John Lax had pointed over his shoulder so clearly in the direction of the Arch Physician's residence, that I could not but understand. Yet I pretended.

'He, John ? Who is he ?'

'The Arch Physician is in it. There ! Now, Suffragan, bring out that bottle and a glass, and I can then tell you the story, without fear of ill consequences to my throat, that was once delicate.'

I gave him the bottle and a glass, and, after drinking a tumblerful of whisky (forbidden to the People) he began.

Certain reasons, he said, had made him suspicious as to what went on at night in the Museum during the last few weeks. The lights were up until late at night. Once he tried the doors, and found that they were locked. He heard the playing of music within, and the sound of many voices.

Now there is, as I told John Lax at this point, no law against the assemblage of the People, nor against their sitting up, or singing and playing together. I had, to be sure, hoped that they had long ceased to desire to meet together, and had quite forgotten how to make music.

He remembered, John Lax went on to say, that there was a door leading into the Picture Gallery from the College Garden—a door of which he held the key.

He opened this door quietly, and then, night after night, he crept into the Picture Gallery, and watched what went on through the door which opened upon the Museum. He had found, in fact, a place close by the door, where, hidden behind a group of statuary, he could watch and listen in almost perfect security.

I then heard, to my amazement, how a small company of the People were every night carrying on a revival of the Past; not with the laudable intention of disgusting themselves with the horrors of that time, but exactly the contrary. It was only the pleasant side of that time—the evening life of the rich and careless—which these foolish persons reproduced.

They had, in fact, gone so far, John Lax told me, as to fall in love with that time, to deride the Present, and to pour abuse upon my name—mine—as the supposed chief author of the Social Equality. This was very well for a beginning. This was a startling awakener out of a Fools' Paradise. True, the company was small; they might be easily dispersed or isolated; means might be found to terrify them into submission. Yet it gave me a rude shock.

'I've had my suspicions,' John Lax continued, 'ever since one morning when I looked into the Museum and see that young gal dressed up and carrying on before the looking-glass, more like—well, more like an actress at the Pav, as they used to make 'em, than like a decent woman. But now there's more.' He stopped, and whispered hoarsely : 'Suffragan, I've just come from a little turn about the Garden. Outside the Picture Gallery, where there's a bit o' turf and a lot of trees all standin' around, there's a very curious sight to see this minute ; and if you'll get up and go along o' me, Suffragan, you'll be pleased—you will, indeed—astonished and pleased you will be.'

I obeyed. I arose and followed this zealous servant. He led me to a part of the Garden which I did not know ; it was the place of which I have spoken. Here, amid a great thick growth of under-woods, he took me into the ruins of an old garden or tool-house, built of wood ; but the planks were decaying and were starting apart.

'Stand there, and look and listen,' whispered John Lax, grinning.

The open planks commanded a view of a semicircular lawn, where the neglected grass had grown thick and rank. Almost under my eyes there was sitting upon a fallen trunk a woman, fantastically dressed—against the Rules—and at her feet lay none other than the Arch Physician himself! Then, indeed, I pricked up my ears and listened with all my might.

'Are we dreaming, Mildred ?' he murmured—'are we dreaming ?'

'No, Harry ; we have all been dreaming for a long, long time—

never mind how long. Just now we are not dreaming ; we are truly awake. You are my old playfellow, and I am your old sweet-heart,' she said, with a little blush. 'Tell me what you are doing —always in your laboratory. I suppose, always finding some new secrets. Does it make you any happier, Harry, to be always find-ing something new ?'

'It is the only thing that makes life endurable—to discover the secrets of nature. For what other purpose do we live ?'

'Then, Harry, for what purpose do the rest of us live, who do not investigate those secrets ? Can women be happy in no other way ? We do not prosecute any kind of research, you know.'

'Happy ? Are we in the Present or the Past, Mildred ?'

He looked about him, as if expecting to see the figures of the Pictures in the Gallery walking about upon the grass.

'Just now, Harry, we are in the Past. We are back—we two together—in the glorious and beautiful Past, where everything was delightful. Outside this place there is the horrible Present. You have made the Present for us, and therefore you ought to know what it is. Let me look at you, Harry. Why, the old look is coming back to your eyes. Take off that black gown, Harry, and throw it away, while you are with me. So. You are now my old friend again, and we can talk. You are no longer the President of the Holy College, the terrible and venerable Arch Physician, the Guardian of the House of Life. You are plain Harry Linister again. Tell me, then, Harry, are you happy in this beautiful Present that you have made ?'

'No, Mildred ; I am never happy.'

'Then why not unmake the Present ? Why not return to the Past ?'

'It is impossible. We might go back to the Past for a little ; but it would become intolerable again, as it did before. Formerly, there was no time for any of the fleeting things of life to lose their rapture. All things were enjoyed for a moment, and then vanished. Now,' he sighed wearily, 'they last—they last. So that there is nothing left for us but the finding of new secrets. And for you, Mildred ?'

'I have been in a dream,' she replied. 'Oh ! a long, long night-mare, that has never left me, day or night. I don't know how long it has lasted ; but it has lifted at last, thank GOD !'

The Arch Physician started and looked astonished.

'It seems a long time,' he said, 'since I heard those words. I thought we had forgotten——'

'It was a dream of no change, day after day. Nothing happened. In the morning we worked ; in the afternoon we rested ; in the evening we took food ; at night we slept. And the mind was dead. There were no books to read ; there was nothing to talk about ; there was nothing to hope. Always the same work—a piece of work that nobody cared to do—a mechanical piece of work. Always the same dress—the same hideous, horrible dress. We were all alike ; there was nothing at all to distinguish us. The Past seemed forgotten.'

'Nothing can be ever forgotten,' said Dr. Linister ; 'but it may be put away for a time.'

'Oh ! when I think of all that we had forgotten, it seems terrible. Yet we lived—how could we live ?—it was not life. No thought, no care, about anything. Everyone centred in himself, careless of his neighbour. Why, I did not know so much as the occupants of the rooms next to my own. Men looked on women, and women on men, without thought or emotion. Love was dead—Life was Death ! Harry, it was a most dreadful dream. And in the night there used to come a terrible nightmare of nothingness ! It was as if I floated alone in ether, far from the world or life, and could find nothing— nothing—for the mind to grasp or think of. And I woke at the point of madness. A dreadful dream ! And yet we lived. Rather than go back to that most terrible dream, I would—I would——'

She clasped her forehead with her hand and looked about her with haggard eyes.

'Yes, yes,' said Dr. Linister ; 'I ought to have guessed your sufferings—by my own. Yet I have had my laboratory.'·

'Then I was shaken out of the dream by a girl—by Christine. And now we are resolved—some of us—at all costs and hazards— yes, even if we are debarred from the Great Discovery—to—live— again—to live—again !' she repeated slowly. 'Do you know, Harry, what that means ? To go back—to live again ! Only think what that means.'

He was silent.

'Have you forgotten, Harry,' she asked softly, 'what that means ?'

'No,' he said. 'I remember everything ; but I am trying to understand. The accursed Present is around and above me, like a horrible black Fog. How can we lift it ? How can we live again ?'

'Some of us have found out a way. In the morning we put on the odious uniform, and do our allotted task among the poor wretches who are still in that bad dream of never-ending monotony. We sit among them, silent ourselves, trying to disguise the new light that has come back to our eyes, in the Public Hall. In the evening we come here, put on the old dresses, and live the old life.'

'It is wonderful,' he said. 'I knew all along that human nature would one day assert itself again. I told Grout so. He has always been quite wrong!'

'Grout! What does Grout know of civilized life? Grout! Why, he was your own bottle-washer—a common servant. He thought it was justice to reduce everybody to his own level, and happiness for them to remain there! Grout! Why, he has only one idea—to make us mere machines. Oh, Harry!' she said, reproach in her eyes, 'you are Arch Physician, and you cannot alter things!'

'No; I have the majority of the College against me.'

'Am I looking well, Harry, after all these years?'

She suddenly changed her voice and manner and laughed, and turned her face to meet his. Witch! Abominable Witch!

'Well, Mildred, was it yesterday that I loved you? Was the Great Discovery made only yesterday? Oh, you look lovelier than ever!'

'Lovely means worthy of love, Harry. But you have killed love.'

'No, no. Love died; we did not kill love. Why did the men cease to love the women? Was it that they saw them every day, and so grew tired of them?'

'Perhaps it was because you took from us the things that might have kept love alive : music, art, literature, grace, culture, society —everything.'

'We did not take them ; they died.'

'And then you dressed us all alike, in the most hideous costume ever invented.'

'It was Grout's dress.'

'What is the good of being Arch Physician if one cannot have his own way?'

Harry sighed.

'My place is in the laboratory,' he said. 'I experiment and I discover ; the Suffragan administers. It has always been the rule. Yet you live again, Mildred. Tell me more. I do not understand how you contrive to live again.'

'We have a little company of twenty or thirty, who meet together in the evening after the supper is over. No one else ever comes to the Museum. As soon as it is dark, you know very well, the People all creep home and go to bed. But my friends come here. It was Christine who began it. She found or made the dresses for us; she beguiled us into forgetting the Present and going back to the Past. Now we have succeeded in caring nothing at all about the Present. We began by pretending. It is no longer pretence. The Past lives again; and we hate the Present. Oh, we hate and loathe it!'

'Yes—yes. But how do you revive the Past?'

'We have dances. You used to dance very well formerly, my dear Harry. That was before you walked every day in a grand Procession, and took the highest place in the Public Hall. I wonder if you could dance again? Natures' secrets are not so heavy that they would clog your feet, are they? We sing and play: the old music has been found, and we are beginning to play it properly again. We talk; we act little drawing-room plays; sometimes we draw or paint; and—oh, Harry!—the men have begun again to make Love—real, ardent Love! All the dear old passions are reviving. We are always finding other poor creatures like ourselves, who were once ladies and gentlemen, and now are aimless and soulless; and we recruit them.'

'What will Grout say when he finds it out?'

'He can never make us go back to the Present again. So far, I defy Grout, Harry.'

The Arch Physician sighed.

'The old life!' he said; 'the old life! I will confess, Mildred, that I have never forgotten it—not for a day; and I have never ceased to regret that it was not continued.'

'Grout pulled it to pieces; but we will revive it.'

'If it could be revived! But that is impossible.'

'Nothing is impossible—to you, nothing—to you. Consider, Harry,' she whispered. 'You have the Secret.'

He started and changed colour.

'Yes—yes,' he said. 'But what then?'

'Come and see the old life revived. Come this evening—come, dear Harry.' She laid a hand upon his arm. 'Come, for auld lang syne. Can the old emotions revive again, even in the breast of the Arch Physician?'

His eyes met hers. He trembled: a sure sign that the old spirit was reviving in him. Then he spoke, in a kind of murmur:

'I have been living alone so long—so long—that I thought there was nothing left but solitude for ever. Grout likes it. He will have it that loneliness belongs to the Higher Life.'

'Come to us,' she replied, her hand still on his arm, her eyes turned so as to look into his. Ah! shameless Witch! 'We are not lonely: we talk; we exchange looks and smiles. We have begun again to practise the old arts; we have begun to read in each other's souls. Old thoughts that we had long forgotten are pouring back into our minds. It is strange to find them there again. Come, Harry! Forget the laboratory for awhile and come with us. But come without Grout. The mere aspect of Grout would cause all our innocent joys to take flight and vanish. Come! Be no more the Sacred Head of the Holy College, but my dear old friend and companion, Harry Linister, who might have been, but for the Great Discovery—but that is foolish. Come, Harry—come this evening.'

CHAPTER VIII.

THE ARCH TRAITOR.

I DISMISSED John Lax, charging him with the most profound secrecy. I knew, and had known for a long time, that this man, formerly the avowed enemy of aristocrats, nourished an extraordinary hatred for the Arch Physician, and therefore I was certain that he would keep silence.

I resolved that I would myself keep watch, and, if possible, be present at the meeting of this evening. What would happen I knew not, nor could I tell what to do: there are no laws in our community to prevent such meetings. If the Arch Physician chooses to attend such a play-acting, how is he to be prevented? But I would myself watch. You shall hear how I was rewarded.

Dr. Linister was, as usual, melancholy and preoccupied at Supper. He said nothing of what he intended. As for me, I looked about the Hall to see if there were any whom I could detect, from any unnatural restlessness, as members of this dangerous company. But I could see none, except the girl Christine, whose vivacity might be allowed on the score of youth. The face of John Lax, it is true, as he sat at the lowest place of our table, betokened an ill-suppressed joy and an eagerness quite interesting to one who understood the meaning of these emotions. Poor John Lax! Never again shall we find one like unto him for zeal and strength and courage!

I waited until half-past nine o'clock. Then I sallied forth.

It was a dark night and still. The moon was hidden; the sky was cloudy; no wind was in the air, and from time to time there were low rumblings of distant thunder.

I made my way cautiously and noiselessly through the dark Garden to the entrance of the Picture Gallery, which the faithful John Lax had left open for me. I ventured, with every precaution, into the Gallery. It seemed quite empty, but at the end there was a door opening into the Museum, which poured a narrow stream of light straight down the middle of the Gallery. I crept along the dark wall, and presently found myself at the end, close to this door. And here I came upon the group of statuary of which John Lax had told me, where I could crouch and hide in perfect safety—unseen myself, yet able to see everything that went on within.

I confess that even the revelations of John Lax had not prepared me for the scene which met my eyes. There were thirty or forty men and women present; the room was lit up; there were flowers in vases set about; there was a musical instrument, at which one sat down and sang. When she had finished, everybody began to laugh and talk. Then another sat down and began to play, and then they went out upon the floor two by two, in pairs, and began to twirl round like teetotums. As for their dresses, I never saw the like. For the women were dressed in frocks of silk — white, pink, cream-coloured — trimmed with lace; with jewels on their arms and necks, and long white gloves, and flowers in their hair. In their hands they carried fans, and their dresses were low, exposing their necks, and so much of their arms as was not covered up with gloves. And they looked excited and eager. The expression which I had striven so long to impart to their faces, that of tranquillity, was gone. The old unhappy eagerness, with flashing eyes, flushed cheeks, and panting breath, was come back to them again. Heavens! what could be done? As for the men, they wore a black-cloth dress—all alike—why, then, did they dislike the regulation blue flannel?—with a large white shirt-front and white ties and white gloves. And they, too, were full of the restless eagerness and excitement. So different were they all from the men and women whom I had observed day after day in the Public Hall, that I could remember not one except the girl Christine, and . . . and . . . yes, among them there was none other than the Arch Physician himself, laughing, talking, dancing among the rest!

I could see perfectly well through the open door, and I was quite certain that no one could see me. But I crouched lower behind the marble group when they began to come out two by two, and to talk together in the dark Gallery.

First came the girl Christine and the sailor, Jack Carera. Him at all events I remembered. They took each other's hands and began to kiss each other, and to talk the greatest nonsense imaginable. No one would ever believe that sane people could possibly talk such nonsense. Then they went back and another pair came out, and went on in the same ridiculous fashion. One has been to a Theatre in the old time and heard a couple of lover talking nonsense on the stage ; but never on any stage did I ever hear such false, extravagant, absurd stuff talked as I did when I lay hidden behind that group in marble.

Presently I listened with interest renewed, because the pair which came into the Gallery was none other than the pair I had that morning watched in the Garden—the Arch Physician and the woman he called Mildred, though now I should hardly have known her, because she was so dressed up and disguised. She looked, indeed, a very splendid creature : not in the least like a plain woman. And this, I take it, was what these would-be great ladies desired, not to be taken as plain women. Yet they were, in spite of their fine clothes, plain and simple women just as much as any wench of Whitechapel in the old time.

'Harry,' she said, 'I thank you from my very heart for coming. Now we shall have hope.'

'What hope ?' he replied, 'what hope ? What can I do for you while the majority of the College continue to side with Grout ? What hope can I bring you ?'

'Never mind the Majority. Consider, Harry. You have the Great Secret. Let us all go away together and found a new colony, where we will have no Grout ; and we will live our own lives. Do you love me, Harry ?'

'Love you, Mildred ? Oh !' he sighed deeply, 'it is a stream that has been dammed up all these years.'

'What keeps us here ?' asked the girl. 'It is that in your hands lies the Great Secret. Our people would be afraid to go without it. If we have it, Jack will take us to some island that he knows of across the seas. But we cannot go without the Secret. You shall bring it with you.'

'When could we go ?' he asked, whispering.

'We could go at any time—in a day—in a week—when you

please. Oh! Harry, will you indeed rescue us? Will you come with us? Some of us are resolved to go—Secret or not. I am one of those. Will you let me go—alone?'

'Is it impossible,' he said, 'that you should go without the Secret?'

'Yes,' she said, 'the people would be afraid. But, oh! To think of a new life ; where we shall no longer be all the same, but different. Everyone shall have his own possessions again—whatever he can win : everyone his own profession : the women shall dress as they please : we shall have Art—and Music—and Poetry again. And—oh! Harry,'—she leaned her head upon his shoulder —'we shall have Love again. Oh! to think of it! Oh! to think of it! Love once more! And with Love, think of all the other things that will come back. *They must* come back, Harry—the old Faith which formerly made us happy. . . .' Her voice choked, and she burst into tears.

I crouched behind the statues, listening. What did she cry about? The old Faith? She could have that if she wanted, I suppose, without crying over it. No law whatever against it.

Dr. Linister said nothing, but I saw that he was shaking— actually shaking—and trembling all over. A most remarkable person! Who would have believed that weakness so lamentable could lie behind so much science?

'I yield,' he said—'I yield, Mildred. The Present is so horrible that it absolves me even from the most solemn oath. Love has been killed—we will revive it again. All the sweet and precious things that made life happy have been killed : Art and Learning and Music, all have been killed—we will revive them. Yes, I will go with you, my dear ; and—since you cannot go without—I will bring the Secret with me.'

'Oh! Harry! Harry!' She flung herself into his arms. 'You have made me more happy than words can tell. Oh! you are mine—you are mine, and I am yours.'

'As for the Secret,' he went on, 'it belongs, if it is to be used at all, to all mankind. Why did the College of Physicians guard it in their own jealous keeping, save to make themselves into a mysterious and separate Caste? Must men always appoint sacred guardians of so-called mysteries which belong to all? My dear, since the Great Discovery, Man has been sinking lower and lower. He can go very little lower now. You have been rescued from the appalling fate which Grout calls the Triumph of Science. Yes ... yes ... .' he repeated, as if uncertain, 'the Secret belongs to

all or none.   Let all have it and work out their destiny in freedom :
or let none have it, and so let us go back to the old times, when
such great things were done against the fearful odds of so short
and uncertain a span.   Which would be the better ?'

'Only come with us, my lover.   Oh ! can a simple woman make
you happy ?   Come with us ; but let our friends know—else they
will not come with us—that wherever we go, we have the Secret.'

'It belongs to all,' he repeated.   'Come with me then, Mildred,
to the House of Life.   You shall be the first to whom the Secret
shall be revealed.   And you, if you please, shall tell it to all our
friends.   It is the Secret, and that alone, which keeps up the
Authority of the College.   Come.   It is dark : but I have a key
to the North Postern.   Come with me.   In the beginning of this
new Life which lies before us, I will, if you wish, give the Secret
to all who share it.   Come, my Love, my Bride.'

He led her by the hand quickly down the Picture Gallery and
out into the Garden.

I looked round.   The silly folk in the Museum were going on
with their masquerade — laughing, singing, dancing.   The girl
Christine ran in and out among them with bright eyes and eager
looks.   And the eyes of the sailor, Jack Carera, followed her
everywhere.   Oh! yes.   I knew what those eyes meant—the old
selfishness—the subjection of the Woman.   She was to be his
Property.   And yet she seemed to like it.   For ever and anon she
made some excuse to pass him, and touched his hand as she passed
and smiled sweetly.   I dare say that she was a beautiful girl—but
Beauty has nothing at all to do with the Administration of the
People.   However, there was no time to be lost.   The Arch
Physician was going to betray the Great Secret.

Happily he would have to go all the way round to the North
Postern.   There was time, if I was quick, to call witnesses, and to
seize him in the very act.   And then—the Penalty.   Death !
Death !   Death !

CHAPTER IX.

IN THE INNER HOUSE.

THE House of Life, you have already learned, is a great and
venerable building.   We build no such houses now.   No one but
those who belong to the Holy College—viz., the Arch Physician,

the Suffragan, the Fellows or Physicians, and the Assistants—are permitted to enter its doors or to witness the work that is carried on within these walls. It is, however, very well understood that this work concerns the prolongation of the Vital Forces first, the preservation of Health next, and the enlargement of scientific truth generally. The House is, in fact, the great laboratory in which the Fellows conduct those researches of which it is not permitted to speak outside. The prevention of disease, the cure of hereditary and hitherto incurable diseases, the continual lowering of the hours of labour, by new discoveries in Chemistry and Physics, are now the principal objects of these researches. When, in fact, we have discovered how to provide food chemically out of simple matter, and thereby abolish the necessity for cultivation, no more labour will be required, and Humanity will have taken the last and greatest step of all—freedom from the necessity of toil. After that, there will be no more need for labour, none for thought, none for anxiety. At stated intervals food, chemically prepared, will be served out : between those intervals man will lie at rest—asleep, or in the torpor of unthinking rest. This will be, as I have said before, the Triumph of Science.

The House, within, is as magnificent as it is without ; that is to say, it is spacious even beyond our requirements, and lofty even beyond the wants of a laboratory. All day long the Fellows and the Assistants work at their tables. Here is everything that Science wants : furnaces, electric batteries, retorts, instruments of all kinds, and collections of everything that may be wanted. Here —behind the Inner House—is a great workshop where our glass vessels are made, where our instruments are manufactured and repaired. The College contains two or three hundred of Assistants working in their various departments. These men, owing to the restlessness of their intellect, sometimes give trouble, either because they want to learn more than the Fellows think sufficient for them, or because they invent something unexpected, or because they become dissatisfied with the tranquil conditions of their life. Some of them from time to time have gone mad. Some, who threatened more trouble, have been painlessly extinguished.

Within the House itself is the Inner House, to enter which is forbidden, save to the Arch Physician, the Suffragan, and the Fellows.

This place is a kind of House within a House. Those who enter from the South orch see before them, more than half-way up the immense building, steps, upon which stands a high screen of woodwork. This screen, which is very ancient, protects the Inner House from entrance or observation. It runs round the whole enclosure, and is most profusely adorned with carved work representing all kinds of things. For my own part, I have never examined into the work, and I hardly know what it is that is here figured. What does it advance science to carve bunches of grapes (which, everybody understands not to be grapes) in wood? All these things in the House of Life—the carved wood, the carved stone, the carved marble, the lofty pillars, the painted windows—irritate and offend me. Yet the Arch Physician, who loved to sit alone in the Inner House, would contemplate these works of Art with a kind of rapture. Nay, he would well-nigh weep at thinking that now there are no longer any who can work in that useless fashion.

As for what is within the Inner House I must needs speak with caution. Suffice it, therefore, to say that round the sides of the screen are ancient carved seats under carved canopies, which are the seats of the Fellows ; and that on a raised stone platform, approached by several steps, is placed the Coffer which contains the Secret of the Great Discovery. The Arch Physician alone had the key of the Coffer: he and his Suffragan alone possessed the Secret: the Fellows were only called into the Inner House when a Council was held on some new Discovery or some new adaptation of Science to the wants of Mankind.

Now, after overhearing the intended treason of the Arch Physician, and witnessing his degradation and fall, I made haste to act ; for I plainly perceived that if the miraculous Prolongation of the Vital Force should be allowed to pass out of our own hands, and to become public property, an end would at once be put to the Order and Discipline now so firmly established : the Authority of the College would be trampled under foot : everybody would begin to live as they pleased : the old social conditions might be revived : and the old social inequalities would certainly begin again, because the strong would trample on the weak. This was, perhaps, what Dr. Linister designed. I remembered, now, how long it was before he could forget the old distinctions : nay, how impossible it was for him ever to bring himself to regard me, though his Suffragan —whom he had formerly made his serving-man—as his equal. Thinking of that time, and of those distinctions, strengthened my purpose. What I did and how I prevented the treachery will approve itself to all who have the best interests of mankind at heart.

The House of Life after nightfall is very dark : the windows are high, for the most part narrow, and, though there are a great many of them, most are painted ; so that even on a clear and bright day there is not more light than enough to carry on experiments, and, if I had my way, I would clear out all the painted glass. It is, of course, provided with the electric light ; but this is seldom used except in the short and dark days of winter, when work is carried on after nightfall. In the evening the place is absolutely empty. John Lax, the Porter, occupies the south porch and keeps the keys. But there is another and smaller door in the north transept. It leads to a Court of Cloisters, the ancient use of which has long been forgotten, the key of which is kept by the Arch Physician himself.

It was with this key—at this entrance—that he came into the House. He opened the door and closed it behind him. His footstep was not the only one : a lighter step was heard on the stones as well. In the silence of the place and time the closing of the door rumbled in the roof overhead like distant thunder, and the falling of the footsteps echoed along the walls of the great building.

The two companions did not speak.

A great many years ago, in the old times, there was a Murder done here—a foul murder by a band of soldiers, who fell upon a Bishop or Saint or Angel—I know not whom. The memory of the Murder has survived the name of the victim and the very religion which he professed—it was, perhaps, that which was still maintained among the aristocracy when I was a boy. Not only is the memory of the murder preserved, but John Lax—who, soon after the Great Discovery, when we took over the building from the priests of the old religion, was appointed its Porter and heard the old stories— would tell all those who chose to listen how the Murderers came in at that small door, and how the murder was committed on such a spot, the stones of which are to this day red with the blood of the murdered man. On the spot, however, stands now a great electrical battery.

The Arch Physician, now about to betray his trust, led his companion, the woman Mildred Carera, by the hand past this place to the steps which lead to the Inner House. They ascended those steps. Standing there, still outside the Inner House, Dr. Linister bade the woman turn round and look upon the Great House of Life.

The clouds had dispersed, and the moonlight was now shining through the windows of the South, lighting up the coloured glass, painting bright pictures and patterns upon the floor, and pouring white light through those windows, which are not painted, upon the clustered pillars and old monuments of the place. Those who were now gathered in the Inner House listened, holding their breath in silence.

'Mildred,' said Dr. Linister, 'long, long years ago we stood together upon this spot. It was after a Service of Praise and Prayer to the God whom then the world worshipped. We came from town with a party to see this Cathedral. When service was over, I scoffed at it in the light manner of the time, which questioned everything and scoffed at everything.'

'I remember, Harry; and all through the service my mind was filled with—you.'

'I scoff no more, Mildred. We have seen to what a depth men can sink when the Hope of the Future is taken from them. The memory of that service comes back to me, and seems to consecrate the place and the time. Mildred,' he said after a pause—oh! the House was very silent—'this is a solemn and a sacred moment for us both. Here, side by side, on the spot once sacred to the service of the God whom we have long forgotten, let us renew the vows which were interrupted so long ago. Mildred, with all my heart with all my strength, I love thee.'

'Harry,' she murmured, 'I am thine—even to Death itself.'

'Even to Death itself,' he replied. 'Yes, if it comes to that. If the Great Discovery itself must be abandoned: if we find that only at that price can we regain the things we have lost.'

'It was Grout who destroyed Religion—not the Great Discovery,' said the girl.

We kept silence in the House. But we heard every word; and this was true, and my heart glowed to think how true it was.

'Nay, not Grout, nor a thousand Grouts. Without the certainty of parting, Religion droops and dies. There must be something not understood, something unknown, beyond our power of discovery, or the dependence which is the ground of religion dies away in man's heart. He who is immortal and commands the secrets of Nature, so that he shall neither die, nor grow old, nor become feeble, nor fall into any disease, feels no necessity for any religion. This House, Mildred, is the expression of religion at the time of man's greatest dependence. To the God in whom, short-lived, ignorant, full of disease, he trusted he built this splendid place, and put into it all the beauty that he could command of sculpture and of form. But it speaks no longer to the People for whom it was built. When the Great Discovery was made, it would surely have been better to have found out whither it was going to lead us before we consented to receive it.'

'Surely——' said Mildred, but the other interrupted her.

'We did not understand—we were blind—we were blind.'

'Yet—we live.'

'And you have just now told me how. Remember the things that men said when the Discovery was made. We were to advance continually: we were to scale heights hitherto unapproached: we were to achieve things hitherto unknown in Art as well as in Science. Was it for the Common Meal, the Common Dress, the Common Toil, the vacant face, the lips that never smile, the eyes that never brighten, the tongue that never speaks, the heart that beats only for itself, that we gave up the things we had ?'

'We did not expect such an end, Harry.'

'No—we had not the wit to expect it. Come, Mildred, I will give you the Secret, and you may give it, if you please, to all the world. Oh! I feel as if the centuries had fallen away. I am full of hope again. I am full of the old life once more : and, Mildred —oh! my sweet—I am full of Love.'

He stooped and kissed her on the lips. Then he led her into the Inner House.

Now, just before Dr. Linister turned the key of the postern, the door of the South Porch was softly closed, and a company of twenty men walked lightly and noiselessly, in slippers, up the nave of the House. Arrived at the Inner House, they ascended the steps and entered that dark Chapel, every man making straight for his own seat and taking it without a word or a breath. This was the College of Physicians hastily called by me, and gathered together to witness the Great Treachery of the Chief. They sat there silent and breathless, listening to their talk.

The Secret was kept in a cipher, intelligible only to the two who then guarded it, in a fireproof chest upon the stone table which was once the altar of the old Faith.

Dr. Linister stood before the chest—his key in his hand.

'It would be better,' he said, 'if the new departure could be made without the Secret. It would be far—far better if we could start again under the old conditions. But if they are afraid to go without the Secret, why——' he unlocked the chest. Then he paused again.

'How many years have I been the guardian of this Secret? Mildred, when I think of the magnificent vistas which opened up before our eyes when this Great Discovery was made: when I think of the culture without bound or limit: the Art in which the hand was always to grow more and more dexterous: the Science which was to advance with gigantic strides—my child, I feel inclined to sink into the earth with shame, only to compare that dream with the awful, the terrible, the disgraceful reality! Let us all go away. Let us leave this place, and let us make a new beginning, with sadder minds, yet with this experience of the Present to guide us and to keep us from committing worse follies. See, dear—here is the Secret. The cipher in which it is written has a key which is in this paper. I place all in your hands. If accident should destroy me, you have the Secret still for yourself and friends. Use it well—use it better than we have used it. Kiss me, Mildred. Oh! my dear!'

Then, as they lay in each other's arms, I turned on the electric light and discovered them. The chest stood open: the papers, cipher, key and all, were in the girl's hands: the Arch Physician was caught in the very act of his supreme Treachery!

And lo! the Fellows of the Holy College were in the Inner House; every man in his place; every man looking on; and every man standing upright, with eyes and gestures of scorn.

'Traitor!' they cried one and all.

John Lax appeared at the door, halberd in hand.

CHAPTER X.

THE COUNCIL IN THE HOUSE.

'BROTHERS of the Holy College!' I cried, 'you have beheld the crime—you are witnesses of the Fact—you have actually seen the Arch Physician himself revealing the Great Secret, which none of yourselves, even of the College, hath been permitted to learn—the Secret confined by the Wisdom of the College to himself and to his Suffragan.'

'We are witnesses,' they cried with one consent. To my great satisfaction, even those who were of Dr. Linister's party, and who voted with him against the Administration and Policy of the College, spoke, on this occasion, for the plain and undeniable truth.

'What,' I asked, 'is the Penalty when one of the least amongst us, even an Assistant only, betrays to the People any of the secrets—even the least secret—of the work carried on in this House ?'

'It is DEATH,' they replied with one voice.

'It is DEATH,' I repeated, pointing to the Arch Physician.

At such a moment, when nothing short of annihilation appeared in view, one would have expected from the guilty pair an appearance of the greatest consternation and dismay. On the contrary, the Arch Physician, with an insensibility—or a bravado—which one would not have expected of him, stood before us all, his arms folded, his eyes steady, his lips even smiling. Beside him stood the girl, dressed in the ridiculous mummery of the nineteenth century, bowed down, her face in her hands.

'It is I,' she murmured—'it is I, Harry, who have brought you to this. Oh ! forgive me. Let us die together. Since I have awakened out of the stupid torpor of the Present—since we remembered the Past—and Love—let us die together. For I could not live without you.' She knelt at his feet and laid her head upon his arm. 'My Love,' she said, 'my Lord and Love ! Let me die with you.'

At this extraordinary spectacle I laughed aloud. Love ? I thought the old wives' tales of Love and Lordship were long, long since dead and forgotten. Yet here was a man for the sake of a woman—actually because she wanted to go away and begin again the old pernicious life—breaking his most sacred vows : and here was a woman—for the sake of this man—actually and truly for his sake—asking for death—death with him ! Since, when they were both dead, there could be no more any feeling one for the other, why ask for death ? What good could that do for either ?

'Your wish,' I said to this foolish woman, 'shall be gratified, in case the Judges of your case decide that your crime can be expiated by no less a penalty. Fellows of the College, let this guilty pair be confined for the night, and to-morrow we will try them solemnly in the College Court according to ancient custom.'

I know not how many years had elapsed since that Court was held. The offences of the old time were for the most part against property—since there had been no property, there had been no crimes of this kind. Another class of old offences consisted of violence rising out of quarrels : since almost all these quarrels originated in disputes about property—every man in the old time who had property was either a thief or the son of a thief, so that disputes were naturally incessant—there could be no longer any such quarrels or any such violence. A third class of crimes were caused by love, jealousy, and the like : these two had happily, as we believed, disappeared for ever.

The last class of crimes to vanish were those of mutiny. When the People grew gradually to understand that the welfare of all was the only rule of the governing body, and that selfishness, individualism, property, privilege, would no longer be permitted, they left off murmuring, and mutiny ceased. You have seen how orderly, how docile, how tranquil, is the life of the People as it has been ordered by the Sacred College. Alas! I thought that this order, this sheep-like freedom from Thought, was going to be henceforth universal and undisturbed.

Our prisoners made no opposition. John Lax, the Porter, bearing his halberd of office, marched beside them. We closed in behind them, and in this order we led them to the strong room over the South Porch, which is provided with bars and a lock. It is the sleeping chamber of John Lax, but for this night he was to remain on the watch below.

Then, as Suffragan, I called a Council of Emergency in the Inner House, taking the Presidency in the absence of the Arch Physician.

I told my brethren briefly what had happened : how my attention had been called to the fact that a company of the People, headed by the young girl called Christine, had begun to assemble every night in the Museum, there to put on clothes which belonged to the old time, and to masquerade in the manners, language, and amusements (so called) of that time : that this assemblage, which might have been innocent and even laudable if it led, as it should have done, to a detestation of the old times, had proved mischievous, because, strangely enough, it had exactly the opposite effect : that, in fact, everybody in the company had fallen into an ardent yearning after the Past, and that all the bad features of that bad time—the Social inequality, the Poverty, the Injustice—were carefully ignored.

Upon this, one of Dr. Linister's Party arose, and begged permission to interrupt the Suffragan. He wished to point out that memory was indestructible : that even if we succeeded in reducing Mankind, as the Suffragan wished, to be a mere breathing and feeding machine—the Ultimate Triumph of Science—any one of these machines might be at any time electrified into a full and exact memory of the Past : that, to the average man, the Emotion of the Past would always be incomparably preferable to the Tranquillity of the Present. What had just been done would be done again.

I went on, after this interruption, to narrate how I set myself to watch, and presently saw the Arch Physician himself enter the Museum : how he exchanged his gown for the costume in which the men disfigured themselves, play-acted, pretended, and masqueraded with them ; danced with them, no external respect whatever being paid to his rank ; and afterwards had certain love passages —actually love passages between the Arch Physician and a Woman of the People !—which I overheard, and repeated as far as I could remember them. The rest my brethren of the College knew already : how I hastily summoned them, and led them into the Inner House just before the arrival of the Criminals.

Thereupon, without any attempt of Dr. Linister's friends to the contrary, it was Resolved that the Trial of the Arch Physician and his accomplices should be held in the morning.

I next invited their attention to the behaviour of the girl Christine. She it was, I told them, who had instigated the whole of the business. A culpable curiosity it was, no doubt, that first led her to consider and study the ways of the ancient world : what should be the ways of the Past to an honest and loyal person, satisfied with the Wisdom which ruled the Present ? She read the old books, looked at the old pictures, and lived all day long in the old Museum. There were many things which she could not understand : she wanted to understand these things ; and she conceived a violent, unreasoning admiration for the old time, which appeared to this foolish girl to be a continual round of pleasure and excitement. Therefore she gathered together a company of those who had belonged to the richer class in the days when property was permitted. She artfully awakened them out of their contentment, sowed the seeds of dissatisfaction among them, caused them to remember the Past with a vehement longing to reproduce the worse part of it—namely, the manners and customs of the richer class—the people for whom the bulk of mankind toiled, so that the privileged few might have nothing to do but to feast, dance, sing, and make love. I asked the College, therefore, what should be done with such a girl, warning them that one Penalty, and one only, would meet the case and render for the future such outbreaks impossible.

Again the Physician who had spoken before rose up and remarked that such outbreaks were inevitable, because the memory is indestructible.

'You have here,' he said, 'a return to the Past, because a young girl, by reading the old books, has been able to stimulate the memory of those who were born in the Past. Other things may bring about the same result : a dream, the talking together of two former friends. Let the girl alone. She has acted as we might have expected a young girl—the only young girl among us—to have acted. She has found that the Past, which some of us have represented as full of woe and horror, had its pleasant side : she asks why that pleasant side could not be reproduced. I, myself, or any of us, might ask the same question. Nay, it is well known that I protest—and always shall protest, my friends and I—against the Theory of the Suffragan. His Triumph of Science we consider horrible to the last degree. I, for one, shall never be satisfied until the Present is wholly abolished, and until we have gone back to the good old system of Individualism, and begun to encourage the People once more to cultivate the old happiness by the old methods of their own exertion.'

I replied that my own recollection of the old time was perfectly clear, and that there was nothing but unhappiness in it. As a child, I lived in the street : I never had enough to eat : I was cuffed and kicked : I could never go to bed at night until my father, who always came home drunk, was asleep : the streets were full of miserable children like myself. Where was the happiness described by my learned brother ? Where was the pleasant side ? More I said, but it suffices to record that by a clear majority it was Resolved to arrest the girl Christine in the morning, and to try all three prisoners, as soon as the Court could be prepared for them, according to ancient usage.

Early in the morning I sought an interview with the Arch Physician. I found him, with the woman Mildred, sitting in the Chamber over the Porch. There was no look of terror, or even of dejection, on the face of either. Rather there was an expression as of exultation. Yet they were actually going to die—to cease breathing—to lose consciousness !

I told the prisoner that I desired to represent my own conduct in its true light. I reminded him that, with him, I was guardian of the Holy Secret. The power and authority of the College, I pointed out, were wholly dependent upon the preservation of that Secret in its own hands. By divulging it to the People he would make them as independent of the Physician as the Great Discovery itself had made them independent of the Priest. The latter had, as he pretended, the Keys of the After Life. The former did actually hold those of the Actual Life. The authority of the Physician gone, the People would proceed to divide among themselves, to split up into factions, to fight and quarrel, to hold private property, and in fact would speedily return to the old times, and all the work that we had accomplished would be destroyed. Every man would have the knowledge of the Secret for himself and his family. They would all begin to fight again—first for the family, next for the Commune, and then for the tribe or nation. All this would have been brought about by this treachery had not I prevented it.

'Yes,' he said, 'doubtless you are quite right, Grout.' He spoke quite in the old manner, as if I had been still his servant in the old laboratory. It was not until afterwards that I remembered this and became enraged to think of his arrogance. 'We will not argue the matter. It is not worth while. You acted after your kind, and as I might have expected.' Again it was not until afterwards that I considered what he meant and was enraged. 'When we allowed gentlehood to be destroyed, gentle manners, honour, dignity, and such old virtues went too. You acted—for yourself—very well, Grout. Have you anything more to say? As for us, we have gone back to the old times, this young lady and I—quite to the old, old times.' He took her hand and kissed it, while his eyes met hers, and they were filled with a tenderness which amazed me. 'This lady, Grout,' he said, 'has done me the honour of accepting my hand. You will understand that no greater happiness could have befallen me. The rest that follows is of no importance—none—not the least. My dear, this is Grout, formerly employed in my laboratory. Unfortunately he has no experience of Love, or of any of the Arts or Culture of the good old Time. But a man of great intelligence. You can go, Grout.'

CHAPTER XI.

THE TRIAL AND SENTENCE.

I was greatly pleased with the honest zeal shown by John Lax, the Porter, on this occasion. When, after snatching three or four hours' sleep, I repaired to the House, I found that worthy creature polishing at a grindstone nothing less than a great, heavy Execution Axe, which had done service many times in the old, old days on Tower Hill, and had since peacefully reposed in the Museum.

'Suffragan,' he said, ' I am making ready.' His feet turned the treadle, and the wheel flew round, and the sparks showered from the blunt old weapon. He tried the edge with his finger. ''Tis not so sharp as a razor,' he said, ' but 'twill serve.'

' John Lax, methinks you anticipate the sentence of the Court.'

'Suffragan, with submission, it is Death to divulge any secret of this House. It is Death even for me, Porter of the House, to tell them outside of any Researches or Experiments that I may observe in my service about the House. And if so great a Penalty is pronounced against one who would reveal such trifles as I could divulge, what of the Great Secret itself ?'

' Lax, you are a worthy man. Know, therefore, that this Secret once divulged, the Authority of the College would vanish ; and we, even the Physicians themselves—to say nothing of the Assistants, the Bedells, and you yourself—would become no better than the Common People. You do well to be zealous.'

John Lax nodded his head. He was a taciturn man habitually ; but now he became loquacious. He stopped the grindstone, laid down the axe, and rammed his hands into his pockets.

' When I see them women dressed up like swells——' he began, grinning.

' John, this kind of language belongs to the old days, when even speech was unequal.'

' No matter ; you understand it. Lord ! Sammy Grout, the brewer's boy—we were both Whitechapel pets ; but I was an old 'un of five-and-thirty, while you were on'y beginning to walk the Waste with a gal on your arm—p'r'aps—and a ha'penny fag in your mouth. Hold on, now. It's like this——'

What with the insolence of Dr. Linister, and the sight of the old dresses, and the sound of the old language, I myself was carried away. Yes, I was once more Sam Grout : again I walked upon the pavement of the Whitechapel Road : again I was a boy in the great brewery of Mile End Road.

' Go on, John Lax,' I said, with condescension. ' Revive, if it is possible, something of the Past. I give you full leave. But when you come to the Present, forget not the reverence due to the Suffragan.'

' Right, guv'nor. Well, then, it's like this. I see them men and women dressed up in the old fallals, and goin' on like I've seen 'em goin' on long ago with their insolence and their haw-haws—damn

16

'em—and all the old feelings came back to me, and I thought I was spoutin' again on a Sunday mornin', and askin' my fellow-country-men if they always meant to sit down and be slaves. And the memory came back to me—ah! proper it did—of a speech I made 'em one mornin' all about the French Revolution. "Less 'ave our own Revolution," I sez, sez I. "Less bring out all the Bloomin' Kings and Queens," I sez, "the Dooks and Markisses, the fat Bishops and the lazy Parsons. Less do what the French did. Less make 'em shorter by the 'ed," I sez. That's what I said that mornin'. Some of the people laughed, and some of 'em went away. There never was a lot more difficult to move than them White-chapellers. They'd listen—and then they'd go away. They'd too much fine speeches given 'em—that was the matter with 'em—too much. Nothing never came of it. That night I was in the Public havin' a drop, and we began to talk. There was a row, and a bit of a fight. But before we was fired out I up and said plain, for every-body to hear, that when it came to choppin' off their noble 'eds I'd be the man to do it—and joyful, I said. Well now, Sammy Grout, you were in that Public Bar among that crowd—maybe, you've forgotten it. But I remember you very well. You was standing there, and you laughed about the choppin'. You've forgotten, Sammy. Think. It was a fine summer evenin': you weren't in Church. Come now—you can't say you ever went to Church, Sammy Grout.'

'I never did. But go on, John Lax. Recall as much of the Past as you wish, if it makes you love the Present more. I would not say aught to diminish an honest zeal.'

'Right, guv'nor. Well, I never got that chance. There was no choppin' of 'eds at all. When we had to murder the old people, your Honour would have it done scientifically ; and there was as many old working men killed off as swells, which was a thousand pities, an' made a cove's heart bleed. What I say is this. Here we've got a return to the old Times. Quite unexpected it is. Now we've got such a chance, which will never come again, let 'em just see how the old Times worked. Have a Procession, with the Executioner goin' before the criminals, his axe on his shoulder ready to begin. If you could only be Sammy Grout again—but that can't be, I'm afraid—what a day's outing you would have had to be sure! Suffragan, let us show 'em how the old Times worked. And let me be the Executioner. I'll do it, I promise you, proper. I've got the old spirit upon me—ah! and the old strength, too— just as I had then. Oh! It's too much!' He sat down and hugged the axe. I thought he would have kissed it. 'It's too much! To think that the time would ever come when I should execute a swell—and that swell the Arch Physician himself. Damn him! He's always looked as if everybody else was dirt beneath his feet.'

'I know not,' I told him gently, 'what may be the decision of the Court. But, John Lax, continue to grind your axe. I would not throw cold water on honest zeal. Your strength, you say, is equal to your spirit. You will not flinch at the last moment? Ah! we have some honest men left.'

The Court was held that morning in the nave of the House itself. The Judges, who were the whole College of Physicians, sat in a semicircle; whereas the three prisoners stood in a row—the Arch Physician carrying himself with a haughty insolence which did not assist his chances; clinging to his arm, still in her silk dress, with her bracelets and chains, and her hair artfully arranged, was the woman called Mildred. She looked once, hurriedly, at the row of Judges, and then turned with a shudder—she found small comfort in those faces—to her lover, and laid her head upon his shoulder, while he supported her with his arm. The degradation and folly of the Arch Physician, apart from the question of his guilt, as shown in this behaviour, were complete.

Beside Mildred stood the girl Christine. Her face was flushed; her eyes were bright; she stood with clasped hands, looking steadily at the Judges; she wore, instead of the Regulation Dress, a frock of white stuff, which she had found, I suppose, in the Museum—as if open disobedience of our laws would prove a passport to favour. She had let her long fair hair fall upon her shoulders and down her back. Perhaps she hoped to conquer her Judges by her beauty— old time phrase! Woman's beauty, indeed, to Judges who know every bone and every muscle in woman's body, and can appreciate the nature of her intellect, as well as of her structure! Woman's Beauty! As if that could ever again move the world!

Behind the President's Chair—I was the President— stood John Lax, bearing his halberd of office.

The Doors of the House were closed; the usual sounds of Laboratory work were silent; the Assistants, who usually at this hour would have been engaged in Research and Experiment, were crowded outside the Court.

I have been told, since, that there were omitted at the Trial many formalities which should have been observed at such a Trial. For instance, there should have been a Clerk or two to make notes of the proceedings ; there should have been a Formal Indictment, and there should have been Witnesses. But these are idle forms. The guilt of the Prisoners was proved ; we had seen it with our own eyes. We were both Judges and Witnesses.

I was once, however, in the old days, charged (and fined) before a magistrate in Bow Street for assaulting a Constable, and, there-fore, I know something of how a Criminal Court should proceed. So, without any unnecessary formalities, I conducted the Trial according to Common Sense.

'What is your name?' I asked the Arch Physician.

'Harry Linister—once M.D. of Cambridge, and Fellow of the Royal Society.'

'What are you by trade?'

'Physicist and Arch Physician of the Holy College of the Inner House.'

'We shall see how long you will be able to describe yourself by those titles. Female Prisoner—you in the middle—what is your name?'

'I am the Lady Mildred Carera, daughter of the Earl of Thordisá.'

'Come—come—none of your Ladyships and Earls here. We are now all equal. You are plain Mildred. And yours—you girl in the white frock? How dare you, either of you, appear before us in open violation of the Rules?'

'I am named Christine,' she replied. 'I have put on the white frock because it is becoming.'

At this point I was interrupted by a whisper from John Lax.

'Christine's friends,' he said, 'are gathering in the Museum, and they are very noisy. They threaten to give trouble.'

'When the Trial and Execution are over,' I told him, 'arrest them every one. Let them all be confined in the Museum. To-morrow, or perhaps this afternoon, we will try them as well.'

The man grinned with satisfaction. Had he known what a fatal mistake I was making, he would not have grinned. Rather would his face have expressed the most dreadful horror.

Then the Trial proceeded.

'Dr. Linister,' I said, 'it is a very singular point in this case that we have not to ask you whether you plead " guilty " or " not guilty," because we have all seen you with our own eyes engaged in the very act with which you are charged. You *are* guilty.'

'I am,' he replied calmly.

'Your companion is also guilty. I saw her practising upon you those blandishments, or silly arts, by which women formerly lured men. We also saw her on the point of receiving from you the Great Secret, which must never be suffered to leave this Building.'

'Yes,' she said, 'if he is guilty, I am guilty as well.'

'As for you' (I turned to Christine), 'you have been so short a time in the world—only nineteen years or so—that to leave it will cause little pain to you. It is not as if you had taken root with all the years of life which the others have enjoyed. Yet the Court would fail in its duty did it not point out the enormity of your offence. You were allowed to grow up undisturbed in the old Museum ; you spent your time in developing a morbid curiosity into the Past. You were so curious to see with your own eyes what it was to outward show, that you cast about to find among the tranquil and contented People some whose minds you might disturb and lead back to the restless old times. This was a most guilty breach of confidence. Have you anything to say ? Do you confess ?'

'Yes, I confess.'

'Next, you, with this woman and a Company who will also be brought to Justice before long, began to assemble together, and to revive, with the assistance of books, pictures, dress, and music, a portion of the Past. But what portion ? Was it the portion of the vast majority, full of disease, injustice, and starvation ? Did you show how the old Times filled the houses with struggling needlewomen and men who refused to struggle any longer ? Did you show the Poor and the Unemployed ? Not at all. You showed the life of the Rich and the Idle. And so you revived a longing for what shall never—never—be permitted to return—the Period of Property and the Reign of Individualism. It was'your crime to misrepresent the Past, and to set forth the Exception as the Rule. This must be made impossible for the future. What have you to say, Christine ?'

'Nothing. I told you before. Nothing. I have confessed. Why keep on asking me ?'

She looked round the Court with no apparent fear. I suppose it was because she was so young, and had not yet felt any apprehension of the Fate which was now so near unto her.

'Dr. Linister,' I said, 'before considering its sentence, the Court will hear what you may have to say.'

'I have but little to say,' he replied. 'Everybody in the College knows that I have always been opposed to the methods adopted by the Suffragan and the College. During the last few days, however,

I have been enabled to go back once more to the half-forgotten Past, and have experienced once more the Emotions of which you have robbed Life. I have seen once more, after many, many years, the Fighting Passion, the Passion of Private Rights, and '—his voice dropped to a whisper—'I have experienced once more the Passion of Love.' He stooped and kissed the woman Mildred on the forehead. 'I regret that we did not succeed. Had we not been caught, we should by this time have been beyond your power —the Secret with us, to use or not, as we pleased—with a company strong enough to defy you, and with the old Life again before us, such as we enjoyed before you robbed us of it. We should have welcomed the old Life, even under the old conditions : we welcome, instead of it, the Thing which, only to think of, makes your hearts almost to stop beating with fear and horror.'

He stopped. That was a speech likely to win indulgence from the Court, was it not ?

I turned to the woman Mildred.

'And you ?' I asked.

'What have I to say? The Present I loathe—I loathe—I loathe ! I would not go back to it if you offered me instant release with that condition. I have found Love. Let me die—let me die —let me die !'

She clung to her lover passionately, weeping and sobbing. He soothed her and caressed her. John Lax, behind me, snorted.

Then I asked the girl Christine what she wished to say.

She laughed—she actually laughed.

'Oh !' she said, 'in return for the past weeks, there is no punishment which I would not cheerfully endure. We have had—oh ! the most delightful time. It has been like a dream. Oh ! Cruel, horrid, wicked men ! You found such a Life in the old Time, and you destroyed it ; and what have you given us in return ? You have made us all equal who were born unequal. Go, look at the sad and heavy faces of the People. You have taken away every-thing, deliberately. You have destroyed all—all. You have left nothing worth living for. Why, I am like Mildred. I would not go back to the Present again if I could ! Yes, for one thing I would—to try and raise a Company of Men — not sheep—and hound them on to storm this place, and to kill—yes, to kill '—the girl looked so dangerous that any thought of mercy was impossible —'everyone who belongs to this Accursed House of Life !'

Here was a pretty outcome of study in the Museum ! Here was a firebrand let loose among us straight from the bad old Nineteenth Century!   And we had allowed this girl actually to grow up in our very midst.

Well, she finished, and stood trembling with rage, cheeks burning, eyes flashing—a very fury.

I invited the Court to retire to the Inner House, and took their opinions one by one.

They were unanimous on several points—first, that the position of things was most dangerous to the Authority of the College and the safety of the People ; next, that the punishment of Death alone would meet the case ; thirdly, that, in future, the Museum, with the Library and Picture Galleries, must be incorporated with the College itself, so that this danger of the possible awakening of memory should be removed.

Here, however, our unanimity ceased.   For the Fellow, of whom I have already spoken as having always followed the Arch Physician, arose and again insisted that what had happened to-day might very well happen again : that nothing was more uncertain in its action, or more indestructible, than human memory ; so that, from time to time, we must look for the arising of some Leader or Prophet who would shake up the people and bring them out of their torpor to a state of discontent and yearning after the lost.   Wherefore he exhorted us to reconsider our Administration, and to provide some safety valve for the active spirits. As to the Death of the three criminals, he would not—he could not—oppose it.   He proposed, however, that the mode of Death should be optional.   So great a light of Science as the Arch Physician had many secrets, and could doubtless procure himself sudden and painless death if he chose.   Let him have that choice for himself and his companions ; and, as regards the girl, let her be cast into a deep sleep, and then painlessly smothered by gas, without a sentence being pronounced upon her at all.   This leniency, he said, was demanded by her youth and her inexperience.

In reply, I pointed out that, as regards our Administration, we were not then considering it at all : that as for the mode of punishment, we had not only to consider the criminals, but also the People, and the effect of the punishment upon them : we were not only to punish, but also to deter.   I therefore begged the Court to go back to one of the former methods, and to one of the really horrible and barbarous, yet comparatively painless, methods.   I showed that a mere report or announcement, made in the Public Hall, that the Arch Physician had been executed for Treason, would produce little or no effect upon the public mind, even if it were added that the two women, Mildred and Christine, had suffered with him : that our people needed to see the thing itself, in order to feel its true horror and to remember it. If Death alone were wanted, I argued, there were dozens of ways in which Life might be painlessly extinguished. But it was not Death alone that we desired—it was Terror that we wished to establish, in order to prevent another such attempt.

'Let them,' I concluded, 'be taken forth in solemn Procession to the open space before the Public Hall—we ourselves will form part of that Procession. Let them in that place, in the sight of all the People, be publicly decapitated by the Porter of the House, John Lax.'

There was a good deal of opposition, at first, to this proposition, because it seemed barbarous and cruel ; but the danger which had threatened the Authority—nay, the very existence—of the College, caused the opposition to give way. Why, if I had not been on the watch, the Secret would have been gone : the College would have been ruined. It was due to me that my proposals should be accepted. The sentence was agreed upon.

I am bound to confess that, on being brought back to receive the sentence of the Court, the Prisoners behaved with unexpected Fortitude. The male criminal turned pale, but only for a moment, and the two women caught each other by the hand. But they offered no prayer for mercy.

They were led back to their prison in the South Porch, until the necessary Preparations could be made.

CHAPTER XII.

THE REBELS.

It is useless to regret a thing that is done and over ; otherwise, one might very bitterly regret two or three steps in these proceedings. At the same time, it may be argued that what happened was the exact opposite of what we had every reason to expect, and therefore we could not blame ourselves with the event. After uncounted years of blind obedience, respect for authority, and unquestioning submission, had we not a full right to expect a continuance of the same spirit ? What we did not know or suspect was the violence of the reaction that had set in. Not only had these revolutionaries gone back to the Past, but to the very worst traditions of the Past.

They had not only become anxious to restore these old traditions ; they had actually become men of violence, and were ready to back up their new convictions by an appeal to arms. We ought to have arrested the conspirators as soon as they assembled ; we ought to have locked them up in the Museum and starved them into submission ; we ought to have executed our criminals in private ; in short, we ought to have done just exactly what we did not do.

While the Trial was proceeding, the new Party of Disorder were, as John Lax reported, gathered together in the Museum, considering what was best to be done.

They now knew all. When John Lax, in the morning, arrested the girl Christine, by my orders, he told her in plain language what had already happened.

'The Arch Physician is a Prisoner,' he said. 'He has been locked up all night in my room, over the South Porch. I watched below. Ha ! If he had tried to escape, my instructions were to knock him on the head, Arch Physician or not. The woman Mildred is a Prisoner, as well. She was locked up with him. They may hold each other's hands and look into each other's eyes, in my room, as much as they please. And now, young woman, it is your turn.'

'Mine ?'

'Yours, my gal. So march along o' me.'

'Why, what have I done that I should be arrested ?'

'That you shall hear. March, I say. You are my Prisoner. You will stand your Trial—ah !' He smacked his lips to show his satisfaction, and wagged his head. He was a true Child of the People, and could not conceal his gratification at the discomfiture of traitors. 'You will hear what the Court has to say—ah !' Again he repeated this sign of satisfaction. 'You will be tried, and you will hear the Sentence of the Court—ah, ah ! Do you know what it will be ? Death !' he whispered. 'Death for all ! I see the sentence in the Suffragran's face. Oh ! he means it.'

The girl heard without reply ; but her cheeks turned pale.

'You won't mind much,' he went on. 'You hardly know what it is to live. You haven't been alive long enough to feel what it means. You're only a chit of a girl. If it wasn't for the example, I dare say they would let you off. But they won't—they won't. Don't try it on. Don't think of going on your knees, or anything else. Don't go weeping or crying. The Court is as hard as nails.'

The honest fellow said this in his zeal for justice, and in the hope that nothing should be said or done which might avert just punishment. Otherwise, had this girl, who was, after all, young and ignorant, thrown herself fully and frankly upon our mercy, perhaps—I do not say—some of us might have been disposed to spare her. As it was—but you have seen.

'We waste time,' he said. 'March !'

She was dressed, as I have already related, in a masquerade white dress of the old time, with I know not what of ribbon round her waist, and wore her hair floating down her back.

The old man—her grandfather, as she called him—sat in his arm-chair, looking on and coughing. John Lax paid no attention to him at all.

'Good-bye, grandad,' she said, kissing him. 'You will not see me any more, because they are going to kill me. You will find your inhaler in its place ; but I am afraid you will have to manage for the future without any help. No one helps anybody in this beautiful Present. They are going to kill me. Do you understand ? Poor old man ! Good-bye !'

She kissed him again and walked away with John Lax through the Picture Gallery, and so into the College Gardens, and by the North Postern into the House of Life.

When she was gone, the old man looked about him feebly. Then he began to understand what had happened. His grandchild, the nurse and stay of his feebleness, was gone from him. She was going to be killed.

He was reckoned a very stupid old man always. To keep the cases in the Museum free from dust was all that he could do. But the revival of the Past acted upon him as it had acted upon the others : it took him out of his torpor and quickened his perceptions.

'Killed ?' he cried. 'My grandchild to be killed ?'

He was not so stupid as not to know that there were possible protectors for her, if he could find them in time. Then he seized his stick and hurried as fast as his tottering limbs would carry him to the nearest field, where he knew the sailor, named John, or Jack, Carera, was employed for the time among the peas and beans.

'Jack Carera !' he cried, looking wildly about him and flourishing his stick. 'Jack ! they are going to kill her ! Jack—Jack Carera !—I say,' he repeated. 'Where is Jack Carera ? Call him, somebody. They are going to kill her ! They have taken my child a prisoner to the House of Life. I say, Jack—Jack ! Where is he ? Where is he ?'

The men were working in gangs. Nobody paid the least heed to the old man. They looked up, saw an old man—his hat blown off, his long white hair waving in the wind—brandishing wildly his stick, and shrieking for Jack. Then they went on with their work; it was no business of theirs. Docile, meek, und unquestioning are the People.

By accident, however, Jack was within hearing, and presently ran across the field.

'What is it?' he cried. 'What has happened?'

'They have taken prisoner,' the old man gasped, 'the—the—Arch Physician—and—Lady Mildred—— They are going to try them to-day before the College of Physicians. And now they have taken my girl—my Christine—and they will try her too. They will try them all, and they will kill them all.'

'That shall be seen,' said Jack, a fierce look in his eyes. 'Go back to the Museum, old man, and wait for me. Keep quiet, if you can : wait for me.'

In half an hour he had collected together the whole of tho company, men and women, which formed their Party. They were thirty in number, and they came in from work in the Regulation Dress.

The sailor briefly related what had happened.

'Now,' he said, 'before we do anything more, let us put on the dress of the nineteenth century. That will help us to remember that our future depends upon ourselves, and will put heart in us.'

This done, he made them a speech.

First, he reminded them how, by the help of one girl alone, the memory of the Past had been restored to them ; next, he bade them keep in their minds the whole of that Past—every portion of it—and to brace up their courage with the thought of it—how delightful and desirable it was. And then he exhorted them to think of the Present, which he called loathsome, shameful, vile, and other bad names.

'We are in the gravest crisis of our fortunes,' he concluded. 'On our action this day depends our whole future. Either we emerge from this crisis free men and women, or we sink back into the Present, dull and dismal, without hope and without thought. Nay, there is more. If we do not rescue ourselves, we shall be very speedily finished off by the College. Do you think they will ever forgive us? Not so. As they deal with the Arch Physician and these two ladies, so they will deal with us. Better so. Better a thousand times to suffer Death at once, than to fall back into that wretched condition to which we were reduced. What! You, who have learned once more what is meant by Love, will you give that up? Will you give up these secret assemblies where we revive the glorious Past, and feel again the old thoughts and the old ambitions? Never—swear with me—never! never! never!'

They shouted together; they waved their hands; they were resolved. The men's eyes were alive again; in short, they were back again to the Past of their young days.

'First,' said Jack, 'let us arm.'

He led them to a part of the Museum where certain old weapons stood stacked. Thanks to the Curator and to Christine, they had been kept bright and clear from rust by the application of oil.

'Here are swords, lances, rifles—but we have no ammunition—bayonets. Let us take the rifles and bayonets. So. To every man one. Now, the time presses. The Trial is going on. It may be too late in a few minutes to save the prisoners. Let us resolve.'

Two plans suggested themselves at once. The first of these was to rush before the House of Life, break open the gates, and tear the prisoners from the hands of the Judges. The next was to ascertain, somehow, what was being done. The former counsel prevailed, and the men were already making ready for the attack when the great Bell of the House began to toll solemnly.

'What is that?' cried the women, shuddering.

It went on tolling, at regular intervals of a quarter of a minute. It was the knell for three persons about to die.

Then the doors of the South Porch flew open, and one of the Bedells came forth.

'What does that mean?' they asked.

The Bedell walked across the great Garden and began to ring the Bell of the Public Hall—the Supper Bell.

Instantly the People began to flock in from the workshops and the fields, from all quarters, in obedience to a summons rarely issued. They flocked in slowly, and without the least animation, showing not the faintest interest in the proceedings. No doubt there was something or other—it mattered not what—ordered by the College.

'Go, somebody," cried Jack—'go, Hilda,' he turned to one of the girls: 'slip on your working dress; run and find out what is being done. Oh! if we are too late, they shall pay—they shall pay! Courage, men! Here are fifteen of us, well armed and stout. We are equal to the whole of that coward mob. Run, Hilda, run!'

Hilda pushed her way through the crowd.

'What is it?' she asked the Bedell eagerly. 'What has happened?'

'You shall hear,' he replied. 'The most dreadful that can happen—a thing that has not happened since. . . . But you will hear.'

He waited a little longer, until all seemed to be assembled. Then he stood upon a garden-bench and lifted up his voice :

'Listen! listen! listen!' he cried. 'By order of the Holy College, listen! Know ye all that, for his crimes and treacheries, the Arch Physician has been deposed from his sacred office. Know ye all that he is condemned to die.' There was here a slight movement —a shiver—as of a wood, on a still autumn day, at the first breath of the wind. 'He is condemned to die. He will be brought out without delay, and will be executed in the sight of the whole People.' Here they trembled. 'There are also condemned with him, as accomplices in his guilt, two women—named respectively Mildred, or Mildred Carera in the old style, and the girl Christine. Listen! listen! listen! It is forbidden to any either to leave the place during the time of punishment, or to interfere in order to stay punishment, or in any way to move or meddle in the matter. Listen! Listen! Long live the Holy College!'

With that he descended and made his way back to the House ; but Hilda ran to the Museum with the news.

'Why,' said Jack, 'what could happen better? In the House, no one knows what devilry of electricity and stuff they may have ready to hand. Here, in the open, we can defy them. Nothing remains but to wait until the prisoners are brought out, and then— then,' he gasped, 'remember what we were. Geoffrey, you wear the old uniform. Let the spirit of your old regiment fire your heart again. Ay, ay, you will do. Now, let us drill a little and practice fighting together, shoulder to shoulder. Why, we are invincible.'

Said I not that we might, if we ever regretted anything, regret that we did not lock these conspirators in the Museum before we brought out our prisoners to their death ?

The great Bell of the House tolled ; the People stood about in their quiet way, looking on, apparently unmoved, while the carpenters quickly hammered together a scaffold some six feet high.

Well. I confess it. The whole business was a mistake ; the People were gone lower down than I had ever hoped ; save for the shudder which naturally seized them on mention of the word Death, they showed no sign of concern. If, even then, I had gone forth to see how they took it, I might have reversed the order, and carried out the execution within. They wanted no lesson. Their Past, if it were once revived, would for the most part be a past of such struggling for life, and so much misery, that it was not likely they would care to revive it. Better the daily course, unchanged, unchangeable. Yet we know not. As my colleague in the House said, the memory is perhaps a thing indestructible. At a touch, at a flash of light, the whole of their minds might be lit up again; and the emotions, remembered and restored, might again seem what once they seemed, worth living for.

Still the great Bell tolled, and the carpenters hammered, and the scaffold, strong and high, stood waiting for the criminals; and on the scaffold a block, brought from the butcher's shop. But the People said not a single word to each other, waiting, like sheep —only, unlike sheep, they did not huddle together. In the chamber over the Porch the prisoners awaited the completion of the preparations; and in the Museum the fifteen conspirators stood waiting, armed and ready for their Deed of Violence.

CHAPTER XIII.

THE EXECUTION.

As the clock struck two, a messenger brought the news that the Preparations were complete.

The College was still sitting in Council. One of the Physicians proposed that before the Execution the Arch Physician should be brought before us to be subjected to a last examination. I saw no use for this measure, but I did not oppose it; and presently John Lax, armed with his sharpened axe, brought the Prisoner before the Conclave of his late brethren.

'Dr. Linister,' I said, 'before we start upon that Procession from which you will not return, have you any communication to make to the College? Your Researches——'

'They are all in order, properly drawn up, arranged in volumes, and indexed,' he replied. 'I trust they will prove to advance the Cause of Science—true Science—not the degradation of Humanity.'

'Such as they are, we shall use them,' I replied, 'according to the Wisdom of the College. Is there anything else you wish to communicate? Are there ideas in your brain which you would wish to write down before you die? Remember, in a few minutes you will be a senseless lump of, clay, rolling round and round the world for ever, like all the other lumps which form the crust of the Earth.'

'I have nothing more to communicate. Perhaps, Suffragan, you are wrong about the senseless lumps of clay. And now, if you please, do not delay the end longer, for the sake of those poor girls waiting in suspense.'

I could have wished more outward show of horror—prayers for forgiveness. No : Dr. Linister was always, in his own mind, an Aristocrat. The aristocratic spirit ! How it survives even after the whole of the Past might have been supposed to be forgotten ! Well : he was a tall and manly man, and he looked a born leader— a good many of them in the old days used to have that look. For my own part, I am short and black of face. No one would call me a leader born. But I deposed the Aristocrat. And as for him —what has become of him ?

' What would you have done for the People ?' I asked him, ' that would have been better for them than forgetfulness and freedom from pain and anxiety ? You have always opposed the Majority. Tell us, at this supreme moment, what you would have done for them.'

'I know not now,' he replied. 'A month ago I should have told you that I would have revived the ancient order ; I would have given the good things of the world to them who were strong enough to win them in the struggle : hard work, bad food, low condition should have been, as it used to be, the lot of the in-competent. I would have recognised in women their instinct for fine dress : I would have encouraged the revival of Love : I would have restored the Arts. But now—now——'

' Now,' I said, ' that you have begun to make the attempt, you recognise at last that there is nothing better for them all than forgetfulness and freedom from anxiety, struggle, and thought.'

' No so,' he replied. ' Not at all. I understand that unless the Spirit of Man mounts higher continually, the earthly things must grow stale and tedious, and so must perish. Yea : all the things which once we thought so beautiful—Music, Art, Letters, Philo-sophy, Love, Society—they must all wither and perish, if Life be prolonged, unless the Spirit is borne continually upwards. And this we have not tried to effect.'

' The Spirit of Man ? I thought that old superstition was cleared away and done with long ago. I have never found the Spirit in my Laboratory. Have you ?'

'No, I have not.   That is not the place to find it.'

'Well.   Since you have changed your mind——'

'With us, the Spirit of Man has been sinking lower and lower, till it is clean forgotten.   Man now lives for himself alone.   The Triumph of Science, Suffragan, is yours.   No more death; no more pain; no more ambition: equality absolute and the ultimate lump of human flesh incorruptible, breathing, sleeping, absorbing food, living.   Science can do no more.'

'I am glad, even at this last moment, to receive this submission of your opinions.'

'But,' he said, his eye flashing, 'remember.   The Spirit of Man only sleeps: it doth not die.   Such an awakening as you have witnessed among a few of us will some day—by an accident, by a trick of memory—how do I know? by a Dream!—fly through the heads of these poor helpless sheep and turn them again into Men and Women who will rend you.   Now take me away.'

It is pleasant to my self-esteem, I say, to record that one who was so great an inquirer into the Secrets of Nature should at such a moment give way and confess that I was right in my administration of the People.   Pity that he should talk the old nonsense.   Why, I learned to despise it in the old days when I was a boy and listened to the fiery orators of the Whitechapel Road.

The Procession was formed.   It was like that of the Daily March to the Public Hall, with certain changes.   One of them was that the Arch Physician now walked in the middle instead of at the end: he was no more clothed in the robes of office, but in the strange and unbecoming garb in which he was arrested.   Before him walked the two women.   They held a book between them, brought out of the Library by Christine, and one of them read aloud.   It was, I believe, part of the incantation or fetish worship of the old time: and as they read, the tears rolled down their cheeks; yet they did not seem to be afraid.

Before the Prisoners marched John Lax, bearing the dreadful axe, which he had now polished until it was like a mirror or a laboratory tool for brightness.   And on his face there still shone the honest satisfaction of one whose heart is joyed to execute punishment upon traitors.   He showed this joy in a manner perhaps unseemly to the gravity of the occasion, grinning as he walked and feeling the edge of the axe with his fingers.

The way seemed long.   I, for one, was anxious to get the business over and done with.   I was oppressed by certain fears— or doubts—as if something would happen.   Along the way on either side stood the People, ranged in order, silent, dutiful, stupid. I scanned their faces narrowly as I walked. In most there was not a gleam of intelligence. They understood nothing. Here and there a face showed a spark of uneasiness or terror. For the most part, nothing. I began to understand that we had made a blunder in holding a Public Execution. If it was meant to impress the People, it failed to do so. That was certain, so far.

What happened immediately afterwards did, however, impress them as much as they could be impressed.

Immediately in front of the Public Hall stood the newly-erected scaffold. It was about six feet high, with a low hand-rail round it, and it was draped in black. The block stood in the middle.

It was arranged that the Executioner should first mount the Scaffold alone, there to await the criminals. The College of Physicians were to sit in a semicircle of seats arranged for them on one side of it, the Bedells standing behind them ; the Assistants of the College were arranged on the opposite side of the scaffold. The first to suffer was to be the girl Christine. The second, the woman Mildred. Last, the greatest criminal of the three, the Arch Physician himself.

The first part of the programme was perfectly carried out. John Lax, clothed in red, big and burly, his red face glowing, stood on the scaffold beside the block, leaning on the dreadful axe. The Sacred College were seated in their places : the Bedells stood behind them : the Assistants sat on the other side. The Prisoners stood before the College. So far all went well. Then I rose and read in a loud voice the Crimes which had been committed and the sentence of the Court. When I concluded I looked around. There was a vast sea of heads before me. In the midst I observed some kind of commotion as of people who were pushing to the front. It was in the direction of the Museum. But this I hardly noticed, my mind being full of the Example which was about to be made. As for the immobility of the People's faces, it was something truly wonderful.

' Let the woman Christine,' I cried, ' mount the scaffold and meet her doom !'

The girl threw herself into the arms of the other woman, and they kissed each other. Then she tore herself away, and the next moment she would have mounted the steps and knelt before the block, but . . . .

The confusion which had sprung up in the direction of the Museum increased suddenly to a tumult. Right and left the

17

people parted, flying and shrieking. And there came running through the lane thus formed a company of men, dressed in fantastic garments of various colours, armed with ancient weapons, and crying aloud, 'To the Rescue! To the Rescue!'

Then I sprang to my feet, amazed. Was it possible—could it be possible—that the Holy College of Physicians should be actually defied?

It was possible; more, it was exactly what these wretched persons proposed to dare and to do.

As for what followed, it took but a moment. The men burst into the circle thus armed and thus determined. We all sprang to our feet and recoiled. But there was one who met them with equal courage and defiance. Had there been—but how could there be?—any more, we should have made a wholesome example of the Rebels.

John Lax was this one.

He leaped from the scaffold with a roar like a lion, and threw himself upon the men who advanced, swinging his heavy axe around him as if it had been a walking-stick. No wild beast deprived of its prey could have presented such a terrible appearance. Baffled revenge—rage—the thirst for battle—all showed themselves in this giant as he turned a fearless front to his enemies and swung his terrible axe.

I thought the rebels would have run. They wavered; they fell back; then at a word from their leader—it was none other than the dangerous man, the sailor called Jack, or John, Carera—they closed in and stood shoulder to shoulder, every man holding his weapon in readiness. They were armed with the ancient weapon called the rifle, with a bayonet thrust on at the end of it.

'Close in, my men; stand firm!' shouted the sailor. 'Leave John Lax to me. Ho! ho! John Lax, you and I will fight this out. I know you. You were the spy who did the mischief. Come on. Stand firm, my men; and if I fall, make a speedy end of this spy and rescue the Prisoners.'

He sprang to the front, and for a moment the two men confronted each other. Then John Lax, with another roar, swung his axe. Had it descended upon the sailor's head, there would have been an end of him. But—I know little of fighting; but it is certain that the fellow was a coward. For he actually leaped lightly back and dodged the blow. Then, when the axe had swung round so as to leave his adversary's side in a defenceless position, the disgraceful coward leaped forward and took a shameful advantage of this accident, and drove his bayonet up to the hilt in the unfortunate Executioner's body!

John Lax dropped his axe, threw up his arms, and fell heavily backwards. He was dead. He was killed instantaneously. Anything more terrible, more murderous, more cowardly, I never witnessed. I know, I say, little of fighting and war. But this, I must always maintain, was a foul blow. John Lax had aimed his stroke and missed, it is true, owing to the cowardly leap of his enemy out of the way. But in the name of common fairness his adversary should have permitted him to resume his fighting position. As it was, he only waited, cowardly, till the heavy axe swinging round exposed John's side, and then stepped in and took his advantage. This I call murder, and not war.

John Lax was quite dead. Our brave and zealous servant was dead. He lay on his back; there was a little pool of blood on the ground : his clothes were stained with blood : his face was already white. Was it possible? Our servant—the sacred servant of the Holy House—was dead! He had been killed! A servant of the Holy College had been killed! What next? What dreadful thing would follow? And the Criminals were rescued!

By this time we were all standing bewildered, horrified, in an undignified crowd, Fellows and Assistants together. Then I spoke, but I fear in a trembling voice.

'Men !' I said. 'Know you what you do? Go back to the place whence you came, and await the punishment due to your crime. Back, I say !'

'Form in Square !' ordered the murderer, paying no heed at all to my commands.

The Rebels arranged themselves—as if they had rehearsed the thing for weeks—every man with his weapon ready : five on a side, forming three sides of a square, of which the scaffold formed the fourth. Within the Square stood the three prisoners.

'Oh ! Jack !' cried Christine. 'We never dreamed of this.'

'Oh ! Harry !' murmured Mildred, falling into the arms of the rescued Dr. Linister. At such a moment, the first thing they thought of was this new-found love. And yet there are some who have maintained that human nature could have been continued by Science on the old lines ! Folly at the bottom of everything ! Folly and Vanity !

'Sir,' the Sailor man addressed Dr. Linister, 'you are now our Chief. Take this sword and the command.'

He threw a crimson sash over the shoulders of him who but a

minute before was waiting to be executed, and placed in his hands a drawn sword.

Then the Chief—I am bound to say that he looked as if he was born to command—mounted the scaffold and looked round with eyes of authority.

'Let the poor People be dismissed,' he said. 'Bid them disperse—go home—go to walk, and rest or sleep, or anything that is left in the unhappy blank that we call their mind.'

Then he turned to the College.

'There were some among you, my former Brethren,' he said, 'who in times past were friends of my own. You voted with me against the degradation of the People, but in vain. We have often communed together on the insufficiency of Science and the unwisdom of the modern methods. Come out from the College, my friends, and join us. We have the Great Secret, and we have all the knowledge of Science that there is. Cast in your lot with mine.'

Five or six of the Fellows stepped forth—they were those who had always voted for the Arch Physician—among them was the man who had spoken on the uncertainty of memory. These were admitted within the line of armed men. Nay, their gowns of office were taken from them and they presently received weapons. About twenty or thirty of the Assistants also fell out and were admitted to the ranks of the Rebels.

'There come no more?' asked the Chief. 'Well, choose for yourselves. Captain Heron, make the crowd stand back—clear them away with the butt ends of your rifles, if they will not go when they are told. So. Now let the rest of the College return to the House. Captain Carera, take ten men and drive them back. Let the first who stops, or endeavours to make the others stop, or attempts to address the People, be run through, as you despatched the man John Lax. Fellows and Assistants of the College—back to the place whence you came. Back, as quickly as may be, or it will be the worse for you.'

The ten armed men stepped out with lowered bayonets. We saw them approaching with murder in their eyes, and we turned and fled. It was not a retreat : it was a helter-skelter run—one over the other. If one fell, the savage Rebels prodded him in fleshy parts and roared with laughter. Fellows, Assistants, and Bedells alike—we fell over each other, elbowing and fighting, until we found ourselves at last—some with bleeding noses, some with black eyes, some with broken ribs, all with torn gowns—within the House of Life.

The Rebels stood outside the South Porch, laughing at our discomfiture.

'Wardens of the Great Secret,' said Captain Carera, 'you have no longer any Secret to guard. Meantime, until the pleasure of the Chief, and the Sentence of the Court is pronounced, REMEMBER. He who endeavours to escape from the House will assuredly meet his death. Think of John Lax, and do not dare to resist the authority of the Army.'

Then he shut the door upon us and locked it, and we heard the footsteps of the men as they marched away in order.

This, then, was the result of my most fatal error. Had we, as we might so easily have done, executed our prisoners in the House itself, and locked up the Rebels in the Museum, these evils would not have happened. It is futile to regret the past, which can never be undone. But it is impossible not to regret a blunder which produced such fatal results.

CHAPTER XIV.

PRISONERS.

THUS, then, were the tables turned upon us. We were locked up, prisoners—actually the Sacred College, prisoners—in the House of Life itself, and the Great Secret was probably by this time in the hands of the Rebels, to whom the Arch Traitor had no doubt given it, as he had proposed to do when we arrested him. Lost to us for ever ! What would become of the College, when the Great Mystery was lost to it ? Where would be its dignity ? Where its authority ?

The first question—we read it in each other's eyes without asking it—was, however, not what would become of our authority, but of ourselves. What were they going to do with us ? They had killed the unfortunate John Lax solely because he stood up manfully for the College. What could we expect ? Besides, we had fully intended to kill the Rebels. Now we were penned up like fowls in a coop, altogether at their mercy. Could one have believed that the Holy College, the Source of Health, the Maintainer of Life, would ever have been driven to its House, as to a prison, like a herd of swine to their sty ; made to run head over heels, tumbling over one another, without dignity or self-respect ; shoved, bundled, cuffed, and kicked into the House of Life, and locked up, with the promise of instant Death to any who should endeavour to escape ? But did they mean to kill us ? That was the Question before us. Why should they not ? We should have killed the Arch Physician, had they suffered it ; and now they had all the power.

I confess that the thought of this probability filled my mind with so great a terror, that the more I thought of it the more my teeth chattered and my knees knocked together. Nay, the very tears—the first since I was a little boy—came into my eyes in thinking that I must abandon my Laboratory and all my Researches, almost at the very moment when the Triumph of Science was well within my grasp, and I was ready—nearly—to present Mankind at his last and best. But at this juncture the Assistants showed by their behaviour and their carriage—now greatly wanting in respect—that they looked to us for aid, and I hastily called together the remaining Fellows in the Inner House.

We took our places, and looked at each other with a dismay which could not be concealed.

'Brothers,' I said, because they looked to me for speech, 'it cannot be denied that the Situation is full of Danger. Never before has the College been in danger so imminent. At this very instant they may be sending armed soldiers to murder us.'

At this moment there happened to be a movement of many feet in the nave, and it seemed as if the thing was actually upon us. I sat down, pale and trembling. The others did the same. It was several minutes before confidence was so far restored that we could speak coherently.

'We have lived so long,' I said, 'and we have known so long the pleasure of Scientific Research, that the mere thought of Death fills us with apprehensions that the common people cannot guess. Our superior nature makes us doubly sensitive. Perhaps—let us hope—they may not kill us—perhaps they may make demands upon us to which we can yield. They will certainly turn us out of the College and House of Life and install themselves, unless we find a way to turn the tables. But we may buy our lives ; we may even become their assistants. Our knowledge may be placed at their disposal——'

'Yes, yes,' they all agreed. 'Life before everything. We will yield to any conditions.'

'The Great Secret has gone out of our keeping,' I went on. 'Dr. Linister has probably communicated it to all alike. There goes the whole Authority, the whole Mystery, of the College.'

'We are ruined !' echoed the Fellows in dismay.

'Half-a-dozen of our Fellows have gone over, too. There is not now a Secret, or a Scientific Discovery, or a Process, concerning Life, Food, Health, or Disease, that they do not know as well as ourselves. And they have all the Power. What will they do with it ? What can we do to get it out of their hands ?'

Then began a Babel of suggestions and ideas. Unfortunately every plan proposed involved the necessity of someone risking or losing his life. In the old times, when there were always men risking and losing their lives for some cause or other, I suppose there would have been no difficulty at all. I had been accustomed to laugh at this foolish sacrifice of one's self—since there is but one life—for pay, or for the good of others. Now, however, I confess that we should have found it most convenient if we could have persuaded some to risk—very likely they would not actually have lost—their lives for the sake of the Holy College. For instance, the first plan that occurred to us was this. We numbered, even after the late defections, two hundred strong in the College. This so-called 'Army' of the Rebels could not be more than seventy, counting the deserters from the College. Why should we not break open the doors and sally forth, a hundred—two hundred— strong, armed with weapons from the laboratory, provided with bottles of nitric and sulphuric acid, and fall upon the Rebel army suddenly while they were unprepared for us ?

This plan so far carried me away that I called together the whole of the College—Assistants, Bedells, and all—and laid it before them. I pointed out that the overwhelming nature of the force we could hurl upon the enemy would cause so great a terror to fall upon them, that they would instantly drop their arms and fly as fast as they could run, when our men would have nothing more to do but to run after and kill them.

The men looked at one another with doubtful eyes. Finally, one impudent rascal said that as the Physicians themselves had most to lose, they should themselves lead the assault. 'We will follow the Suffragan and the Fellows,' he said.

I endeavoured to make them understand that the most valuable lives should always be preserved until the last. But in this I failed.

The idea, therefore, of a sortie in force had to be abandoned.

It was next proposed that we should dig a tunnel under the Public Hall and blow up the Rebels with some of the old explosives. But to dig a tunnel takes time, and then who would risk his life with the explosive ?

It was further proposed to send out a deputation of two or three, who should preach to the Rebels and point out the terrible consequences of their continued mutiny. But this appeared impracticable, for the simple reason that no one could be found to brave the threat of Captain Carera of death to any who ventured out. Besides, it was pointed out, with some reason, that if our messengers were suffered to reach the Rebels, no one would be moved by the threats of helpless prisoners unable to effect their own release. As for what was proposed to be done with electricity, hand grenades, dynamite, and so forth, I pass all that over. In a word, we found that we could do nothing. We were prisoners.

Then an idea occurred to me. I remembered how, many years before, Dr. Linister, who had always a mind full of resource and ingenuity, made a discovery by means of which one man, armed with a single weapon easy to carry, could annihilate a whole army. If war had continued in the world, this weapon would have put an immediate stop to it. But war ceased, and it was never used. Now, I thought, if I could find that weapon or any account or drawing of its manufacture, I should be able from the commanding height of the Tower, with my own hand, to annihilate Dr. Linister and all his following.

I proceeded, with the assistance of the whole College, to hunt among the volumes of Researches and Experiments. There were thousands of them. We spent many days in the search. But we found it not. When we were tired of the search we would climb up into the Tower and look out upon the scene below, which was full of activity and bustle. Oh! if we could only, by simply pointing the weapon, only by pressing a knob, see our enemies swiftly and suddenly overwhelmed by Death!

But we could not find that Discovery anywhere. There were whole rows of volumes which consisted of nothing but indexes. But we could not find it in any of them. And so this hope failed.

They did not kill us. Every day they opened the doors and called for men to come forth and fetch food. But they did not kill us.

Yet the danger was ever present in our minds. After a week the College resolved that, since one alone of the body knew the Great Secret, that one being the most likely to be selected for execution if there were any such step taken, it was expedient that the Secret should be revealed to the whole College. I protested, but had to obey. To part with that Secret was like parting with all my power. I was no longer invested with the sanctity of one who held that Secret; the Suffragan became a simple Fellow of the College; he was henceforth only one of those who conducted Researches into Health and Food and the like.

This suspense and imprisonment lasted for three weeks. Then the Rebels, as you shall hear, did the most wonderful and most unexpected thing in the world. Why they did it, when they had the House of Life, the College, and all in their own hands, and could have established themselves there and done whatever they pleased with the People, I have never been able to understand.

CHAPTER XV.

THE RECRUITING SERGEANT.

WHEN the College had thus ignominiously been driven into the House and the key turned upon us, the Rebels looked at each other with the greatest satisfaction.

'So far,' said Jack, 'we have succeeded beyond our greatest hopes. The Prisoners are rescued; the only man with any fight in him has been put out of the temptation to fight any more; the Holy College are made Prisoners; ourselves are masters of the field, and certain to remain so; and the People are like lambs—nothing to be feared from them—nothing, apparently, to be hoped.'

They had been reduced to terror by the violence of the Rebels in pushing through them; they had rushed away, screaming: those of them who witnessed the horrible murder of John Lax were also seized with panic and fled. But when no more terrifying things befell, they speedily relapsed into their habitual indifference, and crept back again, as if nothing had happened at all, to dawdle away their time in the sunshine and upon the garden benches— every man alone, as usual. That the Holy College were Prisoners —that Rebels had usurped the Authority—affected them not a whit, even if they understood it. My administration had been even too successful. One could no longer look to the People for anything. They were now, even more rapidly than I had thought possible, passing into the last stages of human existence.

'Ye Gods!' cried Dr. Linister, swearing in the language of the Past and by the shadows long forgotten. 'Ye Gods! How stupid they have become! I knew not that they were so far gone. Can nothing move them? They have seen a victorious Rebellion—a Revolution, not without bloodshed. But they pay no heed. Will nothing move them? Will words? Call some of them together,

Jack. Drive them here. Let us try to speak to them. It may be that I shall touch some chord, which will recall the Past. It was thus that you—we—were all awakened from that deadly Torpor.'

Being thus summoned, the People—men and women—flocked about the scaffold, now stripped of its black draperies, and listened while Dr. Linister harangued them. They were told to stand and listen, and they obeyed, without a gleam in their patient, sheep-like faces to show that they understood.

*   *   *   *   *

'I can do no more !' cried Dr. Linister, after three-quarters of an hour.

He had drawn a skilful and moving picture of the Past ; he had depicted its glories and its joys, compared with the dismal realities of the Present. He dwelt upon their loveless and passionless existence ; he showed them how they were gradually sinking lower and lower—that they would soon lose the intelligence necessary even for the daily task. Then he asked them if they would join his friends and himself in the new Life which they were about to begin : it should be full of all the old things—endeavour, struggle, ambition, and Love. They should be alive, not half dead.

More he said—a great deal more—but to no purpose. If they showed any intelligence at all, it was terror at the thought of change.

Dr. Linister descended.

'It is no use,' he said. 'Will you try, Jack ?'

'Not by speaking. But I will try another plan.'

He disappeared, and presently came back again, having visited the cellars behind the Public Halls. After him came servants, rolling barrels and casks at his direction.

'I am going to try the effect of a good drink,' said Jack. 'In the old days they were always getting drunk, and the trades had each its favourite liquor. It is now no one knows how long since these poor fellows have had to become sober, because they could no longer exceed their ration. Let us encourage them to get drunk. I am sure that ought to touch a chord.'

This disgraceful idea was actually carried out. Drink of all kinds—spirits, beer, and every sort of intoxicating liquor—was brought forth, and the men were invited to sit down and drink freely, after the manner of the old time.

When they saw the casks brought out and placed on stands, each ready with its spigot, and, besides the casks, the tables and benches spread for them—on the benches, pipes and tobacco—gleams of intelligence seemed to steal into their eyes.

'Come,' said Jack, 'sit down, my friends ; sit down, all of you. Now then, what will you drink? What shall it be? Call for what you like best. Here is a barrel of beer : here is stout ; here are gin, whisky, rum, Hollands, and brandy. What will you have? Call for what you please. Take your pipes. Why, it is the old time over again.'

They looked at each other stupidly. The very names of these drinks had been long forgotten by them. But they presently accepted the invitation, and began to drink greedily. At seven o'clock, when the Supper Bell rang, there were at least three hundred men lying about, in various stages of drunkenness. Some were fast asleep, stretched at their full length on the ground ; some lay with their heads on the table ; some sat, clutching at the pewter mugs ; some were vacuously laughing or noisily singing.

'What do you make of your experiment?' asked Dr. Linister. 'Have you struck your chord?'

'Well, they have done once more what they used to do,' said Jack despondently ; 'and they have done it in the same old way. I don't think there could ever have been any real jolliness about the dogs who got drunk as fast as ever they could. I expected a more gradual business. I thought the drink would first unloose their tongues and set them talking. Then I hoped that they would, in this way, be led to remember the Past ; and I thought that directly they began to show any recollection at all, I would knock off the supply and carry on the memory. But the experiment has failed, unless '—here a gleam of hope shone in his face— 'to-morrow's hot coppers prove a sensation so unusual as to revive the memory of their last experience in the same direction—never mind how many years ago. Hot coppers *may* produce that result.'

He ordered the casks to be rolled back to the cellars. That evening the Rebels, headed by Dr. Linister—all dressed in scarlet and gold, with swords—and with them the ladies (they were called ladies now, nothing less—not women of the People any more)— came to the Public Hall, dressed for the evening in strange garments, with bracelets, necklaces, jewels, gloves, and things which most of the People had never seen. But they seemed to take no heed of these things.

'They are hopeless,' said Jack ; 'nothing moves them. We shall have to begin our new life with our own company of thirty.'

'Leave them to us,' said Mildred. 'Remember, it was by dress that Christine aroused us from our stagnant condition; and it was by us that you men were first awakened. Leave them to us.'

After the evening meal, the ladies went about from table to table, talking to the women. Many of these, who had belonged to the working classes in the old Time, and had no recollection at all of fine dress, looked stupidly at the ladies' dainty attire. But there were others whose faces seemed to show possibilities of other things, and to these the ladies addressed themselves. First, they asked them to look at their fine frocks and bangles and things; and next, if any admiration was awakened, they begged them to take off their flat caps and to let down their hair. Some of them consented, and laughed with new-born pride in showing off their long-forgotten beauty. Then the ladies tied ribbons round their necks and waists, put flowers into their hair, and made them look in the glass. Not one of those who laughed and looked in the glass but followed the ladies that evening to the Museum.

They came—a company of Recruits fifty strong, all girls. And then the whole evening was devoted to bringing back the Past. It came quickly enough to most. To some, a sad Past, full of hard, underpaid work; to some, a Past of enforced idleness; to some, a Past of work and pay and contentment. They were shop-girls, work-girls, ballet-girls, barmaids—all kinds of girls. To every one was given a pretty and becoming dress; not one but was rejoiced at the prospect of changing the calm and quiet Present for the emotions and the struggles of the Past.

But they were not allowed to rest idle. Next day these girls again, with the ladies, went out and tried the effect of their new dress and their newly-restored beauty upon other women first, and the men afterwards. As they went about, lightly and gracefully, singing, laughing, daintily dressed, many of the men began to lift their sleepy eyes, and to look after them. And when the girls saw these symptoms, they laid siege to such a man, two or three together; or perhaps one alone would undertake the task, if he was more than commonly susceptible. As for those on whom bright eyes, smiles, laughter, and pretty dresses produced no effect, they let them alone altogether. But still Recruits came in fast.

Every night they did all in their power to make the Past live again. They played the old Comedies, Melodramas, and Farces in the Public Hall; they sang the old songs; they encouraged the Recruits to sing; they gave the men tobacco and beer; they had dances and music. Every morning the original company of Rebels sat in Council. Every afternoon the Recruits, dressed like soldiers of the Past, were drawn up, drilled, and put through all kinds of bodily exercises.

We were Prisoners, I said, for three weeks.

One morning, at the end of that time, a message came to us from the 'Headquarters of the Army.' This was now their official style and title. The Chief ordered the immediate attendance of the Suffragan and two Fellows of the College of Physicians.

At this terrifying order, I confess that I fell into so violent a trembling—for, indeed, my last hour seemed now at hand—that I could no longer stand upright ; and, in this condition of mind, I was carried—being unable to walk, and more dead than alive—out of the House of Life to the Headquarters of the Rebel Army.

CHAPTER XVI.

A MOST UNEXPECTED CONCLUSION.

I CONFESS, I say, that I was borne in a half-fainting condition from the House of Life.

'Farewell, Suffragan, farewell !' said my Brethren of the College, gathered within the South Porch, where a guard of armed Rebels waited for us. 'Your turn to-day, ours to-morrow ! Farewell ! Yet if any concessions can be made——'

Yes—yes—if any concessions could be made, only to save life, they might be certain that I should make them. The two Fellows of the College upon whom the lot—they drew lots—had fallen, accompanied me, with cheeks as pallid and hearts as full of terror as my own.

A company of twenty men, armed, escorted us. I looked on the way for lines of People to witness the Downfall of the College and the Execution of its Heads. I looked for the scaffold which we had erected, and for the executioner whom we had provided. I listened for the Great Bell which we had caused to be rung.

Strange ! There were no People at all: the way from the House was quite clear: the People were engaged as usual at their work. I saw no scaffold, and no executioner. I heard no Great Bell. Yet the absence of these things did not reassure me in the least.

But everything, even in these short three weeks, was changed. Nearly the whole of the open space before the Public Hall was now covered with rows of gay-coloured tents, over which flew bright little flags. They were quite small tents, meant, I learned afterwards, for sleeping. Besides these there were great tents open at the sides, and spread, within, with tables and benches, at which sat men smoking tobacco and drinking beer, though it was as yet only the forenoon. Some of them were playing cards, some were reading books, and some—a great many—were eagerly talking. They were all dressed in tunics of scarlet, green, and gray, and wore leathern belts with helmets—the costume seemed familiar to me. Then I remembered: it was the old dress of a soldier. Wonderful! After Science had lavished all her resources in order to suppress and destroy among the People the old passions—at the very first opportunity, the Rebels had succeeded in awakening them again in their worst and most odious form!

There were also large open spaces upon which, regardless of the flower-beds, some of the men were marching up and down in line, carrying arms, and performing evolutions to the command of an officer.

Some of the men, again, lay sprawling about on benches, merely looking on and doing nothing—yet with a lively satisfaction in their faces. They ought to have been in the fields or the workshops. And everywhere among the men, looking on at the drill, sitting in the tents, walking beside them, sitting with them on the benches, were the girls, dressed and adorned after the bad old false style, in which the women pretended to heighten and set off what they are pleased to call their charms by garments fantastically cut, the immodest display of an arm or a neck, hair curiously dressed and adorned, coloured ribbons, flowers stuck in their hats, and ornaments tied on wherever it was possible. And such joy and pride in these silly decorations! No one would believe how these girls looked at each other and themselves. But to think that the poor silly men should have fallen into the nets thus clumsily spread for them! And this, after all our demonstrations to show that woman bears in every limb the mark of inferiority, so that contempt, or at least pity, and not admiration at all, to say nothing of the extraordinarily foolish passion of Love, should be the feeling of man for woman! However, at this moment I was naturally too much occupied with my own danger to think of these things.

One thing, however, one could not avoid remarking. The Rebellion must have spread with astonishing rapidity. It was no longer a company of fifteen or sixteen men—it was a great Army that we saw. And there was no longer any doubt possible as to the movement. The Past was restored. In the faces of the young men and the girls, as we passed through them, I remarked, sick with terror as I was, the old, old expression which I hoped we had abolished for ever—the eagerness, the unsatisfied desire, and the Individualism. Yes—the Individualism. I saw on their faces, plain to read, the newly-restored Rights of Property.

Why, as I walked through one of the groups, composed of men and women, one of the men suddenly rushed forward and struck another in the face with his fist.

'She's my girl!' he cried hoarsely. 'Touch her if you dare.'

They closed round the pair and led them off.

'Going to fight it out,' said one of our Guards.

To fight it out! What a Fall! To fight it out! To call a woman—or anything else—your own after all our teaching! And to fight it out! And all this arrived at in three weeks!

These things I observed, I say, as one observes things in a dream, and remembers afterwards.

My heart failed me altogether, and I nearly fainted, when we stopped at a long tent before which floated a great flag on a flagstaff.

They carried me within and placed me in a chair. As soon as my eyes recovered the power of sight, I saw, sitting at the head of the table, Dr. Linister, dressed in some sort of scarlet coat, with a sash and gold lace. Then, indeed, I gave myself up for lost. It was the Court, and we were called before it to receive sentence. At his side sat half a dozen officers bravely dressed. The tent was filled with others, including many women richly dressed—I observed the woman Mildred, clad in crimson velvet, and the girl Christine, in white, and I thought they regarded me with vindictive eyes.

When we were seated, Dr. Linister looked up—his face was always grave, but it was no longer melancholy. There was in it, now, something of Hope or Triumph or Resolution—I know not what.

'Brothers,' he said gravely, 'once my brothers of the College, I have called you before us in order to make a communication of the greatest importance, and one which will doubtless cause you considerable surprise. What is the matter, Suffragan? Hold him up, somebody. We desire that you should hear from our own lips what we propose to do.

'First—will somebody give Dr. Grout a glass of wine or brandy, or something? Pray be reassured, gentlemen. No harm, I promise, shall happen to any of you. First, in a day or two the doors of the House will be thrown open, and you shall be free again to renew your old life—if you still feel disposed to do so. I repeat that no violence is intended towards you. Grout, pull yourself together, man. Sit up, and leave off shaking. You will be able without opposition, I say, to carry on again your Administration of the People on the old lines. I trust, however, that you will consider the situation, and the condition to which you have reduced unfortunate Humanity, very seriously.

'In short, though we are absolute masters of the situation, and now command a Force against which it would be absurd for you to contend, we are going to abandon the Field, and leave everything to you.' Were we dreaming? 'The Present is so odious to our People: the surroundings of this place are so full of the horrible and loathsome Present, that we have resolved to leave it altogether. We find, in fact, that it will be impossible to begin the new Life until all traces of your Administration are removed or lost. And we shall be so much clogged by your Public Halls, your houses, your system, and the miserable lives to which you have reduced most of the men and women, that we must either send them—and you—away, or go away ourselves. On the whole, it will give us less trouble to go away ourselves. Therefore, as soon as our Preparations are ready, we shall go.

'We shall carry with us from the Common Stores all that we shall be likely to want in starting our New Community. We shall leave you to work out, undisturbed, the Triumph of Science, as you understand it, upon these poor wretches, already more than half stupefied by your treatment.

'We shall take with us all those whom by any means—by the beauty of woman, the splendour of arms, the ancient dresses, the ancient music, the ancient dances—we have been able to awaken from their torpor. They amount in all to no more than a thousand or so of young men and as many maidens. As for the rest, they are sunk in a lethargy so deep that we have been unable to rouse them. They are already very near to the condition which you desire.

'Yet I know not. These poor dull brains may be swiftly and suddenly fired with some contagion which may at any time ruin your calculations and destroy the boasted Triumph. Do not rely too much upon the Torpor of this apparently helpless herd. You had at the beginning a grand weapon with which to enslave them. You could keep them alive, and you could save them from disease —if only they were obedient. If they once get beyond the recollection or the fear of either, what will you do?

'We go'—he paused, and looked round the room, filled with the eager faces which brought the Past back to me—futile eagerness! ever pressing on, gaining nothing, sinking into the grave before there was time to gain anything! That had come back—that! 'We go,' he repeated—his face had long been so melancholy that one hardly knew him for the same man, so triumphant was it now ; 'we go to repair the mistakes of many, many years. We go to lead Mankind back into the ancient paths. It was not altogether you, my friends, who destroyed Humanity: it was mainly the un-fortunate Discovery of the German Professor. We were working admirably in the right direction: we were making life longer, which was then far too short: we were gradually preventing diseases, which had been beyond the control of our wisest men : we were, by slow degrees, in the only true way—through the Revelation of Nature—feeling our way to Health and Prolongation of Life. Yet, whatever happened—whatever we might discover, the First Law of Life—which we did not understand—was that to all things earthly there must come an End.

'Then happened the event by which that End was indefinitely postponed.

'Again, I say, I blame not you so much as the current of events which bore you along. It seemed logical that everybody, able or imbecile, weak or strong, healthy or sickly, skilled or incompetent, should alike reap the Fruits of the Great Discovery. If he did so, he was also entitled to his equal share in the world's goods. This was the Right of Man, put forward as if there could be no question at all about it. Every child was to inherit an equal share of every-thing. It was a false and mischievous claim. What every child inherited was the right of fighting for his share, without danger of injustice or oppression. And the next step, after the Slaughter of the Old, was the forbidding of more births. What that has done for the world, look round and see for yourselves in the torpor of the women and the apathy of the men.

'The People by this time had learned the great lesson that you wished to teach them—that Death and Disease were the only two evils. Then the College of Physicians took the place of the former Priesthood, with its own Mysteries to guard and its gifts to dis-tribute. I do not deny that you—we—have done the work well. The Prevention of the old Diseases is nearly perfect. Yet, at any moment, a new class of Disease may spring up, and baffle all your Science.'

He had often talked in this way before, but never with so much authority. Yet he was going to abandon the whole—all that he and his friends had gained! Were we dreaming? His talk about my Administration affected me not one whit. I knew all his arguments. But the thought that he was going away, that he would actually leave us in Power and Possession, filled me with amazement.

The others looked and listened as if he was speaking for them.

'The Right of Man to an equal share in everything has been carried out. Look around you, and ask yourselves if the result is satisfactory. I have often asked you that question. You have replied that the Present is only a stage in the Triumph of Science. What is the next stage? To that question also you have a reply.

'Well, we give it back to you—the whole of your Present; your People, so stupid, so docile, so sluggish; your House; your College; your Secrecy; your Mystery; your Authority. Take them. You shall have them again, to do with them as seems fit to you.'

At these words my heart welled over with joy. Would he really —but on what conditions?—would he really give us back the whole?

There were no conditions. He meant exactly what he said. He would give everything back to us. Were we dreaming? Were we dreaming?

'As for me and my fr[iends,' he] said, 'we shall sally forth to found a new Settlement, and to govern it by the ideas of the Past. No one in our Settlement will be obliged to work; but if he does not, he shall certainly starve. Nobody will inherit any share to anything except what he may win by struggle. There will be no equality at all, but every man shall have what he can honestly get for himself. No women shall be compelled to work; but they may work if they please, and at such things as they please. Many old and long-forgotten things have been already revived; such as Love: we are in love again—we, who actually forgot what love was like for all the years which we have ceased to number or to chronicle. It is impossible to describe to you, my former Brother Suffragan, who never even in the old days felt the passion—the intense joy, the ecstasy—of Love.' The other men murmured approval. 'But Love is a plant which, while it is hardy to endure many things, withers and dies under certain conditions. It was found to flourish in the old time, through all the changes of life: it survived the time of youth and beauty: it lasted through middle age; it lived through the scenes of old age; it lasted beyond the grave. It endured changes of fortune, decay of health, poverty, sickness, and even helplessness. But one thing kills

Love. It cannot endure the dull monotony which has followed the Great Discovery : it cannot live long while the face and form know no change ; while the voice never changes; while the dress, the hours of work, the work itself, the food, know no change. These are things which kill the Flower of Love. Now, all things desirable—this is a saying too hard for you, Suffragan—depend upon Love. With Love, they have revived : the courtesy of man to woman ; the deference of the stronger to the weaker ; the stimulus of work ; hope and ambition ; self-sacrifice ; unselfishness ; devotion ; the sweet illusions of imagination—all these things have been born again within the last three weeks. They have been born again, and, with them, the necessity of an End. All things earthly must have an end.' The Chief looked round him : the men murmured approval, and tears stood in the eyes of the women. 'We cannot let them die. And since the First Law of Love is change—and the Certain End—we have resolved, Suffragan, on forgetting the Grand Discovery.' Could this be our late Arch Physician ? Were we dreaming ? 'We shall forego any share in it. Only the chiefs here gathered together know as yet what has been resolved. Little by little the truth will get possession of our people that an End is ordained.'

We made no reply to this extraordinary announcement. What could we say ? We only gasped with wonder.

'You cannot understand this, Grout. I do not expect that you should. For long years past I have understood that the Great Discovery was the greatest misfortune that ever happened to mankind. For all things must have an End : else all that is worth preserving will wither and die.

'I have nearly done. You can go back to your House, and you can carry on your Administration as you please. But there is a warning which we have first to pronounce before we let you go. Your Ultimate Triumph of Science is too great a degradation of Humanity to be endured. In years to come, when our successors rule in our place, they shall send an army here to inquire into the conduct of your Trust. If we find the People more brutish, deeper sunk in apathy and torpor, that army will seize the House of Life and the College of Physicians, and will destroy your laboratories, and will suffer all—men and women of the People and Fellows of the Sacred College alike—to die. Never forget this warning. You shall surely die.

'One more point and I have done. I mention it with diffidence, Grout, because I cannot hope for your sympathy. Your own convictions on the subject were arrived at—you have often told us—when you were a boy, and were based upon the arguments of a Sunday-morning Spouter in the Whitechapel Road. I believe that John Lax, deceased, was the Learned Authority who convinced you. Therefore, you will not understand me, Grout, when I tell you that we have found the Soul again—the long-lost Soul. All earthly things must have an End. But there are things beyond that end. Most astonishing results are likely to follow from this discovery. Long thought and great hopes have already begun to spring up in our minds. Our people are reading again—the old Literature is full of the Soul : they are reading the great Poets of old, and are beginning to understand what they mean. I cannot make this intelligible to you, Grout. You will not understand all that this discovery brings with it. You will never, never understand that it is a Discovery ten times—a million times—greater and better for mankind than the Great Discovery itself, of which you and I alone held the Secret.

' I take that Secret with me because I cannot forget it. But, I repeat, we shall never use it. Soon, very soon, the new active life will make men once more familiar with the old figure who carried a scythe. There will be accidents ; new diseases will arrive ; age will creep slowly on—the Great Discovery will be quietly forgotten in minds which you had made so dull that they could not understand when we rescued them what it meant. But we, the leaders, shall know well that their happiness must have an End. All earthly things,' he repeated, for the fifth time, 'must have an End. That is all, Grout ; but when you hear from me again, unless the Administration is changed indeed, the People—the College—and you, my Suffragan—shall all die together. You shall die, Grout ! You and your friends shall die ! And so, Farewell. Guard ! Take them back to the House.'

We returned to the House relieved of our terror, but much amazed. I had heard, in the old days, how men would be so blockishly possessed by the thought of a woman—a creature inferior to man—that they would throw away everything in the world for her sake. And now Dr. Linister himself—with all those who followed after him—had given up everything ; because if Life goes, what is there left ? And for the sake of a woman ! What could it mean ? How to explain this madness on any scientific theory ? We told our Colleagues, and they marvelled ; and some suspected a trick. But Dr. Linister was not a man to play tricks. As for the Soul and all that rubbish, if Dr. Linister was so mad as to give up everything for a woman, he might just as well adopt all the old Creeds together. That was no concern of ours. And as for this precious discovery about things earthly coming to an end, what had that to do with the calm and tranquil state of pure existence which we were providing for mankind? Why should that ever have an end?

That threatened army has never come. For some time the thought of it gave us considerable uneasiness. But it has never come; and I believe, for my own part, that now it never will come. As for the People, there has been no such outbreak of Memory as was prophesied. On the contrary, they have approached more and more, in docility, meekness, mindlessness, and absence of purpose, to the magnificent Ideal which I cherish for them. I know not when it will arrive; but the time is as certain to come as the morrow's sun is to dawn, when the last stage of Humanity will be reached—an inert mass of breathing, feeding, sleeping flesh, kept by the Holy College—the Triumph of Science —free from Decay and Death.

They went away in the afternoon, three or four days later. They took with them everything from the Public Stores which they thought would be useful: provisions of all kinds; wine, beer, and cider in casks; stuff for clothing; furniture; everything that they could think of. They took the pictures out of the Gallery, the books from the Library, and nearly everything that was in the Museum. From the laboratory in the House they took a great number of volumes and a quantity of instruments. At the last moment, nearly all the Assistants and the workmen agreed to join them; so that we were left with numbers greatly reduced It is impossible to enumerate the vast quantities of things which they took with them. The waggons in which they were packed covered a couple of miles of road: the drivers were taken from the People, and ordered to discharge their duty; and, as they never came back, these poor wretches probably perished with the Rebels. They went forth in perfect order: first, an advance guard of mounted men; then a portion of the main body, among whom rode the Chief with his staff. After them came the women, some riding on horseback, among whom were the woman Mildred and the girl Christine, showing in their faces that foolish and excited happiness which is so different from the sweet tranquillity which we have introduced. Indeed, all the women were beyond themselves with this silly happiness. They sang, they laughed, they talked. Some sat in carriages of all kinds, some in waggons; some walked; and, what with their chatter and their dresses, one would have thought them a company of monkeys dressed up. After the women came the waggons, and, lastly, the rest of the men. I forgot to say that they had bands of music with them—drums, fifes, cornets, and all kinds of musical instruments—and that they carried flags, and that the men sang as they marched.

Whither they went, or what became of them—whether they carried out the desperate resolve of giving up the Great Discovery —I know not. They marched away, and we returned to our former life.

One thing more I must relate.

We—that is, the College—were seated, reassured as to our safety, watching this great Departure.

Five minutes or so after the women had passed, I observed two of my own friends—learned Fellows of the College, who had always followed my lead and voted with me—eagerly whispering each other, and plucking one another by the sleeve. Then they suddenly rose and pulled off their black gowns, and fled swiftly in the direction of the waggons and carriages where the women sat.

We have never seen or heard of these two unfortunate men since.

I am now myself the Arch Physician.

EVEN WITH THIS.

I stood to-day beside the grave of my dear old friend Paul ——
(his name will be known by his friends, and for those who were
not his friends his name may remain unknown). The vicar read
the funeral service while the birds were singing on the trees, the
sun shone on the laburnum and the lilac, and from below the cliff
came the roll of the waves along the shore. His remains were
laid beside those of his wife, and while the words of the solemn
service fell upon my ears, I was thinking how it would have fared
with Paul had it not been for his marriage. It will harm no one
now to tell the story of that marriage.

Paul died at the age of fifty-two, a time of life when most men
look forward to many more years of successful work. There was
only one reason why he should not have lived to three-score years
and ten—namely, that his wife was dead. She died twelve months
before him, and he could not endure life without her companionship. He looked more than fifty-two, because he had gone completely gray, and he stooped and walked slowly, as one who is
drawing near to the grave. When first he met his wife, in the
year 1857, he was—well, he was twenty-five years of age to begin
with. It seems as if merely to be twenty-five is enough, but I
suppose some other things are desirable as well. He had just been
called to the Bar ; he was a fellow of his college, a hard-headed
reader, and an athlete, such as athletes then were. That is to say,
he neither ran nor leaped, and took no heed of running or leaping,
but he tugged a manful oar in his college boat, went to Switzerland
after every 'long,' climbed high mountains, and made light of in-
accessible peaks, and at home took great walks. He was popular
because he possessed a pleasant voice, a pleasant face, and a
pleasant manner ; because he was not small and petty in speech
or thought ; and because he was strong. Nobody among under-
graduates is so popular as the man who is strong. It was also

known to Paul's friends that he was ambitious as well as strong. In order to further his ambitious aims, he read mathematics, and came out in the first half-dozen wranglers. Though he had no real genius or love for that many-headed science, yet he knew that a good degree and a fellowship are good things for a barrister to begin with. They recommend a man. Further, in order to acquire facility in speaking, he spoke regularly at the Union, and learned to speak well. Whatever he attempted, he either did well or abandoned altogether.

For instance, he played racquets admirably, but would never play billiards ; he played whist well, but would not play chess ; and in conversation he spoke only about things in which he was tolerably well ' posted.' There are in every generation of under-graduates two or three men such as Paul, who have determined beforehand for themselves that they have a great career before them : it will generally be found that they are not mistaken.

I have said that in the year 1857 Paul was twenty-five years of age. It was in that year that he took the step which subsequently led to his early retirement. And it happened in this way.

In the month of September we started together upon a walking expedition. In those days we had a project for walking round the coast of Great Britain, taking a fortnight here and another there, according to season and opportunity, and reckoning that we should complete the task—allowing for sinuosities and creeks—in three hundred and seventy-three years exactly. We carried a white round pebble. At the end of each walk, we buried it and marked the place : at the beginning of a new walk we dug it up again. By this method one was quite sure of passing over the whole ground without the possibility of self-deception. We began very well, with capital weather and high spirits. On the afternoon of the third day an accident happened of a very common and uninteresting nature. Paul twisted his ankle on a loose stone. We were then about a mile and a half distant from a certain small village through which we had to pass, but we had not intended to rest a night there. When we reached it, however, the trouble of the ankle became so bad that it was absolutely necessary to stop. Fortunately we found a decent inn, with better accommodation than might have been expected. It was an old thatched and rustic village public-house, to which had been built a new modern wing containing three or four bedrooms, a coffee-room, and a billiard-room.

After laying my man upon the sofa in the coffee-room, I went out to explore the place. It was more considerable than I had expected ; there was a single long street running up a gentle hill from the seashore ; on the top of the hill was a church with an ancient square rubble tower and a square brick 'temple' of the period of George II. ; beyond the church were two roads, and beside them certain villas, which looked very pretty amid the woods and trees and gardens. At the lower end of the town was the port. Here the sea runs inland and makes a little creek for the reception of a stream ; they have built out a brick jetty and constructed a wharf, along which are generally lying half a dozen small vessels ; a few boats were hauled upon the beach, with two or three fishing-smacks and a row of fisher-folk's cottages, the women sitting at work in the doors, the men leaning against posts, and the children playing barefooted on the sand. Looking up the creek, one saw trees and fields and houses behind the masts, producing effects unusual in England ; you can see it on the Dart, and at Bridgwater, and on the quay at Yarmouth.

There was not much to observe. I walked to the end of the jetty, where three ancient mariners were sitting in a row, each with a pipe in his mouth. Far out to sea, one saw a steamer, low down on the horizon, the following of smoke looking as solid as the hull and many miles long ; so that one wondered why the craft, with this top-heavy gear, did not capsize. There was a gentle ripple on the water, and a soft westerly breeze. On the right of the creek there rose a bold headland, such as are so common on the white coasts of Albion ; on the left the land was low for a mile or two, and then rose gradually, and there was a great bay with a sweep of cliff after cliff, very beautiful. As I looked there came swiftly round the headland a little boat—not a common dingy or fisher-man's boat, but a miniature yacht—quite a dainty little craft, flying foresail and mainsail. A girl was steering her, and a boy sat beside the mast, ready to lower sail. The boat ran merrily up the creek, alongside the jetty. The boy lowered sail, unshipped mast and rudder, and tied the painter with the quickness of him who understands his work. Then both sprang out and ran up the steps of the jetty, and one of the fishermen touched his hat, and went slowly down to take the boat to her moorings. The pair were clearly brother and sister ; he a lad of eighteen, she a year or two older, perhaps twenty-one. They were curiously alike, and the girl's face was her brother's, glorified. There is no other word which can express the difference between the two faces. She had the same face as her brother, but glorified. Every face, if you come to think of it, has its best and most delightful type in the womanly form ; in

the old days every god had a corresponding goddess, though, sometimes, so great became the admiration and love of the goddess,
that the god dropped out and was forgotten. Who remembereth the
male Astarte ? Now, you may buy a block of marble and commission almost any sculptor to carve out of it a boy's head, beautiful,
brave, and manly. But, if you want the girl's head corresponding
to this, you must find out a sculptor of poetic temperament, and
you will not get what you want unless you do find the right man.
This girl, then, had the same face as her brother, but it was different.
Thus, the boy's hair was light and curly, hers was darker ; his eyes
were a light blue, and hers a dark blue and deeper ; his mouth was
weak, and hers was strong ; in her walk and bearing there was more
strength and character than seemed to belong to her brother. All
these things I did not observe at the moment when she passed
quickly up the pier, but I found them out afterwards. As for her
figure, she was nearly as tall as her brother, who was certainly five
feet eight, and in shape she resembled the goddess Artemis, who
was of thinner and slighter build, and had a more slender waist
than Aphroditê. Her admirers, in fact, invented the corset and the
practice of tight-lacing.

The girl passed me with just the slight glance of curiosity which
one bestows upon an unexpected stranger, and I presently left the
pier and walked slowly back to our inn, wondering why girls so
beautiful are so rarely seen in the world. Do they all live in the
country and blush unseen beside the hedges, like the wood-
anemones? Why, just to look upon such a face fills the mind
with all kinds of sweet fancies. But she passed before me and was
gone, and only the remembrance of her was left.

In the evening after dinner we took refuge in the billiard-room,
as there was nothing at all in the house to read. The only occupant of the room was the young fellow whom I had seen in the
boat with the extraordinarily beautiful girl. He was knocking the
balls about for amusement. There was no marker. I observed
that he blushed violently when I invited him to play a game—more
violently, that is, than a boy of eighteen ought to blush. He accepted, however, and we played five games, Paul watching the
play in a chair. Presently we began to talk about the village.
The boy said that, partly because it was eight miles from a station,
and partly because there were no lodgings except at the inn, visitors
very rarely found their way to the place. As for society, he said,
blushing crimson—we could not say why—a few people lived in
the villas beyond the church outside the little town—his own people

among them ; but it was a very dull and quiet place. For his own part—but here he blushed again and did not complete his sentence.

'For your own part,' said Paul, 'you do not desire to hear anything but the beating of the waves on the shore and the cry of the sea-birds all your life.'

'And yet,' the boy replied, with a touch of sadness in his voice, 'I do not know how I am to get anything else. But that does not matter to you,' he added quickly.

Then, as if afraid of saying more than he desired to say, he wished us good-night, and went away.

'Why can't he expect anything else ?' Paul asked. 'The boy wants to go to sea, I suppose, or on the stage, or into the army, or to become a poet, or to do something which his father won't let him do. He's a pretty pink and white sort of boy ; sometimes they turn out well, that sort of make. And he's a gentleman. Well, I shall go and put a compress on my ankle. Help me upstairs, old man.'

He went upstairs and I returned to the coffee-room. It was then about ten o'clock. The place was so quiet and still that the silence oppressed me. There are times when one cannot bear a complete silence. I even opened the door for the purpose of hearing the low buzz of voices from the bar, where half-a-dozen men were slowly and solemnly drinking and talking.

Then I heard steps outside the house and in the hall, and a man appeared at the door. He peered round, saw me sitting beside a couple of candles, hesitated for a moment, and then came in. It was a public room, and I suppose he had a perfect right to use it if he pleased ; but I resented his intrusion. When he took off his hat I perceived by the light of my two candles that he was perfectly bald, that his whiskers and eyebrows were white, that his eyes were red, his lips thick, his cheeks as fiercely red as his eyes, and his nose swollen. I declare that the very first aspect of this man made me tremble and shiver ; I cannot tell why—it may have been a presentiment of mischief, yet he did no harm to me. Sometimes I have thought that this natural loathing was caused by the inexpressible wickedness of the man's face. Why he looked so wicked I cannot tell ; it may have been some evil thought lurking like a devil in his eyes. I do not know what it is that betrays the evil disposition of a man ; certain I am, however, that the man's face was altogether most remarkably evil. Now you cannot, in the coffee-room of an inn, say to a stranger, even if he carries hoofs and a tail, 'Sir, your appearance impresses me with so unfavourable an idea of your moral character that I must request you to withdraw, or at least not to speak to me.' I did not say that to him, and he did not withdraw, but opened a conversation with me.

'I think,' he said—his voice was raspy and grating—'I think that I saw young Robert Reeve leave the inn a little while ago.'

'There was a young gentleman here,' I replied, 'who played a game of billiards with me, and is gone.'

'Yes, the same, the same. Nice boy, sir, ain't he?'

'He appears to be so.'

'Are you a friend of his—of the family, may I ask?' He leaned forward and grinned horribly. Why did he grin? 'An old friend, perhaps, of former and happier times? Yet not quite old enough, I should say——'

'I have not the pleasure of knowing them.'

'Ah!' He leaned back in his chair and breathed another sigh, apparently of satisfaction. 'Ah! a thousand pities for him, poor boy; but of course it is worse, much worse, for the girl. But you do not know the family yet. You would be interested——'

'Not at all,' I said. 'Pray do not waste village scandals upon me.'

'Village scandals? My dear sir, you are greatly mistaken—greatly mistaken. It is a world-wide—why, I could tell scandals—why, I could tell you things about this village which——'

'Good-night, sir.'

I interrupted his confidences, not on account of dislike to village gossip, which might be interesting, but because the fellow looked so malignant that I could no longer endure his company.

'You are wrong, sir,' he said. 'As a stranger you are wrong to go; I could have told you some very interesting things indeed about the people in this town. Mary—Mary—I say. Some more whisky, girl. Very interesting things indeed I could have told you.'

I perceived then that the old fellow had been drinking, which was perhaps the cause of his familiarity and his strange confidences. However, I left him.

In the morning, Paul's ankle was still swollen, and I agreed to leave him and go on with the walk alone. He, for his own part, thought he would send to town for some books and stay where he was. The place was quiet, the inn was comfortable, he should be neither lonely nor dull. I thought of the boy—this Robert Reeve, if that was the name—perhaps he would turn up at the inn; and then I thought of the girl. There was certainly one possibility which might make a stay at this place very far from dull. But I said nothing about her.

After breakfast I strapped my knapsack and started for the solitary walk of five-and twenty miles a day for a fortnight or so. When one is young so many friends are made at every halt that there is no time to feel lonely. My way took me first over the high headland of which I have spoken. Halfway up the hill I passed, sitting on the grass, my acquaintance of the previous night. He was sober, apparently, and yet somehow he looked more malignant than before.

'Good morning, sir,' he said, without, apparently, bearing any malice for my abruptness of the previous evening, 'you are off ? And alone, I see. Your friend remains behind, I suppose.'

'He remains behind.' I pushed on, not caring to converse any longer with the man.

'Ah ! Don't be in a hurry, my good sir. Stop half a minute now. You wouldn't listen to me last night. Well, I forgive you ; I always forgive people ; though I do think it is a bit rude to go off to bed when a gentleman offers to tell you all there is to be told.'

'Pardon me, you offered to tell me the scandals of the town. I am not fond of Paul Pry in a country village.'

'There again,' he said, 'you do me an injury. Without intention, doubtless—without intention,' he smiled in a ghastly way. 'So your friend stays. It is to be hoped that young Robert Reeve, as he calls himself, will not thrust himself upon your friend. Otherwise, it will be my duty to warn your friend solemnly ; yes, though I knew young Reeve's father at what I may call a very critical period of his life, it will be my duty to warn him.'

'It seems to me,' I said, with as much sternness as is possible at five-and-twenty—'it seems to me that you are proposing to meddle in what does not belong to you.'

'You do me another injury, young man,' he replied, spreading out his hands. 'You do me another injury. But I forgive you. It is from ignorance. You do not know me, indeed you do not. I forgive everybody ; I am accustomed to injury. People have all my life been resolved to injure me, who never harmed a fly—not a fly.'

I left this man and pushed on my way up the hill. Presently I came to the top—not a very lofty eminence after all—and sat down. Below me was the little port up the creek, with the fishing boats, and, if one could have seen them, the fishermen themselves. I remember thinking that if one had to choose a profession, one might think twice about becoming a fisherman. It is, to be sure, a hard life ; a good many get drowned ; there is too much moaning of the harbour bar, and more rolling up of the night rack than is pleasant ; and fish do certainly smell ; and it is very often horribly cold at sea ; and nobody can pretend to dine in comfort in a tossing boat on a rough sea ; probably, too, no other life offers so many facilities for getting wet ; and yet, all deductions made, what other life offers so many opportunities for repose, either sitting in the boat, or leaning against a post, or standing, hands in pocket, gazing at the sky ? In London we never see the sky. We must never look up at it, for fear of being run over. Besides, fishermen wear a most convenient and picturesque costume ; a great woollen jersey, lying in thick folds and rollers several inches thick, seems, when you come to think of it, the only costume possible for all weathers, except perhaps the simple dress of John Chinaman.

While I was meditating in this foolish fashion, I became aware of a grating raspy voice.

'You are unjust, dear sir, you are indeed. If you knew all I know——'

Here I sprang to my feet and fairly bolted. But this dreadful-looking old person with the cringing manner, the raspy voice, and the evil eyes, left a bad impression upon me. Not as regards Paul. If anybody in the world could take care of himself, it was Paul.

Three weeks later, having forgotten this person and, indeed, the village itself, I found waiting for me, on my arrival at a certain town which was on our proposed route, a letter from Paul. It was short, and without explanation begged me to get back to him as soon as I received the letter. This request gave me an uneasy feeling.

What should Paul—Paul the Self-Reliant—want with me or with anyone ? If a man wanted counsel he generally went to Paul for it, but Paul himself asked no man's counsel. It could not be that Paul was in a scrape of any kind.

It was not till nine in the evening that I reached the place. Paul was not in the inn. The landlord told me, however, that he was quite well, and that he was most probably at Mr. Reeve's. This he said with a meaning smile, and added that he would be certainly back again before eleven o'clock. I went into the coffee-room, and sat down to wait.

The old bald head again, the man with the red eyes and the white eyebrows ; he followed me into the coffee-room.

'Back again, my dear sir?' he began cheerfully. 'Back again? I hardly expected this. Yes; I saw you drive down the street. The horse and cart belong to old Poulton, the man who burned down his own hay-ricks for the insurance. The fellow who drove you is said to be reformed. A very violent character once, and in prison many times.'

I paid no attention to these revelations. He took a chair, however, called for some brand-and-water, and went on talking.

'Strange doings!' he said—'strange doings, since you went away. Your friend, sir—ah! poor young man. Trapped, I am afraid, trapped!' He drank half his glass of brandy-and-water and drummed the table with his fingers, repeating with great satisfaction that my poor young friend was trapped.

'Now'—I grew pretty hot at this interference—'if you have come here to tell me stories and made-up scandal, walk straight out of the door—or, old as you are, I shall put you out.'

'Don't be violent, young man: pray don't be violent. Why, you are like your friend—I warned him a week ago—I thought it my duty to warn him—and what was the consequence? Language more rude than I thought possible for a barrister and a gentleman to employ.'

'I dare say you deserved it.'

'What? For warning a young man on the edge of a precipice? Oh! what a world is this! What an ungrateful world!'

'I think,' I said, 'that you are a very meddlesome and impertinent person. Why do you speak to me at all?'

'Because I *must* speak. Young man, if you have any friendship for your friend—the other young man who swears—drag him away.'

He looked and spoke so much in earnest that I began to fear there might be some danger of an unknown and unsuspected kind.

'What danger?' I asked.

'The danger'—he leaned across the table and shook a warning forefinger in my face, 'the danger of a most lamentable connection. You do not know—how should you?—the nature of this village and its residents.'

I began to wonder if the man was mad, or if there was method in his madness. 'This place, sir, is the refuge of those who can no longer live among their fellow-men. Here, all alike have a disgraceful past and can meet on equal terms; in fact, it would be in the highest degree unmannerly to speak of what may have happened. Some words—such as detection, punishment, justice, and the like—are never used here ; be careful not to use them.'

'Good heavens !'

'Why not ? People must live somewhere. Surely it is best when a man " comes out " to join a community of others who have either come out or been driven from society. Ah! my young friend, I have now been here six months and more, and I have as yet regarded the possession of this knowledge as a sacred secret ; but to see a young gentleman trapped—I cannot longer remain silent, I cannot indeed.'

I wanted to ask him if he had recently ' come out,' but I forbore.

' In the very first villa outside the town,' this agreeable person went on, ' there lives a lady who was once tried for her life in Scotland ; she got off because the verdict was *Not proven*. But she did it, my dear sir, she did it. I have read the evidence, and I think I may be allowed some experience in evidence. She did it.'

' Well ?'

' And on the other side of my house lives a man who was cashiered —drummed out of the army, sir, and he a major—for cowardice. Oh, yes ! My house is between them.'

' And what have you done ?' I asked impudently.

He shook his head sadly, as if I was greatly to blame for asking so indiscreet a question.

' Opposite to us there lives an aged clergyman. Ask him—I am not a libellous person—I say, only ask him why he holds no bene- fice *now—ask him that*. To say of *his* neighbour that he is a fraudulent bankrupt, and lives upon the profits, would not surprise you, I suppose. And of the Honourable Mr. Arthur Mompesson, another of our neighbour residents, that he was expelled all his clubs for cheating at cards, would not strike you, perhaps, as at all an unusual incident in a gentleman's career.'

' But what did *you* do ?' For the man was reeling out these accusations with a malignant joy which made one's brain turn. ' What is it that you have done ?'

He shook his head again.

' And there's another man, who made his fortune by wrecking ships, over-insuring them and then overloading them. He is a churchwarden now—Ho ! ho ! And as for old Reeve, as he calls himself now, who wants to throw over his old friends, refuses to speak to me if he meets me, and has forbidden me the house—why, I defended him, sir, I defended him, and this is gratitude.'

'You—you defended him ? ˙ What were you, then ?'

'What was I, sir ? I would have you to know, sir, that I was a barrister, sir, and a Queen's Counsel, sir. What do you think of that ?'

'You were a barrister and a Queen's Counsel. Then, why are you no longer either ? What did you do ?' I asked again.

He shook his head no longer, but sprang to his feet with a fierce gesture, and for a moment I thought he would have made for me.

'Why,' I said, looking him steadily in the face, 'if you are no longer a Q.C., what is it that you have done ?'

He made no reply, but actually fled from the room : he ran out of it, and down the street, and I saw him no more.

At eleven Paul came home. He was evidently in a state of high excitement. 'I sent for you,' he said, 'because I *must* tell someone, and I know I can trust you. Sit down and listen to me without speaking one word.'

As for the substance of his tale, it was what one might have expected. He was in love, madly in love, and with the very girl, the beautiful creature, whom I had seen on the river. Her name was Isabel. The largest and finest house in the place belonged to her father, who was, it appeared, a man of considerable wealth. So far all seemed plain and easy sailing.

'You love her, Paul,' I said. 'No occasion to repeat it. And —if one may have the impertinence to ask—does the young lady——'

'She refuses me,' he replied. All this time he had been walking about the room in a violent agitation. 'She refuses me.'

'Refuses you ?' At twenty-five one knows little about women, but one thing everybody knows—that when a clever, handsome, and in every way eligible young man makes love to a girl— especially to a girl in a dull country place—his chances of refusal are not—well—not equal to the chances of acceptance. You can't go beyond a man who is a gentleman, clever, hard-working, am- bitious, and of good heart. They don't make young men any better than that. 'Refused you, Paul ?'

'Refused me. Mind, there is a reason. The dear girl owned to-day that if it were not for this reason—she—she——' Here he choked.

'Is the reason insurmountable ?'

'Oh !' he replied. 'The reason is unreasonable ; it is a mere trick of the brain ; it matters really nothing. I cannot tell you, though she has told me the whole, God bless her! and it tore her heart to tell it. She told me the whole story two days ago. I wrote to you at once, because I felt that I must speak to some one or die. Yet I cannot tell you all of it—only this : there is upon her past a cloud. Yes, I admit it is a very dreadful cloud. Through no fault of her own—none, mind. No one can blame her in the least ; no one would dare to throw it in her teeth. By Heaven! I would kill such a man where he stood. It is on account of this cloud that she refuses. She says that she will never consent to bring her burden of shame to weigh down the life of a man she loved. O Isabel! my dear!——' Here again he choked.

'Yet, Paul, if you would take her—even with this—this——'

'*Even with this!*' he said solemnly. 'Why it would be nothing in the world to me ; less than nothing ; just a secret between husband and wife ; just a painful reminiscence of the past, never to be mentioned between us.'

'Is there,' I asked, 'anyone who knows the secret?'

'Her brother knows, of course, poor fellow! Well for him if he did not know, because the knowledge of it will poison his life wherever he goes. I am sorry, truly sorry, for the boy. But as for Isabel, I can take her away from all of it.'

'And does no one else know?'

'There is a dreadful man who lives here—a most horrible beast. I threatened to cowhide him last week because he threw out hints that he knew something about the previous history of this family not altogether to their credit. He is a man named Brundish ; he was formerly, it appears, in very good practice at the Bar, and had taken silk, was a Q.C., and a bencher of Lincoln's Inn, and was then found out to have appropriated, embezzled, or made away with certain trust-moneys. This was a horrible scandal, and they disbenched and disbarred him. He is a man of infamous private character, and drinks, I believe. Probably he will drink himself into the grave before long. I am afraid he knows something, but I do not know how much. What does that creature signify?'

I thought it unnecessary to tell Paul of my experience with Mr. Brundish ; but I felt relieved to think that he had not told me more. We went on talking of the young lady's perfections. In fact, we talked half through the night.

The next morning he took me to the house. It was a beautiful villa, furnished with admirable taste, heaped with books, pictures, and all kinds of pretty things. Isabel herself—I have always called her, by gracious permission, by her Christian name—received us, and presently her brother joined us. There was some constraint upon the whole party, which was natural under the circumstances, and I was glad when we all went out together and climbed to the top of the headland. Here, presently, I found myself—whether by accident or design I know not—standing alone with Isabel, the other two slowly going on before us down the hill. She looked grave and anxious, her cheek rather pale; I knew that her mind was full of her lover and her refusal. I had no right to speak, yet I did speak to her about it. First, I told her what Paul had told me, that he loved her and that she would not accept him, for a reason.

'Did he tell you the reason?' she asked, her cheek flushing suddenly.

'No; only in general terms. There is a cloud upon some part of your past.'

'A cloud indeed,' she replied.

'Which would not in any way affect the life of the man you married.'

'But it would,' she said; 'oh! it would. You do not know what it is, or you would say that I am right.'

'Nay, I cannot think, Miss Reeve, that you are right, for you make the man who loves you—the best man in the world—you do not know what a clever, brave, and good-hearted man he is—you make him wretched when you might make him happy.' And so I continued, she shaking her head, though the tears came into her eyes, and murmuring:

'Oh! I refuse him because I would not make him unhappy.'

Then I said it all over again. The only way to agree with a woman, especially with a woman who in her heart wishes to be convinced, is to repeat your proposition until she gets it well into her head. I said that, in the first place, nobody would know the thing which she was afraid would injure Paul; and secondly, that if all the world knew it, nobody would care; that in all cases of this kind the real injury to one was in suspicion that there was injury; that it was like a man's being ashamed of low origin, a thing which could not be prevented, and which no one, certainly, would ever cast in a man's teeth. Then I begged her to put this consideration out of her mind altogether, and, if she could, to make Paul happy.

She shook her head with less firmness than before, and I saw that she was shaken.   When a lovely woman has thoroughly made up her mind, she does not keep on crying.   Then we descended the hill, and found Paul and Robert in the boat.   I remember that we went sailing in the pretty little boat.   I do not know where, or whither, or for how long.   I was thinking over the position of things, and admiring the sight of a man desperately in love and a girl ready to receive his homage but for one thing that seemed to stand in the way.   Yet in every look, and in every gesture, she said, so plainly that all could read,

> ' Ask me no more, for at a touch I yield :
>   Ask me no more.'

When we walked back to the house the boy came with me, and Paul walked beside Isabel.

'I wish it may come off,' he said, blushing as usual.   'I say— I know I can talk freely with you, because Paul says so.   He has told you something about us—hasn't he ?   Not much, he says, but I dare say it is quite enough.   Isabel wrote it all down, so that he should not think he had been deceived—all, she says—everything. Good God !' here he gasped.   'If Paul likes to show it to you, he may.   But I hope he will not.   As for me, I am done for ; I can do nothing, the history is round my neck like a millstone ; I must sit in the background all my life, and make myself as little conspicuous as I can.   I cannot go into the army or the university.   I have not been to a public school.   I have no friends and I can make none.   I can never marry.'   Here he stopped for a while, and walked on at a great rate, swinging his arms.

'As for Isabel,' he went on, 'it really cannot matter to her when once she is married.   Paul will take her away : no one will trouble their heads to ask who she was.   She swears that nothing would ever induce her to spoil a man's life, but I don't think it would hurt his career.   Let Paul persevere ; if she can once be got to think that it will not do him mischief, I think she will give in.   And, oh ! I cannot bear to think that she should stay on here, wasted, her life spoiled ; living in vain.'

She had already given in, though we did not know it.   The word was spoken, and she was promised.   I saw it in her blushing face and softened eyes, when we reached the house : I saw it in Paul's absurdly triumphant air when we walked away.

'It is settled,' he said, pressing my arm.   'She has accepted me.   My dear boy ! I am the happiest man in the world.'

He went on to explain at great length how very happy he was

already, and how very much happier he meant to be in the immediate future. They were to be married at once—in a few weeks ;
there was no need to wait ; and so on. Meantime there was a
small dinner-party at the house that evening, and I was invited by
Isabel.

In the nature of things, it was impossible that I could avoid
being interested not only in the love-affair of my friend, and
that most beautiful girl, Isabel, but also in her father. From
Paul I learned that Something had been done which must be
concealed ; from the boy, that Something had been done which
would make it impossible for him to go into any kind of public
life ; from the wicked old man, Mr. Brundish, that he had himself
'defended' the father of this interesting pair at a critical juncture,
when he himself had been a Q.C. All this, put together, did not
inform one of much ; yet it made me curious, not so much to
know more, as to see, in the flesh, the man who had caused this
terrible cloud to hang over his children's lives, the man who had
'done something.'

Well, I was introduced to him : I saw him ; he was a singularly
handsome man, portly, dignified, well dressed, and possessed of a
manner perfectly charming ; not only at ease with himself, but able
to set his guests at their ease. He was apparently about sixty
years of age ; his abundant hair was of a splendid creamy white ;
his features were sharp and clear ; his eyes singularly bright—
they were of a deep blue, like those of his daughter ; he not only
looked, but he was, a perfectly polished and delightful man. At
the very sight of him, all the injurious suspicion and doubts one
had entertained of him vanished ; as he talked, one was lifted out
of one's self and carried into circles and among people one had
never thought to know. Perhaps he talked too continuously, but
nobody else present could have talked half so well, and I, for one,
was content to listen. He seemed to know, or to have met—
because he did not profess friendship with any of them—all the
great men of the day ; he knew the secret history of everything
that had taken place ten, twenty, thirty years before—such as the
Reform Bill of 1832, or the great railway bubble of 1846 ; he knew
the great men of the City ; he knew, as well, the best literary
men and artists of the day, and even the great statesmen. He
talked, in fact, through the whole dinner, and we neither grew
tired of him, nor did the dinner languish.

There were six or seven guests, besides Paul and myself ; it
was an excellent dinner, admirably served, and with admirable

wine. At first I gave myself up entirely to the enjoyment of the delightful talk, and thought of nothing else. But a strange thing happened : in the very middle of the dinner I caught a sharp and curiously suggestive glance from Isabel. It seemed to ask me what I thought, now, of her father, and if I really knew that——

I felt myself blushing like her brother, and my mind suddenly went back to what I had heard. Of what nature was the 'cloud'? Had the ex-Q.C. really defended our host? and if so, on what occasion? And all the other scandalous statements returned to my brain : why had the venerable clergyman opposite to me no longer a cure of souls? Why had the gallant major next to him left the army? Was it true that the Honourable Arthur Mompesson had been expelled his club for cheating at cards? And this middle-aged lady, whom I had taken in to dinner, could she really have poisoned her lover? And while I pondered these things our host's pleasant genial voice went flowing on, so that one felt the strangest incongruity between these absurd questions and the place, the talk, and the people.

Three weeks later the pair were quietly married, without any party, bridesmaids, or ceremony at all. What Paul said to Isabel's father I know not, but at the wedding the old man seemed strangely shaken and agitated, trembling at every footfall. He had become aged, one knew not why. The bride and bridegroom drove from the church to the nearest station. Mr. Reeve went home, and I went back to the inn. I found there the man Brundish, who had been drinking already, though it was not yet noon.

'I told the old man I would interrupt the ceremony,' he said with a grin, 'and make him marry the girl under her true name, but he begged me not. I am to dine with him to night instead. Ha! now that the girl is gone, he says, he does not care who comes to his house. Wanted to keep his own children from their father's old friends, you see. There's gratitude! Why, who defended him? Who made such a speech that all England rang with it—eh?'

'Well,' I said, 'now that Mr. Reeve's daughter has married, you have done with her, at any rate, and with me, too.'

'I don't know, young man, I don't know,' he replied. 'I am, it is true, a forgiving person, which is lucky for the happy bridegroom. But then he once shook a cane over my shoulders. I don't know if I have done with them. And I wasn't good enough to be invited to the house. Respectable company you met there,

wasn't it?   The man drummed out of his regiment; the man
expelled from the clubs; the woman tried——'

'Go to the devil!' I said, and left him.

A month or two later I heard from Paul that his father-in-law
had been found dead in his bed. It appeared that he had no money
of his own, but was living on his late wife's fortune, which had
been settled upon herself, and was held in trust. The share of it
which now came to Isabel put the newly-married pair at once into
a position of great material comfort, if not wealth. But Paul was
already making way in his profession.

'I must be a judge by forty-five,' he said to me, laughing;
'otherwise I shall think that I have failed.'

'And then, Paul?' asked Isabel.

'Then I must be made Lord Chancellor, and I shall pass great
measures for the law of the land, and shall become immortal.'

I never knew any couple so entirely happy as they were during
the first twelve months of their marriage. They had very few
friends, and these were all Paul's own friends; they lived on
Campden Hill—remember that it was long before Campden Hill
was covered with houses—and they were just as selfishly and as
completely happy as love could make them. Gradually the pensive
and troubled look vanished from Isabel's eyes: the 'Cloud,' the
'Thing,' the Secret, whatever it had been, was wholly put away
and forgotten. As for me, I sometimes thought of it involuntarily.
Was the malignant old man truthful in his account of the village
and its residents? Could they really be all of them outcasts by
reason of having been found out in something disgraceful? Had
Isabel's father really been 'defended' by the man Brundish in a
speech that made all England ring? One would not pry into the
matter, but the doubt remained which it was impossible to kill. In
Isabel's society, however, it vanished completely. She was one of
those rare women whose friendship is a great possession for a man,
and whose love is a gift of the gods; a woman whom one regarded
with a daily increasing respect and admiration; a woman to whom
goodness of all kinds came by nature.

Isabel's brother came to town soon after his father's death, and
called upon me.

'I have made up my mind,' he said to me soon after his sister's
marriage, 'what I shall do. So long as I remain in this country,
Isabel will always have somebody to remind her of the past. If I
once go away she will belong entirely to her husband. While I
am here I shall always be in terror of the Thing being found out.

I shall go away, then, and travel.   After a year or two I shall con-
vey to Isabel the news that I am dead.   Then she will have broken
altogether with the past.   I shall settle down somewhere, perhaps,
some day.   I am not sure where or when, and if I am quite sure
that I can never be identified, I shall marry, perhaps.   But never,
never will I come back to England.'

So we shook hands and we parted.   Six months afterwards there
came a note to Isabel in pencil from her brother, saying that he
was dying of fever on the African coast, and that the letter would
be sent on after his death.   Isabel wept over the letter, but she
dried her tears soon, and I think it was better that the last link
which reminded her of the shame of her childhood should have
been broken.

As for their happiness, however, it was rudely shaken.

One day, Paul, the junior counsel in a case of no apparent importance, found himself unexpectedly called upon to maintain a
legal position against the opinion of the Court ; he displayed, in
his argument, so much ability and knowledge of the law as to
call forth an expression of admiration from the judge himself.   I
was myself present in my quality of briefless barrister.   On the
termination of the case we came out, and stood for a few minutes
talking over the point which had been raised.   Paul's senior joined
us, and congratulated him, prophesying that his table would never
be without briefs after that morning's work.   Others came to shake
hands with him, and there was quite a little scene of congratula-
tion and triumph.   In the midst of our talk I saw, bearing straight
down upon us, with the evident intention of speaking, no other
than that terrible ex-Q.C.   He was clearly half-drunk.   One of
the men among us whispered in disgust : 'Good heavens ! here's
that miserable man Brundish !'   Everybody stood aside to make
way for him, as one makes way for a leper.   Worse than a leper,
in the courts of Lincoln's Inn, is a man who has been disbarred.
As well should a man who has been stripped of his commission
and drummed out of his regiment for cowardice, show himself
again upon parade.

This man, then, with a half-drunken laugh, walked straight to
Paul and held out his hand.

'How are you, Paul, my boy ?' he cried, addressing him inde-
pendently by his Christian name ; 'Isabel quite well ?'

Paul turned perfectly white.

'How dare you,' he cried, 'how dare you speak to me ?   How
dare you address me by my Christian name ?'

'How dare I ? Ho ! ho ! Not use his Christian name to the man who married my dear old friend's only daughter ? How do you do, Sir John ?' He addressed one of the group, a well-known counsel of very high standing and ex-Solicitor-General, who made no reply. 'Gentlemen, you know me, all of you. I have been in Court to-day, and I declare I never heard a better argument than my young friend's here. Why, I never put a point better myself.'

'Your friend ! Yours !' cried Paul, with a gesture of loathing.

'Come, come !' cried the man. 'This is rather too much. Why, Paul, you forget that you married the only daughter of my old friend, Sir Robert Reeve Byrne, baronet, whom I defended. You remember my famous defence, gentlemen. I am sure it nearly pulled him through, but not quite, for he got his five years' penal servitude.'

Then there was a dead silence, and nobody dared to look at his neighbour. As for me, I understood it all. The case of Sir Robert Byrne was a *cause célèbre*. He had been, I remembered, defended by Mr. Brundish, Q.C., with marvellous skill and ingenuity. My delightful host was, then, no other than that famous baronet, then ! and the rest of his guests—were they also what the ex-Q.C. had described them ?

Paul recovered himself.

'It is quite true,' he said proudly ; 'I married the daughter of Sir Robert Byrne, but this man I know nothing of, except that he is a rogue.'

Mr. Brundish looked round him ; he saw on every face loathing clearly written. Half-drunk though he was, he was cowed. He said no more, but slunk away.

It was Sir John himself who laid his hand upon Paul's shoulder and said, kindly :

'We are all sorry you should have been troubled by this scoundrel, whom once I called my friend. As for your private affairs—but of them we need not speak.'

They all murmured something, the group broke up, and I took Paul by the arm and walked with him to his chambers. He threw his papers upon the table, and sank into a chair.

'It is all over,' he groaned ; 'my career is finished.'

'Paul, this is absurd.'

'No,' he said. 'I have already made up my mind what will happen. These men are my private friends—they are part of our social circle ; for Isabel, poor child, had no friends of her own.

They are good fellows, and at first they will say that it doesn't make any difference, and think it too.   But then, you see, there are the women.   They will resent the thing, and show their resentment, too.   Isabel must be spared this, at any cost.   Go away now, my dear fellow, and leave me to think.'

'For heaven's sake, Paul,' I said, 'do nothing rash.   Think of your profession first.'

'No,' he replied.   'Isabel must be first thought of.'

I lingered awhile, unwilling to leave him.

'Now you know all,' he said.   'It is something like a cloud, isn't it?'

'Is it possible that the courtly and polished—— ?'

'Quite possible.   Sometimes I tried to think what he would look like in prison dress, but I never could.   There was another side to him, though.   I saw it on the day when I asked him for his daughter.   "Do you," he said, "know the story of my past?" I assured him that he need not open a painful chapter, because I knew everything.   And then—then he broke down, burst into a fit of weeping like any woman, and thanked God solemnly that I had come to take his daughter away from him.   "For myself," he said, "I suppose I am sorry.   That matters nothing.   But for my children's sake, and especially for my daughter's sake, I am—sometimes I am mad."   I think that when he was left alone after our marriage he was really mad, and I am nearly sure that he killed himself.   However, that is done with.   Isabel must not know what has happened.   And she must not be made to suspect that our friends, her new friends, know her secret.   Women are not always considerate towards each other.   I must think—I must think what is best to do.'

Next morning, I was not surprised to receive a note from Isabel.   She said that her husband was suddenly prostrated with some kind of nervous breakdown, though he looked very well, and that the doctor ordered him to give up all work, break off all engagements, and go away for three months at least.   They were going the same day.

The three months became six, and the six became twelve: they were travelling about in unfrequented places, where Paul's health would not suffer from noise and talk of travellers: they stayed only in towns where there were no English residents, and so on.   Then Paul wrote to me that he had given up his chambers and bought a cottage in the country, where he proposed to stay, his health, he said, being too wretched to think of his practising any more.

I made many visits to the cottage. It was three or four miles from any village or house. It was on the seaside, and they had a boat. They had no children, and the only people who ever visited them were the family of the nearest clergyman, who came often to them. Isabel was their friend, unpaid governess, adviser, everything.

Remark, here, a very strange thing. This man, my friend Paul, to whom at the outset life without success would have seemed intolerable, who gave up the most promising prospects solely on his wife's account, who was endowed with every quality which success requires, was perfectly happy in this obscure retreat. He wanted no other kind of life : to sail in his boat, to wander on the sands, to meditate in his garden, always with Isabel beside him, was enough for him. His love for Isabel was absorbing and sufficient for both. Other married people continue to pay each other the attentions of their first love : but this pair seemed to live wholly for each other. As for me, who knew their secret, it seemed to me as if Paul spent his life in a perpetual care to ward off from his wife the danger of being reminded of that dreadful story. It had destroyed his career—that mattered nothing. It had driven him from the world—that mattered nothing, provided his wife was never reminded of it, never made to feel it. Needs must that so terrible a thing should bring a burden and a curse upon the children—Paul accepted it and bore the burden without a murmur or a sigh. And as they lived together among books, and nourishing thoughts sacred and lofty, their home became as a church in which one might fitly meditate, and the conversation was unlike what one heard outside.

They lived in this way for five-and-twenty years. Then the greatest possible misfortune fell upon Paul. For Isabel caught a fever and died. Then Paul began to break up. He was only just past fifty, and should have been in the vigorous enjoyment of his manhood ; but he began to fail. In the last months of his life I stayed a great deal with him, and he talked freely about his old ambitions and their sudden end.

'I am sure,' he said, 'that I did right in giving all up. Sooner or later Isabel would have found out—would have been made to feel, somehow—that other people knew the truth. In such a case the only safety lies in flight.'

'But if you had stayed, your own career was certain.'

'Perhaps : with the explanation, whenever my name was mentioned, "You know, I suppose, that he married Sir Robert Byrne's daughter." And she would have heard it.'

'Tell me,' I said, 'who were the residents of the village—the people we met at dinner——'

'I do not know. Why do you ask?'

Evidently Isabel knew nothing of them. Perhaps, after all, the wicked old man lied about them.

'I am glad to think,' Paul went on, 'that we never met any of them afterwards, because perhaps they knew. Thank God! never, never for a moment after the marriage did Isabel feel that her father's sins were visited upon her.'

'Why, Paul,' I said, 'they were; but you shifted the burden to your own-shoulders and bore it for her. Did Isabel ever learn why you left London?'

'No, she never knew and she never suspected. The man Brundish died a very little while after—of drink, I believe.'

'And you never regretted all that you lost?'

'Never—not for a moment. What is it that I gave up for Isabel's sake? Why, she has done far, far more for me than I ever did for her. There is something better than ambition, my friend. Isabel gave me that, in return for the burden which, as you say, I shifted to my own shoulders. It pleases me now to think of what I might have become; but if all were to be done over again, I would have it as it has been.'

What it was that Isabel gave him and did for him I do not know, for I did not ask, and now I shall never learn, because he is dead.

CAMILLA'S LAST STRING.

I.

' Oh ! you silly boy,' she said, but not withdrawing her hand, which
he held, enraptured : nor refusing her sunny brow when he
ventured to stoop and kiss that feature. 'You silly boy ! You
only fancy you love me.'

'Fancy ? Camilla ! You cannot guess the depth and the—the—
constancy—and—oh ! Camilla, who could help falling in love with
such an angel of goodness ?'

'M—m—m !' she murmured softly, accepting the character.
'How noble it is—Mr.—well—then—Harry—how truly noble it is
to see good qualities in others ! And ah ! how generous to love a
woman for her qualities and not for her looks or her fortune !'

'For her looks ? Camilla—you are as lovely as you are good.
Oh ! Camilla—Heaven framed your face to show the angelic soul
behind it.'

This was the beginning of it—that is to say, not quite the beginning, but near it. The Rev. Mr. Estill took one pupil only, at
£250 a-year, to prepare for the University. Mr. Harry Ambrose
Strange was then this fortunate pupil. He was better at loafing,
playing croquet—the middle-aged reader understands that we are
now in the sixties, which to the young are like unto the year before
the Deluge for remoteness—cricket, shooting, riding, and dancing,
than he was at books. At this time he was eighteen years of age.
Camilla, the Vicar's only child, was, as she candidly confessed,
already past twenty. She had made the same confession to six
pupils before Harry : when a girl so long persists in a statement
there is generally some truth in it.

'Yes, Harry,' she said, 'I will wait for you, though you are only eighteen, and I am—alas!—past twenty. Since I have suffered you to—to take my hand'—that is how she put it. He had, in fact, kissed that hand, fondled it, knelt to it, and mumbled over it —'it is because I feel that you are worth waiting for if I am worth working for.'

'Worth working for! Oh! good Heavens!'

'Every girl,' said Camilla calmly, 'has her own ideal in the kind of man to whom she would consent to surrender herself. Mine is, I confess, a lofty ideal. My favoured lover, Harry, must be a Galahad for perfect purity, a Lancelot for bravery, an Arthur for wisdom——'

'Yes,' said Harry meekly.

'For such a man—you will make yourself such a man, dear Harry—only for such a man would I consent to enter into the union which shall confer upon him earthly happiness.'

She was short in figure and dumpy—quite one of Leech's girls— she wore a lovely great crinoline, which made her lower half like a large football : her light, even sandy, hair was in a bag : her cheeks wanted colour, her eyes were a light blue, her eyebrows were faint indications, her nose was uncertain, and her mouth a little too large. Otherwise, as Sancho Panza said, she was doubtless a miracle of beauty. She read great quantities of poetry, sang senti-mental songs, with a reedy voice, and played 'pieces' such as *L'Hirondelle, L'Invitation à la valse,* Weber's last waltz, the *Copen-hagen,* the *Blue Danube,* and other choice pieces. She also interested herself in the village choir. To the youths who succeeded each other year after year in her father's study she was a fairy, an angel, a wood nymph, everything that the romance of eighteen is able to imagine. We have all been young once, I suppose. If we are of the fairer sex, we have found it pleasing to be worshipped and called all kinds of lovely names : if of the other, we do not blush in thinking of the time when every young woman clearly belonged to that now unknown land called Heaven.

'My dear,' said the Vicar's wife, that evening, 'I think you should put a question to that young man as to his future prospects. I suspect that he and Camilla——'

'For the sixth time, Maria, or is it the seventh? Mind, I cannot countenance any engagement. It shall not be said that any young man under my charge——'

'You need countenance nothing, my dear. But you may, for all that, ascertain what his position really is. So far, all you know is that he is a ward and that he pays rather less than you are accus-tomed to take.'

'It is, I am certain, the seventh engagement, and nothing ever comes of it. The road to Church might be paved with Camilla's broken engagements.'

'Well, dear, it is the poor girl's only chance, and it's another string to her bow, even if it prove the last. And besides, my dear, something may come out of all these affairs, and I never heard of Camilla breaking off any of her engagements. She is still, for aught we know, engaged to all the young gentlemen. Of course, that's nonsense—but still——'

The Vicar blew out the light.

Next day, however, he had quite a fatherly conversation with his pupil.

'Seriously,' he said in conclusion, 'if your fortune will do little more for you than complete your course at Oxford, I should advise you to give up the University. There are other careers open to youth. We cannot all of us become country clergymen and private tutors. Some of us must be content with lesser ambitions. Your degree—even an ordinary degree—is to you, my dear boy, a dubious —a very dubious matter. I strongly advise you to devote your— your energies, which are undoubted—to something practical. Think it over.'

'My dear,' he said to his wife, 'the boy has only two or three thousand pounds for all his fortune. His guardians are paying for his education out of the principal. They want him to go into the Church because they think it's a safe profession. Safe starvation, I call it, and the boy is a fool, too, about books. You will tell Camilla whatever you think best.'

His wife sighed.

'I am sorry,' she said. 'A fool he may be, but an honourable fool is sometimes a better catch than a clever man. Some of the happiest women are married to the greatest fools. After all, it may still be another string to her bow. Who knows? Let us leave it to Camilla.'

Harry turned things over in his mind. The immediate result was a tearful leave-taking in the Vicarage garden. It was a large garden full of retired corners, arbours, and retreats, which always gave an opportunity for the exchange of confidences with Camilla —every successive pupil, if he had been asked, could have testified to the convenience of the garden.

'You will really wait for me?' he asked, with the tears in his eyes. 'Oh! angel! Oh! Camilla! I never dared to think——'

She laid her hand on his arm and smiled sweetly, pensively, tenderly.

' You poor boy !' she said. 'It seems so hard to part, doesn't it ? You will work for me?'

' Oh ! to work for you, Camilla—to work—to work for you !'

The prospect was too much—he could not find words—he only caught her hand and began to kiss it.

' You *shall* work for me, Harry. We must not correspond—but, remember, I am waiting for you.'

II.

THE Sixties have gone, and the Seventies. Alas! what a multitude of youthful faces have gone with them! Only to think of the poor things who were then in the twenties and are now in the fifties, brings tears into the eyes, especially when one looks into the glass. As for the other poor things who were already in their fifties and their sixties, where are they now? Perhaps they have by this time recovered their youth and their beauty. I am sure I hope so, for all our sakes.

It was in the summer of 1884, which was a long hot summer, such as dries up rheumatism and makes the old people so strong again that they see their way clear to another summer. And it was at Broadstairs, which that year was so full that the children on the beach could not paddle without jostling each other, and in bathing the ranks were so thick that those who were behind got no water. It was also the middle of August, when the place is at its fullest. Therefore, those who came down by the evening train were rash in expecting room at any of the hotels. I believe there are three hotels at Broadstairs, without counting the Tartar Frigate. No beds were to be had. All the lodgings in the town were also said to be quite full. Some of the baffled voluptuaries, who had been looking for a comfortable room after a toothsome dinner at the table d'hôte, began wandering from house to house. Others, more artful, confided their case to the hotel porters, the head waiter, and the manager.

Among the latter was a gentleman whose appearance revealed nothing at all about his antecedents, his age, his temper, his habits, or his profession. Formerly, there was generally something in the appearance, habits, or dress of a man which told a tale. Now there is nothing. Anybody, at and above a certain level, is exactly alike. All we can say of a man is that he appears to have reached that level. It is one where the clothes are well made and the bearing of the man who wears them is quiet ; where the age may be anywhere between five-and-thirty and fifty, and the man's profession may be anything you please ; but if it is a shop it must be a large shop. For this man was big and well set up; he wore a moustache but no beard ; he was quite quiet and well-bred ; and he looked as if he was accustomed to be obeyed ; there was the look in his face, not only of the master, but also of the hereditary master, one whose forefathers had been accustomed to command. We belong to a democratic age, but we must not deny heredity.

He had his portmanteau set down in the hall of the hotel and informed the hall porter that good largesse would be his on the finding of a room. Very shortly, while the other houseless wretches were beginning to beat their bedless heads against the street-doors in despair, and to ask what price for bathing machines, his portmanteau was carried to a lodging-house hard by.

He was shown into a room on the ground-floor by the landlady, a middle-aged woman, dressed in the rusty black which is the uniform of her profession ; she was small and thin ; her face was worn and anxious, and she wore an obvious front of very light hair. This was just a little pushed out of place, which gave the poor woman something of a rakish air.

'My ground-floor,' she began, 'left this morning. I can let it till the 1st of September ; not longer, nor for less ; not for a single night or two.'

'Very good. I will take it until the 1st of September.'

When her new lodger spoke the landlady started. Then she looked quickly at the portmanteau on which was written his name in large letters—'Mr. H. Ambrose Strange'—and she suddenly turned quite white and dropped into a chair.

'You are ill ?' asked the man.

She jumped up and ran—fluttering like a scared hen—ran as quickly as she could. He looked after her, wondering what hornet had stung her, and where, that she should thus scuttle away, leaving her bargain only half concluded.

Then there appeared a girl who seemed to be three or four and twenty years of age. The lodger observed that she carried her head with great haughtiness, and that she was deeply resentful, as all daughters of lodging-house keepers are, at having to do or to say anything to the lodgers. What little services they are obliged to render to the establishment are done in the privacy of the kitchen or in the bedrooms, where, being unseen, they do not affect the social status of the young ladies.

'Mother isn't very well,' she said. Mr. Strange observed further that she really was a very pretty girl, with something of the

Spanish darkness, not being in the least like the lady with the flaxen front. 'Mother has sent me. The rent, she says, is three guineas. Kitchen fire, gas, and attendance extra. She will let the rooms for a fortnight, no more and no less.'

'I take them,' he said, 'and I pay in advance.'

He counted out six pounds and six shillings and laid them on the table.

'Mother will give you a receipt.' She swept up the money scornfully. 'Mother told me to ask you if you are the Mr. Harry Strange who was a pupil of the Rev. Mr. Estill at Hilsea Vicarage twenty years ago.'

'Pupil? At Hilsea Vicarage? Twenty years ago? Oh! old Estill's. Yes, yes; I believe it must be about that time. Yes, I was. Why?'

'I don't know. I was told to ask. What time do you take dinner?'

'I am going to dine at the hotel.'

'Oh! the attendance and the kitchen fire will be charged all the same.'

'Very good,' said the lodger.

And the young lady withdrew.

'Pupil at Hilsea Vicarage,' he repeated. 'Of course. Who's the old woman, and why did she ask that question? It was the last place where I wasted time and money over Latin and Greek before I went out. Old Estill. Old Estill. I remember, with his infernal grammar. And Mother Estill and Camilla. Yes, Camilla; she had sandy hair, I remember, and light blue eyes, without any eyebrows; and she had a squeaky voice. She was romantic and sentimental. I believe I fancied myself in love with her. Camilla. Yes. Oh! yes. Camilla.'

Then the girl came back again.

'Mother's compliments,' she said, presenting an envelope.

He opened it. Within the envelope was a carte-de-visite, representing a dumpy young lady in a very wide crinoline, carrying a hat with ribbons, her hair in a bag. Time, the destroyer, had made sad work of this portrait. The Alps among which the young lady was standing (as is customary in English villages) still reared their snowy peaks an inch or so above her head; the hands were visible, though ghostly; and the hat remained; the graceful curve of the crinoline still bulged out; but the face—the face—where was that? Two pale cavities for eyes; the faintest indication of a nose; and a mouth which had lost not only its north and south outlines, but had also widened from ear to ear.

'What is this?' he asked, looking at it in astonishment.

'It is mother, I believe, as she was twenty years ago.. She says so, but nobody would know it.'

'What the—I mean why, child, does your mother send this thing to me?'

'She says, ask him if he remembers the likeness.'

'Remember the likeness? What likeness?' He looked again. Then a glimmer shone upon his brain. It was a ray of light struck by the crinoline—as by a Bryant and May. 'By George!' he laughed, 'I believe it is Camilla.'

'That,' said the girl, 'is my mother's Christian name. Am I to tell her that you do remember it?'

'Good Lord!' cried Mr. Strange. 'She said she would wait for me! Is she waiting still?'

III.

CAMILLA herself appeared to answer the question. She had put off her robe of stuff, and, like a barrister, had taken silk. She was now dressed in her best frock, that in which she went to evening church; she had a gold chain—it had been her husband's—round her neck, and a lace shawl over her shoulders : she had also put her front straight, washed her hands and got rid of the lodging-house keeper. She was once more, as she was fond of telling her children when the season was over, 'the lady.' She stood at the door smiling sweetly, quite in her old style, with her head on one side, as if pondering piously on the poetry and the beauty of every-thing, and she put out both her hands with a modest uplifting and then a more modest depression of the eyes that was most maidenly, and reminded the man ridiculously of the past.

'Harry!' she said. 'At last! Is it possible?'

He took one of the proffered hands.

'Miss Estill,' he remarked coldly, without note of interrogation or of admiration.

'Oh! after so many years! not Camilla—as of old?'

'After so many years,' he replied coldly, 'one hardly ventures on names once familiar.'

'You mean that I have changed. Perhaps even more than you. From eighteen to thirty-eight is indeed a great jump.'

He remembered, at this point, that unless she was out in her dates in the old days she must be credited with two more years at least.

'It is indeed a great jump,' he said, still coldly.

'The heart of a woman wears out her frame,' she sighed pen-sively. 'We live and die by our affections.' She clasped her hands and inclined her head in the old sentimental way which brought back the old time. 'It is a great price to pay, but who would wish it otherwise? You are still young at thirty-eight. I am old. Don't say that I am not,' she put up her hands also in the old manner. 'Don't, Harry—because I feel that I am old. I look old. The heart may still be fresh, but when one looks old——' she paused to be assured that she did not look old.

Her lodger did not respond in the expected manner. He only bowed, still with great coldness. He was asking himself how in the world he could ever have found this poor little withered creature pretty? The little affectations of speech and carriage were the same ; she had not forgotten the old tricks : they were now so feeble and so old and so ridiculous ; yet they recalled the past. He remembered the Camilla whom for twenty years he had clean forgotten ; he remembered how he had once heard that she was six-and-twenty, fully struck, in the days of his flirtation ; he also remembered, vaguely, that someone had told him somewhere how all the pupils had to fall in love with Camilla—she expected it—that was before he went to read with old Estill. All these thoughts crossed his mind as the little woman smiled and played off her poor, faded old-fashioned graces before him. I do not know what she was saying to him, but when she finished he bowed again, replying nothing, because he had heard nothing, his mind having wandered back to twenty years before. She coloured, and was silent for a brief space, rebuffed at his coldness.

Then she began again, with an assumption of brightness.

'But tell me—to what happy accident do I owe your arrival, Harry? Oh! if I had only known that you were arriving I would have had my two boys home to be presented to you—my step-daughter you have already seen—my Isabel. But I know, it was a little device of your own. You would have your little romance. It was like my Harry. You heard I was living at Broad-stairs—you came down, you asked my address at the hotel, you walked over suddenly without sending in your name, thinking to surprise me. You would catch me at home, just as the children play at hide-and-seek. It was pretty of you, Harry. It was delicate, nobly delicate.'

'On the contrary,' he said, 'my coming here was a pure acci-dent.'

'Then it was Providential. Everything, as you should know who have been my father's pupil, is Ordered. As for me, Harry, I have been waiting—you remember how you went away—I have been waiting, as I promised. I said to my children : he has gone away to work for me——'

Harry began to feel as if the round world was really turning, but the wrong way. Was she married? Was she a widow? How could a married woman wait for her old lover ?

'Oh !' she clasped her hands, 'to work for me ! I knew not in what far off island of the ocean. Papa told me that you—that he had gone abroad. "He is working for me," I said. Papa is dead· He had but one more pupil after you. I think he pined when you went away. "He is working for me," I told the children.'

'Why ?' said Harry ; 'considering everything——'

The woman rose with great dignity.

'We exchanged a solemn promise,' she said. 'I undertook to wait for you. I have been waiting for you. For your part you promised to work for me. Is that true, Mr. Strange ? Is that true, Harry ?' she dropped her voice and laid her hand upon his arm. 'Oh ! Harry, have you forgotten ?'

'Forgotten? No. You make me remember that some such foolery was exchanged.'

'Then it is true—it is true. Say only that it is true ?'

'Of course it is true—if you come to that.'

'Then—Harry—Oh ! my Harry——' She threw herself upon his shoulder, though she had to stand on tiptoe, being so much shorter. But she did not mind that, so great was her resolution. 'I am yours at last. Oh ! oh ! oh !' She burst into the tears proper for the occasion. 'I am yours at last.'

'Oh ! get off—get off, I say.' He hitched this fair burden off his shoulder by a movement, neither graceful nor polite, but effective. She fell back upon the sofa, where she lay murmuring thanks to Heaven for thus bringing back to her the only man she had ever really loved—and for whom she had waited so long.

He, for his part, stood over her with perplexed face. Anyone will understand that when a man comes home, unmarried, still under forty, with a really fine thing out in New Zealand, he does not wish to marry a lodging-house keeper of Broadstairs, a widow close upon fifty, her personal attractions wholly gone, and with three children.

'I am too much overcome, Harry,' she said, rising, 'to continue this interview any longer. The o'erwrought heart may break its fragile cell ; the strings may snap. Oh ! Harry. Are we young again ? To-morrow we will renew this talk. It is my greatest happiness to feel that I have to do with a man of the strictest honour. You have worked for me—oh !' She clasped her hands and turned her eyes to Heaven. 'You have worked for me. You will tell me to-morrow—how well—and I—Oh! Harry—have waited—Oh ! with what constancy have I waited—for you——'

She disappeared.

He looked after her with bewildered face. Then he clutched his portmanteau and put on his hat. Then he put down his portmanteau again.

'No,' he said, 'never shall it be said that I ran away—even from a woman.'

IV.

HE went over to the hotel, dined there, spent the evening on the Cliff listening to the band, watching the people as they walked about, and wondering whether at eight-and-thirty he too could begin again the charming amusement which seemed to please so many of the young people. And at the thought of the widow he laughed.

At eleven o'clock he walked back to his lodgings, and went to bed. In the dead of night he thought he heard the lady weeping and blessing Heaven on the landing outside his door. It might have been the wind in the chimney, but the lodger crept out of bed and made sure that the bolt was fast.

In the morning he rang the bell for hot water, and on dressing found that his breakfast was spread for him by invisible hands and with evident desire to gratify him. Broadstairs is not a city of luxury ; in fact, at crowded times there are stories of stand-up fights over a neck of mutton or an ornamental block, but this table groaned, actually groaned, with the unwonted load of fried fish, ham, eggs, shrimps, toast, marmalade and jam.

'Camilla !' he murmured. 'Thus she thinks to soften my heart.'

He made an excellent breakfast, and then he lit a pipe and sat at the open window looking over the terrace. He was a self-reliant person, and was quite at ease as regards the lady, being, in fact, only anxious to put things right by personal explanation.

Presently the door opened and the girl—Camilla's Isabel—appeared. 'I'm to ask if there is anything more that you want ?' she asked ungraciously.

'Nothing—only—stay. Shut the door, child, and come here. Now, sit down and let us talk.'

She hesitated.

'If you will not, go and tell your mother that I want to speak to her at once.'

'She cannot see you now. She is busy. She isn't dressed. You are not the only lodger to be looked after. Mother is upstairs helping to do the rooms. Then there's the early dinners to get ready—and——'

'Well, then, sit down and talk for her.'

The girl obeyed, but with suspicion.

'What is your name ?' he began, 'and who was your father ?'

'My name is Isabel Pendlebury and my father was in Orders.'

'Pendlebury! I know now—he was one of my predecessors—two between him and me—at old Estill's. There he met Camilla and became engaged to her.'

'I do not know. He married her after my mother died.'

'Yes—yes. You have no resemblance to Camilla. You are her step-daughter,' he said. 'Now tell me more.'

In a few minutes he was master of the leading facts ; that the Rev. Pendlebury, deceased, was one of those brilliantly successful clergymen who arrive at a district church in a poor quarter at £300 a year ; that Isabel herself had been educated by a kindly maiden aunt, who unfortunately forgot to make a new will in Isabel's behalf before she died ; that when her father died, there was left for his widow, his daughter, and the two boys of the second marriage, exactly £500, the amount of his insurance. The Pendlebury relations, it appeared, belonged, as mostly happens, to the class which never has any money for the luxury of helping other people; they therefore applauded strenuously when the widow con-sented to 'sink the lady,' as she nicely put it, and bought the fur-niture and good will of a Broadstairs lodging, which she was still conducting with the sunshine and shower, the good season and the bad season, the fat time and the lean time, which attend on those who thus wait upon fortune. But Isabel, constrained to assist, or else to join the ranks of the nursery governess, or the shop-girl, remembered the maiden aunt's house and was unhappy.

So much Harry learned from her lips, or judged from her manner, which gradually softened as she perceived the sympathy which he felt. Perhaps instinct itself whispered in her ear that sympathy flows more easily towards a lovely damsel in distress than towards an elderly widow who wears a front, and this feeling may have given her freedom of speech.

'And you don't like your share in the business?' said Mr. Strange, at this point.

It certainly helped Isabel to larger utterance that he was one of those men who by reason of a soft voice, a kindly eye, and of a right feeling as to the proper moment for interruption, speedily win the confidence of those with whom they talk.

'Like it! oh!' she answered with infinite meaning in the long drawn breath. 'Like it! It is horrible—horrible.' She dropped her voice to a whisper. 'Think! the lodgers are always cheated, and I've got to draw out their bills. They must be cheated—you'll be cheated. Otherwise, what with the rent and taxes, we couldn't live out of the three months' season.'

'Yes; that is very bad—very bad. And all the time you would like—what would you like?'

'I don't know. We have always been poor. While father lived, we were honest—at least, I suppose so. Now——' she got up impatiently. 'What is the use? I have never had time even to wish for anything except for more money. What does mother mean?' she changed her manner suddenly. 'She says you have been working for her.'

'She is mistaken. I have been working for myself.'

'Oh! but she came out yesterday crying, and she said that her troubles were over, because you had been working for her.'

'She shall understand presently,' said the lodger, 'that she is quite mistaken.'

'May I go now?' she asked, chilled by the sudden coldness of his voice.

In the afternoon, when the tea was off her mind, Camilla was once more able to dress herself in order to resume her conversation with her old lover. Harry—who looked much more like Mr. Strange—rose politely and offered her a chair. But his face was stony. The widow sat down and shivered. All night she had been glowing under the rosy sunshine of hope and imagination. Now she watched his stony face and she shivered.

'Harry,' she said, smiling, as if in the sunshine of welcome, 'were you able to sleep at all last night? For myself, feeling that I was once more under the same roof after twenty years——'

'Mrs. Pendlebury,' he said, calling her by her married name, 'will you have the goodness at once, and without further rigmarole, to descend to common sense?'

She turned her eyes, those blue eyes once so fatal, upon him; she tried to smile; she laughed feebly; but she encountered a hard fixed face; she trembled again, and a tear stole down her cheek.

'No more nonsense,' he said. 'It is by the purest accident that I am here. I did not know you were living. I have clean—long since—forgotten your very existence. I have thought nothing about you ever since I sailed for New Zealand.'

'But your promise, Harry, your promise!'

'Good Lord! How dare you speak of my promise—you—who are a widow—actually a widow, with three children?'

'Cruel!' she folded her hands and raised streaming eyes to Heaven. 'He reproaches me with my marriage. And yet it was but an Incident in my life—only an Incident. Nothing but an Incident.'

'Only an Incident? What in the name of wonder do you mean?'

'And there were not three children but two—only two. Isabel is not my own. I have only Cyril and Augustine—Ril and Gus—dear children!'

'It is really too good!' he laughed aloud and remained totally unmoved by her tears. 'Besides, I know all about you, now. I had forgotten until after you left me. Shall I recall to you your own history? Jack Bolder told me—surely you remember Jack —if he were to drop in casually you would send him your faded photograph and ask if he was still working for you.'

'Cruel! Cruel!'

'You were twenty when you were engaged to the first of the pupils. You were still twenty when you were engaged, a year after, to the third. That was Jack Bolder. He's a Colonial Bishop now, and outside his ecclesiasticums he's a very good fellow. You were twenty when you were engaged to Pendlebury, the fourth or fifth. And you were twenty when you were engaged to me, the seventh.'

She shook her head sorrowfully.

'When Pendlebury met you after his first wife died, it was thirteen years since he had gone away and forgotten you. You reminded him that you were still waiting. Your fidelity touched him. But I believe that even he had not the courage to pretend that he was still waiting for you.'

'If you only knew! If I could only tell you! But the heart knows its own secrets—even when I stood at the altar with that good man. The heart knew, Harry—I mean Mr. Strange—and it never faltered in its allegiance—never—never.'

Harry quoted something incongruous about a man's heart being true to Poll in spite of many similar Incidents.

'And—and—when I saw you again—Oh! Oh! Oh!—my memory carried me back and I thought I was once more young and beautiful and loved by the only man in the world who ever touched my heart. Oh! and I thought I had found a friend at last. Oh! and I am so poor and friendless. Oh! and I have my two boys—my Ril and my Gus—and no one to help.' There was no mockery in the tears that she shed now, or in the disappointment which filled her heart.

'I shall be here for a fortnight, Mrs. Pendlebury,' he said ; 'we need have no more interviews. If I can help you—perhaps——' he rose and opened the door.

'You were always truth and honour itself. What that villain Jack Bolder—Oh! I could almost turn Primitive Methodist to think that such a man is a Bishop!—what he told you about all those pupils is dreadful lying and slandering. To think that a Bishop should condescend to slander a weak, helpless, unhappy woman!'

'Good-morning, Mrs. Pendlebury,' he said, opening the door wider.

'Isabel,' said the widow presently, 'Mr. Strange is an old friend. He will not go away without helping us, I am quite sure of that. Let us make him as comfortable as we can. I only wish he would dine at home. I remember that he was fond of roast veal when I stuffed it with my own hands—and he would lose himself in plum tart if he thought I had made it. I would give him, Isabel, just to recall the happy past, a knuckle of veal roasted, with a delicious stuffing, and a plum tart—plums are cheap now — beautifully browned.'

V.

It was the last day of the fortnight. Mr. Strange was to go on the morrow in order to make room for the new comers. In the evening he walked on the cliff, but not alone. With him walked Isabel Pendlebury. The band finished : the people began to disperse and to go home : there were left only a few couples strolling up and down ; the moon shone on the waters and the air was balmy.

They walked to the far end, where there was no one but themselves ; and they sat down on the very last bench, on the very edge of the cliff.

'Isabel,' said the lodger, 'I have had a most delightful fortnight.'

So had she. For her the fortnight had been like a little breath of Heaven. For it had been wholly spent in the society of a man who had nothing to do, apparently, but to make her happy.

Was it not the most natural thing in the world? This man,

twenty years from home, who had long since broken from his old ties, with no mother or sisters, and possessed of a tender heart, found a truly beautiful damsel in great unhappiness. Of course he pitied her; of course he began to devise means to make her happy; therefore he gave her gloves—which is a safe way to begin when you are rich and nearly forty, and can always fall back, in case of misunderstanding, upon a fatherly interest. Then he took her for drives—Broadstairs lends itself to drives; then to larger excursions, with little dinners, to Canterbury, Dover, Deal, Sandwich, Ramsgate, Westgate, even Margate. And, quite naturally, the girl being clever, sympathetic, beautiful, and easily pleased, he began to ask himself what sort of a wife he should like to have at his fine house in New Zealand.

As for the girl, I don't think she cared so much for the things he showed her, as for the thoughts that now filled her brain. For she began, after two or three days of this fine pleasuring, to recognise a certain gleam or ray, as of half understood perception; this kindled into tumultuous hope, which fired her brain and kept her awake all night and lit up her eyes, naturally very good, and put colour into her cheek, and then, in its turn, changed into a quaggy slough of despond, which, once passed, gave place to hope again, and finally rose to certainty. And then, like the glass, it was set fair. This evening it was certainly absolute. For she was not blind; she could not but see—the most innocent girl ever created could not but see—that Mr. Strange regarded his companion with greater admiration than he bestowed even upon the Cathedral of Canterbury, or upon the quaint old streets of Sandwich. It was not on the scenery that he gazed when he walked beside this interesting damsel left so friendless with a stepmother in a lodging-house.

'Thanks to you,' he went on. He was now much too old and experienced to fall a-trembling over any woman. His voice was quite steady, and his words were measured. Yet he was thinking all the time how well this girl would look at the head of his table attired in crimson velvet. 'I think,' he said, 'I am quite sure, Isabel, that your father must have been the best of men. Perhaps also the loveliest.'

She laughed. She expected something much more sentimental. Her saintly parent may have been quite the best, but certainly he was not the loveliest of mankind.

'Then it was your mother. Isabel, child,' at this point he laid an affectionate hand round a willing and a yielding waist, 'I am going back to New Zealand. If you will come with me, I will do my best to make you happy.'

Go with him? Leave the dingy lodging-house and the cheating bills? Go to a land of plenty, with horses and carriages, and silk frocks and kid gloves? Go with a real man, strong enough to have made his own way, and sweet-tempered as well? Of course she would go. But she did not express all the joy she felt. Not so. She only murmured faintly—though she would have liked to jump up and shout and dance for joy—that she would go with him.

They went home together hand-in-hand. Harry took his betrothed into his own room and rang the bell. Camilla herself obeyed the call.

'Mrs. Pendlebury,' he said, 'pray sit down. We agreed a fortnight ago not to return to the old familiar names. We may now do so, however. You shall henceforth be once more Camilla to me, and I will be Harry to you in future, if you like.'

'What do you mean?' She was now quite subdued. There was hardly any jealousy even in her mind, though it is not in human nature to stand by and look on quite unmoved when such a comedy is played under your very eyes. 'What am I to understand? Will you explain, Isabel?'

'We will be friends again. In short, Camilla, you may henceforth regard me as one of the family, because I am going to marry your step-daughter. Isabel has consented to become my wife. And all we have to arrange now is to make up to you, somehow, for the loss of her assistance. I daresay we can do something for the boys, you know—your Gus and Ril.'

That is a happy moment—too rare—too seldom vouchsafed to mortals—when all misunderstandings are cleared up and all hearts made to rejoice.

'My Ril and Gus, Harry—dear Cyril and dear Augustine! Oh! when I saw you, the moment I saw you, though the past was forgotten, I knew—I felt—I recognised, that a crisis in my life was at hand. Isabel, dear child—I said a crisis was at hand. It came with your arrival. I knew that in a consecrated and a holy sense, Harry, not in the low and earthly sense—no—no—that was gone—I knew, I say, and I told you, that I was waiting for you—my dear future stepson-in-law—and that you were working for me.'

THE END.

BILLING AND SONS, PRINTERS, GUILDFORD.

A LIST OF BOOKS

PUBLISHED BY

CHATTO & WINDUS

214, PICCADILLY, LONDON, W.

Sold by all Booksellers, or sent post-free for the published price by the Publishers.

Abbé Constantin (The) By LUDOVIC HALEVY, of the French Academy. Translated into English. With 36 Photogravure Illustrations by GOUPIL & Co., after the Drawings of Madame MADELEINE LEMAIRE. Only 250 copies of this choice book have been printed (in large quarto) for the English market, each one numbered. The price may be learned from any Bookseller.

About.—The Fellah: An Egyp- tian Novel. By EDMOND ABOUT. Translated by Sir RANDAL ROBERTS. Post 8vo, illustrated boards, **2s.**; cloth limp, **2s. 6d.**

Adams (W. Davenport), Works by:
A Dictionary of the Drama. Being a comprehensive Guide to the Plays, Playwrights, Players, and Playhouses of the United Kingdom and America, from the Earliest to the Present Times. Crown 8vo, halfbound, **12s. 6d.** [*Preparing.*
Quips and Quiddities. Selected by W. DAVENPORT ADAMS. Post 8vo, cloth limp, **2s. 6d.**

Agony Column (The) of "The Times," from 1800 to 1870. Edited, with an Introduction, by ALICE CLAY. Post 8vo, cloth limp, **2s. 6d.**

Aidé (Hamilton), Works by:
Post 8vo, illustrated boards, **2s.** each.
Carr of Carrlyon. | Confidences.

Alexander (Mrs.), Novels by:
Post 8vo, illustrated boards, **2s.** each.
Maid, Wife, or Widow?
Valerie's Fate.

Allen (Grant), Works by:
Crown 8vo, cloth extra, **6s.** each.
The Evolutionist at Large.
Vignettes from Nature.
Colin Clout's Calendar.

Crown 8vo, cloth extra, **6s.** each; os 8vo, illustrated boards., **2s.** each.
Strange Stories. With a Frontispiece by GEORGE DU MAURIER.
The Beckoning Hand. With a Frontispiece by TOWNLEY GREEN.

Philistia. Crown 8vo, cloth extra, **3s. 6d.**; post 8vo, illustrated bds., **2s.**

Post 8vo, illustrated boards, **2s.** each
Babylon: A Romance.
For Maimie's Sake.
In all Shades.

Crown 8vo, cloth extra, **3s. 6d.** each.
The Devil's Die. | This Mortal Coil.
The Tents of Shem. With a Frontispiece by G. F. BREWTNALL.
[*Shortly.*

Architectural Styles, A Hand- book of. Translated from the German of A. ROSENGARTEN, by W. COLLETT-SANDARS. Crown 8vo, cloth extra, with 639 Illustrations, **7s. 6d.**

Arnold.—Bird Life in England. By EDWIN LESTER ARNOLD. Crown 8vo, cloth extra, **6s.**

Art (The) of Amusing: A Col- lection of Graceful Arts, Games, Tricks, Puzzles, and Charades. By FRANK BELLEW. With 300 Illustrations. Cr 8vo, cloth extra, **4s. 6d.**

Artemus Ward:

Artemus Ward's Works: The Works of CHARLES FARRER BROWNE, better known as ARTEMUS WARD. With Portrait and Facsimile. Crown 8vo, cloth extra, 7s. 6d.

The Genial Showman: Life and Adventures of Artemus Ward. By EDWARD P. HINGSTON. With a Frontispiece. Cr. 8vo, cl. extra, 3s. 6d.

Ashton (John), Works by:

Crown 8vo, cloth extra, 7s. 6d. each.

A History of the Chap-Books of the Eighteenth Century. With nearly 400 Illustrations, engraved in facsimile of the originals.

Social Life in the Reign of Queen Anne. From Original Sources. With nearly 100 Illustrations.

Humour, Wit, and Satire of the Seventeenth Century. With nearly 100 Illustrations.

English Caricature and Satire on Napoleon the First. With 115 Illustrations.

Modern Street Ballads. With 57 Illustrations

Bacteria.—A Synopsis of the

Bacteria and Yeast Fungi and Allied Species. By W. B. GROVE, B.A. With 87 Illusts. Crown 8vo, cl. extra, 3s. 6d.

Bankers, A Handbook of Lon-

don; together with Lists of Bankers from 1677. By F. G. HILTON PRICE. Crown 8vo, cloth extra, 7s. 6d.

Bardsley (Rev. C.W.), Works by:

English Surnames: Their Sources and Significations. Third Edition, revised. Crown 8vo, cl. ex., 7s. 6d.

Curiosities of Puritan Nomenclature. Second Edition. Crown 8vo, cloth extra, 6s.

Barrett.—Fettered for Life.

By FRANK BARRETT, Author of "Lady Biddy Fane," &c. Three Vols., crown 8vo.

Beaconsfield, Lord: A Biogra-

phy. By T. P. O'CONNOR, M.P. Sixth Edition, with a New Preface. Crown 8vo, cloth extra, 5s.

Beauchamp. — Grantley

Grange: A Novel. By SHELSLEY BEAUCHAMP. Post 8vo, illust. bds., 2s.

Beautiful Pictures by British

Artists: A Gathering of Favourites from our Picture Galleries. All engraved on Steel in the highest style of Art. Edited, with Notices of the Artists, by SYDNEY ARMYTAGE, M.A. Imperial 4to, cloth extra, gilt and gilt edges, 21s.

Bechstein. — As Pretty as

Seven, and other German Stories. Collected by LUDWIG BECHSTEIN. With Additional Tales by the Brothers GRIMM, and 100 Illusts. by RICHTER. Small 4to, green and gold, 6s. 6d.; gilt edges, 7s. 6d.

Beerbohm. — Wanderings in

Patagonia; or, Life among the Ostrich Hunters. By JULIUS BEERBOHM. With Illusts. Crown 8vo, cloth extra, 3s. 6d.

Bennett (W.C., LL.D.), Works by:

Post 8vo, cloth limp, 2s. each.

A Ballad History of England.

Songs for Sailors.

Besant (Walter) and James

Rice, Novels by. Crown 8vo, cloth extra, 3s. 6d. each; post 8vo, illust. bds., 2s. each; cl. limp, 2s. 6d. each.

Ready-Money Mortiboy.

My Little Girl.

With Harp and Crown.

This Son of Vulcan.

The Golden Butterfly.

The Monks of Thelema.

By Celia's Arbour.

The Chaplain of the Fleet.

The Seamy Side.

The Case of Mr. Lucraft, &c.

'Twas in Trafalgar's Bay, &c.

The Ten Years' Tenant, &c.

Besant (Walter), Novels by:

Crown 8vo, cloth extra, 3s. 6d. each; post 8vo, illust. boards, 2s. each; cloth limp, 2s. 6d. each.

All Sorts and Conditions of Men: An Impossible Story. With Illustrations by FRED. BARNARD.

The Captains' Room, &c. With Frontispiece by E. J. WHEELER.

All in a Garden Fair. With 6 Illustrations by HARRY FURNISS.

Dorothy Forster. With Frontispiece by CHARLES GREEN.

Uncle Jack, and other Stories.

Children of Gibeon.

The World Went Very Well Then. With Illustrations by A. FORESTIER

BESANT (WALTER), *continued—*
Herr Paulus: His Rise, his Greatness, and his Fall. With a NEW PREFACE. Cr. 8vo, cloth extra, 3s. 6d.
For Faith and Freedom. With Illustrations by A. FORESTIER and F. WADDY. Cheaper Edition. Crown 8vo, cloth extra, 3s. 6d.
To Call her Mine, &c. With Nine Illustrations by A. FORESTIER. Cr. 8vo, cloth extra, 6s.
The Holy Rose, &c. With Illusts. Cr 8vo, cloth extra, 6s.   [*Shortly.*
The Bell of St. Paul's. Three Vols., crown 8vo.
Fifty Years Ago. With 137 full-page Plates and Woodcuts. Demy 8vo, cloth extra, 16s.
The Eulogy of Richard Jefferies. With Photograph Portrait. Second Edition. Cr. 8vo, cloth extra, 6s.
The Art of Fiction. Demy 8vo, 1s.

New Library Edition of
Besant and Rice's Novels.
The whole 12 Volumes, printed from new type on a large crown 8vo page, and handsomely bound in cloth, are now ready, price Six Shillings each.
1. Ready - Money Mortiboy. With Etched Portrait of JAMES RICE.
2. My Little Girl.
3. With Harp and Crown.
4. This Son of Vulcan.
5. The Golden Butterfly. With Etched Portrait of WALTER BESANT.
6. The Monks of Thelema.
7. By Celia's Arbour.
8. The Chaplain of the Fleet.
9. The Seamy Side.
10. The Case of Mr. Lucraft, &c.
11. 'Twas in Trafalgar's Bay, &c.
12. The Ten Years' Tenant, &c.

Betham-Edwards (M.)—Felicia
By M. BETHAM-EDWARDS. Cr. 8vo, cloth extra, 3s. 6d.; post 8vo, illust. bds., 2s.

Bewick (Thomas) and his
Pupils. By AUSTIN DOBSON. With 95 Illusts. Square 8vo, cloth extra, 6s.

Blackburn's (Henry) Art Handbooks.
Academy Notes, separate years, from 1875 to 1887, and 1889, each 1s.
Academy Notes, 1890. With numerous Illustrations. 1s. [*Preparing.*
Academy Notes, 1875-79. Complete in One Volume, with about 600 Facsimile Illustrations. Cloth limp, 6s.
Academy Notes, 1880-84. Complete in One Volume, with about 700 Facsimile Illustrations. Cloth limp, 6s.
Academy Notes, 1885-89. Complete in One Vol., with about 600 Illustrations. Cloth limp, 7s. 6d.

BLACKBURN (HENRY), *continued—*
Grosvenor Notes, 1877. 6d.
Grosvenor Notes, separate years, from 1878 to 1889, each 1s.
Grosvenor Notes, 1890. With numerous Illusts. 1s.   [*Preparing.*
Grosvenor Notes, Vol. I., 1877-82. With upwards of 300 Illustrations. Demy 8vo, cloth limp, 6s.
Grosvenor Notes, Vol. II., 1883-87. With upwards of 300 Illustrations. Demy 8vo, cloth limp, 6s.
The New Gallery, 1888. With numerous Illustrations. 1s.
The New Gallery, 1889. With numerous Illustrations. 1s.
The English Pictures at the National Gallery. 114 Illustrations. 1s.
The Old Masters at the National Gallery. 128 Illustrations. 1s. 6d.
A Complete Illustrated Catalogue to the National Gallery. With Notes by H. BLACKBURN, and 242 Illusts. Demy 8vo, cloth limp, 3s.

The Paris Salon, 1890. With 300 Facsimile Sketches. 3s.   [*Preparing.*

Blake (William): Etchings from
his Works. By W. B. SCOTT. With descriptive Text. Folio, half-bound boards, India Proofs, 21s.

Blind.—The Ascent of Man:
A Poem. By MATHILDE BLIND. Crown 8vo, printed on hand-made paper, cloth extra, 5s.

Bourne (H. R. Fox), Works by:
English Merchants: Memoirs in Illustration of the Progress of British Commerce. With numerous Illustrations. Cr. 8vo, cloth extra, 7s. 6d.
English Newspapers: Chapters in the History of Journalism. Two Vols., demy 8vo, cloth extra, 25s.

Bowers'(G.) Hunting Sketches:
Oblong 4to, half-bound boards, 21s. each
Canters in Crampshire.
Leaves from a Hunting Journal
Coloured in facsimile of the originals.

Boyle (Frederick), Works by:
Crown 8vo, cloth extra, 3s. 6d. each; post 8vo, illustrated boards, 2s. each.
Camp Notes: Stories of Sport and Adventure in Asia, Africa, America.
Savage Life: Adventures of a Globe-Trotter.

Chronicles of No-Man's Land. Post 8vo, illust. boards, 2s.

Brand'sObservations on Popular Antiquities, chiefly Illustrating the Origin of our Vulgar Customs, Ceremonies, and Superstitions. With the Additions of Sir HENRY ELLIS. Crown 8vo, with Illustrations, 7s. 6d.

Bret Harte, Works by:
LIBRARY EDITION, Complete in Five Vols., cr. 8vo, cl.extra, 6s. each.
Bret Harte's Collected Works: LIBRARY EDITION. Arranged and Revised by the Author.
Vol. I. COMPLETE POETICAL AND DRAMATIC WORKS. With Steel Portrait, and Introduction by Author.
Vol. II. EARLIER PAPERS—LUCK OF ROARING CAMP, and other Sketches —BOHEMIAN PAPERS — SPANISH AND AMERICAN LEGENDS.
Vol. III. TALES OF THE ARGONAUTS —EASTERN SKETCHES.
Vol. IV. GABRIEL CONROY.
Vol. V. STORIES — CONDENSED NOVELS, &c.

The Select Works of Bret Harte, in Prose and Poetry. With Introductory Essay by J. M. BELLEW, Portrait of the Author, and 50 Illustrations. Crown 8vo, cloth extra. 7s. 6d

Bret Harte's Complete Poetical Works. Author's Copyright Edition. Printed on hand-made paper and bound in buckram. Cr. 8vo, 4s. 6d.

The Queen of the Pirate Isle. With 28 original Drawings by KATE GREENAWAY, Reproduced in Colours by EDMUND EVANS. Sm. 4to, bds., 5s.

Post 8vo, illustrated boards, 2s. each.
Gabriel Conroy.
An Heiress of Red Dog, &c.
The Luck of Roaring Camp, and other Sketches.
Californian Stories (including THE TWINS OF TABLE MOUNTAIN, JEFF BRIGGS'S LOVE STORY, &c.)

Post 8vo, illustrated boards, 2s. each; cloth, 2s. 6d. each.
Flip. | Maruja.
A Phyllis of the Sierras.
A Waif of the Plains.   [Shortly.

Fcap. 8vo, picture cover, 1s. each.
The Twins of Table Mountain.
Jeff Briggs's Love Story.

Brewer (Rev. Dr.), Works by:
The Reader's Handbook of Allusions, References, Plots, and Stories. Twelfth Thousand. With Appendix, containing a COMPLETE ENGLISH BIBLIOGRAPHY. Cr. 8vo, cloth 7s. 6d.

BREWER (Rev. Dr.), *continued—*
Authors and their Works, with the Dates: Being the Appendices to "The Reader's Handbook," separately printed. Cr. 8vo, cloth limp, 2s.
A Dictionary of Miracles: Imitative, Realistic, and Dogmatic. Crown 8vo, cloth extra 7s. 6d.

Brewster (Sir David), Works by:
Post 8vo, cloth extra, 4s. 6d. each.
More Worlds than One: The Creed of the Philosopher and the Hope of the Christian. With Plates.
The Martyrs of Science: Lives of GALILEO, TYCHO BRAHE, and KEPLER. With Portraits.
Letters on Natural Magic. A New Edition, with numerous Illustrations, and Chapters on the Being and Faculties of Man, and Additional Phenomena of Natural Magic, by J. A. SMITH.

Brillat-Savarin.—Gastronomy as a Fine Art. By BRILLAT-SAVARIN. Translated by R. E. ANDERSON, M.A. Post 8vo, printed on laid-paper and half-bound, 2s.

Brydges. — Uncle Sam at Home. By HAROLD BRYDGES. Post 8vo, illust. boards, 2s.; cloth, 2s. 6d.

Buchanan's (Robert) Works:
Crown 8vo, cloth extra, 6s. each.
Ballads of Life, Love, and Humour. With a Frontispiece by ARTHUR HUGHES.
Selected Poems of Robert Buchanan. With a Frontispiece by T. DALZIEL.
The Earthquake; or, Six Days and a Sabbath.
The City of Dream: An Epic Poem. With Two Illusts. by P. MACNAB. Second Edition.

Robert Buchanan'sComplete Poetical Works. With Steel-plate Portrait. Crown 8vo, cloth extra, 7s. 6d.

Crown 8vo, cloth extra, 3s. 6d. each; post 8vo, illust. boards, 2s. each.
The Shadow of the Sword.
A Child of Nature. With a Frontispiece.
God and the Man. With Illustrations by FRED. BARNARD.
The Martyrdom of Madeline. With Frontispiece by A. W. COOPER.
Love Me for Ever. With a Frontispiece by P. MACNAB.
Annan Water. | The New Abelard.
Foxglove Manor.
Matt: A Story of a Caravan.
The Master of the Mine.
The Heir of Linne.

Burton (Captain).—The Book of the Sword: Being a History of the Sword and its Use in all Countries, from the Earliest Times. By RICHARD F. BURTON. With over 400 Illustrations. Square 8vo, cloth extra, 32s.

Burton (Robert):

The Anatomy of Melancholy. A New Edition, complete, corrected and enriched by Translations of the Classical Extracts. Demy 8vo, cloth extra, 7s. 6d.

Melancholy Anatomised: Being an Abridgment, for popular use, of BURTON'S ANATOMY OF MELANCHOLY. Post 8vo, cloth limp, 2s. 6d.

Caine (T. Hall), Novels by:

Crown 8vo, cloth extra, 3s. 6d. each; post 8vo, illustrated boards, 2s. each.

The Shadow of a Crime.

A Son of Hagar.

The Deemster: A Romance of the Isle of Man.

Cameron (Commander).— The Cruise of the "Black Prince" Privateer. By V. LOVETT CAMERON, R.N., C.B. With Two Illustrations by P. MACNAB. Crown 8vo, cl. ex., 5s.; post 8vo, illustrated boards, 2s.

Cameron (Mrs. H. Lovett), Novels by:

Crown 8vo, cloth extra, 3s. 6d. each post 8vo, illustrated boards, 2s. each.

Juliet's Guardian. | Deceivers Ever.

Carlyle (Thomas):

On the Choice of Books. By THOMAS CARLYLE. With a Life of the Author by R. H. SHEPHERD. New and Revised Edition, post 8vo, cloth extra, Illustrated, 1s. 6d.

The Correspondence of Thomas Carlyle and Ralph Waldo Emerson, 1834 to 1872. Edited by CHARLES ELIOT NORTON. With Portraits. Two Vols., crown 8vo, cloth extra, 24s.

Chapman's (George) Works: Vol. I. contains the Plays complete, including the doubtful ones. Vol. II., the Poems and Minor Translations, with an Introductory Essay by ALGERNON CHARLES SWINBURNE. Vol. III., the Translations of the Iliad and Odyssey. Three Vols., crown 8vo, cloth extra, 18s. or separately, 6s. each.

Chatto & Jackson.—A Treatise on Wood Engraving, Historical and Practical. By WM. ANDREW CHATTO and JOHN JACKSON. With an Additional Chapter by HENRY G. BOHN; and 450 fine Illustrations. A Reprint of the last Revised Edition. Large 4to, half-bound, 28s.

Chaucer :

Chaucer for Children: A Golden Key. By Mrs. H. R. HAWEIS. With Eight Coloured Pictures and numerous Woodcuts by the Author. New Ed., small 4to, cloth extra, 6s.

Chaucer for Schools. By Mrs. H. R. HAWEIS. Demy 8vo, cloth limp, 2s. 6d.

Clodd.—Myths and Dreams. By EDWARD CLODD, F.R.A.S., Author of "The Story of Creation," &c. Crown 8vo, cloth extra, 5s.

Cobban.—The Cure of Souls : A Story. By J. MACLAREN COBBAN. Post 8vo, illustrated boards, 2s.

Coleman (John), Works by:

Players and Playwrights I have Known. Two Vols., demy 8vo, cloth extra, 24s.

Curly: An Actor's Romance. With Illustrations by J. C. DOLLMAN. Crown 8vo, cloth, 1s. 6d.

Collins (Churton).—A Monograph on Dean Swift. By J. CHURTON COLLINS. Crown 8vo, cloth extra, 8s. [*Shortly.*

Collins (C. Allston).—The Bar Sinister: A Story. By C. ALLSTON COLLINS. Post 8vo, illustrated bds., 2s.

Collins (Mortimer), Novels by : Crown 8vo, cloth extra, 3s. 6d. each; post 8vo, illustrated boards, 2s. each.

Sweet Anne Page.

Transmigration.

From Midnight to Midnight.

A Fight with Fortune. Post 8vo, illustrated boards, 2s.

Collins (Mortimer & Frances), Novels by : Crown 8vo, cloth extra, 3s. 6d. each; post 8vo, illustrated boards, 2s. each.

Blacksmith and Scholar.

The Village Comedy.

You Play Me False.

Post 8vo, illustrated boards, 2s. each.

Sweet and Twenty.

Frances.

Collins (Wilkie), Novels by:
Crown 8vo, cloth extra, 3s. 6d. each;
post 8vo, illustrated boards, 2s. each;
cloth limp, 2s. 6d. each.
Antonina. Illust. by Sir John Gilbert.
Basil. Illustrated by Sir John Gilbert and J. Mahoney.
Hide and Seek. Illustrated by Sir John Gilbert and J. Mahoney.
The Dead Secret. Illustrated by Sir John Gilbert.
Queen of Hearts. Illustrated by Sir John Gilbert.
My Miscellanies. With a Steel-plate Portrait of Wilkie Collins.
The Woman in White. With Illustrations by Sir John Gilbert and F. A. Fraser.
The Moonstone. With Illustrations by G. Du Maurier and F. A. Fraser.
Man and Wife. Illust. by W. Small.
Poor Miss Finch. Illustrated by G. Du Maurier and Edward Hughes.
Miss or Mrs.? With Illustrations by S. L. Fildes and Henry Woods.
The New Magdalen. Illustrated by G. Du Maurier and C. S. Reinhardt.
The Frozen Deep. Illustrated by G. Du Maurier and J. Mahoney.
The Law and the Lady. Illustrated by S. L. Fildes and Sydney Hall.
The Two Destinies.
The Haunted Hotel. Illustrated by Arthur Hopkins.
The Fallen Leaves.
Jezebel's Daughter.
The Black Robe.
Heart and Science: A Story of the Present Time.
"I Say No."
The Evil Genius.
Little Novels.

The Legacy of Cain. Cheap Edition. Crown 8vo, cloth, 3s. 6d.
Blind Love. With a Preface by Walter Besant, and Illustrations by A. Forestier. Three Vols., crown 8vo.   [*Shortly.*

Colman's Humorous Works:
"Broad Grins," "My Nightgown and Slippers," and other Humorous Works, Prose and Poetical, of George Colman. With Life by G. B. Buckstone, and Frontispiece by Hogarth. Crown 8vo cloth extra, gilt, 7s. 6d.

Colquhoun.—Every Inch a Soldier: A Novel. By M. J. Colquhoun. Post 8vo, illustrated boards, 2s.

Convalescent Cookery: A Family Handbook. By Catherine Ryan. Crown 8vo, 1s.; cloth, 1s. 6d.

Conway (Moncure D.), Works by:
Demonology and Devil-Lore. Third Edition. Two Vols., royal 8vo, with 65 Illustrations, 28s.
A Necklace of Stories. Illustrated by W. J. Hennessy. Square 8vo, cloth extra, 6s.
Pine and Palm: A Novel. Cheaper Ed. Post 8vo, illust. bds., 2s. [*Shortly.*

Cook (Dutton), Novels by:
Leo. Post 8vo, illustrated boards, 2s.
Paul Foster's Daughter. Crown 8vo, cloth extra, 3s. 6d.; post 8vo, illustrated boards, 2s.

Copyright.—A Handbook of English and Foreign Copyright in Literary and Dramatic Works. By Sidney Jerrold. Post 8vo, cl., 2s. 6d.

Cornwall.—Popular Romances of the West of England; or, The Drolls, Traditions, and Superstitions of Old Cornwall. Collected and Edited by Robert Hunt, F.R.S. New and Revised Edition, with Additions, and Two Steel-plate Illustrations by George Cruikshank. Crown 8vo, cloth extra, 7s. 6d.

Craddock. — The Prophet of the Great Smoky Mountains. By Charles Egbert Craddock. Post 8vo illust. bds., 2s.; cloth limp, 2s. 6d.

Cruikshank (George):
The Comic Almanack. Complete in Two Series: The First from 1835 to 1843; the Second from 1844 to 1853. A Gathering of the Best Humour of Thackeray, Hood, Mayhew, Albert Smith, A'Beckett, Robert Brough, &c. With 2,000 Woodcuts and Steel Engravings by Cruikshank, Hine, Landells, &c. Crown 8vo, cloth gilt, two very thick volumes, 7s. 6d. each.
The Life of George Cruikshank. By Blanchard Jerrold, Author of "The Life of Napoleon III.," &c. With 84 Illustrations. New and Cheaper Edition, enlarged, with Additional Plates, and a very carefully compiled Bibliography. Crown 8vo, cloth extra, 7s. 6d.

Cumming (C. F. Gordon), Works by:
Demy 8vo, cloth extra, 8s. 6d. each.
In the Hebrides. With Autotype Facsimile and numerous full-page Illusts.
In the Himalayas and on the Indian Plains. With numerous Illusts.

Via Cornwall to Egypt. With a Photogravure Frontispiece. Demy 8vo, cloth extra, 7s. 6d.

Cussans.—Handbook of Heraldry; with Instructions for Tracing Pedigrees and Deciphering Ancient MSS., &c. By JOHN E. CUSSANS. Entirely New and Revised Edition, illustrated with over 400 Woodcuts and Coloured Plates. Crown 8vo, cloth extra, 7s. 6d.

Cyples.—Hearts of Gold: A Novel. By WILLIAM CYPLES. Crown 8vo, cloth extra, 3s. 6d.; post 8vo, illustrated boards, 2s.

Daniel. — Merrie England in the Olden Time. By GEORGE DANIEL. With Illustrations by ROBT. CRUIKSHANK. Crown 8vo, cloth extra, 3s. 6d.

Daudet.—The Evangelist; or, Port Salvation. By ALPHONSE DAUDET. Translated by C. HARRY MELTZER. With Portrait of the Author. Crown 8vo, cloth extra, 3s. 6d.; post 8vo, illust. boards, 2s.

Davenant.—Hints for Parents on the Choice of a Profession or Trade for their Sons. By FRANCIS DAVENANT, M.A. Post 8vo, 1s.; cloth limp, 1s. 6d.

Davies (Dr. N. E.), Works by: Crown 8vo, 1s. each; cloth limp, 1s. 6d. each.
One Thousand Medical Maxims.
Nursery Hints: A Mother's Guide.
Foods for the Fat: A Treatise on Corpulency, and a Dietary for its Cure.

Aids to Long Life. Crown 8vo, 2s.; cloth limp, 2s. 6d.

Davies' (Sir John) Complete Poetical Works, including Psalms I. to L. in Verse, and other hitherto Unpublished MSS., for the first time Collected and Edited, with Memorial-Introduction and Notes, by the Rev. A. B. GROSART, D.D. Two Vols., crown 8vo, cloth boards, 12s.

Daylight Land: The Adven- tures, Humorous and Otherwise, of Judge JOHN DOE, Tourist; CEPHAS PEPPERELL, Capitalist; Colonel GOFFE, and others, in their Excursion over Prairie and Mountain. By W. H. MURRAY. With 140 Illusts. in colours. Small 4to, cloth extra, 12s. 6d.

De Maistre.—A Journey Round My Room. By XAVIER DE MAISTRE. Translated by HENRY ATTWELL. Post 8vo, cloth limp, 2s. 6d.

De Mille.—A Castle in Spain: A Novel. By JAMES DE MILLE. With a Frontispiece. Crown 8vo, cloth extra, 3s. 6d.; post 8vo, illust. bds., 2s.

Derwent (Leith), Novels by: Crown 8vo, cloth extra, 3s. 6d. each; post 8vo, illustrated boards, 2s. each.
Our Lady of Tears. | Circe's Lovers.

Dickens (Charles), Novels by: Post 8vo, illustrated boards, 2s. each.
Sketches by Boz. | Nicholas Nickleby.
Pickwick Papers. | Oliver Twist.

The Speeches of Charles Dickens, 1841-1870. With a New Bibliography, revised and enlarged. Edited and Prefaced by RICHARD HERNE SHEPHERD. Cr. 8vo, cloth extra, 6s.—Also a SMALLER EDITION, in the *Mayfair Library*. Post 8vo, cloth limp, 2s. 6d.

About England with Dickens. By ALFRED RIMMER. With 57 Illustrations by C. A. VANDERHOOF, ALFRED RIMMER, and others. Sq. 8vo, cloth extra, 7s. 6d.

Dictionaries:

A Dictionary of Miracles: Imitative, Realistic, and Dogmatic. By the Rev. E. C. BREWER, LL.D. Crown 8vo, cloth extra, 7s. 6d.

The Reader's Handbook of Allusions, References, Plots, and Stories. By the Rev. E. C. BREWER, LL.D. With an Appendix, containing a Complete English Bibliography. Eleventh Thousand. Crown 8vo, 1,400 pages, cloth extra, 7s. 6d.

Authors and their Works, with the Dates. Being the Appendices to "The Reader's Handbook," separately printed. By the Rev. Dr. BREWER. Crown 8vo, cloth limp, 2s.

A Dictionary of the Drama: Being a comprehensive Guide to the Plays, Playwrights, Players, and Playhouses of the United Kingdom and America, from the Earliest to the Present Times. By W. DAVENPORT ADAMS. A thick volume, crown 8vo, half-bound, 12s. 6d. *[In preparation.*

Familiar Short Sayings of Great Men. With Historical and Explanatory Notes. By SAMUEL A. BENT, M.A. Fifth Edition, revised and enlarged. Cr. 8vo, cloth extra, 7s. 6d.

The Slang Dictionary: Etymological, Historical, and Anecdotal. Crown 8vo, cloth extra, 6s. 6d.

Women of the Day: A Biographical Dictionary. By FRANCES HAYS. Cr. 8vo, cloth extra, 5s.

Words, Facts, and Phrases: A Dictionary of Curious, Quaint, and Out-of-the-Way Matters. By ELIEZER EDWARDS. Crown 8vo, cloth extra, 7s. 6d.

Diderot.—The Paradox of Acting. Translated, with Annotations, from Diderot's "Le Paradoxe sur le Comédien," by WALTER HERRIES POLLOCK. With a Preface by HENRY IRVING. Cr. 8vo, in parchment, **4s. 6d.**

Dobson (W. T.), Works by :
Post 8vo, cloth limp, **2s. 6d.** each.
Literary Frivolities, Fancies, Follies, and Frolics.
Poetical Ingenuities and Eccentricities.

Donovan (Dick), Detective Stories by:
Post 8vo, illustrated boards, **2s.** each; cloth limp, **2s. 6d.** each.
The Man-hunter: Stories from the Note-book of a Detective.
Caught at Last!

Drama, A Dictionary of the. Being a comprehensive Guide to the Plays, Playwrights, Players, and Playhouses of the United Kingdom and America, from the Earliest to the Present Times. By W. DAVENPORT ADAMS. (Uniform with BREWER'S "Reader's Handbook.") Crown 8vo, half-bound, **12s. 6d.** [*In preparation.*

Dramatists, The Old. Cr. 8vo, cl. ex., Vignette Portraits, **6s.** per Vol.
Ben Jonson's Works. With Notes Critical and Explanatory, and a Biographical Memoir by WM. GIFFORD. Edit. by Col. CUNNINGHAM. 3 Vols.
Chapman's Works. Complete in Three Vols. Vol. I. contains the Plays complete, including doubtful ones; Vol. II., Poems and Minor Translations, with Introductory Essay by A. C. SWINBURNE; Vol. III., Translations of the Iliad and Odyssey.
Marlowe's Works. Including his Translations. Edited, with Notes and Introduction, by Col. CUNNINGHAM. One Vol.
Massinger's Plays. From the Text of WILLIAM GIFFORD. Edited by Col. CUNNINGHAM. One Vol.

Dyer. — The Folk - Lore of Plants. By Rev. T. F. THISELTON DYER, M.A. Crown 8vo, cloth extra, **6s.**

Edgcumbe. — Zephyrus : A Holiday in Brazil and on the River Plate. By E. R. PEARCE EDGCUMBE. With 41 Illusts. Cr. 8vo, cl. extra, **5s.**

Eggleston.—Roxy: A Novel. By EDWARD EGGLESTON. Post 8vo, illust. boards, **2s.**

Early English Poets. Edited, with Introductions and Annotations, by Rev. A. B. GROSART, D.D. Crown 8vo, cloth boards, **6s.** per Volume.
Fletcher's (Giles, B.D.) Complete Poems. One Vol.
Davies' (Sir John) Complete Poetical Works. Two Vols.
Herrick's (Robert) Complete Collected Poems. Three Vols.
Sidney's (Sir Philip) Complete Poetical Works. Three Vols.

Edwardes (Mrs. A.), Novels by:
A Point of Honour. Post 8vo, illustrated boards, **2s.**
Archie Lovell. Crown 8vo, cloth extra, **3s. 6d.**; post 8vo, illust. bds., **2s.**

Emanuel.—On Diamonds and Precious Stones: their History, Value, and Properties ; with Simple Tests for ascertaining their Reality. By HARRY EMANUEL, F.R.G.S. With numerous Illustrations, tinted and plain. Crown 8vo, cloth extra, gilt, **6s.**

Ewald (Alex. Charles, F.S.A.), Works by:
The Life and Times of Prince Charles Stuart, Count of Albany, commonly called the Young Pretender. From the State Papers and other Sources. New and Cheaper Edition, with a Portrait, crown 8vo, cloth extra, **7s. 6d.**
Stories from the State Papers. With an Autotype Facsimile. Crown 8vo, cloth extra, **6s.**

Englishman's House, The : A Practical Guide to all interested in Selecting or Building a House ; with full Estimates of Cost, Quantities, &c. By C. J. RICHARDSON. Fourth Edition. With Coloured Frontispiece and nearly 600 Illustrations. Crown 8vo, cloth extra, **7s. 6d.**

Eyes, Our: How to Preserve Them from Infancy to Old Age. By JOHN BROWNING, F.R.A.S., &c. Seventh Edition (Twelfth Thousand). With 70 Illustrations. Crown 8vo, cloth, **1s.**

Familiar Short Sayings of Great Men. By SAMUEL ARTHUR BENT, A.M. Fifth Edition, Revised and Enlarged. Cr. 8vo, cl. ex., **7s. 6d.**

Farrer (James Anson), Works by:
Military Manners and Customs. Crown 8vo, cloth extra, **6s.**
War: Three Essays, Reprinted from "Military Manners." Crown 8vo, **1s.**; cloth, **1s. 6d.**

Faraday (Michael), Works by:
Post 8vo, cloth extra, 4s. 6d. each.
The Chemical History of a Candle:
Lectures delivered before a Juvenile
Audience at the Royal Institution.
Edited by WILLIAM CROOKES, F.C.S.
With numerous Illustrations.
On the Various Forces of Nature,
and their Relations to each other:
Lectures delivered before a Juvenile
Audience at the Royal Institution.
Edited by WILLIAM CROOKES, F.C.S.
With numerous Illustrations.

Fin-Bec. — The Cupboard
Papers: Observations on the Art of
Living and Dining. By FIN-BEC. Post
8vo, cloth limp, 2s. 6d.

Fireworks, The Complete Art
of Making; or, The Pyrotechnist's
Treasury. By THOMAS KENTISH. With
267 Illustrations. A New Edition, Revised throughout and greatly Enlarged.
Crown 8vo, cloth extra, 5s.

Fitzgerald (Percy), Works by:
The World Behind the Scenes.
Crown 8vo, cloth extra, 3s. 6d.
Little Essays: Passages from the
Letters of CHARLES LAMB. Post
8vo, cloth limp, 2s. 6d.
A Day's Tour: A Journey through
France and Belgium. With Sketches
in facsimile of the Original Draw-
ings. Crown 4to picture cover, 1s.
Fatal Zero: A Homburg Diary. Cr.
8vo, cloth extra, 3s. 6d.; post 8vo,
illustrated boards, 2s.

Post 8vo, illustrated boards, 2s. each.
Bella Donna. | Never Forgotten.
The Second Mrs. Tillotson.
Seventy-five Brooke Street
Polly. | The Lady of Brantome.

Fletcher's (Giles, B.D.) Com-
plete Poems: Christ's Victorie in
Heaven, Christ's Victorie on Earth,
Christ's Triumph over Death, and
Minor Poems. With Memorial-Intro-
duction and Notes by the Rev. A. B.
GROSART, D.D. Cr. 8vo, cloth bds., 6s.

Fonblanque. — Filthy Lucre: A
Novel. By ALBANY DE FONBLANQUE.
Post 8vo, illustrated boards, 2s.

Frederic. — Seth's Brother's
Wife: A Novel. By HAROLD FREDERIC.
Post 8vo, illust. bds., 2s.

French Literature, History of.
By HENRY VAN LAUN. Complete in
3 Vols., demy 8vo, cl. bds., 7s. 6d. each.

Francillon (R. E.), Novels by.
Crown 8vo, cloth extra, 3s. 6d. each;
post 8vo, illust. boards, 2s. each.
One by One. | A Real Queen.
Queen Cophetua. |

Olympia. Post 8vo, illust. boards, 2s.
Esther's Glove. Fcap. 8vo, 1s.
King or Knave: A Novel. Cheaper
Edition. Cr. 8vo, cloth extra, 3s. 6d
Romances of the Law. Frontispiece
by D. H. FRISTON. Cr.8vo, cl. ex., 6s.

Frenzeny.—Fifty Years on the
Trail: The Adventures of JOHN Y.
NELSON, Scout, Guide, and Interpreter,
in the Wild West. By HARRINGTON
O'REILLY. With over 100 Illustrations
by PAUL FRENZENY. Crown 8vo, picture
cover, 3s. 6d.; cloth extra, 4s. 6d.

Frere.—Pandurang Hari; or,
Memoirs of a Hindoo. With a Preface
by Sir H. BARTLE FRERE, G.C.S.I., &c.
Crown 8vo, cloth extra, 3s. 6d.

Friswell.—One of Two: A Novel.
By HAIN FRISWELL. Post 8vo, illustrated boards, 2s.

Frost (Thomas), Works by:
Crown 8vo, cloth extra, 3s. 6d. each.
Circus Life and Circus Celebrities.
The Lives of the Conjurers.
Old Showmen and Old London Fairs.

Fry's (Herbert) Royal Guide
to the London Charities, 1888-9,
Showing their Name, Date of Founda-
tion, Objects, Income, Officials, &c.
Edited by JOHN LANE. Published Annually. Crown 8vo, cloth, 1s. 6d.

Gardening Books:
Post 8vo, 1s. each; cl. limp, 1s. 6d. each.
A Year's Work in Garden and Green-
house: Practical Advice to Amateur
Gardeners as to the Management of
the Flower, Fruit, and Frame Garden.
By GEORGE GLENNY.
Our Kitchen Garden: The Plants we
Grow, and How we Cook Them.
By TOM JERROLD.
Household Horticulture: A Gossip
about Flowers. By TOM and JANE
JERROLD. Illustrated.
The Garden that Paid the Rent.
By TOM JERROLD.

My Garden Wild, and What I Grew
there. By F. G. HEATH. Crown 8vo,
cloth extra, 5s.; gilt edges, 6s.

Garrett.—The Capel Girls: A
Novel. By EDWARD GARRETT. Cr. 8vo,
cl. ex., 3s. 6d.; post 8vo, illust. bds., 2s.

Gentleman's Magazine (The)
for 1889.—1s. Monthly.—In addition
to the Articles upon subjects in Literature, Science, and Art, for which this
Magazine has so high a reputation,
"Table Talk" by SYLVANUS URBAN
appears monthly.

. *Bound Volumes for recent years are
kept in stock, cloth extra, price 8s. 6d.
each; Cases for binding,* 2s. *each*

Gentleman's Annual (The).
Published Annually in November. In
picture cover Demy 8vo 1s. The
Annual for 1889 is written by T. W.
SPEIGHT, Author of "The Mysteries of
Heron Dyke," and is entitled "There-
by Hangs a Tale."

German Popular Stories Collected by the Brothers GRIMM, and
Translated by EDGAR TAYLOR. Edited
with an Introduction, by JOHN RUSKIN.
With 22 Illustrations or Steel by
GEORGE CRUIKSHANK. Square 8vo,
cloth extra, 6s. 6d.; gilt edges, 7s 6d.

Gibbon (Charles), Novels by:
Crown 8vo, cloth extra, 3s. 6d. each
post 8vo, illustrated boards, 2s. each.

Robin Gray	The Braes of Yar-
What will the	row.
World Say?	A Heart's Prob-
Queen of the	lem.
Meadow	The Golden Shaft.
The Flower of the	Of High Degree.
Forest	Loving a Dream.
In Honour Bound	

Post 8vo, illustrated boards, 2s. each.
  The Dead Heart
  For Lack of Gold
  For the King | In Pastures Green.
  In Love and War
  By Mead and Stream.
  A Hard Knot | Heart's Delight.
  Blood-Money   [*Preparing.*

Gilbert (William), Novels by:
Post 8vo, illustrated boards, 2s. each.
  Dr. Austin's Guests
  The Wizard of the Mountain.
  James Duke, Costermonger.

Gilbert (W. S.), Original Plays
by: In Two Series, each complete in
itself, price 2s. 6d. each.

  The FIRST SERIES contains—The
Wicked World—Pygmalion and Ga-
latea—Charity—The Princess · The
Palace of Truth—Trial by Jury.

  The SECOND SERIES contains—Bro-
ken Hearts—Engaged—Sweethearts—
Gretchen—Dan'l Druce—Tom Cobb—
H.M.S. Pinafore—The Sorcerer—The
Pirates of Penzance.

GILBERT (W. S.), *continued*—
Eight Original Comic Operas. Writ-
ten by W. S. GILBERT. Containing:
The Sorcerer—H.M.S. "Pinafore"
—The Pirates of Penzance—Iolanthe
— Patience.— Princess Ida — The
Mikado—Trial by Jury. Demy 8vo,
cloth limp, 2s. 6d

Glenny.—A Year's Work in
Garden and Greenhouse: Practical
Advice to Amateur Gardeners as to
the Management of the Flower, Fruit,
and Frame Garden. By GEORGE
GLENNY. Post 8vo, 1s.; cloth, 1s. 6d.

Godwin.—Lives of the Necro-
mancers. By WILLIAM GODWIN.
Post 8vo, limp, 2s.

Golden Library, The:
Square 16mo (Tauchnitz size) cloth
    limp, 2s. per Volume.
Bayard Taylor's Diversions of the
  Echo Club.
Bennett's (Dr W. C.) Ballad History
  of England.
Bennett's (Dr.) Songs for Sailors.
Godwin's (William) Lives of the
  Necromancers.
Holmes's Autocrat of the Break-
  fast Table. Introduction by SALA.
Holmes's Professor at the Break-
  fast Table.
Hood's Whims and Oddities. Com-
  plete. All the original Illustrations.
Jesse's (Edward) Scenes and Oc-
  cupations of a Country Life.
Leigh Hunt's Essays: A Tale for a
  Chimney Corner, and other Pieces.
  With Portrait, and Introduction by
  EDMUND OLLIER.
Mallory's (Sir Thomas) Mort
  d'Arthur: The Stories of King
  Arthur and of the Knights of the
  Round Table. Edited by B. MONT-
  GOMERIE RANKING.
Pascal's Provincial Letters. A New
  Translation, with Historical Intro-
  duction and Notes, by T. M'CRIE, D.D.
Pope's Poetical Works. Complete.
Rochefoucauld's Maxims and Moral
  Reflections. With Notes, and In-
  troductory Essay by SAINTE-BEUVE.

Golden Treasury of Thought,
The: An ENCYCLOPÆDIA OF QUOTA-
TIONS from Writers of all Times and
Countries. Selected and Edited by
THEODORE TAYLOR. Crown 8vo, cloth
gilt and gilt edges, 7s. 6d.

Gowing. — Five Thousand
Miles in a Sledge: A Mid-winter
Journey Across Siberia. By LIONEL
F. GOWING. With a Map by E. WEL-
LER, and 30 Illustrations by C. J. WREN.
Large cr. 8vo, cloth extra, 8s. [*Shortly.*

Graham. — The Professor's Wife: A Story. By LEONARD GRAHAM. Fcap. 8vo, picture cover, 1s.

Greeks and Romans, The Life of the, Described from Antique Monuments. By ERNST GUHL and W. KONER. Translated from the Third German Edition, and Edited by Dr. F. HUEFFER. 545 Illusts. New and Cheaper Edition, large crown 8vo, cloth extra, 7s. 6d.

Greenaway (Kate) and Bret Harte.—The Queen of the Pirate Isle. By BRET. HARTE. With 25 original Drawings by KATE GREEN-AWAY, Reproduced in Colours by E. EVANS. Sm. 4to, bds., 5s.

Greenwood (James), Works by: Crown 8vo, cloth extra, 3s. 6d. each.
The Wilds of London.
Low-Life Deeps: An Account of the Strange Fish to be Found There.

Greville (Henry), Novels by: Crown 8vo, cloth extra, 6s. each.
Nikanor: A Russian Novel. Translated by ELIZA E. CHASE.
A Noble Woman. Translated by A. VANDAM. [Shortly.

Habberton (John), Author of "Helen's Babies," Novels by: Post 8vo, illustrated boards, 2s. each; cloth limp, 2s. 6d. each.
Brueton's Bayou.
Country Luck.

Hair (The): Its Treatment in Health, Weakness, and Disease. Translated from the German of Dr. J. PINCUS. Crown 8vo, 1s.; cloth, 1s. 6d.

Hake (Dr. Thomas Gordon), Poems by: Crown 8vo, cloth extra, 6s. each.
New Symbols.
Legends of the Morrow.
The Serpent Play.

Maiden Ecstasy. Small 4to, cloth extra, 8s.

Hall.—Sketches of Irish Cha-racter. By Mrs. S. C. HALL. With numerous Illustrations on Steel and Wood by MACLISE, GILBERT, HARVEY, and G. CRUIKSHANK. Medium 8vo, cloth extra, gilt, 7s. 6d.

Halliday.—Every-day Papers. By ANDREW HALLIDAY. Post 8vo, illustrated boards, 2s.

Handwriting, The Philosophy of. With over 100 Facsimiles and Explanatory Text. By DON FELIX DE SALAMANCA. Post 8vo, cl. limp, 2s. 6d.

Hanky-Panky: A Collection of Very Easy Tricks, Very Difficult Tricks, White Magic, Sleight of Hand, &c. Edited by W. H. CREMER. With 200 Illusts. Crown 8vo, cloth extra, 4s. 6d.

Hardy (Lady Duffus). — Paul Wynter's Sacrifice: A Story. By Lady DUFFUS HARDY. Post 8vo, illust. bs., 2s.

Hardy (Thomas).—Under the Greenwood Tree. By THOMAS HARDY, Author of "Far from the Madding Crowd." With numerous Illustrations. Post 8vo, illustrated boards, 2s.

Harwood.—The Tenth Earl. By J. BERWICK HARWOOD. Post 8vo, illustrated boards, 2s.

Haweis (Mrs. H. R.), Works by: Square 8vo, cloth extra, 6s. each.
The Art of Beauty. With Coloured Frontispiece and numerous Illusts.
The Art of Decoration. With numerous Illustrations.
Chaucer for Children: A Golden Key. With Eight Coloured Pictures and numerous Woodcuts.

The Art of Dress. With numerous Illustrations. Small 8vo, illustrated cover, 1s.; cloth limp, 1s. 6d.
Chaucer for Schools. Demy 8vo, cloth limp, 2s. 6d.

Haweis (Rev. H. R.).—American Humorists: WASHINGTON IRVING, OLIVER WENDELL HOLMES, JAMES RUSSELL LOWELL, ARTEMUS WARD, MARK TWAIN, and BRET HARTE. By Rev. H. R. HAWEIS, M.A. Cr. 8vo. 6s.

Hawley Smart. — Without Love or Licence: A Novel. By HAWLEY SMART. Three Vols., crown 8vo. [Shortly.

Hawthorne (Julian), Novels by. Crown 8vo, cloth extra, 3s. 6d. each; post 8vo, illustrated boards, 2s. each.

Garth.	Sebastian Strome.
Ellice Quentin.	Dust.
Fortune's Fool.	Beatrix Randolph.

David Poindexter's Disappearance.
Post 8vo, illustrated boards, 2s. each.
Miss Cadogna. | Love—or a Name.
Mrs. Gainsborough's Diamonds. Fcap. 8vo, illustrated cover, 1s.
The Spectre of the Camera. Crown 8vo, cloth extra, 3s. 6d.
A Dream and a Forgetting. Post 8vo, cloth, 1s. 6d.

Hays.—Women of the Day: A Biographical Dictionary of Notable Contemporaries. By FRANCES HAYS. Crown 8vo, cloth extra, 5s.

Heath (F. G.). — My Garden Wild, and What I Grew There. By FRANCIS GEORGE HEATH, Author of "The Fern World," &c. Crown 8vo, cloth extra, 5s.; cl. gilt, gilt edges, 6s.

Helps (Sir Arthur), Works by: Post 8vo, cloth limp, 2s. 6d. each.
Animals and their Masters.
Social Pressure.

Ivan de Biron: A Novel. Crown 8vo, cloth extra, 3s. 6d.; post 8vo, illustrated boards, 2s.

Henderson.—Agatha Page: A Novel. By ISAAC HENDERSON, Author of "The Prelate." Cheaper Edition. Crown 8vo, cloth extra, 3s. 6d.

Herman.—One Traveller Re- turns: A Romance. By HENRY HERMAN and D. CHRISTIE MURRAY. Crown 8vo, cloth extra, 6s.

Herrick's (Robert) Hesperides, Noble Numbers, and Complete Collected Poems. With Memorial-Introduction and Notes by the Rev. A. B. GROSART, D.D., Steel Portrait, Index of First Lines, and Glossarial Index, &c. Three Vols., crown 8vo, cloth, 18s.

Hesse-Wartegg (Chevalier Ernst von), Works by:
Tunis: The Land and the People. With 22 Illusts. Cr. 8vo, cl. ex., 3s. 6d.
The New South-West: Travelling Sketches from Kansas, New Mexico, Arizona, and Northern Mexico. With 100 fine Illustrations and Three Maps. Demy 8vo, cloth extra, 14s. *[In preparation.*

Hindley (Charles), Works by:
Tavern Anecdotes and Sayings: Including the Origin of Signs, and Reminiscences connected with Taverns, Coffee Houses, Clubs, &c. With Illustrations. Crown 8vo, cloth extra, 3s. 6d.
The Life and Adventures of a Cheap Jack. By One of the Fraternity. Edited by CHARLES HINDLEY. Crown 8vo, cloth extra, 3s. 6d.

Hoey.—The Lover's Creed. By Mrs. CASHEL HOEY. Post 8vo, illustrated boards, 2s.

Holmes (O. Wendell), Works by:
The Autocrat of the Breakfast-Table. Illustrated by J. GORDON THOMSON. Post 8vo, cloth limp, 2s. 6d.—Another Edition in smaller type, with an Introduction by G. A. SALA. Post 8vo, cloth limp, 2s.
The Professor at the Breakfast-Table; with the Story of Iris. Post 8vo, cloth limp, 2s.

Holmes. — The Science of Voice Production and Voice Preservation: A Popular Manual for the Use of Speakers and Singers. By GORDON HOLMES, M.D. With Illustrations. Crown 8vo, 1s.; cloth, 1s. 6d.

Hood (Thomas):
Hood's Choice Works, in Prose and Verse. Including the Cream of the COMIC ANNUALS. With Life of the Author, Portrait, and 200 Illustrations. Crown 8vo, cloth extra, 7s. 6d.
Hood's Whims and Oddities. Complete. With all the original Illustrations. Post 8vo, cloth limp, 2s.

Hood (Tom).—From Nowhere to the North Pole: A Noah's Arkæological Narrative. By TOM HOOD. With 25 Illustrations by W. BRUNTON and E. C. BARNES. Square crown 8vo, cloth extra, gilt edges, 6s.

Hook's (Theodore) Choice Hu- morous Works, including his Ludicrous Adventures, Bons Mots, Puns and Hoaxes. With a New Life of the Author, Portraits, Facsimiles, and Illusts. Cr. 8vo, cl. extra, gilt, 7s. 6d.

Hooper.—The House of Raby: A Novel. By Mrs. GEORGE HOOPER. Post 8vo, illustrated boards, 2s.

Horse (The) and his Rider: An Anecdotic Medley. By "THORMANBY." Crown 8vo, cloth extra, 6s.

Hopkins—"'Twixt Love and Duty:" A Novel. By TIGHE HOPKINS. Post 8vo, illustrated boards, 2s.

Horne.—Orion: An Epic Poem, in Three Books. By RICHARD HENGIST HORNE. With Photographic Portrait from a Medallion by SUMMERS. Tenth Edition, crown 8vo, cloth extra, 7s.

Hunt (Mrs. Alfred), Novels by:
Crown 8vo, cloth extra, 3s. 6d. each; post 8vo, illustrated boards, 2s. each.
Thornicroft's Model.
The Leaden Casket.
Self-Condemned.
That other Person.

Hunt.—Essays by Leigh Hunt.
A Tale for a Chimney Corner, and other Pieces. With Portrait and Introduction by EDMUND OLLIER. Post 8vo, cloth limp, 2s.

Hydrophobia: an Account of M.
PASTEUR'S System. Containing a Translation of all his Communications on the Subject, the Technique of his Method, and the latest Statistical Results. By RENAUD SUZOR, M.B., C.M. Edin., and M.D. Paris, Commissioned by the Government of the Colony of Mauritius to study M. PASTEUR'S new Treatment in Paris. With 7 Illusts. Cr. 8vo, cloth extra, 6s.

Indoor Paupers. By ONE OF THEM. Crown 8vo, 1s.; cloth, 1s. 6d.

Ingelow.—Fated to be Free: A Novel. By JEAN INGELOW. Crown 8vo, cloth extra, 3s. 6d.; post 8vo, illustrated boards, 2s.

Irish Wit and Humour, Songs of. Collected and Edited by A. PERCEVAL GRAVES. Post 8vo, cl. limp, 2s. 6d.

James.—A Romance of the Queen's Hounds. By CHARLES JAMES. Post 8vo, picture cover, 1s.; cl., 1s. 6d.

Janvier.—Practical Keramics for Students. By CATHERINE A. JANVIER. Crown 8vo, cloth extra, 6s.

Jay (Harriett), Novels by:
Post 8vo, illustrated boards, 2s. each.
  The Dark Colleen.
  The Queen of Connaught.

Jefferies (Richard), Works by:
Nature near London. Crown 8vo, cl. ex, 6s.; post 8vo, cl. limp, 2s. 6d.
The Life of the Fields. Post 8vo, cloth limp, 2s. 6d.
The Open Air. Crown 8vo, cloth extra, 6s.; post 8vo, cl. limp, 2s. 6d.
The Eulogy of Richard Jefferies. By WALTER BESANT. Second Ed. Photo. Portrait. Cr. 8vo, cl. ex., 6s.

Jennings (H. J.), Works by:
Curiosities of Criticism. Post 8vo, cloth limp, 2s. 6d.
Lord Tennyson: A Biographical Sketch. With a Photograph-Portrait. Crown 8vo, cloth extra, 6s.

Jerrold (Tom), Works by:
Post 8vo, 1s. each; cloth, 1s. 6d. each.
The Garden that Paid the Rent.
Household Horticulture: A Gossip about Flowers. Illustrated.
Our Kitchen Garden: The Plants we Grow, and How we Cook Them.

Jesse.—Scenes and Occupations of a Country Life. By EDWARD JESSE. Post 8vo, cloth limp, 2s.

Jeux d'Esprit. Collected and Edited by HENRY S. LEIGH. Post 8vo, cloth limp, 2s. 6d.

"John Herring," Novels by the Author of:
Red Spider. Crown 8vo, cloth extra, 3s. 6d.; post 8vo, illust. boards, 2s.
Eve. Crown 8vo, cloth extra, 3s. 6d.

Jones (Wm., F.S.A.), Works by:
Crown 8vo, cloth extra, 7s. 6d. each.
Finger-Ring Lore: Historical, Legendary, and Anecdotal. With over Two Hundred Illustrations.
Credulities, Past and Present; including the Sea and Seamen, Miners, Talismans, Word and Letter Divination, Exorcising and Blessing of Animals, Birds, Eggs, Luck, &c. With an Etched Frontispiece.
Crowns and Coronations: A History of Regalia in all Times and Countries. One Hundred Illustrations.

Jonson's (Ben) Works. With Notes Critical and Explanatory, and a Biographical Memoir by WILLIAM GIFFORD. Edited by Colonel CUNNINGHAM. Three Vols., crown 8vo, cloth extra, 18s.; or separately, 6s. each.

Josephus, The Complete Works of. Translated by WHISTON. Containing both "The Antiquities of the Jews" and "The Wars of the Jews." Two Vols., 8vo, with 52 Illustrations and Maps, cloth extra, gilt, 14s.

Kempt.—Pencil and Palette: Chapters on Art and Artists. By ROBERT KEMPT. Post 8vo, cloth limp, 2s. 6d.

Kershaw.—Colonial Facts and Fictions: Humorous Sketches. By MARK KERSHAW. Post 8vo, illustrated boards, 2s.; cloth, 2s. 6d.

Keyser.—Cut by the Mess: A Novel. By ARTHUR KEYSER. Cr. 8vo, picture cover, 1s.; cl., 1s. 6d. [*Shortly.*

King (R. Ashe), Novels by:
Crown 8vo, cloth extra, 3s. 6d. each; post 8vo, illustrated boards, 2s. each.
A Drawn Game.
"The Wearing of the Green."

Passion's Slave. Three Vols. Crown 8vo.

Kingsley (Henry), Novels by:
Oakshott Castle. Post 8vo, illustrated boards, 2s.
Number Seventeen. Crown 8vo, cloth extra, 3s. 6d.

Knight.—The Patient's Vade Mecum: How to get most Benefit from Medical Advice. By WILLIAM KNIGHT, M.R.C.S., and EDW. KNIGHT, L.R.C.P. Cr. 8vo, 1s.; cloth, 1s. 6d.

Knights (The) of the Lion: A
Romance of the Thirteenth Century.
Edited, with an Introduction, by the
MARQUESS of LORNE, K.T. Crown
8vo, cloth extra, 6s.

Lamb (Charles):
Lamb's Complete Works, in Prose
and Verse, reprinted from the Ori-
ginal Editions, with many Pieces
hitherto unpublished. Edited, with
Notes and Introduction, by R. H.
SHEPHERD. With Two Portraits and
Facsimile of Page of the "Essay on
Roast Pig." Cr. 8vo, cl. extra, 7s. 6d.
The Essays of Elia. Both Series
complete. Post 8vo, laid paper,
handsomely half-bound, 2s.
Poetry for Children, and Prince
Dorus. By CHARLES LAMB. Care-
fully reprinted from unique copies.
Small 8vo, cloth extra, 5s.
Little Essays: Sketches and Charac-
ters by CHARLES LAMB. Selected
from his Letters by PERCY FITZ-
GERALD. Post 8vo, cloth limp, 2s. 6d.

Lane's Arabian Nights.—The
Thousand and One Nights: com-
monly called, in England, "THE
ARABIAN NIGHTS' ENTERTAIN-
MENTS." A New Translation from
the Arabic with copious Notes, by
EDWARD WILLIAM LANE. Illustrated
by many hundred Engravings on
Wood, from Original Designs by
WM. HARVEY. A New Edition, from
a Copy annotated by the Translator,
edited by his Nephew, EDWARD
STANLEY POOLE. With a Preface by
STANLEY LANE-POOLE. Three Vols.,
demy 8vo, cloth extra, 7s. 6d. each.

Larwood (Jacob), Works by:
The Story of the London Parks.
With Illusts. Cr. 8vo, cl. ex., 3s. 6d.

Post 8vo, cloth limp, 2s. 6d. each.
Forensic Anecdotes.
Theatrical Anecdotes.

Leigh (Henry S.), Works by:
Carols of Cockayne. A New Edition,
printed on fcap. 8vo, hand-made
paper, and bound in buckram, 5s.
Jeux d'Esprit. Collected and Edited
by HENRY S. LEIGH. Post 8vo, cloth
limp, 2s. 6d.

Leys.—The Lindsays: A Ro-
mance of Scottish Life. By JOHN K.
LEYS. Cheaper Edition. Post 8vo,
illustrated boards, 2s.

Life In London; or, The History
of Jerry Hawthorn and Corinthian
Tom. With the whole of CRUIK-
SHANK'S Illustrations, in Colours, after
the Originals. Cr. 8vo, cl. extra, 7s. 6d.

Linskill.—In Exchange for a
Soul. By MARY LINSKILL, Author of
"The Haven Under the Hill," &c.
Cheaper Edit. Post 8vo, illust. bds., 2s.

Linton (E. Lynn), Works by:
Post 8vo, cloth limp, 2s. 6d. each.
Witch Stories.
The True Story of Joshua Davidson.
Ourselves: Essays on Women.
Crown 8vo, cloth extra, 3s. 6d. each; post
8vo, illustrated boards, 2s. each.
Patricia Kemball.
The Atonement of Leam Dundas.
The World Well Lost.
Under which Lord?
"My Love!" | Ione.
Paston Carew, Millionaire & Miser.
Post 8vo, illustrated boards, 2s. each.
With a Silken Thread.
The Rebel of the Family.

Longfellow's Poetical Works.
Carefully Reprinted from the Original
Editions. With numerous fine Illustrations on Steel and Wood. Crown 8vo,
cloth extra, 7s. 6d.

Long Life, Aids to: A Medical,
Dietetic, and General Guide in Health
and Disease. By N. E. DAVIES,
L.R.C.P. Cr. 8vo, 2s.; cl. limp, 2s. 6d.

Lucy.—Gideon Fleyce: A Novel.
By HENRY W. LUCY. Crown 8vo,
cl. ex., 3s. 6d.; post 8vo, illust. bds., 2s.

Lusiad (The) of Camoens.
Translated into English Spenserian
Verse by ROBERT FFRENCH DUFF.
Demy 8vo, with Fourteen full-page
Plates, cloth boards, 18s.

Macalpine (Avery), Novels by:
Teresa Itasca, and other Stories.
Crown 8vo, bound in canvas, 2s. 6d.
Broken Wings. With Illusts. by W. J.
HENNESSY. Cr. 8vo, cloth extra, 6s.

McCarthy (Justin H., M.P.),
Works by:
An Outline of the History of Ireland,
from the Earliest Times to the Pre-
sent Day. Cr. 8vo, 1s.; cloth, 1s. 6d.
Ireland since the Union: Sketches
of Irish History from 1798 to 1886.
Crown 8vo, cloth extra, 6s.
England under Gladstone, 1880-85.
Second Edition, revised. Crown
8vo, cloth extra, 6s.
Hafiz in London: Poems. Choicely
printed. Small 8vo, gold cloth, 3s. 6d.
Harlequinade: Poems. Small 4to,
Japanese vellum, 8s.
Our Sensation Novel. Edited by
JUSTIN H. MCCARTHY. Crown 8vo,
1s.; cloth, 1s. 6d.
Dolly: A Sketch. Crown 8vo, picture
cover, 1s.; cloth, 1s. 6d.

McCarthy (Justin, M.P.), Works by:

Lily Lass: A Romance. Crown 8vo, picture cover, 1s.; cl., 1s. 6d. [*Shortly.*

A History of Our Own Times, from the Accession of Queen Victoria to the General Election of 1880. Four Vols. demy 8vo, cloth extra, 12s. each.—Also a POPULAR EDITION, in Four Vols. cr. 8vo, cl. extra, 6s. each. —And a JUBILEE EDITION, with an Appendix of Events to the end of 1886, complete in Two Vols., square 8vo, cloth extra, 7s. 6d. each.

A Short History of Our Own Times. One Vol., crown 8vo, cloth extra, 6s.

History of the Four Georges. Four Vols. demy 8vo, cloth extra, 12s. each. [Vol. II. *nearly ready.*

Crown 8vo, cloth extra, 3s. 6d. each; post 8vo, illustrated boards, 2s. each.
Dear Lady Disdain.
The Waterdale Neighbours.
A Fair Saxon.
Miss Misanthrope.
Donna Quixote.
The Comet of a Season.
Maid of Athens.
Camiola: A Girl with a Fortune.

Post 8vo, illustrated boards, 2s. each.
Linley Rochford.
My Enemy's Daughter.

"The Right Honourable:" A Romance of Society and Politics. By JUSTIN McCARTHY, M.P., and Mrs. CAMPBELL-PRAED. New and Cheaper Edition, crown 8vo, cloth extra, 6s.

MacColl.—Mr. Stranger's Sealed Packet: A Story of Adventure. By HUGH MACCOLL. Crown 8vo, cloth extra, 5s.

MacDonald.—Works of Fancy and Imagination. By GEORGE MAC-DONALD, LL.D. Ten Volumes, in handsome cloth case, 21s. — Vol. 1. WITHIN AND WITHOUT. THE HIDDEN LIFE.—Vol. 2. THE DISCIPLE. THE GOSPEL WOMEN. A BOOK OF SONNETS, ORGAN SONGS.—Vol. 3. VIOLIN SONGS. SONGS OF THE DAYS AND NIGHTS. A BOOK OF DREAMS. ROADSIDE POEMS. POEMS FOR CHILDREN. Vol. 4. PARABLES. BALLADS. SCOTCH SONGS.— Vols. 5 and 6. PHANTASTES: A Faerie Romance.—Vol. 7. THE PORTENT.— Vol. 8. THE LIGHT PRINCESS. THE GIANT'S HEART. SHADOWS.—Vol. 9. CROSS PURPOSES. THE GOLDEN KEY. THE CARASOYN. LITTLE DAYLIGHT.— Vol. 10. THE CRUEL PAINTER. THE WOW O' RIVVEN. THE CASTLE. THE BROKEN SWORDS. THE GRAY WOLF. UNCLE CORNELIUS.
The Volumes are also sold separately in Grolier-pattern cloth 2s. 6d. each.

Macdonell.—Quaker Cousins: A Novel. By AGNES MACDONELL. Crown 8vo, cloth extra, 3s. 6d.; post 8vo, illustrated boards, 2s.

Macgregor. — Pastimes and Players. Notes on Popular Games. By ROBERT MACGREGOR. Post 8vo, cloth limp, 2s. 6d.

Mackay.—Interludes and Undertones; or, Music at Twilight. By CHARLES MACKAY, LL.D. Crown 8vo cloth extra, 6s.

Maclise Portrait-Gallery (The) of Illustrious Literary Characters; with Memoirs—Biographical, Critical, Bibliographical, and Anecdotal—illustrative of the Literature of the former half of the Present Century. By WILLIAM BATES, B.A. With 85 Portraits printed on an India Tint. Crown 8vo, cloth extra, 7s. 6d.

Macquoid (Mrs.), Works by:

Square 8vo, cloth extra, 7s. 6d. each.
In the Ardennes. With 50 fine Illustrations by THOMAS R. MACQUOID.
Pictures and Legends from Normandy and Brittany. With numerous Illusts. by THOMAS R. MACQUOID.
Through Normandy. With 90 Illustrations by T. R. MACQUOID.
Through Brittany. With numerous Illustrations by T. R. MACQUOID.
About Yorkshire. With 67 Illustrations by T. R. MACQUOID.

Post 8vo, illustrated boards, 2s. each.
The Evil Eye, and other Stories.
Lost Rose.

Magician's Own Book (The): Performances with Cups and Balls, Eggs Hats, Handkerchiefs, &c. All from actual Experience. Edited by W. H. CREMER. With 200 Illustrations. Crown 8vo, cloth extra, 4s. 6d.

Magic Lantern (The), and its Management: including full Practical Directions for producing the Limelight, making Oxygen Gas, and preparing Lantern Slides. By T. C. HEPWORTH. With 10 Illustrations. Crown 8vo, 1s. ; cloth, 1s. 6d.

Magna Charta. An exact Facsimile of the Original in the British Museum, printed on fine p'ate paper, 3 feet by 2 feet, with Arms and Seals emblazoned in Gold and Colours. 5s.

Mallock (W. H.), Works by:

The New Republic; or, Culture, Faith and Philosophy in an English Country House. Post 8vo, cloth limp, 2s. 6d.; Cheap Edition, illustrated boards, 2s.

The New Paul and Virginia; or, Positivism on an Island. Post 8vo, cloth limp, 2s. 6d.

Poems. Small 4to, in parchment, 8s.

Is Life worth Living? Crown 8vo, cloth extra, 6s.

Mallory's (Sir Thomas) Mort d'Arthur: The Stories of King Arthur and of the Knights of the Round Table. Edited by B. MONTGOMERIE RANKING. Post 8vo, cloth limp, 2s.

Man - Hunter (The): Stories from the Note-book of a Detective. By DICK DONOVAN. Post 8vo, illustrated boards, 2s.; cloth, 2s. 6d.

Mark Twain, Works by:

Crown 8vo, cloth extra, 7s. 6d. each.

The Choice Works of Mark Twain. Revised and Corrected throughout by the Author. With Life, Portrait, and numerous Illustrations.

Roughing It, and The Innocents at Home. With 200 Illustrations by F. A. FRASER.

The Gilded Age. By MARK TWAIN and CHARLES DUDLEY WARNER. With 212 Illustrations by T. COPPIN.

Mark Twain's Library of Humour. With numerous Illustrations.

A Yankee at the Court of King Arthur. With 250 Illustrations by DAN BEARD. [*Dec. 6.*

Crown 8vo, cloth extra, (illustrated), 7s. 6d. each; post 8vo (without Illustrations), illustrated boards, 2s. each.

The Innocents Abroad; or, The New Pilgrim's Progress: "MARK TWAIN'S PLEASURE TRIP."

The Adventures of Tom Sawyer. With 111 Illustrations.

The Prince and the Pauper. With nearly 200 Illustrations.

A Tramp Abroad. With 314 Illusts.

Life on the Mississippi. With 300 Illustrations.

The Adventures of Huckleberry Finn. With 174 Illustrations by E. W. KEMBLE.

The Stolen White Elephant, &c. Crown 8vo, cloth extra, 6s.; post 8vo, illustrated boards, 2s.

Marlowe's Works. Including his Translations. Edited, with Notes and Introductions, by Col. CUNNINGHAM. Crown 8vo, cloth extra, 6s.

Marryat (Florence), Novels by:

Crown 8vo, cloth, 3s. 6d.; post 8vo, picture boards, 2s.
Open! Sesame!

Post 8vo, illustrated boards, 2s. each.
A Harvest of Wild Oats.
Fighting the Air. | Written in Fire.

Massinger's Plays. From the Text of WM. GIFFORD. Edited by Col. CUNNINGHAM. Cr. 8vo, cloth extra, 6s.

Masterman.—Half a Dozen Daughters: A Novel. By J. MASTERMAN. Post 8vo, illustrated boards, 2s.

Matthews.—A Secret of the Sea, &c. By BRANDER MATTHEWS. Post 8vo, illust. bds., 2s.; cloth, 2s. 6d.

Mayfair Library, The:

Post 8vo, cloth limp, 2s. 6d. per Volume.

A Journey Round My Room. By XAVIER DE MAISTRE. Translated by HENRY ATTWELL.

Quips and Quiddities. Selected by W. DAVENPORT ADAMS.

The Agony Column of "The Times," from 1800 to 1870. Edited, with an Introduction, by ALICE CLAY.

Melancholy Anatomised: A Popular Abridgment of "Burton's Anatomy of Melancholy."

The Speeches of Charles Dickens.

Literary Frivolities, Fancies, Follies, and Frolics. By W. T. DOBSON.

Poetical Ingenuities and Eccentricities. Selected and Edited by W. T. DOBSON.

The Cupboard Papers. By FIN-BEC.

Original Plays by W. S. GILBERT. FIRST SERIES. Containing: The Wicked World — Pygmalion and Galatea—Charity — The Princess—The Palace of Truth—Trial by Jury.

Original Plays by W. S GILBERT. SECOND SERIES. Containing: Broken Hearts — Engaged — Sweethearts—Gretchen—Dan'l Druce—Tom Cobb—H.M.S. Pinafore — The Sorcerer—The Pirates of Penzance.

Songs of Irish Wit and Humour. Collected and Edited by A. PERCEVAL GRAVES.

Animals and their Masters. By Sir ARTHUR HELPS.

Social Pressure. By Sir A. HELPS.

Curiosities of Criticism. By HENRY J. JENNINGS.

The Autocrat of the Breakfast-Table. By OLIVER WENDELL HOLMES. Illustrated by J. GORDON THOMSON.

Pencil and Palette. By R. KEMPT.

Little Essays: Sketches and Characters. By CHAS. LAMB. Selected from his Letters by PERCY FITZGERALD.

Forensic Anecdotes; or, Humour and Curiosities of the Law and Men of Law. By JACOB LARWOOD.

MAYFAIR LIBRARY, *continued—*
Post 8vo, cloth limp, 2s. 6d. per Volume.
Theatrical Anecdotes. By JACOB LARWOOD. [LEIGH.
Jeux d'Esprit. Edited by HENRY S.
True History of Joshua Davidson. By E. LYNN LINTON.
Witch Stories. By E. LYNN LINTON.
Ourselves: Essays on Women. By E. LYNN LINTON. [MACGREGOR.
Pastimes and Players. By ROBERT
The New Paul and Virginia. By W. H. MALLOCK.
New Republic. By W. H. MALLOCK.
Puck on Pegasus. By H. CHOLMONDE-LEY-PENNELL.
Pegasus Re-Saddled. By H. CHOLMONDELEY-PENNELL. Illustrated by GEORGE DU MAURIER.
Muses of Mayfair Edited by H. CHOLMONDELEY-PENNELL.
Thoreau: His Life and Aims. By H. A. PAGE.
Puniana. By the Hon. HUGH ROWLEY.
More Puniana. By Hon. H. ROWLEY.
The Philosophy of Handwriting. By DON FELIX DE SALAMANCA.
By Stream and Sea By WILLIAM SENIOR.
Leaves from a Naturalist's Note-Book. By Dr. ANDREW WILSON.

Mayhew.—London Characters and the Humorous Side of London Life. By HENRY MAYHEW. With numerous Illusts. Cr. 8vo, cl. extra, 3s. 6d.

Medicine, Family.—One Thousand Medical Maxims and Surgical Hints, for Infancy, Adult Life, Middle Age, and Old Age. By N. E. DAVIES, L.R.C.P. Lond. Cr. 8vo, 1s.; cl., 1s. 6d.

Menken.—Infelicia: Poems by ADAH ISAACS MENKEN. A New Edition, with a Biographical Preface, numerous Illustrations by F. E. LUMMIS and F. O. C. DARLEY, and Facsimile of a Letter from CHARLES DICKENS. Beautifully printed on small 4to ivory paper, with red border to each page, and handsomely bound. Price 7s. 6d.

Mexican Mustang (On a), through Texas, from the Gulf to the Rio Grande. A New Book of American Humour. By A. E. SWEET and J. ARMOY. KNOX, Editors of "Texas Siftings." With 265 Illusts. Cr. 8vo, cl. extra, 7s. 6d.

Middlemass (Jean), Novels by:
Post 8vo, illustrated boards, 2s. each.
Touch and Go. | Mr. Dorillion.

Miller.—Physiology for the Young; or, The House of Life: Human Physiology, with its application to the Preservation of Health. With numerous Illusts. By Mrs. F. FENWICK MILLER. Small 8vo, cloth limp, 2s. 6d.

Milton (J. L.), Works by.
Sm. 8vo, 1s. each; cloth ex., 1s. 6d. each.
The Hygiene of the Skin. Rules for the Management of the Skin; with Directions for Diet, Soaps, Baths,&c.
The Bath in Diseases of the Skin.
The Laws of Life, and their Relation to Diseases of the Skin.

Minto.—Was She Good or Bad? A Romance. By WILLIAM MINTO. Cr. 8vo, picture cover, 1s.; cloth, 1s. 6d.

Molesworth (Mrs.), Novels by:
Hathercourt Rectory. Post 8vo, illustrated boards, 2s.
That Girl in Black. Crown 8vo, picture cover, 1s.; cloth, 1s. 6d.

Moncrieff. — The Abdication; or, Time Tries All. An Historical Drama. By W. D. SCOTT-MONCRIEFF. With Seven Etchings by JOHN PETTIE, R.A., W. Q. ORCHARDSON, R.A., J. MACWHIRTER, A.R.A., COLIN HUNTER, A.R.A., R. MACBETH, A.R.A., and TOM GRAHAM, R.S.A. Large 4to, bound in buckram, 21s.

Moore (Thomas).—Prose and Verse, Humorous, Satirical, and Sentimental, by THOMAS MOORE; with Suppressed Passages from the Memoirs of Lord Byron. Edited, with Notes and Introduction, by R. HERNE SHEPHERD. With Portrait. Cr. 8vo, cl. extra, 7s. 6d.

Muddock (J. E.), Stories by:
Stories Weird and Wonderful. Post 8vo, illust. boards, 2s.; cloth, 2s. 6d.
The Dead Man's Secret; or, The Valley of Gold: Being a Narrative of Strange and Wild Adventure. Compiled and Written from the Papers of the late HANS CHRISTIAN FELDGE, Mate. Crown 8vo, cloth extra, 5s. [*Preparing.*

Murray (D. Christie), Novels by. Crown 8vo, cloth extra, 3s. 6d. each; post 8vo, illustrated boards, 2s. each.
A Life's Atonement. | A Model Father.
Joseph's Coat. | Coals of Fire.
By the Gate of the Sea.| Hearts.
Val Strange. | Cynic Fortune
A Bit of Human Nature.
First Person Singular.
The Way of the World.
Old Blazer's Hero. With Three Illustrations by A. McCORMICK. Crown 8vo, cloth ex., 6s.—Cheaper Edition, post 8vo, illust. boards, 2s.
One Traveller Returns. By D. CHRISTIE MURRAY and HENRY HERMAN. Crown 8vo, cloth extra, 6s.
Paul Jones's Alias, &c. By D. CHRISTIE MURRAY and HENRY HERMAN. Crown 8vo, cloth extra, 6s. [*Preparing.*

Murray.—A Game of Bluff: A
Novel. By HENRY MURRAY, Joint
Author with CHRISTIE MURRAY of "A
Dangerous Catspaw." Post 8vo, pic-
ture boards, 2s.; cloth, 2s. 6d. [*Shortly.*

Novelists. — Half-Hours with
the Best Novelists of the Century:
Choice Readings from the finest Novels.
Edited, with Critical and Biographical
Notes, by H. T. MACKENZIE BELL.
Crown 8vo, cl. ex., 3s. 6d. [*Preparing.*

Nursery Hints: A Mother's
Guide in Health and Disease. By N. E.
DAVIES, L.R.C.P. Cr.8vo, 1s.; cl., 1s.6d.

O'Connor.—Lord Beaconsfield:
A Biography. By T. P. O'CONNOR, M.P.
Sixth Edition, with a New Preface.
Crown 8vo, cloth extra, 5s.

O'Hanlon (Alice), Novels by:
Post 8vo, illustrated boards, 2s. each.
The Unforeseen.
Chance? or Fate?   [*Preparing.*

Ohnet (Georges), Novels by:
Doctor Rameau. Translated by Mrs.
CASHEL HOEY. With 9 Illustrations
by E. BAYARD. Cr.8vo, cloth extra, 6s.
A Last Love. Trans. by Mrs. CASHEL
HOEY. Cr. 8vo, cl. ex., 5s. [*Shortly.*

Oliphant (Mrs.) Novels by:
Whiteladies.   With Illustrations by
ARTHUR HOPKINS and H. WOODS.
Crown 8vo, cloth extra, 3s. 6d.;
post 8vo, illustrated boards, 2s.

Post 8vo, illustrated boards, 2s. each.
The Primrose Path.
The Greatest Heiress in England.

O'Reilly.—Phœbe's Fortunes:
A Novel. With Illustrations by HENRY
TUCK. Post 8vo, illustrated boards, 2s.

O'Shaughnessy (A.), Poems by:
Songs of a Worker. Fcap. 8vo, cloth
extra, 7s. 6d.
Music and Moonlight.   Fcap. 8vo,
cloth extra, 7s. 6d.
Lays of France. Cr.8vo, cl. ex., 10s. 6d.

Ouida, Novels by. Crown 8vo,
cloth extra, 3s. 6d. each; post 8vo,
illustrated boards, 2s. each.

Held in Bondage.	Pascarel.
Strathmore.	Signa. | Ariadne.
Chandos	In a Winter City.
Under Two Flags.	Friendship.
Cecil Castle-	Moths. | Bimbi.
maine's Gage.	Pipistrello.
Idalia.	In Maremma
Tricotrin.	A Village Com-
Puck.	mune.
Folle Farine.	Wanda.
Two Little Wooden	Frescoes. [ine.
Shoes.	Princess Naprax-
A Dog of Flanders.	Othmar.

Ouida—*continued.*
Guilderoy. Crown 8vo, cloth extra,
3s. 6d.

Wisdom, Wit, and Pathos, selected
from the Works of OUIDA by F.
SYDNEY MORRIS. Sm.cr.8vo,cl.ex.,5s.
CHEAPER EDITION, illust. bds., 2s.

Page (H. A.), Works by :
Thoreau: His Life and Aims: A Study.
With Portrait. Post 8vo,cl.limp, 2s.6d.
Lights on the Way: Some Tales with-
in a Tale. By the late J. H. ALEX-
ANDER, B.A. Edited by H. A. PAGE.
Crown 8vo, cloth extra, 6s.
Animal Anecdotes. Arranged on a
New Principle. Cr. 8vo, cl. extra, 5s.

Parliamentary Elections and
Electioneering in the Old Days (A
History of). Showing the State of
Political Parties and Party Warfare at
the Hustings and in the House of
Commons from the Stuarts to Queen
Victoria. Illustrated from the original
Political Squibs, Lampoons, Pictorial
Satires, and Popular Caricatures of
the Time. By JOSEPH GREGO, Author
of "Rowlandson and his Works,"
"The Life of Gillray," &c. A New
Edition, crown 8vo, cloth extra, with
Coloured Frontispiece and 100 Illus-
trations, 7s. 6d.   [*Preparing.*

Pascal's Provincial Letters. A
New Translation, with Historical In-
troduction and Notes, by T. M'CRIE,
D.D. Post 8vo, cloth limp, 2s.

Patient's (The) Vade Mecum:
How to get most Benefit from Medical
Advice. By W. KNIGHT, M.R.C.S., and
E. KNIGHT, L.R.C.P. Cr.8vo, 1s.; cl. 1/6.

Paul Ferroll : why he killed his
Wife. Post 8vo, illustrated boards, 2s.

Payn (James), Novels by.
Crown 8vo, cloth extra, 3s. 6d. each;
post 8vo, illustrated boards, 2s. each.
Lost Sir Massingberd.
Walter's Word.
Less Black than we're Painted.
By Proxy. | High Spirits.
Under One Roof.
A Confidential Agent.
Some Private Views.
A Grape from a Thorn.
The Talk of the Town.
From Exile. | The Canon's Ward
Holiday Tasks. | Glow-worm Tales

Post 8vo, illustrated boards, 2s. each.
Kit: A Memory. | Carlyon's Year.
A Perfect Treasure.
Bentinck's Tutor. | Murphy's Master.
The Best of Husbands.

PAYN (JAMES), *continued—*
Post 8vo, illustrated boards, **2s. each.**
For Cash Only.
What He Cost Her. | Cecil's Tryst.
Fallen Fortunes. | Halves.
A County Family. | At Her Mercy.
A Woman's Vengeance.
The Clyffards of Clyffe.
The Family Scapegrace.
The Foster Brothers. | Found Dead.
Gwendoline's Harvest.
Humorous Stories.
Like Father, Like Son.
A Marine Residence.
Married Beneath Him.
Mirk Abbey. | Not Wooed, but Won.
Two Hundred Pounds Reward.
Crown 8vo, cloth extra, 3s. 6d. each.
In Peril and Privation: Stories of
Marine Adventure Re-told. With 17
Illustrations.
The Mystery of Mirbridge. With a
Frontispiece by ARTHUR HOPKINS.

Paul.—Gentle and Simple. By
MARGARET AGNES PAUL. With a
Frontispiece by HELEN PATERSON.
Cr. 8vo, cloth extra, 3s. 6d. ; post 8vo,
illustrated boards, 2s.

Pears.—The Present Depres-
sion in Trade: Its Causes and Reme-
dies. Being the "Pears" Prize Essays
(of One Hundred Guineas). By EDWIN
GOADBY and WILLIAM WATT. With
an Introductory Paper by Prof. LEONE
LEVI, F.S.A., F.S.S. Demy 8vo, 1s.

Pennell (H. Cholmondeley),
Works by:
Post 8vo, cloth limp, 2s. 6d. each.
Puck on Pegasus. With Illustrations.
Pegasus Re-Saddled. With Ten full-
page Illusts. by G. DU MAURIER.
The Muses of Mayfair. Vers de
Société, Selected and Edited by H.
C. PENNELL.

Phelps (E. Stuart), Works by:
Post 8vo, 1s. each ; cl. limp, 1s. 6d. each.
Beyond the Gates. By the Author
of "The Gates Ajar."
An Old Maid's Paradise.
Burglars in Paradise.

Jack the Fisherman. With Twenty-
two Illustrations by C. W. REED.
Cr. 8vo, picture cover, 1s. ; cl. 1s. 6d.

Pirkis (C. L.), Novels by:
Trooping with Crows. Fcap. 8vo,
picture cover, 1s.
Lady Lovelace. Post 8vo, illustrated
boards, 2s.

Plutarch's Lives of Illustrious
Men. Translated from the Greek,
with Notes Critical and Historical, and
a Life of Plutarch, by JOHN and
WILLIAM LANGHORNE. Two Vols.,
8vo, cloth extra, with Portraits, 10s. 6d.

Planché (J. R.), Works by:
The Pursuivant of Arms; or, Her-
aldry Founded upon Facts. With
Coloured Frontispiece and 200 Illus-
trations. Cr. 8vo, cloth extra, 7s. 6d.
Songs and Poems, from 1819 to 1879.
Edited, with an Introduction, by his
Daughter, Mrs. MACKARNESS. Crown
8vo, cloth extra, 6s.

Poe (Edgar Allan):
The Choice Works, in Prose and
Poetry, of EDGAR ALLAN POE. With
an Introductory Essay by CHARLES
BAUDELAIRE, Portrait and Fac-
similes. Crown 8vo, cl. extra, 7s. 6d.
The Mystery of Marie Roget, and
other Stories. Post 8vo, illust. bds., 2s.

Pope's Poetical Works. Complete in One Vol. Post 8vo, cl. limp, 2s.

Praed (Mrs. Campbell-).—"The
Right Honourable:" A Romance of
Society and Politics. By Mrs. CAMP-
BELL-PRAED and JUSTIN MCCARTHY,
M.P. Cr. 8vo, cloth extra, 6s.

Price (E. C.), Novels by:
Crown 8vo, cloth extra, 3s. 6d. each ;
post 8vo, illustrated boards, 2s. each.
Valentina. | The Foreigners.
Mrs. Lancaster's Rival.

Gerald. Post 8vo, illust. boards, 2s.

Princess Olga—Radna; or, The
Great Conspiracy of 1881. By the
Princess OLGA. Cr. 8vo, cl. ex., 6s.

Proctor (Rich. A.), Works by:
Flowers of the Sky. With 55 Illusts.
Small crown 8vo, cloth extra, 3s. 6d.
Easy Star Lessons. With Star Maps
for Every Night in the Year, Draw-
ings of the Constellations, &c.
Crown 8vo, cloth extra, 6s.
Familiar Science Studies. Crown
8vo, cloth extra, 6s.
Saturn and Its System. New and
Revised Edition, with 13 Steel Plates.
Demy 8vo, cloth extra, 10s. 6d.
Mysteries of Time and Space. With
Illusts. Cr. 8vo, cloth extra, 6s.
The Universe of Suns, and other
Science Gleanings. With numerous
Illusts. Cr. 8vo, cloth extra, 6s.
Wages and Wants of Science
Workers. Crown 8vo, 1s. 6d.

Rambosson.—Popular Astro-
nomy. By J. RAMBOSSON, Laureate of
the Institute of France. Translated by
C. B. PITMAN. Crown 8vo, cloth gilt,
numerous Illusts., and a beautifully
executed Chart of Spectra, 7s. 6d.

Reade (Charles), Novels by:
Cr. 8vo, cloth extra, illustrated, 3s. 6d. each; post 8vo, illust. bds., 2s. each.
Peg Woffington. Illustrated by S. L. FILDES, A.R.A.
Christie Johnstone. Illustrated by WILLIAM SMALL.
It is Never Too Late to Mend. Illustrated by G. J. PINWELL.
The Course of True Love Never did run Smooth. Illustrated by HELEN PATERSON.
The Autobiography of a Thief; Jack of all Trades; and James Lambert. Illustrated by MATT STRETCH.
Love me Little, Love me Long. Illustrated by M. ELLEN EDWARDS.
The Double Marriage. Illust. by Sir JOHN GILBERT, R.A., and C. KEENE.
The Cloister and the Hearth. Illustrated by CHARLES KEENE.
Hard Cash. Illust. by F. W. LAWSON.
Griffith Gaunt. Illustrated by S. L. FILDES, A.R.A., and WM. SMALL.
Foul Play. Illust. by DU MAURIER.
Put Yourself in His Place. Illustrated by ROBERT BARNES.
A Terrible Temptation. Illustrated by EDW. HUGHES and A. W. COOPER.
The Wandering Heir. Illustrated by H. PATERSON, S. L. FILDES, A.R.A., C. GREEN, and H. WOODS, A.R.A.
A Simpleton. Illustrated by KATE CRAUFORD.   [COULDERY.
A Woman-Hater. Illust. by THOS.
Singleheart and Doubleface: A Matter-of-fact Romance. Illustrated by P. MACNAB.
Good Stories of Men and other Animals. Illustrated by E. A. ABBEY, PERCY MACQUOID, and JOSEPH NASH.
The Jilt, and other Stories. Illustrated by JOSEPH NASH.
Readiana. With a Steel-plate Portrait of CHARLES READE.

Bible Characters: Studies of David, Nehemiah, Jonah, Paul, &c. Fcap. 8vo, leatherette, 1s.

Reader's Handbook (The) of Allusions, References, Plots, and Stories. By the Rev. Dr. BREWER. Fifth Edition, revised throughout, with a New Appendix, containing a COMPLETE ENGLISH BIBLIOGRAPHY. Cr. 8vo, 1,400 pages, cloth extra, 7s. 6d.

Rimmer (Alfred), Works by:
Square 8vo, cloth gilt, 7s. 6d. each.
Our Old Country Towns. With over 50 Illustrations.
Rambles Round Eton and Harrow. With 50 Illustrations.
About England with Dickens. With 58 Illustrations by ALFRED RIMMER and C. A. VANDERHOOF.

Riddell (Mrs. J. H.), Novels by:
Crown 8vo, cloth extra, 3s. 6d. each; post 8vo, illustrated boards, 2s. each.
Her Mother's Darling.
The Prince of Wales's Garden Party.
Weird Stories.

Post 8vo, illustrated boards, 2s. each.
The Uninhabited House.
Fairy Water.
The Mystery in Palace Gardens.

Robinson (F. W.), Novels by:
Crown 8vo, cloth extra, 3s. 6d. each; post 8vo, illustrated boards, 2s. each.
Women are Strange.
The Hands of Justice.

Robinson (Phil), Works by:
Crown 8vo, cloth extra, 7s. 6d. each.
The Poets' Birds.
The Poets' Beasts.
The Poets and Nature: Reptiles, Fishes, and Insects.   [Preparing.

Rochefoucauld's Maxims and Moral Reflections. With Notes, and an Introductory Essay by SAINTE-BEUVE. Post 8vo, cloth limp, 2s

Roll of Battle Abbey, The; or, A List of the Principal Warriors who came over from Normandy with William the Conqueror, and Settled in this Country, A.D. 1066-7. With the principal Arms emblazoned in Gold and Colours. Handsomely printed, 5s.

Rowley (Hon. Hugh), Works by
Post 8vo, cloth limp, 2s. 6d. each.
Puniana: Riddles and Jokes. With numerous Illustrations.
More Puniana. Profusely Illustrated.

Runciman (James), Stories by:
Post 8vo, illustrated boards, 2s. each; cloth limp, 2s. 6d. each.
Skippers and Shellbacks.
Grace Balmaign's Sweetheart.
Schools and Scholars.

Russell (W. Clark), Works by:
Crown 8vo, cloth extra, 6s. each; post 8vo, illustrated boards, 2s. each.
Round the Galley-Fire.
In the Middle Watch.
A Voyage to the Cape.
A Book for the Hammock.

On the Fo'k'sle Head. Post 8vo, illustrated boards, 2s.
The Mystery of the "Ocean Star," &c. Crown 8vo, cloth extra, 6s.
The Romance of Jenny Harlowe, and Sketches of Maritime Life. With a Frontispiece by F. BARNARD. Crown 8vo, cloth extra, 6s.

An Ocean Tragedy: A Novel. Three Vols., crown 8vo.   [Shortly

Sala.—Gaslight and Daylight.
By GEORGE AUGUSTUS SALA. Post
8vo, illustrated boards, 2s.

Sanson.—Seven Generations
of Executioners: Memoirs of the
Sanson Family (1688 to 1847). Edited
by HENRY SANSON. Cr.8vo, cl.ex. 3s. 6d.

Saunders (John), Novels by:
Crown 8vo, cloth extra, 3s. 6d. each;
post 8vo, illustrated boards, 2s. each.

  Guy Waterman. | Lion in the Path.
  The Two Dreamers.

  Bound to the Wheel. Crown 8vo,
  cloth extra, 3s. 6d.

Saunders (Katharine), Novels
by. Cr. 8vo, cloth extra, 3s. 6d. each;
post 8vo, illustrated boards, 2s. each.
Margaret and Elizabeth.
The High Mills.
Heart Salvage. | Sebastian.

  Joan Merryweather. Post 8vo, illustrated boards, 2s.
  Gideon's Rock. Crown 8vo, cloth
  extra, 3s. 6d.

Science-Gossip for 1889: An
Illustrated Medium of Interchange
for Students and Lovers of Nature.
Edited by Dr. J. E. TAYLOR, F.L.S.,&c.
Devoted to Geology, Botany, Physiology, Chemistry, Zoology, Micros-
copy, Telescopy, Physiography, &c.
Price 4d. Monthly; or 5s. per year,
post free. Vols. I. to XIX. may be
had at 7s. 6d. each; and Vols. XX. to
date, at 5s. each. Cases for Binding,
1s. 6d. each.

Seguin (L. G.), Works by:
Crown 8vo, cloth extra, 6s. each.
The Country of the Passion Play,
and the Highlands and Highlanders
of Bavaria. With Map and 37 Illusts.
Walks in Algiers and its Surroundings. With 2 Maps and 16 Illusts.

"Secret Out" Series, The:
Cr. 8vo, cl. ex., Illusts., 4s. 6d. each.
The Secret Out: One Thousand
Tricks with Cards, and other Re-
creations; with Entertaining Experi-
ments in Drawing-room or "White
Magic." By W. H. CREMER. 300 Illusts.
The Art of Amusing: A Collection of
Graceful Arts, Games, Tricks, Puzzles,
and Charades By FRANK BELLEW.
With 300 Illustrations.
Hanky-Panky: Very Easy Tricks,
Very Difficult Tricks, White Magic,
Sleight of Hand. Edited by W. H.
CREMER. With 200 Illustrations.

"SECRET OUT" SERIES—*continued.*
  Magician's Own Book: Performances
  with Cups and Balls, Eggs, Hats,
  Handkerchiefs, &c. All from actual
  Experience. Edited by W. H. CRE-
  MER. 200 Illustrations.

Senior.—By Stream and Sea.
By W. SENIOR. Post 8vo, cl. limp, 2s. 6d.

Seven Sagas (The) of Prehis-
toric Man. By JAMES H. STODDART,
Author of "The Village Life." Crown
8vo, cloth extra, 6s.

Shakespeare:
  The First Folio Shakespeare.—MR.
  WILLIAM SHAKESPEARE'S Comedies,
  Histories, and Tragedies. Published
  according to the true Originall Copies
  London, Printed by ISAAC IAGGARD
  and ED. BLOUNT. 1623.—A Repro-
  duction of the extremely rare original,
  in reduced facsimile, by a photographic process—ensuring the strictest
  accuracy in every detail. Small 8vo,
  half-Roxburghe, 7s. 6d.
  Shakespeare for Children: Tales
  from Shakespeare. By CHARLES
  and MARY LAMB. With numerous
  Illustrations, coloured and plain, by
  J. MOYR SMITH. Cr. 4to, cl. gilt, 6s.

Sharp.—Children of To-mor-
row: A Novel. By WILLIAM SHARP.
Crown 8vo, cloth extra, 6s.

Sheridan (General).—Personal
Memoirs of General P. H. Sheridan:
The Romantic Career of a Great
Soldier, told in his Own Words. With
22 Portraits and other Illustrations, 27
Maps and numerous Facsimiles of
Famous Letters. Two Vols. of 500
pages each, demy 8vo, cloth extra, 24s.

Sheridan:—
  Sheridan's Complete Works, with
  Life and Anecdotes. Including his
  Dramatic Writings, printed from the
  Original Editions, his Works in
  Prose and Poetry, Translations,
  Speeches, Jokes, Puns, &c. With a
  Collection of Sheridaniana. Crown
  8vo, cloth extra, gilt, with 10 full-
  page Tinted Illustrations, 7s. 6d.
  Sheridan's Comedies: The Rivals,
  and The School for Scandal.
  Edited, with an Introduction and
  Notes to each Play, and a Bio-
  graphical Sketch of Sheridan, by
  BRANDER MATTHEWS. With Decora-
  tive Vignettes and 10 full-page Illusts.
  Demy 8vo, half-parchment, 12s. 6d.

Shelley.—The Complete Works in Verse and Prose of Percy Bysshe Shelley. Edited, Prefaced and Annotated by R. HERNE SHEPHERD. Five Vols., cr. 8vo, cloth bds., 3s. 6d. each.

Poetical Works, in Three Vols.

Vol. I. An Introduction by the Editor; The Posthumous Fragments of Margaret Nicholson; Shelley's Correspondence with Stockdale; The Wandering Jew (the only complete version); Queen Mab, with the Notes; Alastor, and other Poems; Rosalind and Helen; Prometheus Unbound; Adonais, &c.

Vol. II. Laon and Cythna (as originally published, instead of the emasculated "Revolt of Islam"); The Cenci; Julian and Maddalo (from Shelley's manuscript); Swellfoot the Tyrant (from the copy in the Dyce Library at South Kensington); The Witch of Atlas; Epipsychidion; Hellas.

Vol. III. Posthumous Poems, published by Mrs. SHELLEY in 1824 and 1839; The Masque of Anarchy (from Shelley's manuscript); and other Pieces not brought together in the ordinary editions.

Prose Works, in Two Vols.

Vol. I. The Two Romances of Zastrozzi and St. Irvyne; the Dublin and Marlow Pamphlets; A Refutation of Deism; Letters to Leigh Hunt, and some Minor Writings and Fragments.

Vol. II. The Essays; Letters from Abroad; Translations and Fragments, Edited by Mrs. SHELLEY, and first published in 1840, with the addition of some Minor Pieces of great interest and rarity, including one recently discovered by Professor DOWDEN. With a Bibliography of Shelley, and an exhaustive Index of the Prose Works.

Sherard.—Rogues: A Novel of Incident. By R. H. SHERARD. Crown 8vo, picture cover, 1s.; cloth, 1s. 6d.
[Shortly.

Sidney's (Sir Philip) Complete Poetical Works, including all those in "Arcadia." With Portrait, Memorial-Introduction, Notes, &c., by the Rev. A. B. GROSART, D.D. Three Vols., crown 8vo, cloth boards, 18s.

Signboards: Their History. With Anecdotes of Famous Taverns and Remarkable Characters. By JACOB LARWOOD and JOHN-CAMDEN HOTTEN. Crown 8vo, cloth extra, with 100 Illustrations, 7s. 6d.

Sims (George R.), Works by:
Post 8vo, illustrated boards, 2s. each; cloth limp, 2s. 6d. each.

Rogues and Vagabonds.
The Ring o' Bells.
Mary Jane's Memoirs.
Mary Jane Married.
Tales of To-day.

Cr. 8vo, picture cover, 1s. ea.; cl., 1s. 6d. ea.

The Dagonet Reciter and Reader: Being Readings and Recitations in Prose and Verse, selected from his own Works by G. R. SIMS.

How the Poor Live; and Horrible London. In One Volume.

Sister Dora: A Biography. By MARGARET LONSDALE. Popular Edition, Revised, with additional Chapter, a New Dedication and Preface, and Four Illustrations. Sq. 8vo, picture cover, 4d.; cloth, 6d.

Sketchley.—A Match in the Dark. By ARTHUR SKETCHLEY. Post 8vo, illustrated boards, 2s.

Slang Dictionary, The: Etymological, Historical, and Anecdotal. Crown 8vo, cloth extra, gilt, 6s. 6d.

Smart.—Without Love or Licence: A Novel. By HAWLEY SMART. Three Vols., cr. 8vo. [Shortly.

Smith (J. Moyr), Works by:
The Prince of Argolis: A Story of the Old Greek Fairy Time. Small 8vo, cloth extra, with 130 Illusts., 3s. 6d.

Tales of Old Thule. With numerous Illustrations. Cr. 8vo, cloth gilt, 6s.

The Wooing of the Water Witch. With Illustrations. Small 8vo, 6s.

Society in London. By A FOREIGN RESIDENT. Crown 8vo, 1s.; cloth, 1s. 6d.

Society out of Town. By A FOREIGN RESIDENT, Author of "Society in London." Crown 8vo, cloth extra, 6s.
[Preparing.

Society in Paris: The Upper Ten Thousand. By Count PAUL VASILI. Trans. by RAPHAEL LEDOS DE BEAUFORT. Cr. 8vo, cl. ex., 6s. [Preparing.

Somerset.—Songs of Adieu. By Lord HENRY SOMERSET. Small 4to, Japanese vellum, 6s.

Speight (T. W.), Novels by:
The Mysteries of Heron Dyke. With a Frontispiece by M. ELLEN EDWARDS. Crown 8vo, cloth extra, 3s. 6d.; post 8vo, illustrated bds., 2s.

Wife or No Wife? Post 8vo, cloth limp, 1s. 6d.

A Barren Title. Crown 8vo, cl., 1s. 6d.

The Golden Hoop. Post 8vo, illust. boards, 2s.

By Devious Ways; and A Barren Title. Post 8vo, illust. boards, 2s.

Spalding.—Elizabethan Demonology: An Essay in Illustration of the Belief in the Existence of Devils, and the Powers possessed by Them. By T. A. SPALDING, LL.B. Cr. 8vo, cl. ex., 5s.

Spenser for Children. By M. H. TOWRY. With Illustrations by WALTER J. MORGAN. Crown 4to, with Coloured Illustrations, cloth gilt. 6s.

Stageland: Curious Habits and Customs of its Inhabitants. By JEROME K. JEROME. With 64 Illustrations by J. BERNARD PARTRIDGE. Second Edition. Fcap. 4to, illustrated cover, 3s. 6d.

Starry Heavens, The: A Poetical Birthday Book. Square 8vo, cloth extra, 2s. 6d.

Staunton.—Laws and Practice of Chess. With an Analysis of the Openings. By HOWARD STAUNTON. Edited by ROBERT B. WORMALD. Small crown 8vo, cloth extra, 5s.

Stedman (E. C.), Works by:
Victorian Poets. Thirteenth Edition. Crown 8vo, cloth extra, 9s.
The Poets of America. Crown 8vo, cloth extra, 9s.

Sterndale.—The Afghan Knife: A Novel. By ROBERT ARMITAGE STERNDALE. Cr. 8vo, cloth extra, 3s 6d.; post 8vo, illustrated boards, 2s.

Stevenson (R. Louis), Works by:
Post 8vo, cloth limp, 2s. 6d. each.
Travels with a Donkey in the Cevennes. Seventh Edition. With a Frontispiece by WALTER CRANE.
An Inland Voyage. Third Edition. With Frontispiece by WALTER CRANE.

Cr. 8vo, buckram extra, gilt top, 6s. each.
Familiar Studies of Men and Books. Third Edition.
The Silverado Squatters. With Frontispiece.
The Merry Men. Second Edition.
Underwoods: Poems. Fourth Edit.
Memories & Portraits. Second Ed.
Virginibus Puerisque, and other Papers. Fourth Edition.

Cr. 8vo, buckram extra, gilt top, 6s. each; post 8vo, illust. boards, 2s. each.
New Arabian Nights. Tenth Edition.
Prince Otto: Sixth Edition.

Stoddard.—Summer Cruising in the South Seas. By CHARLES WARREN STODDARD. Illust. by WALLIS MACKAY. Crown 8vo, cl. extra, 3s. 6d.

Stories from Foreign Novelists. With Notices of their Lives and Writings. By HELEN and ALICE ZIMMERN. Frontispiece. Crown 8vo, cloth extra, 3s. 6d. post 8vo, illust. bds., 2s.

Strange Manuscript (A) found in a Copper Cylinder. With 19 full-page Illustrations by GILBERT GAUL. Third Edition. Cr. 8vo, cl. extra, 5s.

Strange Secrets. Told by PERCY FITZGERALD, FLORENCE MARRYAT, JAMES GRANT, A. CONAN DOYLE, DUTTON COOK, and others. With 8 Illustrations by Sir JOHN GILBERT, WILLIAM SMALL, W. J. HENNESSY, &c. Crown 8vo, cloth extra, 6s.

Strutt's Sports and Pastimes of the People of England; including the Rural and Domestic Recreations, May Games, Mummeries, Shows, &c., from the Earliest Period to the Present Time. With 140 Illustrations. Edited by WM. HONE. Cr. 8vo, cl. extra, 7s. 6d.

Suburban Homes (The) of London: A Residential Guide to Favourite London Localities, their Society, Celebrities, and Associations. With Notes on their Rental, Rates, and House Accommodation. With Map of Suburban London. Cr. 8vo, cl. ex., 7s 6d.

Swift (Dean):—
Swift's Choice Works, in Prose and Verse. With Memoir, Portrait, and Facsimiles of the Maps in the Original Edition of "Gulliver's Travels." Crown 8vo, cloth extra, 7s. 6d.
A Monograph on Dean Swift. By J. CHURTON COLLINS. Crown 8vo, cloth extra, 8s. [Shortly.

Swinburne (Algernon C.), Works by:
Selections from the Poetical Works of Algernon Charles Swinburne. Fcap. 8vo, cloth extra, 6s.
Atalanta in Calydon. Crown 8vo, 6s.
Chastelard. A Tragedy. Cr. 8vo, 7s.
Poems and Ballads. FIRST SERIES. Cr. 8vo, 9s. Fcap. 8vo, same price.
Poems and Ballads. SECOND SERIES. Cr. 8vo, 9s. Fcap. 8vo, same price.
Poems and Ballads. THIRD SERIES. Crown 8vo, 7s.
Notes on Poems and Reviews. 8vo, 1s
Songs before Sunrise. Cr. 8vo, 10s. 6d.
Bothwell: A Tragedy. Cr. 8vo, 12s. 6d.
George Chapman: An Essay. (See Vol. II. of GEO. CHAPMAN'S Works.) Crown 8vo, 6s.
Songs of Two Nations. Cr. 8vo, 6s.
Essays and Studies. Crown 8vo, 12s.
Erechtheus: A Tragedy. Cr. 8vo, 6s.
Songs of the Springtides. Cr. 8vo, 6s.
Studies in Song. Crown 8vo, 7s.
Mary Stuart: A Tragedy. Cr. 8vo, 8s.
Tristram of Lyonesse, and other Poems. Crown 8vo, 9s.
A Century of Roundels. Small 4to, 8s
A Midsummer Holiday, and other Poems. Crown 8vo, 7s.
Marino Faliero: A Tragedy. Cr. 8vo, 6s.
A Study of Victor Hugo. Cr. 8vo, 6s.
Miscellanies. Crown 8vo, 12s.
Locrine: A Tragedy. Crown 8vo, 6s.
A Study of Ben Jonson. Cr. 8vo, 7s.

Symonds.—Wine, Women, and Song: Mediæval Latin Students' Songs. Now first translated into English Verse, with Essay by J. ADDINGTON SYMONDS. Small 8vo, parchment, **6s.**

Syntax's (Dr.) Three Tours: In Search of the Picturesque, in Search of Consolation, and in Search of a Wife. With the whole of ROWLANDSON's droll page Illustrations in Colours and a Life of the Author by J. C. HOTTEN. Med. 8vo, cloth extra, **7s. 6d.**

Taine's History of English Literature. Translated by HENRY VAN LAUN. Four Vols., small 8vo, cloth boards, **30s.**—POPULAR EDITION, Two Vols., crown 8vo, cloth extra, **15s.**

Taylor's (Bayard) Diversions of the Echo Club: Burlesques of Modern Writers. Post 8vo, cl. limp, **2s.**

Taylor (Dr. J. E., F.L.S.), Works by. Crown 8vo, cloth ex., **7s. 6d.** each.
The Sagacity and Morality of Plants: A Sketch of the Life and Conduct of the Vegetable Kingdom. Coloured Frontispiece and 100 Illust.
Our Common British Fossils, and Where to Find Them: A Handbook for Students. With 331 Illustrations.
The Playtime Naturalist. With 366 Illustrations. Crown 8vo, cl. ex., **5s.**

Taylor's (Tom) Historical Dramas: "Clancarty," "Jeanne Darc," "'Twixt Axe and Crown," "The Fool's Revenge," "Arkwright's Wife," "Anne Boleyn," "Plot and Passion." One Vol., cr. 8vo, cloth extra, **7s. 6d.**
*** The Plays may also be had separately, at **1s.** each.

Tennyson (Lord): A Biographical Sketch. By H. J. JENNINGS. With a Photograph-Portrait. Crown 8vo, cloth extra, **6s.**

Thackerayana: Notes and Anecdotes. Illustrated by Hundreds of Sketches by WILLIAM MAKEPEACE THACKERAY, depicting Humorous Incidents in his School-life, and Favourite Characters in the books of his every-day reading. With Coloured Frontispiece. Cr. 8vo, cl. extra, **7s. 6d.**

Thames.—A New Pictorial History of the Thames, from its Source Downwards. A Book for all Boating Men and for all Lovers of the River. With over 300 Illusts. Post 8vo, picture cover, **1s.**; cloth, **1s. 6d.**

Thomas (Bertha), Novels by: Crown 8vo, cloth extra, **3s. 6d.** each post 8vo, illustrated boards, **2s.** each.
Cressida. | Proud Maisie.
The Violin Player.

Thomas (M.).—A Fight for Life: A Novel. By W. MOY THOMAS. Post 8vo, illustrated boards, **2s.**

Thomson's Seasons and Castle of Indolence. With a Biographical and Critical Introduction by ALLAN CUNNINGHAM, and over 50 fine Illustrations on Steel and Wood. Crown 8vo, cloth extra, gilt edges, **7s. 6d.**

Thornbury (Walter), Works by:
Crown 8vo, cloth extra, **7s. 6d.** each.
Haunted London. Edited by EDWARD WALFORD, M.A. With Illustrations by F. W. FAIRHOLT, F.S.A.
The Life and Correspondence of J. M. W. Turner. Founded upon Letters and Papers furnished by his Friends and fellow Academicians. With numerous Illusts. in Colours, facsimiled from Turner's Original Drawings.

Post 8vo, illustrated boards, **2s.** each.
Old Stories Re-told.
Tales for the Marines.

Timbs (John), Works by:
Crown 8vo, cloth extra, **7s. 6d.** each.
The History of Clubs and Club Life in London. With Anecdotes of its Famous Coffee-houses, Hostelries, and Taverns. With many Illusts.
English Eccentrics and Eccentricities: Stories of Wealth and Fashion, Delusions, Impostures, and Fanatic Missions, Strange Sights and Sporting Scenes, Eccentric Artists, Theatrical Folk, Men of Letters, &c. With nearly 50 Illusts.

Trollope (Anthony), Novels by:
Crown 8vo, cloth extra, **3s. 6d.** each post 8vo, illustrated boards, **2s.** each.
The Way We Live Now.
Kept in the Dark.
Frau Frohmann. | Marion Fay.
Mr. Scarborough's Family.
The Land-Leaguers.

Post 8vo, illustrated boards, **2s.** each.
The Golden Lion of Granpere.
John Caldigate. | American Senator

Trollope (Frances E.), Novels by
Crown 8vo, cloth extra, **3s. 6d.** each; post 8vo, illustrated boards, **2s.** each.
Like Ships upon the Sea.
Mabel's Progress. | Anne Furness.

Trollope (T. A.).—Diamond Cut Diamond, and other Stories. By T. ADOLPHUS TROLLOPE. Post 8vo, illustrated boards, **2s.**

Trowbridge.—Farnell's Folly: A Novel. By J. T. TROWBRIDGE. Post 8vo, illustrated boards, **2s.**

Turgenieff. — Stories from Foreign Novelists. By IVAN TURGENIEFF, and others. Cr. 8vo, cloth extra, 3s. 6d.; post 8vo, illustrated boards, 2s.

Tytler (C. C. Fraser-). — Mistress Judith: A Novel. By C. C. FRASER-TYTLER. Cr. 8vo, cloth extra, 3s. 6d.; post 8vo, illust. boards, 2s.

Tytler (Sarah), Novels by:
Crown 8vo, cloth extra, 3s. 6d. each; post 8vo, illustrated boards, 2s. each.
What She Came Through.
The Bride's Pass. | Noblesse Oblige.
Saint Mungo's City. | Lady Bell.
Beauty and the Beast.
Buried Diamonds.
Post 8vo, illustrated boards, 2s. each.
Citoyenne Jacqueline.
Disappeared. | The Huguenot Family
The Blackhall Ghosts: A Novel. Crown 8vo, cl. ex., 3s. 6d.

Van Laun.—History of French Literature. By H. VAN LAUN. Three Vols., demy 8vo, cl. bds., 7s. 6d. each.

Villari.—A Double Bond. By L. VILLARI. Fcap. 8vo, picture cover, 1s.

Walford (Edw., M.A.), Works by:
The County Families of the United Kingdom (1889). Containing Notices of the Descent, Birth, Marriage, Education, &c., of more than 12,000 distinguished Heads of Families their Heirs Apparent or Presumptive, the Offices they hold or have held, their Town and Country Addresses, Clubs, &c. Twenty-ninth Annual Edition. Cloth gilt, 50s.
The Shilling Peerage (1889). Containing an Alphabetical List of the House of Lords, Dates of Creation, Lists of Scotch and Irish Peers, Addresses, &c. 32mo, cloth, 1s.
The Shilling Baronetage (1889). Containing an Alphabetical List of the Baronets of the United Kingdom, short Biographical Notices, Dates of Creation, Addresses, &c. 32mo, cl., 1s.
The Shilling Knightage (1889). Containing an Alphabetical List of the Knights of the United Kingdom, short Biographical Notices, Dates of Creation, Addresses, &c. 32mo, cl., 1s.
The Shilling House of Commons (1889). Containing List of all Members of Parliament, their Town and Country Addresses, &c. 32mo, cl., 1s.
The Complete Peerage, Baronetage, Knightage, and House of Commons (1889). In One Volume, royal 32mo, cloth extra, gilt edges, 5s.
Haunted London. By WALTER THORNBURY. Edit. by EDWARD WALFORD, M.A. Illusts. by F. W. FAIRHOLT, F.S.A. Cr. 8vo, cloth extra, 7s. 6d.

Walton and Cotton's Complete Angler; or, The Contemplative Man's Recreation; being a Discourse of Rivers, Fishponds, Fish and Fishing, written by IZAAK WALTON; and Instructions how to Angle for a Trout or Grayling in a clear Stream, by CHARLES COTTON. With Original Memoirs and Notes by Sir HARRIS NICOLAS, and 61 Copperplate Illustrations. Large crown 8vo, cloth antique, 7s. 6d.

Walt Whitman, Poems by. Selected and edited, with an Introduction, by WILLIAM M. ROSSETTI. A New Edition, with a Steel Plate Portrait. Crown 8vo, printed on handmade paper and bound in buckram, 6s.

Wanderer's Library, The:
Crown 8vo, cloth extra, 3s. 6d. each.
Wanderings in Patagonia; or, Life among the Ostrich-Hunters. By JULIUS BEERBOHM. Illustrated.
Camp Notes: Stories of Sport and Adventure in Asia, Africa, and America. By FREDERICK BOYLE.
Savage Life. By FREDERICK BOYLE.
Merrie England in the Olden Time. By GEORGE DANIEL. With Illustrations by ROBT. CRUIKSHANK.
Circus Life and Circus Celebrities. By THOMAS FROST.
The Lives of the Conjurers. By THOMAS FROST.
The Old Showmen and the Old London Fairs. By THOMAS FROST.
Low-Life Deeps. An Account of the Strange Fish to be found there. By JAMES GREENWOOD.
The Wilds of London. By JAMES GREENWOOD.
Tunis: The Land and the People. By the Chevalier de HESSE-WARTEGG. With 22 Illustrations.
The Life and Adventures of a Cheap Jack. By One of the Fraternity. Edited by CHARLES HINDLEY.
The World Behind the Scenes. By PERCY FITZGERALD.
Tavern Anecdotes and Sayings: Including the Origin of Signs, and Reminiscences connected with Taverns, Coffee Houses, Clubs, &c. By CHARLES HINDLEY. With Illusts.
The Genial Showman: Life and Adventures of Artemus Ward. By E. P. HINGSTON. With a Frontispiece.
The Story of the London Parks. By JACOB LARWOOD. With Illusts.
London Characters. By HENRY MAYHEW. Illustrated.
Seven Generations of Executioners: Memoirs of the Sanson Family (1688 to 1847). Edited by HENRY SANSON.
Summer Cruising in the South Seas. By C. WARREN STODDARD. Illustrated by WALLIS MACKAY.

Warner.—A Roundabout Journey. By CHARLES DUDLEY WARNER, Author of "My Summer in a Garden." Crown 8vo, cloth extra, 6s.

Warrants, &c. :—
Warrant to Execute Charles I. An exact Facsimile, with the Fifty-nine Signatures, and corresponding Seals. Carefully printed on paper to imitate the Original, 22 in. by 14 in. Price 2s.
Warrant to Execute Mary Queen of Scots. An exact Facsimile, including the Signature of Queen Elizabeth, and a Facsimile of the Great Seal. Beautifully printed on paper to imitate the Original MS. Price 2s.
Magna Charta. An exact Facsimile of the Original Document in the British Museum, printed on fine plate paper, nearly 3 feet long by 2 feet wide, with the Arms and Seals emblazoned in Gold and Colours. 5s.
The Roll of Battle Abbey; or, A List of the Principal Warriors who came over from Normandy with William the Conqueror, and Settled in this Country, A.D. 1066-7. With the principal Arms emblazoned in Gold and Colours. Price 5s.

Wayfarer, The : Journal of the Society of Cyclists. Published at intervals. Price 1s. The Numbers for OCT., 1886, JAN., MAY, and OCT., 1887, and FEB., 1888, are now ready.

Weather, How to Foretell the, with the Pocket Spectroscope. By F. W. CORY, M.R.C.S. Eng., F.R.Met. Soc., &c. With 10 Illustrations. Crown 8vo, 1s. ; cloth, 1s. 6d.

Westropp.—Handbook of Pottery and Porcelain ; or, History of those Arts from the Earliest Period. By HODDER M. WESTROPP. With numerous Illustrations, and a List or Marks. Crown 8vo, cloth limp, 4s. 6d.

Whist. — How to Play Solo Whist: Its Method and Principles Explained, and its Practice Demonstrated. With Illustrative Specimen Hands in red and black, and a Revised and Augmented Code of Laws. By ABRAHAM S. WILKS and CHARLES F. PARDON. Crown 8vo, cloth extra, 3s. 6d.

Whistler's (Mr.) "Ten o'Clock." Crown 8vo, hand-made and brown paper, 1s.

Williams (W. Mattieu, F.R.A.S.), Works by:
Science In Short Chapters. Crown 8vo, cloth extra, 7s. 6d.
A Simple Treatise on Heat. Crown 8vo, cloth limp, with Illusts., 2s. 6d.
The Chemistry of Cookery. Crown 8vo, cloth extra, 6s.

Wilson (Dr. Andrew, F.R.S.E.), Works by:
Chapters on Evolution: A Popular History of Darwinian and Allied Theories of Development. 3rd ed. Cr. 8vo, cl. ex., with 259 Illusts., 7s. 6d.
Leaves from a Naturalist's Note book. Post 8vo, cloth limp, 2s. 6d.
Leisure-Time Studies, chiefly Biological. Third Edit., with New Preface. Cr. 8vo, cl. ex., with Illusts., 6s.
Studies In Life and Sense. With numerous Illusts. Cr. 8vo, cl. ex., 6s.
Common Accidents, and How to Treat them. By Dr. ANDREW WILSON and others. With numerous Illusts. Cr. 8vo, 1s. ; cl. limp, 1s. 6d.

Winter (J. S.), Stories by : Post 8vo, illustrated boards, 2s. each.
Cavalry Life. | Regimental Legends.

Witch, Warlock, and Magician : A Popular History of Magic and Witchcraft in England and Scotland. By W. H. DAVENPORT ADAMS. Demy 8vo, cloth extra, 12s.

Women of the Day : A Biographical Dictionary of Notable Contemporaries. By FRANCES HAYS. Crown 8vo, cloth extra, 5s.

Wood.—Sabina : A Novel. By Lady WOOD. Post 8vo, illust. bds., 2s.

Wood (H.F.), Detective Stories :
The Passenger from Scotland Yard. Crown 8vo, cloth extra, 6s.; post 8vo, illustrated boards, 2s.
The Englishman of the Rue Caïn. Crown 8vo, cloth extra, 6s.

Woolley.—Rachel Armstrong ; or, Love and Theology. By CELIA PARKER WOOLLEY. Post 8vo, illustrated boards, 2s. ; cloth, 2s. 6d.

Words, Facts, and Phrases : A Dictionary of Curious, Quaint, and Out-of-the-Way Matters. By ELIEZER EDWARDS. New and cheaper issue, cr. 8vo, cl. ex., 7s. 6d. ; half-bound, 9s.

Wright (Thomas), Works by : Crown 8vo, cloth extra, 7s. 6d. each.
Caricature History of the Georges. (The House of Hanover.) With 400 Pictures, Caricatures, Squibs, Broadsides, Window Pictures, &c.
History of Caricature and of the Grotesque In Art, Literature, Sculpture, and Painting. Profusely Illustrated by F.W. FAIRHOLT, F.S.A.

Yates (Edmund), Novels by : Post 8vo, illustrated boards, 2s. each.
Land at Last. | The Forlorn Hope.
Castaway.

NEW NOVELS AT ALL LIBRARIES.

The Bell of St. Paul's. By WALTER BESANT. Three Vols.

Blind Love. By WILKIE COLLINS. Three Vols. [*Shortly.*

An Ocean Tragedy. By W. CLARK RUSSELL. Three Vols. [*Shortly.*

Passion's Slave. By RICHARD ASHE KING. Three Vols. [*Shortly.*

Without Love or Licence. By HAWLEY SMART. Three Vols. [*Shortly.*

The Romance of Jenny Harlowe, &c. By W. CLARK RUSSELL. Cr.8vo,cl.ex.6s.

Paul Jones's Alias, &c. By D. CHRISTIE MURRAY and HENRY HERMAN. Crown 8vo, cloth, 6s. [*Shortly.*

The Dead Man's Secret. By J. E. MUDDOCK. Cr. 8vo, cloth, 5s. [*Shortly.*

Strange Secrets. Told by PERCY FITZGERALD, &c. With 8 Illustrations, Crown 8vo, cloth extra, 6s.

Doctor Rameau. By GEORGES OHNET. Nine Illusts. Cr. 8vo, cloth extra, 6s.

A Last Love. By GEORGES OHNET. Crown 8vo, cloth extra, 5s. [*Shortly.*

Children of To-morrow. By WILLIAM SHARP. Crown 8vo, cloth extra, 6s.

Nikanor. From the French of HENRY GREVILLE. With Eight Illustrations, Crown 8vo, cloth extra, 6s.

A Noble Woman. By HENRY GREVILLE. Translated by A. VANDAM. Crown 8vo, cloth extra, 6s. [*Shortly.*

Mr. Stranger's Sealed Packet. By HUGH MACCOLL. Cr. 8vo, cl. extra, 5s.

THE PICCADILLY NOVELS.

Popular Stories by the Best Authors. LIBRARY EDITIONS, many Illustrated crown 8vo, cloth extra, 3s. 6d. each.

BY THE AUTHOR OF "JOHN HERRING."

Red Spider. | Eve.

BY GRANT ALLEN.

Philistia.
The Devil's Die.
The Tents of Shem.

BY WALTER BESANT & J. RICE.

Ready-Money Mortiboy.
My Little Girl.
The Case of Mr. Lucraft.
This Son of Vulcan.
With Harp and Crown.
The Golden Butterfly.
By Celia's Arbour.
The Monks of Thelema.
'Twas in Trafalgar's Bay.
The Seamy Side.
The Ten Years' Tenant.
The Chaplain of the Fleet.

BY WALTER BESANT.

All Sorts and Conditions of Men.
The Captains' Room.
All in a Garden Fair.
Dorothy Forster. | Uncle Jack.
Children of Gibeon.
The World Went Very Well Then.
Herr Paulus.
For Faith and Freedom.

BY ROBERT BUCHANAN.

A Child of Nature.
God and the Man.
The Shadow of the Sword.
The Martyrdom of Madeline.
Love Me for Ever.
Annan Water. | The New Abelard
Matt. | Foxglove Manor.
The Master of the Mine.
The Heir of Linne.

BY HALL CAINE.

The Shadow of a Crime.
A Son of Hagar. | The Deemster.

BY MRS. H. LOVETT CAMERON.

Juliet's Guardian. | Deceivers Ever.

BY MORTIMER COLLINS.

Sweet Anne Page. | Transmigration
From Midnight to Midnight.

MORTIMER & FRANCES COLLINS.

Blacksmith and Scholar.
The Village Comedy.
You Play me False.

BY WILKIE COLLINS.

Antonina.
Basil.
Hide and Seek.
The Dead Secret
Queen of Hearts.
My Miscellanies.
Woman in White.
The Moonstone.
Man and Wife.
Poor Miss Finch.
Miss or Mrs. ?
New Magdalen.
The Frozen Deep.

The Law and the Lady.
The Two Destinies
Haunted Hotel.
The Fallen Leaves
Jezebel'sDaughter
The Black Robe.
Heart and Science
"I Say No."
Little Novels.
The Evil Genius.
The Legacy of Cain.

BY DUTTON COOK.

Paul Foster's Daughter.

BY WILLIAM CYPLES.

Hearts of Gold.

BY ALPHONSE DAUDET.

The Evangelist; or, Port Salvation.

BY JAMES DE MILLE.

A Castle in Spain.

BY J. LEITH DERWENT.

Our Lady of Tears.
Circe's Lovers.

BY M. BETHAM-EDWARDS.

Felicia.

BY MRS. ANNIE EDWARDES.

Archie Lovell.

BY PERCY FITZGERALD.

Fatal Zero.

BY R. E. FRANCILLON.

Queen Cophetua. | A Real Queen.
One by One. | King or Knave ?

Prefaced by Sir BARTLE FRERE.

Pandurang Hari.

PICCADILLY NOVELS, *continued*—

BY EDWARD GARRETT.
The Capel Girls.

BY CHARLES GIBBON.
Robin Gray.
What will the World Say?
In Honour Bound.
Queen of the Meadow.
The Flower of the Forest.
A Heart's Problem.
The Braes of Yarrow.
The Golden Shaft.
Of High Degree.
Loving a Dream.

BY JULIAN HAWTHORNE.
Garth.
Ellice Quentin.
Sebastian Strome.
Dust.
Fortune's Fool.
Beatrix Randolph.
David Poindexter's Disappearance
The Spectre of the Camera.

BY SIR A HELPS.
Ivan de Biron.

BY ISAAC HENDERSON.
Agatha Page.

BY MRS. ALFRED HUNT.
Thornicroft's Model.
The Leaden Casket.
Self-Condemned.
That other Person.

BY JEAN INGELOW.
Fated to be Free.

BY R. ASHE KING.
A Drawn Game.
"The Wearing of the Green."

BY HENRY KINGSLEY.
Number Seventeen.

BY E. LYNN LINTON.
Patricia Kemball.
Atonement of Leam Dundas.
The World Well Lost.
Under which Lord?
"My Love!"
Ione.
Paston Carew.

BY HENRY W. LUCY.
Gideon Fleyce.

BY JUSTIN McCARTHY.
The Waterdale Neighbours.
A Fair Saxon.
Dear Lady Disdain.
Miss Misanthrope.
Donna Quixote.
The Comet of a Season.
Maid of Athens.
Camiola.

BY MRS. MACDONELL.
Quaker Cousins.

PICCADILLY NOVELS *continued*—

BY FLORENCE MARRYAT.
Open! Sesame!

BY D. CHRISTIE MURRAY.
Life's Atonement. | Coals of Fire.
Joseph's Coat. | Val Strange.
A Model Father. | Hearts.
By the Gate of the Sea.
A Bit of Human Nature.
First Person Singular.
Cynic Fortune.
The Way of the World.

BY MRS. OLIPHANT.
Whiteladies.

BY OUIDA.
Held in Bondage. | Two Little Wooden
Strathmore. | Shoes.
Chandos. | In a Winter City.
Under Two Flags. | Ariadne.
Idalia. | Friendship.
Cecil Castle- | Moths.
maine's Gage. | Pipistrello.
Tricotrin | A Village Com-
Puck. | mune.
Folle Farine. | Bimbi.
A Dog of Flanders | Wanda.
Pascarel. | Frescoes.
Signa. | In Maremma
Princess Naprax- | Othmar.
ine. | Guildoroy.

BY MARGARET A. PAUL
Gentle and Simple.

BY JAMES PAYN.
Lost Sir Massing- | A Grape from a
berd. | Thorn.
Walter's Word. | Some Private
Less Black than | Views.
We're Painted | The Canon's Ward.
By Proxy. | Glow-worm Tales.
High Spirits. | Talk of the Town.
Under One Roof. | In Peril and Pri-
A Confidential | vation.
Agent. | Holiday Tasks.
From Exile. | The Mystery of
| Mirbridge.

BY E. C. PRICE.
Valentina. | The Foreigners.
Mrs. Lancaster's Rival.

BY CHARLES READE.
It is Never Too Late to Mend.
Hard Cash. | Peg Woffington.
Christie Johnstone.
Griffith Gaunt. | Foul Play.
The Double Marriage.
Love Me Little, Love Me Long.
The Cloister and the Hearth.
The Course of True Love
The Autobiography of a Thief.
Put Yourself in His Place.
A Terrible Temptation
The Wandering Heir. | A Simpleton.
A Woman-Hater. | Readiana.
Singleheart and Doubleface.
The Jilt
Good Stories of Men and other
Animals.

PICCADILLY NOVELS, *continued*—
BY MRS. J. H. RIDDELL.
Her Mother's Darling.
Prince of Wales's Garden-Party.
Weird Stories.
BY F. W. ROBINSON.
Women are Strange.
The Hands of Justice.
BY JOHN SAUNDERS.
Bound to the Wheel.
Guy Waterman. | Two Dreamers.
The Lion in the Path.
BY KATHARINE SAUNDERS.
Margaret and Elizabeth.
Gideon's Rock. | Heart Salvage.
The High Mills. | Sebastian.
BY T. W. SPEIGHT.
The Mysteries of Heron Dyke.
BY R. A. STERNDALE.
The Afghan Knife.
BY BERTHA THOMAS.
Proud Maisie. | Cressida.
The Violin-Player.

PICCADILLY NOVELS, *continued*—
BY ANTHONY TROLLOPE.
The Way we Live Now.
Frau Frohmann. | Marion Fay.
Kept in the Dark.
Mr. Scarborough's Family.
The Land-Leaguers.
BY FRANCES E. TROLLOPE.
Like Ships upon the Sea.
Anne Furness. | Mabel's Progress.
BY IVAN TURGENIEFF, &c.
Stories from Foreign Novelists.
BY SARAH TYTLER.
What She Came Through.
The Bride's Pass. | Saint Mungo's City.
Beauty and the Beast.
Noblesse Oblige.
Lady Bell. | Buried Diamonds.
The Blackhall Ghosts.
BY C. C. FRASER-TYTLER.
Mistress Judith.

CHEAP EDITIONS OF POPULAR NOVELS.
Post 8vo, illustrated boards, 2s. each.

BY THE AUTHOR OF "MEHALAH."
Red Spider.
BY EDMOND ABOUT.
The Fellah.
BY HAMILTON AÏDÉ.
Carr of Carrlyon. | Confidences.
BY MRS. ALEXANDER.
Maid, Wife, or Widow?
Valerie's Fate.
BY GRANT ALLEN.
Strange Stories.
Philistia.
Babylon.
In all Shades.
The Beckoning Hand.
For Maimie's Sake.
BY SHELSLEY BEAUCHAMP.
Grantley Grange.
BY WALTER BESANT & J. RICE.
Ready-Money Mortiboy.
With Harp and Crown.
This Son of Vulcan. | My Little Girl.
The Case of Mr. Lucraft.
The Golden Butterfly.
By Celia's Arbour.
The Monks of Thelema.
'Twas in Trafalgar's Bay.
The Seamy Side.
The Ten Years' Tenant.
The Chaplain of the Fleet.
BY WALTER BESANT.
All Sorts and Conditions of Men.
The Captains' Room.
All in a Garden Fair.
Dorothy Forster.
Uncle Jack.
Children of Gibeon.
The World Went Very Well Then.

BY FREDERICK BOYLE.
Camp Notes. | Savage Life.
Chronicles of No-man's Land.
BY BRET HARTE.
An Heiress of Red Dog.
The Luck of Roaring Camp.
Californian Stories.
Gabriel Conroy. | Flip.
Maruja. | A Phyllis of the Sierras.
A Waif of the Plains.
BY HAROLD BRYDGES.
Uncle Sam at Home.
BY ROBERT BUCHANAN.
The Shadow of | The Martyrdom
  the Sword. | of Madeline.
A Child of Nature. | Annan Water.
God and the Man. | The New Abelard.
Love Me for Ever. | Matt.
Foxglove Manor. | The Heir of Linne
The Master of the Mine.
BY HALL CAINE.
The Shadow of a Crime.
A Son of Hagar. | The Deemster.
BY COMMANDER CAMERON.
The Cruise of the "Black Prince."
BY MRS. LOVETT CAMERON
Deceivers Ever. | Juliet's Guardian.
BY MACLAREN COBBAN.
The Cure of Souls.
BY C. ALLSTON COLLINS.
The Bar Sinister.
BY WILKIE COLLINS.
Antonina. | My Miscellanies.
Basil. | Woman in White.
Hide and Seek. | The Moonstone.
The Dead Secret. | Man and Wife
Queen of Hearts. | Poor Miss Finch.

CHEAP POPULAR NOVELS, *continued—*
WILKIE COLLINS, *continued.*

Miss or Mrs. ?
New Magdalen.
The Frozen Deep.
The Law and the Lady.
The Two Destinies
Haunted Hotel.
The Fallen Leaves.
Jezebel's Daughter
The Black Robe.
Heart and Science
"I Say No."
The Evil Genius.
Little Novels.

BY MORTIMER COLLINS.

Sweet Anne Page. | From Midnight to
Transmigration. | Midnight.
A Fight with Fortune.

MORTIMER & FRANCES COLLINS.

Sweet and Twenty. | Frances.
Blacksmith and Scholar.
The Village Comedy.
You Play me False.

BY M. J. COLQUHOUN.

Every Inch a Soldier.

BY MONCURE D. CONWAY.

Pine and Palm.

BY DUTTON COOK.

Leo. | Paul Foster's Daughter.

BY C. EGBERT CRADDOCK.

The Prophet of the Great Smoky Mountains.

BY WILLIAM CYPLES.

Hearts of Gold.

BY ALPHONSE DAUDET.

The Evangelist; or, Port Salvation.

BY JAMES DE MILLE.

A Castle in Spain

BY J. LEITH DERWENT.

Our Lady of Tears. | Circe's Lovers.

BY CHARLES DICKENS.

Sketches by Boz. | Oliver Twist.
Pickwick Papers. | Nicholas Nickleby

BY DICK DONOVAN.

The Man-Hunter.
Caught at Last !

BY MRS. ANNIE EDWARDES.

Point of Honour. | Archie Lovell.

BY M. BETHAM-EDWARDS.

Felicia.

BY EDWARD EGGLESTON.

Roxy.

BY PERCY FITZGERALD.

Bella Donna. | Never Forgotten.
The Second Mrs. Tillotson.
Polly. | Fatal Zero.
Seventy-five Brooke Street.
The Lady of Brantome.

BY ALBANY DE FONBLANQUE.

Filthy Lucre.

BY R. E. FRANCILLON.

Olympia. | Queen Cophetua.
One by One. | A Real Queen.

BY HAROLD FREDERIC.

Seth's Brother's Wife.

BY HAIN FRISWELL.

One of Two.

BY EDWARD GARRETT.

The Capel Girls.

CHEAP POPULAR NOVELS, *continued—*
BY CHARLES GIBBON.

Robin Gray.
For Lack of Gold.
What will the World Say ?
In Love and War.
For the King.
In Pastures Green
Queen of the Meadow.
A Heart's Problem
The Dead Heart.
In Honour Bound
The Flower of the Forest.
Braes of Yarrow.
The Golden Shaft.
Of High Degree.
Mead and Stream.
Loving a Dream.
A Hard Knot.
Heart's Delight.
Blood-Money.

BY WILLIAM GILBERT.

Dr Austin's Guests. | James Duke.
The Wizard of the Mountain.

BY JOHN HABBERTON.

Brueton's Bayou. | Country Luck.

BY ANDREW HALLIDAY.

Every-Day Papers.

BY LADY DUFFUS HARDY.

Paul Wynter's Sacrifice.

BY THOMAS HARDY.

Under the Greenwood Tree.

BY J. BERWICK HARWOOD.

The Tenth Earl.

BY JULIAN HAWTHORNE.

Garth.
Ellice Quentin.
Fortune's Fool.
Miss Cadogna.
David Poindexter's Disappearance.
Sebastian Strome
Dust.
Beatrix Randolph.
Love—or a Name.

BY SIR ARTHUR HELPS.

Ivan de Biron.

BY MRS. CASHEL HOEY.

The Lover's Creed.

BY MRS. GEORGE HOOPER.

The House of Raby.

BY TIGHE HOPKINS.

'Twixt Love and Duty.

BY MRS. ALFRED HUNT.

Thornicroft's Model.
The Leaden Casket.
Self-Condemned. | That other Person

BY JEAN INGELOW.

Fated to be Free.

BY HARRIETT JAY.

The Dark Colleen.
The Queen of Connaught.

BY MARK KERSHAW.

Colonial Facts and Fictions.

BY R. ASHE KING.

A Drawn Game.
"The Wearing of the Green."

BY HENRY KINGSLEY.

Oakshott Castle

BY JOHN LEYS.

The Lindsays.

BY MARY LINSKILL.

In Exchange for a Soul.

BY E. LYNN LINTON.

Patricia Kemball.
The Atonement of Leam Dundas.

CHEAP POPULAR NOVELS, *continued—*
E. LYNN LINTON, *continued—*
The World Well Lost.
Under which Lord? | Paston Carew.
With a Silken Thread.
The Rebel of the Family.
"My Love." | Ione.
BY HENRY W. LUCY.
Gideon Fleyce.
BY JUSTIN McCARTHY.

Dear Lady Disdain | MissMisanthrope
The Waterdale | Donna Quixote.
Neighbours. | The Comet of a
My Enemy's | Season.
Daughter. | Maid of Athens.
A Fair Saxon. | Camiola.
Linley Rochford. |

BY MRS. MACDONELL.
Quaker Cousins.
BY KATHARINE S. MACQUOID.
The Evil Eye. | Lost Rose.
BY W. H. MALLOCK.
The New Republic.
BY FLORENCE MARRYAT.

Open! Sesame. | Fighting the Air.
A Harvest of Wild | Written in Fire.
Oats. |

BY J. MASTERMAN.
Half-a-dozen Daughters.
BY BRANDER MATTHEWS.
A Secret of the Sea.
BY JEAN MIDDLEMASS.
Touch and Go. | Mr. Dorillion.
BY MRS. MOLESWORTH.
Hathercourt Rectory.
BY J. E. MUDDOCK.
Stories Weird and Wonderful.
BY D. CHRISTIE MURRAY.

A Life's Atonement | Hearts.
A Model Father. | Way of the World.
Joseph's Coat. | A Bit of Human
Coals of Fire. | Nature,
By the Gate of the | First Person Sin-
Val Strange [Sea. | gular.
Old Blazer's Hero. | Cynic Fortune.

BY ALICE O'HANLON.
The Unforeseen. | Chance? or Fate?
BY MRS. OLIPHANT.
Whiteladies. | The Primrose Path.
The Greatest Heiress in England.
BY MRS. ROBERT O'REILLY.
Phœbe's Fortunes.
BY OUIDA.

Held in Bondage. | Two Little Wooden
Strathmore. | Shoes.
Chandos. | Ariadne.
Under Two Flags. | Friendship.
Idalia. | Moths.
Cecil Castle- | Pipistrello.
maine's Gage. | A Village Com-
Tricotrin. | Puck. | mune.
Folle Farine. | Bimbi. | Wanda.
A Dog of Flanders. | Frescoes.
Pascarel. | In Maremma.
Signa. [Ine. | Othmar.
Princess Naprax- | Wisdom, Wit, and
In a Winter City. | Pathos.

CHEAP POPULAR NOVELS, *continued—*
BY MARGARET AGNES PAUL.
Gentle and Simple.
BY JAMES PAYN.

Lost Sir Massing- | Marine Residence.
berd. | Married Beneath
A Perfect Treasure | Him.
Bentinck's Tutor. | Mirk Abbey.
Murphy's Master. | Not Wooed, but
A County Family. | Won.
At Her Mercy. | Less Black than
A Woman's Ven- | We're Painted.
geance. | By Proxy.
Cecil's Tryst. | Under One Roof.
Clyffards of Clyffe | High Spirits.
The Family Scape- | Carlyon's Year.
grace. | A Confidential
Foster Brothers. | Agent.
Found Dead. | Some Private
Best of Husbands. | Views.
Walter's Word. | From Exile.
Halves. | A Grape from a
Fallen Fortunes. | Thorn.
What He Cost Her | For Cash Only.
Humorous Stories | Kit: A Memory
Gwendoline's Har- | The Canon's Ward
vest. | Talk of the Town.
£200 Reward. | Holiday Tasks.
Like Father, Like | Glow-worm Tales
Son. |

BY C. L. PIRKIS.
Lady Lovelace.
BY EDGAR A. POE.
The Mystery of Marie Roget.
BY E. C. PRICE.
Valentina. | The Foreigners
Mrs. Lancaster's Rival.
Gerald.
BY CHARLES READE.
It is Never Too Late to Mend.
Hard Cash. | Peg Woffington
Christie Johnstone.
Griffith Gaunt.
Put Yourself in His Place.
The Double Marriage.
Love Me Little, Love Me Long.
Foul Play.
The Cloister and the Hearth.
The Course of True Love.
Autobiography of a Thief.
A Terrible Temptation.
The Wandering Heir.
A Simpleton. | A Woman-Hater.
Readiana. | The Jilt.
Singleheart and Doubleface.
Good Stories of Men and other
Animals.
BY MRS. J. H. RIDDELL.
Her Mother's Darling.
Prince of Wales's Garden Party.
Weird Stories. | Fairy Water.
The Uninhabited House.
The Mystery in Palace Gardens.
BY F. W. ROBINSON.
Women are Strange.
The Hands of Justice.

CHEAP POPULAR NOVELS. *continued—*

BY JAMES RUNCIMAN.
Skippers and Shellbacks.
Grace Balmaign's Sweetheart.
Schools and Scholars.

BY W. CLARK RUSSELL
Round the Galley Fire.
On the Fo'k'sle Head.
In the Middle Watch.
A Voyage to the Cape.
A Book for the Hammock.

BY GEORGE AUGUSTUS SALA.
Gaslight and Daylight.

BY JOHN SAUNDERS.
Guy Waterman. | Two Dreamers.
The Lion in the Path.

BY KATHARINE SAUNDERS.
Joan Merryweather. | The High Mills.
Margaret and Elizabeth.
Heart Salvage. | Sebastian.

BY GEORGE R. SIMS.
Rogues and Vagabonds.
The Ring o' Bells. | Mary Jane Married.
Mary Jane's Memoirs.
Tales of To-day.

BY ARTHUR SKETCHLEY.
A Match in the Dark.

BY T. W. SPEIGHT.
The Mysteries of Heron Dyke.
The Golden Hoop. | By Devious Ways.

BY R. A. STERNDALE.
The Afghan Knife.

BY R. LOUIS STEVENSON.
New Arabian Nights. | Prince Otto.

BY BERTHA THOMAS.
Cressida. | Proud Maisie.
The Violin-Player.

BY W. MOY THOMAS.
A Fight for Life.

BY WALTER THORNBURY.
Tales for the Marines.
Old Stories Re-told.

BY T. ADOLPHUS TROLLOPE.
Diamond Cut Diamond.

BY ANTHONY TROLLOPE.
The Way We Live Now.
The American Senator.
Frau Frohmann. | Marion Fay.
Kept in the Dark.
Mr. Scarborough's Family.
The Land-Leaguers. | John Caldigate
The Golden Lion of Granpere.

By F. ELEANOR TROLLOPE.
Like Ships upon the Sea.
Anne Furness. | Mabel's Progress.

BY J. T. TROWBRIDGE.
Farnell's Folly.

BY IVAN TURGENIEFF, &c.
Stories from Foreign Novelists.

CHEAP POPULAR NOVELS, *continued—*

BY MARK TWAIN.
Tom Sawyer. | A Tramp Abroad.
The Stolen White Elephant.
A Pleasure Trip on the Continent
Huckleberry Finn.   [of Europe.
Life on the Mississippi.
The Prince and the Pauper.

BY C. C. FRASER-TYTLER.
Mistress Judith.

BY SARAH TYTLER.
What She Came Through.
The Bride's Pass. | Buried Diamonds.
Saint Mungo's City.
Beauty and the Beast.
Lady Bell. | Noblesse Oblige.
Citoyenne Jacqueline | Disappeared.
The Huguenot Family.

BY J. S. WINTER.
Cavalry Life. | Regimental Legends.

BY H. F. WOOD.
The Passenger from Scotland Yard.

BY LADY WOOD.
Sabina.

BY CELIA PARKER WOOLLEY.
Rachel Armstrong; or, Love & Theology.

BY EDMUND YATES.
Castaway.
The Forlorn Hope. | Land at Last.

ANONYMOUS.
Why Paul Ferroll Killed his Wife.

POPULAR SHILLING BOOKS.
Jeff Briggs's Love Story By BRET HARTE.
The Twins of Table Mountain. By BRET HARTE.
A Day's Tour. By PERCY FITZGERALD.
Mrs. Gainsborough's Diamonds. By JULIAN HAWTHORNE.
A Romance of the Queen's Hounds. By CHARLES JAMES.
Trooping with Crows. By C. L. PIRKIS
The Professor's Wife. By L. GRAHAM.
A Double Bond. By LINDA VILLARI.
Esther's Glove. By R. E. FRANCILLON.
The Garden that Paid the Rent. By TOM JERROLD.
Beyond the Gates. By E. S. PHELPS.
Old Maid's Paradise. By E. S. PHELPS.
Burglars in Paradise. By E. S. PHELPS.
Jack the Fisherman. By E. S. PHELPS.
Our Sensation Novel. Edited by JUSTIN H. McCARTHY, M.P.
Dolly. By JUSTIN H. McCARTHY, M.P.
Lily Lass. By JUSTIN H. McCARTHY, M.P.
That Girl in Black. By Mrs. MOLESWORTH.
Was She Good or Bad? By W. MINTO.
Bible Characters. By CHAS. READE.
Rogues. By R. H. SHERARD.
The Dagonet Reciter. By G. R. SIMS.
How the Poor Live. By G. R. SIMS.